KINGDOM OF ESSENCE

HOLLY KARLSSON

KINGDOM OF ESSENCE

Copyright © 2021 by Holly Karlsson

All rights reserved.

This book is a work of fiction and any resemblance to real persons, living or dead, is purely coincidental.

Cover Art & Design by Tanya Anor
Chapter Header & Line Art by Nathan Hansen
Map by ALTCartography

Proofreading by Maria Fowler

Ebook ISBN: 978-1-7330998-7-5
Paperback ISBN: 978-1-7330998-8-2
Hardcover ISBN: 978-1-7330998-9-9

www.byhollykarlsson.com

For everyone who dreams of adventure.

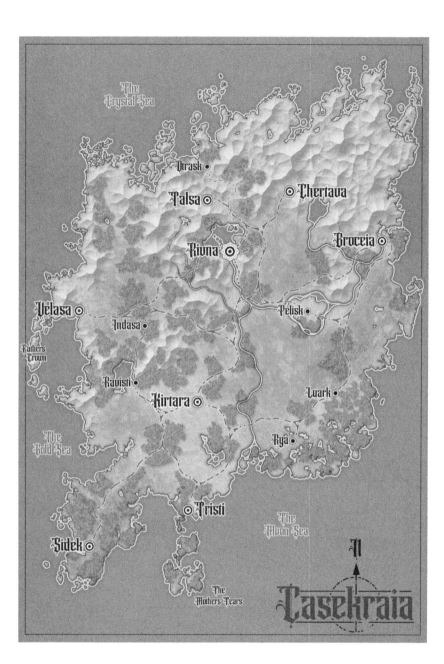

CHAPTER 1

E litsa shoved the door closed with her fist, her eyes sweeping the windowless room as her mark spun around with a startled gasp. The man was dressed as a laborer, his travel-stained clothes rumpled and worn. His face was too lean, the bones of his face sharp beneath sunken eyes. Another essence farmer unable to meet the terms of his contract.

Reclamations had been satisfying once, even fun, but Elitsa's exhilaration had waned long ago. Now it was simply a job, often tedious and thankless, but a means to an end. "Mr. Janso. I'm a Tower reclamation agent, and you're in breach of contract. Give me the relic, and I'll be on my way." She looked him over for weapons. She didn't expect to find any, but it was a habit that'd saved her more than once. Anyone could be dangerous, even a hungry, sweet-faced kid on the street. To survive here, you either grew wings or claws.

Desperation shone in Janso's pale blue eyes, and he fumbled with a chain around his neck, pulling free a silvery medallion. Lightly tarnished, the relic was shaped into the round face of a barn owl.

Elitsa sighed, a hiss of air between her teeth, but he didn't attack. Instead, Janso hesitated, eyes darting from the door behind her to her face. She'd seen that doubtful look before. The assumption that with her small build and quiet reserve, she was more fawn than mountain cat. When she wanted the element of surprise, this often worked to her advantage, but right now, Elitsa had no desire to fight or chase him half across the city. *Please don't underestimate me*, she thought, tiredly.

Janso hadn't been hard to find, though it'd taken two days before she'd caught up with him. Whatever essence he'd been extracting for the Tower, it'd sent him up into the mountains north of Rivna for months at a time. He was foolish to have come back, but perhaps he had a family. Someone who'd miss him if he never came home.

The man's fingers tightened on the relic.

"Careful, Mr. Janso," Elitsa warned, bracing her feet. "Attacking an agent is a bad idea." Especially one who was tired and hungry and longed for a bath. She focused on the magesilver earrings in her ears, past the cool metal to the essences trapped inside. It was like following the limb of a tree, feeling where the trunk became root, growing down into the soil, an expanded awareness of something deep and ignored. Swirls of color bloomed in her mind, the elemental shapes of air, earth, and fire.

Janso licked his lips, his indecision plain, as his eyes moved down her long coat. He was probably searching for relics, but he wouldn't find them. Elitsa's shoulder-length brown hair covered her ears, and as the magesilver pierced her skin, she didn't have to touch them like he did. The farmer should have left the medallion inside his shirt against his skin; perhaps he'd never used it to fight. "How do I know you're from the Tower?"

Elitsa gave him an irritated look, then reached for the scarf around her neck, shifting the patterned fabric so Janso could see the inside of her coat collar. Her agent pin was there, a silver hand holding a curl of flame. "See? I'm not a rogue, Mr. Janso." Was it too much to wish just once they'd believe her?

"Please, I haven't hurt anyone." His voice became soft, imploring. "I'm just trying to provide for my family. You can understand that, can't you?"

What she understood is that he hadn't been clever enough to avoid getting caught. She couldn't help him, and it was unfair for him to think she could. They were all just trying to survive. "Spare me your sob story. You broke the rules, and I'm here to collect. It's as simple as that."

The faint sweet scent of birch and wet moss touched Elitsa's nose as Janso tightened his hand on the medallion. He was drawing on a tree's essence, likely planning to enhance his strength to try and overpower her.

Elitsa raised her hand in warning and readied an essence of air. A blue swirl of light, like a transparent ribbon, fluttered in her mind's eye. She could smell the breeze, remember the mountain she'd gathered it on and how it'd blown through her hair. "Careful. I don't *want* to hurt you, but that doesn't mean I won't. Give me the relic." She held his gaze, saw the flicker of desperate resolve. "Think of your family, Mr. Janso. You can't provide for them if you're injured or dead. I could have taken the relic when I entered this room, but I didn't. I want you to be able to walk home to your family."

Janso stared at her, eyes wide, then his shoulders slumped, the smell of trees fading. "They told me I'd earn enough to support my family, but I can barely pay my contract. The essences they want? The ones they'll actually pay for? They're near impossible to find. I can't afford to harvest, but I can't afford to stop."

Elitsa took a careful step forward, keeping her eyes on his. "This year has been hard for everyone. Your survival is up to you and what you choose to do next." That's all life really was. Choices. Whether to give up or claw your way to the surface.

Janso clutched the medallion as though it held his salvation. "I need the relic to harvest, to feed my family. I know I shouldn't have sold to the Smoke Eyes, but they pay more per essence. It was the only way to pay my fees to the Guild, to eat. Please, Miss. Tell them I won't do it again. I promise!"

Elitsa's stomach murmured as if in shared commiseration. There was a cost to harvesting essence. Despite a relic's assistance, each extraction drew on your body's energy. Eating could replenish what you lost, but if you could barely afford food, how long you could work was limited, even dangerous. She thought longingly of the garlic rye bread in her room, a gift from Pipene. "I'm sorry, Mr. Janso, but the terms of your contract are up to the Tower. I can't speak on your behalf." She took another slow step forward, expecting him to move back, but Janso just stared at her.

"The Smoke Eyes approached me; I didn't seek them out. I was going to say no, but I—"

"Mr. Janso. The relic." Irritation had slipped into her voice. Why did they always think they could convince her to let them go?

"Nevena, my daughter, she's sic—"

Elitsa's hand caught Janso in the center of his chest, driving the air from his lungs. He let go of the medallion as he staggered back, and she ripped it from his neck in a fast, violent motion. Shock and pain twisted Janso's face, and then he fell onto the bed behind him. The faint hope lighting his eyes flickered out, replaced by fear.

Breathing hard, Elitsa stared down at him, a confusing storm of fury and horror tightening her throat. The way he was looking at her twisted her stomach. He was a person, a human being, and she was treating him like a simple transaction. A mark in a ledger. When had she become so callous? So focused on herself that she could ignore the plea in his eyes?

Elitsa looked at the owl-faced medallion in her hand, recalling a story her mother, Branka, had told her as a child. Long ago, when Mother Moon and Father Sun walked Cerana, a man had desired to become a god. He'd stolen the essence from one of

Mother's owls to ascend and, using its claw, rose into the heavens on gray-spotted wings. Instead of welcoming him as he'd expected, Mother Moon cast the man back down, cursing him to live as the creature he'd killed, a messenger of death.

Now, seeing herself through Janso's eyes, the story felt personal. *Is this who I want to be?* A mindless messenger of loss and ruin? Elitsa had fought for her place in the Guild's organization, not because she believed in them, but because she'd thought they were her best chance to find her mother's killer. But instead of justice, she'd only succeeded in protecting the mages' wealth and influence. How many lives had Elitsa helped destroy by being an obedient hound for the Tower?

The guilt and disappointment she should feel didn't come, and that was somehow worse than any self-reproach. She'd allowed herself to stop caring. If she continued on this path, what would she become? The need to do something *good* took stubborn root inside her chest, thorns of urgency digging deep. Elitsa rubbed a finger over the owl's eyes, thinking. The Guild didn't know what essences, if any, Janso currently had. Sometimes Elitsa returned relics with a few still trapped inside, but sometimes she kept them for herself, storing the harvested essence in jars beneath the floorboards of her room. A small act of practical and selfish rebellion with minimal risk. She could help Janso if she wanted, ensure his daughter didn't go to bed hungry.

Elitsa made a decision. "Do you have something to store your essences in, Mr. Janso?"

Janso blinked, a trembling hand pressed against his chest where she'd struck him. "What?"

"Do you have something to store your essences in?" Elitsa repeated impatiently. "I can't let you keep the relic, but I'll leave you with your harvest. I suggest you sell the essences quickly, as the Tower may believe you've found an unregistered relic and are working again."

"You'll let me keep them?" He stared at her, disbelief and suspicion clouding his eyes.

"Yes." Elitsa held out the medallion, dangling it in front of Janso by the broken chain. She could see and understand his mistrust, especially after what she'd done, but she couldn't walk away, leaving him broken. He had to accept her help. She *needed* him to. "Consider it a gift in honor of Mother Moon." Gifts and favors were often traded in the Mother's name in the weeks leading up to the Night of Souls, usually between friends and family, but occasionally strangers. Janso didn't know she was rarely generous. She wiggled her hand, making the medallion sway. "Quickly, Mr. Janso, before I change my mind." She was beginning to regret her impulsiveness when relief flashed across Janso's face, drawing his mouth into a joyous smile.

"Thank you, Miss! Mother's blessings to you!"

Elitsa nodded as Janso stood up, taking the medallion from her hand. As she backed up a step, he stooped down and pulled out a small crate from under the bed, glass bottles clinking against each other as he set it on the threadbare blanket.

It was a risk, letting Janso hold the relic while he transferred the essence, but she'd seen enough to know she could disarm him easily. Still, Elitsa watched him closely as he selected a bottle and pulled free the cork.

Holding the medallion in his other hand, Janso began to move an essence into the bottle. The smell of trees — sweet and earthy like before — filled the room, and Elitsa inhaled reflexively as green and brown light swirled inside the container, shaping itself into a small branch. Replacing the cork, Janso put the bottle back into the crate and reached for another.

Relics, like Janso's medallion and Elitsa's earrings, could hold multiple essences, even different kinds, but glass could only hold one. Elitsa sometimes combined them — she'd learned water with certain plant essences could heal — but it was only possible at the moment you released them from magesilver.

The scent of rain wafted through the air as Janso moved another essence.

Lightly drumming her fingers against her thighs, Elitsa looked at the door. She didn't know how many essences Janso had without touching the medallion, but she hoped he'd finish soon. If the Guild found out what she'd done, she'd lose her contract, but what did they expect? She barely earned enough to keep herself fed and clothed. *This is hardly the worst thing that goes on beneath the Tower's nose*, she thought defiantly, pushing back against the feeling she was doing something wrong.

She'd given the Guild her loyalty for years, and for what? And why did the thought of betraying them bother her more than taking Janso's livelihood? The faintest curl of shame flickered inside her chest, and Elitsa seized it desperately. This is what she'd felt before, what she *should* feel now. Without it, she was no better than the mages, thinking only of themselves.

Janso's knees cracked as he stood up. "Old bones," he said, smiling tiredly. He looked paler than when he'd started, and Elitsa wondered when he'd last eaten.

She looked at the crate. Janso had filled six bottles, one with a tree's essence and the other five with water. Rain was one of the easiest essences to obtain and therefore not worth much, but the sale of all six should earn enough coin to last a week or two. And beyond that? What would Janso do for his family then? *Not my problem*, Elitsa reminded herself harshly.

"That's it," Janso said, but he didn't hand her the medallion. He stared at it in the center of his palm, breathing slowly. Then, shoulders slumping, he held it out.

Elitsa took the relic and slipped it into an inner pocket inside her coat. Relief eased the tightness inside her chest, and she let go of a breath she hadn't realized she was holding. She was glad he'd given in without a fight. All things considered, the retrieval had gone well. There were no injuries or torn clothing to worry about, and she still had all her essences. Janso didn't know how many arms and legs she'd broken chasing contract-breakers. If he did, he wouldn't be looking at her with such gratitude.

Still, she couldn't let her vigilance go until she'd returned the relic to the Tower. Rogues were always on the lookout for relics to grab, which made Elitsa, an agent, a prime target. It was one reason why she didn't wear her badge or relics openly, in addition to the mistrustful and sometimes hateful attitude towards anyone associated with the Guild. It used to bother her before she understood. *I don't like myself much either these days.*

"Thank you, Miss." Janso reached for her suddenly, causing a spike of alarm, but he only grasped her hand.

Surprised, Elitsa almost yanked away from him. "It's nothing. Don't tell anyone."

"I won't." His eyes glistened wetly. "I promise. What's your name?"

She hesitated, though Janso could find out from the Tower if he wanted to. "Elitsa."

"Thank you, Elitsa. You are a good person."

No, she wasn't. It'd been a long time since someone had thanked her, and she stared at Janso awkwardly as he squeezed her fingers then turned back to the crate of essences. Elitsa looked down at her hand, still feeling the warmth his calloused fingers had left behind. It wasn't enough, what she'd done. All it would do was delay the inevitable. A surge of hopelessness overwhelmed her, dragging her down into memories of loss and pain, of being weak, incapable.

Elitsa took a step back, clenching her jaw hard enough that her teeth ached. *This* was why she'd made herself stop caring. It was the only way she could do what she'd done, perform her job, but letting those feelings back in had opened a door, and she couldn't force it closed again. Doubt and regret, and longing gnawed at her. *I've done all I can*, she reminded herself, turning away and striding to the door. Whatever happened next to Janso and his family was not her responsibility.

Elitsa hurried through the dim hall, her footsteps sounding loud to her ears as she hastened to leave the boarding house. A door cracked open, and she sunk into the high collar of her coat, letting her hair shift across her cheek as she passed. Sometimes she was recognized — nosy neighbors and all that— but nothing about her clothing marked her as a reclamation agent.

Unlike most women in town, Elitsa preferred plainer styles, colors and patterns that'd blend into forest and shadow. Her coat was a masculine style, ending at her ankles, with a high collar, buttoned closed at an angle from her left breast to her waist, where it flared open as she walked. Instead of thick, colorful skirts, easy to become tangled in, hers was split at the hips, their only embellishment a band of black and dark blue stripes several inches above the hem and worn over snug brown trousers. Covered by her long, dark green coat and the scarf at her neck, the only light-colored clothing she wore was her white blouse with twining bluebells stitched down the sleeves. Those who didn't recognize Elitsa might assume she was a tracker or one of the Smoke Eyes' runners. There were disadvantages to being marked in that way, but heavy skirts were not helpful in a fight.

Taking the steps down two at a time, Elitsa moved through a narrow entryway — painted white to brighten the small space — and out the front door. She immediately stepped off the stone sill and to the side, boots sinking into the churned mud as she scanned the street. The morning air was brisk, and she could smell cookfires and the stables to the east. Apart from a brown, rough-eared dog scratching at the foundation of the white-washed building across from her, she was alone. Someone had made a half-hearted attempt to paint the window frames a pale gray, but it only made the wooden structure seem sadder some-how. Pipene thought they should use the brighter colors that the wealthier neighborhoods favored, but paint was expensive, so the suburb remained an almost unending sea of white and gray.

Moving out into the center of the street, Elitsa searched the peaked rooftops but saw nothing but chimneys and worn, gray tiles. Turning right, she jumped onto a plank someone had laid down over the mud and headed north. To reach the Guild tower, she had to pass through the merchants' district. Elitsa walked quickly, alert to anyone following. Though she was several streets over from the river that separated the Aerie from the rest of the suburb, she could hear the noisy protestations of ducks as fishers moved their boats through the channels.

A pair of city guards strolling in the opposite direction eyed her but didn't slow, the red-cheeked men carrying on their muted conversation. They were easy to spot in their fur-lined hats and thick uniforms, the king's sigil embroidered on the back of their dark gray coats — a winged wolf beneath a gold sun overlapping a silver half-moon. Though Elitsa had nothing to fear from them, unless she planned to break the law in their presence, she kept her eyes turned down as she hurried past. It was always better to go unnoticed.

The wind quickly chilled her cheeks, and Elitsa knew her nose had turned red from the cold. As she turned a corner, a biting blast of mountain air hit her in the face, blowing her bangs up off her forehead and carrying the scent of fresh-baked bread. Inhaling deeply, Elitsa blinked tears from her eyes and tugged her scarf up over her mouth and nose before shoving her hands into her pockets.

Worn gray cobblestones replaced the dirt beneath Elitsa's feet as she entered the Kurdaima District, and the wooden buildings of the People's Suburb gave way to green and yellow and light blue stone with red peaked roofs. The doors were wider here, bearing etchings of birds and flowers across their paneled surfaces, with transom windows above. Most were painted green or dark brown, but a few were highlighted in striking purple. Those embellishments marked the wealthier merchants, as the rare color came from sea snails from Kreanos, carried on ships from the Queen's homeland across the Gold Sea.

Trees shedding orange-yellow leaves leaned out over the walls of small courtyards, filling the street with color. Her mother had loved this time of year, so Elitsa viewed the change of season as bittersweet. It was hard not to think of the death and decay that would follow.

It was four weeks until the Night of Souls, and shopkeepers had begun to set out carved wooden masks, harvest wreaths, and painted pumpkins. Bouquets of soul bells — small, blood-red flowers that bloomed in fall — marked the mantles of the spirit houses hanging over their doors. Pipene had urged her to place one in her window, but Elitsa knew her mother's soul wouldn't come.

As Elitsa walked through the Lady's Square, she saw that the fountain — a veiled woman holding her hands up to the sky — was dry, the tarnished copper scales of the basin glinting in the cold sunlight. She frowned, stopping to run her fingers along its edge. The Guild had emptied it early this year. One of the Tower's contributions to the city was to keep the fountains running, as there were only a handful of deep wells where citizens could gather clean water. Supposedly in years past — before Elitsa could remember — the mages had kept the fountains running all year round.

Solveiga won't like this, Elitsa thought. If it was dry here in the merchant's quarter, then so was the fountain by the Aerie. A section of the People's Suburb by the Green Gate, the Aerie was protected by Solveiga, the well-respected proprietress of The House of Swans. Thanks to several wealthy patrons, the pleasure house and the attached apartments where Elitsa lived — all owned by Solveiga — had indoor plumbing, but the rest of the neighborhood relied on the nearby fountain. It would not sit well with Solveiga that the people she'd made it her mission to care for would have to walk toward the east gate for water.

Well, if the Guild wanted to make an enemy of Solveiga, that was their business. *As long as it doesn't get me kicked out of the Aerie.*

There wasn't much love for the Tower in the People's Suburb, but Solveiga allowed her presence — supposedly she had history with her mother — and Elitsa liked living close to her childhood friend Pipene. Without her, Elitsa would likely have moved into the Spears after her mother's death, the cramped and spiritless neighborhood east of the Tower that was a favorite for soldiers and guards. Sure, it was supposedly a nicer part of town and closer to the king, but there was no warmth there.

As she passed the candle maker's shop, a black cat dashed across Elitsa's path into the mouth of a narrow side street. She stopped abruptly, catching her footing as she followed the animal's rush down the shadowy corridor to a familiar blue door. The cat disappeared around a corner, but Elitsa continued to stare at the door as memories enfolded her. She knew that workshop well with its warm darkness and book-filled shelves. It was where her mother had restored books, as Elitsa and Pipene dreamed of adventures before they'd grown old enough to know better.

The door's paint was worn and faded. Given the leaves on the threshold, it didn't look like it'd been opened in a long time. Why hadn't Master Davor rented it out? The scribe owned the adjoining building, where Elitsa had apprenticed before she'd quit to work for the Tower. Well, she would have quit if he hadn't first chosen Gordan over her. Becoming a scribe had been her mother's idea, and when she'd died eight years ago, Elitsa couldn't stay there, not when the Guild and their relics could help find her mother's killer.

After four years in the Guild's service, her plan to climb the ranks and solve her mother's murder seemed to be just another youthful dream. Elitsa felt a wave of regret. What would her life be like now if she hadn't left? Hadn't burned herself ragged looking for a ghost? Would she be happier?

The sound of someone's footsteps shattered Elitsa's reverie, and she turned her head, catching the eyes of a tall, bearded man carrying a package under his arm. He inclined his head as he passed, and Elitsa nodded back.

Casting a look skyward, Elitsa resumed walking, mentally scolding herself over her foolishness. It was pointless to wish for something she didn't have. She'd made her choices, and this was her life, like it or not, and if she wanted to eat tonight, she needed to get paid.

CHAPTER 2

Crossing a small courtyard, Elitsa observed a cluster of women outside a seamstress's shop, talking beneath the dark green awning. It was unusual for customers to gather this early in the morning, and she slowed curiously. As Elitsa drew closer, the shop door opened, and two people stepped outside, one joining the crowd and the other brushing past to enter the street. She caught sight of a sharp nose and chin, but the person's heavy blue cloak obscured further details. More interested in the conversation than the departing figure, Elitsa joined the edge of the circle.

"It's terribly sad," a woman said, adjusting the floral scarf over her blonde hair. Given the sweet scent emanating from the cloth-covered basket on her arm, she was on her way home with bread from Oleh's, the bakery a street over.

Another woman with pale blue eyes and dimpled cheeks flushed by the cold, nodded, smoothing her hands along the strings of coral beads at her throat. "Yes, Mistress Dulkai was so young too. And alone, poor thing."

"Young!" A gray-haired woman laughed sharply. "She was hardly young."

The others gave her an askance look, which the older woman ignored. Beside her, a girl with frizzy black hair and sallow skin, who Elitsa guessed couldn't be more than sixteen, shifted uncomfortably.

"What happened?" Elitsa asked.

"The Night Sickness!" the woman wearing the scarf said, seemingly pleased to pass the news along.

"The Night Sickness." Elitsa's breath quickened. The illness that had supposedly killed her mother. Thanks to Vilis, she knew that wasn't true. Someone was behind the death, though they didn't know how or why. "Did Mistress Dulkai have a Guild contract?"

"A contract?" The woman blinked in surprise, exchanging baffled looks with the others. "Certainly not. She had no interest in magic. No time for it. This young woman," she gestured at the girl, "found her this morning."

"Hah," the older woman barked. "Can you imagine? Dulkai, a *mage*. Perhaps if she were, we'd have gotten our dresses faster, hmm?" She seemed pleased when the others bristled like upset birds.

Elitsa looked at the girl, taking in her worn striped skirts and threadbare coat. Her eyes darted up to Elitsa and then away. She seemed more nervous than bereaved. "Has the city guard come yet?" Elitsa asked, noting how quickly the girl's eyes shot back to hers.

"They've been sent for, and the doctor," the woman wearing jewelry said. She raised her chin, studying Elitsa's clothing. "Did you know Mistress Dulkai?"

"She was working on a dress for me," Elitsa lied, relieved when that answer seemed to satisfy them. When the conversation continued, she stepped closer to the girl. "Can I talk to you for a moment?"

The girl nodded, following Elitsa several steps away from the group. As she escaped the cluster of women, the girl's confidence increased markedly. Her eyes slid past Elitsa to the street, and Elitsa took a purposeful step in front of her. If the girl wanted to run, she'd have to push past her or through the women behind them.

"You don't work for Mistress Dulkai, do you," Elitsa said quietly, catching the girl's eyes.

"What? Of course I do!" The girl gripped her skirts with wind-chapped hands. "I'm her ... her assistant."

Elitsa raised an eyebrow. She was clearly too unnerved to lie well. "I've seen you before, in the River District. You're a thief." She raised a hand at the alarm in the girl's eyes. "Relax, I'm not going to tell anyone; I just have some questions."

"I didn't kill her," the girl hissed, glancing back at the women.

"I know." It seemed highly unlikely. "What's your name?"

The girl gave her a sullen look. "Neci."

"When you found her, did you see anything unusual? Or anyone leaving the building?"

Neci frowned. "No one killed her; she died from the Sickness."

"Nothing strange at all?" Elitsa asked impatiently. "No smells?"

"Smells?"

"Did you touch her? See anything on her body?"

Neci's eyes widened in disgust. "I didn't *touch* her," she hissed. "Who are you, exactly? Why are you asking me this?"

"I'm training to be a healer," Elitsa lied, relieved to see Neci's suspicion soften. Releasing a frustrated breath, Elitsa pressed on the skin above her lip. How could there be nothing? How could a rogue kill without leaving any traces behind? No signs of poison or injury? She narrowed her eyes, considering the flustered expression on Neci's face. "Why are you still here? Why didn't you run?"

Neci glanced sideways, crossing her arms. "I would have, but I heard someone at the door and had to hide under the bed."

"So there was someone!"

"Just some rich lady."

Elitsa felt a spark of excitement. "What did she look like? What'd she do?"

"I don't know." The girl shrugged. "All I could see were her legs. She checked if the seamstress was alive, I think? She didn't say anything. She had some kind of silver shield on her calf, under her dress. A relic, maybe? She was only there a few minutes. I waited, thinking she left, but when I slipped out into the hall, she was there. Then all those women arrived, and I told them I was the seamstress's apprentice, so they told me to wait for the guards and ..." She glanced at the women. "I've been stuck here."

Elitsa looked back towards the street, remembering the person who'd brushed past her. *I should have paid more attention*, she thought, dismayed and irritated with herself. Had the woman been wearing a relic? A rogue had walked right by her, and Elitsa didn't even know the color of her eyes or hair.

The sound of a shoe scraping against stone, brought her attention back to the girl, who'd started to shift sideways as if to make a run for it.

"There they are! The city guards," one of the women called out, nodding at two uniformed figures approaching from the east.

Neci paled, eyes rounding like moons, and clutched at her shawl.

"Just tell them what you told the women," Elitsa said quietly. "They'll believe you." She felt sympathetic to the girl's fear, but she couldn't get involved. She'd hoped to get a look at the room, even if there was nothing to find, but it'd be better to be gone before the guards arrived. She had no contract to explain her interest in the death and didn't want to be questioned for half the day. As a reclamation agent for the Tower, Elitsa had equal if not more authority than the city guards, which didn't exactly lead to friendly interactions.

As the women turned towards the guards — after drawing Neci back into their fold — Elitsa slipped into a side alley. They didn't notice her leave, too eager to be the first to offer their thoughts on the seamstress's passing. Exiting onto a broad street that passed beneath the Messengers' tower, currently quiet, Elitsa frowned at the stones beneath her feet. Mistress Dulkai was the thirteenth death this year attributed to the Night Sickness, nearly twice that of the year before. If someone was purposefully killing these people, she could find no reason for it. What connected Mistress Dulkai to her mother? To any of the others? They held different jobs, were of different sexes and ages, and had no familial connection. A few had relic contracts with the Guild, but not all.

And why had the king and Guild, with their resources and money, been unable to catch the assassins? It was maddening. Elitsa could understand why they kept the existence of the killer or killers quiet, why they let everyone believe it was just a mysterious illness, but if they were trying to do anything at all to stop them, she could see no sign of it.

If only I could warn people, she thought bitterly, eyeing the fresh loaves of bread in the baker's window. But what would she say? She had no answers either, nothing beyond 'beware the rogues', which was what the Tower counseled anyway. It was better to keep her head down and eyes open. Was that selfish? Elitsa had hardened herself, discarding compassion to survive, but whatever changes she wanted to make to ease her guilt, she still had to be practical. Her mother would understand that. *You can't save someone from drowning, my love, if they pull you under.*

An unexpected wave of loneliness left her heart feeling hollow, and Elitsa pressed her fingers to her cheek. It'd been years since her mother's passing, but sometimes the ache felt as fresh as an open wound. Right now, all she wanted to do was run back home and lean her head against her mother's knee, feel her strong fingers running through her hair, hear her throaty laughter. Branka had always seemed to know what to do and say.

If I'd died instead, she'd likely already found and hauled my killer before the king. It was a ghastly thought, but it lifted the corner of Elitsa's mouth. The loneliness softened and receded, the longing just a whisper. All Elitsa could do was keep moving forward. For now, that had to be enough.

CHAPTER 3

Climbing a short hill, Elitsa followed the cobbled street beneath a stone archway. On the other side, she checked the shadows as she passed beneath the green-tinged copper hooves of two rearing horses. It was more out of habit than any real threat of ambush — she was in sight of the Tower, after all — but she'd rather be overly cautious than surprised.

Never let your guard down, Lelja's gruff voice rumbled in her mind. *They'll think you're weak, soft, so you'll have to fight more than most.* Despite spending an entire year in the veteran reclamation agent's shadow, Elitsa hadn't seen much of Lelja once she'd signed her own contract. When the older woman retired a year ago, it'd been several months before Elitsa found out she'd left the Tower's service. *She hadn't wanted to teach me anyway,* Elitsa thought.

Training with Lelja had been High Mage Vilis' doing. A Guild mage who'd used to purchase old books from her mother, Vilis was the closest thing to family Elitsa had left, aside from Pipene. His support was the only reason she'd been allowed to become an agent. Irritation tightened Elitsa's jaw. She didn't understand why she still felt hurt over Lelja's indifference. The encouraged competition between agents did not leave much room for friendship.

Shoving aside old memories, Elitsa focused on the broad lawn ahead of her. The Guild tower sat at its center, dark red stone rising high enough into the bright sky that the mages could look down on the entire city, as well as the king's castle to the north. Clustered around its base, like the points of stars, were smaller, single-story buildings that housed the kitchens, stables, and receiving halls, one of which was where Elitsa accepted and returned her contracts. Despite her connection to Vilis, she'd never been in the tower proper itself. From beneath her feet, a ring of white stone ran around the edge of the grassy hilltop, divided by three more archways guarded by stone horses. Wide paths, like the one ahead of her, connected the outer pathway to the courtyard, aligning with the spoke-like buildings around the tower's foundation.

Starting down the path, Elitsa saw a small group of people having a picnic on the trimmed lawn to her right. They were lounging on colorful blankets, laughing and drinking. Based on their rich clothing, they were either nobles from the Moon Court or from The Hearth, the wealthy neighborhoods that separated the king from the rest of Rivna. What were they doing here? The Guild's hill was not a usual spot for gatherings. Why hadn't the guards chased them off?

Elitsa stared at them in confusion as a slim figure with dark brown hair and a long, bright green coat suddenly jumped to their feet. Facing the Tower, they threw their arms wide and howled like a wolf, making several of the others burst into loud laughter. As the figure spun, coat flaring out around their legs, Elitsa recognized the king's angular face, his head thrown back with a wide grin. He was young for a king, only a few years older than Elitsa, but he acted more like a rebellious child than a ruler, planning elaborate pranks and doing ridiculous things like filling the throne room with kittens.

Last summer, a week before the queen's arrival for their wedding, he'd hosted a midnight party during the full moon where he somehow convinced half the younger nobles to strip naked and cover themselves in sugar to attract the moon moths. The king was too busy having fun and thumbing his nose at the Tower, the true power in Rivna, to do anything meaningful.

Lips thinning in distaste, Elitsa continued down the path to where the lawn ended, and the courtyard began, passing through a ring of dead trees with bark the color of bone. It was said they'd been beautiful — blooming with thousands of star-shaped flowers — before the Tower split a hundred years ago, and the rogue mages who'd left drained the essence of everything around it. Afterward, the remaining mages had to replace the dirt as nothing would grow, though Elitsa often wondered why they'd left the dead trees. A reminder, perhaps?

Two guards, in dark green tunics with the Guild's emblem embroidered on it, bracketed the door to the Hall of Reclamation. They were clearly ignoring the king's antics, which seemed to be the Guild's way of dealing with him. Their silver buttons shone in the sunlight, glinting with the telltale pearl shine of magesilver. Unlike the medallion she'd retrieved from Janso, their relics had been created without impurities and could hold more essences. Elitsa had heard the guards carried prepared essence combinations, both offensive and defensive spells, that could be deployed quickly and efficiently, though she'd certainly never attacked one to find out. Rogues would go after agents in the street, but so far, no one had been brazen enough to force their way past the Tower guards. Did they get bored waiting for an attack that never came?

With chin-length brown hair and a face that brought to mind a pine marten, the guard on the left gave Elitsa a curious look, his gloved hand resting on his sword. She'd never seen him before.

Luckily she didn't have to pull her hands from her pockets to show her badge, as the other guard knew her.

"Agent Serlov," Guardsman Oltov said, "welcome back."

"Guardsman Oltov," Elitsa murmured, dipping her head as she reached for the door.

When she first started working for the Tower, Oltov had tried to open the door for her on numerous occasions. It'd perplexed her as the gesture went against the guards' standard procedure of keeping their hands free, and she was the only agent he singled out. Eventually, she'd learned she reminded him of his daughter, and it had taken several requests before he stopped treating her differently.

As Elitsa entered the darkened hall, she heard the younger guard say, "*She's* an agent?" before the door shut behind her and cut off the cold wind.

Rolling her eyes, Elitsa headed for the collections office. There were no windows in the lower rooms of the tower. Lightprisms on the wall provided enough light to see, but they were spaced far enough apart that there were shadows in between. The Guild didn't use torches inside, as anyone with a relic could attempt to grab the fire's essence. Instead, they relied solely on lightprisms — thick glass crystals with fire essence trapped inside. The light never went out, and the glass was thick enough that it would take time to break one. *Difficult, but not impossible*, Elitsa mused. Someone with a strong wood essence could smash a prism to pieces easily enough, but the sound would undoubtedly bring an entire squad of Guild mages down on their head.

Passing through a long room with padded benches pushed up against the walls, Elitsa turned into the adjoining hall and entered the first door on the left. The wallpaper always drew her eye despite how often she'd seen it, a near dizzying pattern of colorful flowers and long-feathered birds. It was so striking that it was almost possible to ignore the wooden desk in the room's center and the occupant in the chair behind it.

Guild Mistress Astraia, of the Hands — which Elitsa thought was an odd name for the administrative branch of the Tower — glanced up from the open ledger on her desk and marked her place with one long-nailed finger. The Guild mage was always a picture of order with never a wrinkle or unplanned crease in her pleated skirt or crisp, embroidered blouse. Her heavy cloak hung neatly from a hook on the wall, and her gloves were perfectly stacked on her desk beside a cup of tea. Beaded necklaces hung around her neck, and her silvering black hair was knotted behind her head. Her pale green eyes looked unimpressed as they passed over Elitsa's rumpled clothing and mud-splattered boots.

Elitsa resisted the urge to squirm.

"Agent Serlov," Astraia said in a throaty voice. "I expected you yesterday. Unforeseen complications?"

Elitsa winced before she could stop herself, then straightened and strode towards Astraia's desk. What was it about the woman that made her feel like a misbehaving child? "Nothing significant." Elitsa removed the medallion and placed it on the table. Astraia didn't bother with extra chairs, so Elitsa was left to stand over her awkwardly. *Always ensuring we know who's in charge*, she thought sourly, crossing her arms. She'd observed that despite Astraia's control of all contracted relics, the mage's position wasn't considered prestigious enough to elevate her within the Guild's hierarchy. So how did the Guild mistress compensate for feeling powerless? *By making me wait.*

Taking her time, Astraia leisurely picked the medallion up. She rolled it between her fingers, the tang of lemon and fresh rain filling Elitsa's nose as the mage probed the relic for essence. Finding nothing — as Elitsa knew she would — Astraia turned a few pages in the ledger and wrote something down. "Mr. Tirin Janso. Contract closed." She opened a drawer and removed a slip of pale gray paper. Making a notation for the amount Elitsa would be paid, she stamped the sheet with the Guild's seal, then held it up without looking.

Elitsa took the paper from Astraia's fingers, recognizing the dismissal, and was turning away when the mage looked up.

"Your term is nearly up," she said.

Elitsa eyed her, unsure what the Guild mistress' interest implied. "Yes, seven days tomorrow."

"I thought High Mage Vilis made a mistake when he sponsored you."

Elitsa blinked at the sudden barb. *Ouch. She certainly sharpened her dagger this morning.* Though Astraia had never been exactly warm, she'd never been rude or malicious. Unsure of how to respond, Elitsa stared at her.

"You proved me wrong." Astraia folded her hands. "You've been quite successful. One of our quickest agents. I hope you'll consider signing a new contract."

Now she was complimenting her? Confused, Elitsa nodded at the unexpected praise. "Thank you, Mistress Astraia."

Astraia pursed her lips — perhaps because Elitsa hadn't confirmed if she would seek an extension of her contract — then looked back at her ledger.

"Is there a new retrieval contract for me?" Elitsa asked after a moment of awkward silence. "I still have time …"

"All current contracts have been assigned. You may check the city boards."

Elitsa nodded, careful to keep relief off her face. She hadn't decided what she was going to do after the end of her contract, and it would be nice to have time to consider. *Especially after today*, she thought, the regret returning. Hunting people like Janso, who she could sympathize with, had worn her thin, and she needed to get away from it before she stopped caring entirely. For how long, she wasn't sure.

The door opened, and a young girl walked in carrying a drink tray. As she set it carefully on the edge of Astraia's desk and turned the teapot's handle towards the mage, Elitsa looked at the dark red apple beside a small plate of cheese. It was large and glossy, a reminder that while Rivna's poorer citizens struggled to fill their bellies with stunted fruit and vegetables, the Guild was successfully growing food and keeping the best for themselves.

And our ridiculous king does nothing, Elitsa thought angrily, clenching her fist. He had the nobles' favor; why not attempt something? Her emotions were heightened, her anger feeling reborn. She needed to leave before she did something she'd regret. "Good day, Mistress Astraia," Elitsa said, barely keeping a growl from her voice.

The mage nodded, not lifting her eyes from her paper.

Leaving Astraia's office, Elitsa followed the hall deeper into the tower towards Accounts, where she could exchange the gray slip for payment. The unassuming door was located between an old bench and a faded tapestry, a hopefully overembellished depiction of mages facing off against an ice wyrm exploding out of the ground. *Glad you're not still around,* she thought, grimacing at the wyrm's gaping mouth filled with thousands of razor-edged teeth. Pulling hard on the door's handle, Elitsa walked straight into someone's chest.

"Feeling a fire, Eli?" a familiar voice laughed as they caught her arm.

Elitsa immediately pulled back and tipped her head to look up into Casimir's face. She sighed as he grinned wickedly. It was just like him to act as if they'd just shared some intimate joke instead of her smacking into him. Tall, with smooth black hair that swept down over his cheek and jaw, Cas had the irritating ability to find amusement in everything. He usually wore a teasing smile, but Elitsa had seen him easily turn off his jovial humor when he wanted to appear tragic and brooding. It was a tactic he frequently employed in taverns, one that earned him numerous drinks and willing companions.

She looked longingly past him to the clerk and thought about the lunch she could buy once she exchanged her stamped ticket for payment. Unfortunately, Cas seemed to have decided to trap her in the doorway. "What do you want, Cas?" Elitsa sighed, frowning up at him.

"Want?" Delight filled his warm brown eyes. "I'm just being friendly to a fellow agent." He braced his arm against the door frame, forcing Elitsa to keep the door open with her shoulder and foot lest it shove her into him.

"Can you let me pass? I need to—Hey!"

Cas plucked the ticket from her fingers and held it up over her head, reading it.

Refusing to be seen jumping in an attempt to reclaim it, Elitsa crossed her arms and deepened her glare.

"Ah, a farmer bounty. A simple one, no?"

"Easy enough."

"Oh yeah? Didn't I see you running after some old man in front of Veselka? You tripped on a—"

Jumping, Elitsa snatched the pay ticket from Cas's hand and caught him around the neck and shoulder, using her momentum to swing him sideways. Surprised, he caught her waist, letting go of the door frame as they turned.

Elbowing Cas sharply in the chest, Elitsa released his shoulder and pushed him back as her boots landed on the floor. Before the door could slam shut, she kicked it open, shoving him hard out into the hall, then yanked the door closed between them, all while ignoring the surprised grin still caught on his face.

Elitsa straightened her coat and turned around, stalking to the high desk where the clerk waited. She slapped the stamped paper onto the counter and glowered at the buttons on the man's vest, refusing to look into his eyes as her cheeks heated. What must he be thinking after seeing her throw herself on Cas? "Contract collection, please," she said quickly.

The man collected the paper with long, pale fingers. "One moment." Fabric rustled as he bent down behind the desk, then she heard the clink of metal and the slide of cloth as he pushed a small bag across the counter towards her.

Grabbing the purse, Elitsa looked up into the clerk's round face. He gave her a bland expression, though she saw the thick mustache above his lip quiver as though he was trying not to smile.

"Thank you." Cheeks flaming, Elitsa whirled around and shoved the purse into her coat. She walked quickly back to the door and yanked it open, relieved the hall was empty. She'd half-expected to find Cas waiting for her, and she did not want to see that damned grin on his face. As she retraced her footsteps to the exit, her mind helpfully reminded her how his hands had felt around her waist. Her blush deepened. *Hells, Elitsa, you'd think a boy's never touched you before.*

Though Cas had received his contract six months after she had four years ago, he liked to pretend that he was the veteran agent. As if being older by two years gave him extra experience. Every job and new skill became a competition, with Cas constantly appearing during her contract collections to goad her or comment on how she was handling things. Whatever charm others saw in him, she did not. He was insufferable and annoying and so damnably arrogant and—

Breathe. It'd be easier if Cas just ignored her as the others did. Before she'd joined, Elitsa had assumed there was some camaraderie between the agents, some familial bond. She'd thought she'd feel part of something. Instead, they did their best to avoid each other, their interactions either indifferent or suspicious. Cas was the only friendly one, and that made it impossible to trust him.

What is his game? Elitsa thought as she stepped outside. He had to want something from her, but she didn't know what. She also didn't understand how he could be so unaffected by their work. It wasn't that she thought him callous or that Cas enjoyed the misfortune and pain of their marks, but he shouldn't still be so light-hearted, so untouched by their reclamations. He seemed to live with ease. Was he somehow more broken than she was, or did he simply know how to live?

Feeling oddly resentful, Elitsa stepped outside. She didn't want to think about Cas anymore. Nodding at the guards, she turned up the collar of her coat against the cold wind, and headed back to the Kurdaima in search of lunch.

CHAPTER 4

Elitsa's door slammed open, prompting her to drop the book she was holding and roll unceremoniously off the bed. She rose up on one knee, the rounded butter knife she'd snatched off the floor grasped in her hand.

The tall blonde woman standing in her doorway giggled as she shoved the door closed. "The look on your face!" Pipene said, wiping tears from her eyes.

Sticking out her tongue, Elitsa tossed the dull knife towards Pipene, who easily evaded it, and picked the book off the floor. She closed it and smoothed her fingers over the spine, her thoughts turning to her mother. The cold brush of grief made her pause. It'd been over eight years since her mother's death, and yet there were moments where the pain returned as sharp as when she'd left. *And I still don't know who took you from me.*

Elitsa set the book back on her bed and turned to Pipene, her sadness subsiding at the affectionate smile on her friend's face. "I could have killed you."

Pipene shook her head, laughing. "Maybe if you'd hit me with that heavy book." She shifted her arm, the white cloak of swan feathers sliding off her pale right shoulder. The cloak looked like it'd be heavy, the cascade of snowy plumes reaching from Pipene's shoulder to the back of her calves, but Elitsa knew from one laughter-filled evening that it was soft and light. Though Pipene often left it draped over her shoulders — revealing whatever diaphanous dress she'd selected for the day — a heavy ribbon could be used to tie it closed.

Sometimes, Elitsa didn't recognize the girl she'd grown up with. Pipene had always been beautiful, but now with her jeweled combs and striking cloak, she'd become something otherworldly, like one of Mother Moon's handmaids from the old stories. It was no surprise that she was thriving as a companion at Solveiga's. Pipene often expressed how much she enjoyed her interactions with the House's varied clientele, especially the people who traveled. Personally, Elitsa thought it'd be exhausting. Sex was one thing, but how did Pipene not run out of things to talk about? Still, if you didn't mind so much social interaction, Solveiga took care of her Swans, and that was invaluable when half the country was starving.

"What are you up to?" Pipene's eyes swept the room and landed on the book Elitsa had rescued from the floor. "One week until you're a free woman, and you're reading?" She wrinkled her nose. "Adventures are out in the wind and on the road, not caught in dusty pages! It's a good thing I came to rescue you."

Throwing open her cloak with a dramatic flourish, Pipene revealed a bottle of clear liquor. "You really need chairs in here."

"You're the only person who visits me, Pippe," Elitsa laughed.

"Well, you do keep it dreadfully cold in here." Pipene shivered, making a show of rewrapping her cloak around her neck and shoulders as she sat cross-legged on Elitsa's bed. "You should move in with me! Solveiga won't mind."

"No, thank you. I like the quiet."

Something thumped overhead, and Pipene arched an eyebrow.

Laughing, Elitsa sat across from her and gave the small room a critical eye. It wasn't much, slightly smaller than the room she'd shared with her mother growing up, but she had a bed, warm blankets, a table — it was rickety, but it served its purpose — and a wooden chest to store her clothes. She even had a small window that looked out over the courtyard. Though Elitsa didn't have a fireplace, Solveiga had run heated pipes through the floors bringing water to the shared bathroom down the hall. It kept the chill away too, which she truly appreciated during winter. There were advantages to your landlord having wealthy clients from the Moon Court and the high mages in the Tower.

Pipene pulled the cork from the liquor bottle and took a drink before handing it to Elitsa. "So," she said, eyes sparkling like sun-lit water, "have you decided what to do with yourself before you sign a new contract?"

Elitsa took a small sip of the honeyed spirits and passed it back. Despite the pleasant taste, she grimaced. It was a question she really should have the answer to by now. And when she'd suggested to Pipene several days ago that she might take a break, she'd thought it'd be a week or two. But now?

The turmoil she'd felt that morning eddied up inside her belly like a poisoned spring. Had Pipene noticed the changes in her? Elitsa had never been as free with her emotions as she was. Pipene often joked that Elitsa was as easy to read as a wind-smoothed stone. She'd never understood that. She'd always thought her feelings were a tangible thing, her sorrow and anger as easy to see as the scattered freckles on her cheeks. Elitsa stared into Pipene's bright eyes until her friend raised a quizzical brow.

"No, not really," she admitted. Elitsa thought about Janso and all the others before him. Should she try to explain? Pipene was kind and good, always willing to help. She would never have done what Elitsa had. Never accept a job where someone could be injured or killed. "I think I need to do something new." She knew it was true as soon as she said it, the need for a different direction rushing like fire through her skin. "I can't do this another four years."

Pipene tilted her head, expression softening as if she might understand. She'd never judged Elitsa for working for the Guild, but Elitsa had always had the impression that she hoped she'd picked something else. Still, Pipene knew her motivation. "You want to leave the Tower."

"Yes ... though it seems unwise, doesn't it? I earn enough to support myself, and if I work for another eight years, I get a bonus that could mean true freedom. It'd be better to quit then." The thought of eight more years sent a chill down her spine, but Elitsa kept that thought to herself.

"You shouldn't stay if you're unhappy."

Elitsa smiled sadly. "That's not often a choice we get to make."

Pipene reached forward and squeezed her hand. "Well, you don't have to decide now. And leaving the Guild doesn't mean giving up on finding your mother's killer."

Sometimes Pipene could see straight through her to where Elitsa's fears hissed and slithered.

"Why not talk to some of the retirees?" Pipene laughed suddenly, and covered her mouth with one hand. "Makes you sound old, doesn't it."

Elitsa grinned. It was impossible not to smile when Pipene did. She thought about the agents who'd left. "Well, there was Aleks who planned to open an inn in Broceia, and I think Minna was going to become a caravan guard? Most don't talk about their plans, you know."

"And the handsome one?"

Elitsa raised an eyebrow. There were over fifteen agents.

"The funny boy, Cas. He's friends with Ieva, you know. I see him at the House sometimes."

Of course she was talking about Cas. Elitsa scowled. "I don't know; I've never asked him."

"Why not?"

"Because he's annoying!"

Pipene smiled knowingly, tucking her bottom lip beneath her teeth. "There must be something you want to do."

Elitsa reached for the book and ran her fingers over the faded title. It was one her mother had restored, about the different seas of Cerana. She'd often wondered if her father, Arno, had ever read it. He'd been a mapmaker, an explorer, and had lived more on ships than on Casekraian land. She didn't remember him. He'd disappeared in the Crystal Sea when she was four. "Maybe I should travel." She glanced up at Pipene with a stab of guilt. They'd always talked about running off on adventures together. "I've never had time to just … enjoy myself, you know?" Elitsa said quickly, feeling like she had to explain. She looked for disappointment or hurt in her friend's face, but it didn't appear.

"A vacation!" Pipene rocked forward, setting the bottle down on the floor, the strands of beads on her shoulders swaying as she moved. "Yes, that sounds like a glorious plan. You should visit the other continent! Explore the jungles of Hibera, or ride one of those big lizards in Xiltarma. There's so much to see!"

"Well, considering the cost of travel and that Hibera is incredibly dangerous—"

"According to a bunch of fussy merchants," Pipene interrupted, rolling her eyes.

"—I probably won't go much farther than Velasa. You could come with me." Hope bloomed for one long heartbeat, until she saw the flicker of regret in her friend's eyes.

Pipene shook her head, still smiling. "No, I can't leave." She glanced towards the door, eyes going distant for a moment. "It's curious there are no retired agents in Rivna, isn't it? At least I've never heard of any."

Elitsa frowned. "Yes, I suppose it is." She'd never really thought about it before, though what Pipene said was true. There were no retired agents in Rivna. Most reclamation agents remained in service until they died, but a few every year chose to move on. Why had they all decided to leave? People usually moved to Rivna, not away from it. As Casekraia's capital, there were more opportunities here than out in the smaller towns and villages, and with the Guild's presence, the agents had access to amenities that those in the country did not. *Well, at least before the Guild started rationing everything.*

Come to think of it, Elitsa hadn't heard of or seen any retired agent return for a visit either. Did they have no ties at all, even those who had been in service for years? Did no one miss their magesilver and being able to use magic? Was it really so easy to give it all up, to walk away without looking back? *I'm thinking of doing so, at least for a little while.* But she had no plans to disappear forever. The answers of who murdered her mother were here, as was Pipene.

Pipene nudged her knee. "You should send a message to the man who wanted an inn."

"Aleks?"

"Yeah, ask him how it is on the other side of Guild employ-ment." Pipene gestured vaguely.

Elitsa wasn't certain Aleks would appreciate her checking in, but they weren't in competition any longer. He'd been a little like Cas, quick to smile, though it'd never quite filled his eyes. *It couldn't hurt talking to him.* "Yes, Broceia could be a good place to start my vacation." Maybe seeing Aleks would give her an idea about what she should do or not do. *And I can ask him why no one seems to stay.*

Pipene nodded eagerly. "Yes. You can take a break, and then decide what to do. I've heard it's very pretty there and not far from the Moon Sea." Her face brightened, a slight dimple appearing in her left cheek. "They're known for their painting. Bring me back a decorative spoon or something!"

Elitsa laughed. "All right." She felt uneasy, but maybe she was just nervous about not knowing what to do next. It'd been a long time since she'd been without a clear plan. And as Pipene said, she didn't have to decide now. If she couldn't find a new way to support herself, she could always come back. But surely the Guild was not the only job for her.

"Well, it sounds like you have a direction." Pipene sprang up onto her feet, shaking the bed and nearly dumping Elitsa onto the floor. "To adventure!" she declared, throwing open her arms.

Laughing, Elitsa leaned back onto her elbow. What she wouldn't give for just a drop of Pipene's happy self-assurance. "To adventure."

The Next Day

"WHAT DO YOU MEAN THERE'S NO ALEKS?" ELITSA ASKED impatiently. She leaned over the counter, receiving a pinched glare from the dark-haired woman on the other side. "Do you know where he went? He was a Guild reclamation agent. He was going to open an inn."

The messenger, Yeva, a surprisingly unfriendly woman considering her profession, gave Elitsa an impatient look, then heaved herself out of her chair and walked back to the east-facing window.

The narrow messengers' tower was taller than the majority of the buildings in the city — though not as high as the Guild tower north of them — and offered a breathtaking view of the land outside the city's walls, including the farmlands to the south and the trees and snow-brushed mountains past Lake Odarka to the north. Broceia, a village on the river that opened to the sea, was several days' ride east of Rivna.

Additional communication towers along the main roads allowed messages to be passed between the capital and the towns and villages beyond. Paid for by the king, the Guild supplied the messengers with magesilver relics and essences. Their service was much faster than sending a rider or bird, though it cost a few coins more. It wasn't always worth the extra money, but as a reclamation agent, Elitsa had saved quite a lot of time using the towers to track people down.

Yeva opened the window, letting in a blast of cold air, and raised a small hooded lantern. Pressing a lever on its side, she began to tap her finger, switching between long and short presses, which resulted in flashes of light. Elitsa could smell the smoky scent of fire and wind, as well as a strange earthy odor of a firebeetle. Whatever mage had figured out how to combine the beetle's essence with fire and wind was very clever.

Watching the window, Elitsa saw a brief flare of light, a signal from the eastern tower that their message had been received. Now they'd have to wait while it was relayed to Broceia and a reply sent back. Yeva had a mirrored device on the counter that would allow her to see if any messages came through one of the windows, but she stayed where she was, perhaps hoping Elitsa would get bored and leave her alone.

Falling back onto her heels, Elitsa paced across the circular room, ignoring the irritated look Yeva shot over her shoulder. Usually, she'd examine the ornamental panels on the walls — exquisite wood carvings of flowers and birds and the curling forms of elemental essence — but today she couldn't focus. She felt restless, her earlier unease growing. It was like the feeling she'd get before a bad storm or when she knew something terrible had happened — like someone was hurt or missing. Her second sight, as her mother called it. *We're all connected, Elitsa, like beads of dew on a spiderweb. If the web thrums, we all feel it.*

There was a thump as Yeva set the lantern down and turned back to the counter. "The last message took hours, and your pacing is giving me a headache. Go get a drink or something."

Elitsa sighed impatiently but headed towards the stairs. Her presence wouldn't hurry Broceia's reply. She rushed down the spiraling staircase and burst out onto the street, startling a passing woman. Giving her a hasty apology, Elitsa headed straight to a small cafe where she ordered tea and a thick, hearty slice of dark bread flavored with caraway seeds and sugar beet syrup. She gulped the bread and sweetened black tea down at the table by the window, then, deciding she'd left Yeva alone long enough, headed back to the messenger tower.

Back at the top, Elitsa found Yeva waiting for her behind the counter. She had an odd expression on her face. Was that sympathy in her green eyes?

"The man is dead," Yeva said carefully.

Elitsa frowned and pressed her hands into the counter. "What do you mean dead? You last told me Aleks wasn't there."

"There have never been any innkeepers in Broceia with the name of Aleks Bondaren; however, they do recall a former Guild agent last year who was robbed and killed a few days after taking residence at The Balodis. There was some confusion over the identity of the body, but perhaps he's the man you're looking for."

Elitsa's skin prickled. "He was never identified? Did they ask the Tower?"

"A request was made, but the Guild only confirmed they were missing no active agents."

Elitsa frowned and bit the inside of her cheek. Could it be Aleks? Active agent or not, why hadn't the Guild sent someone to investigate? She pulled a handful of copper coins from her pocket and set them on the counter. "I need to send another message."

CHAPTER 5

How could they all be dead or missing? Elitsa had spent the entire day with Yeva, much to her irritation, and sent numerous messages to every town with a messenger tower. Even the trade guild in Velasa claimed no one beyond their merchants and bonded sailors had boarded a ship in the last three years. She'd been unable to find a single retired agent anywhere. It was unnerving and improbable.

Entering the hall to her apartment, Elitsa was so caught up in her thoughts that she nearly ran into Sofija Arenko, who was backing out of her doorway. A tall, thin woman, Sofija's clothing was always tidy and neatly pressed, somehow managing to avoid the mud from the street. Even her dark brown hair, graying at the temples, resisted the wind's effort to dishevel it, every strand tucked neatly beneath an embroidered scarf. Her patterned red apron — adorned with green stripes and ribbons of orange and white flowers — covered a dark blue skirt beneath. There were touches of Sofija's skilled embroidery around the hem, small black flowers like the ones on her apron.

"Mother Sofija," Elitsa said in surprise as she watched the

older woman lock her door. "Forgive my hastiness." She leaned in to kiss Sofija's cheeks.

"Elitsa. It is good to see you."

Elitsa felt a stab of guilt at the genuine affection on the older woman's face. She had not been by to visit her in a long time. After Elitsa's mother had died, Pipene's stepmother, Sofija, had opened her home, despite the added expense of caring for a four-teen-year-old girl. It was a generous offer, but not without its complications. Elitsa had ultimately declined, fiercely deter-mined to make her own way despite her grief, but her neighbor had still brought her food and checked up on her. "How is Orson?"

"He is a good boy." Sofija beamed. "Generous and kind like his father, Mother bless him. He's taken extra shifts at the mill to help me. My hands aren't quite as nimble anymore, my joints, you know." She massaged her knuckles, then rested her hands on the woven sash tied around her waist. "And you?" Her brown eyes scanned Elitsa's face. "You are taking care of yourself." She said it more as an expectation than a question.

"Of course," Elitsa lied. As kind as Sofija was, she'd never confided in her like she had with her mother.

Sofija nodded approvingly. "You have done well for yourself, Elitsa. I know not everyone appreciates the Tower's presence in our city, but you have a secure, well-paying job, and that should be respected and commended. Stability is a hard thing to come by. Your mother would be proud of you."

Elitsa smiled tightly but didn't argue. She doubted her mother would be proud of how she'd changed, but would she see her job in the same way that Sofija did? Her mother didn't know Elitsa had given up on her apprenticeship. She'd wanted her to become a scribe. Despite her mother's friendship with Vilis or her handling and repair of books on magic, Elitsa had never gotten the impression her mother approved of the Tower. Was that why she'd refused to teach Elitsa her work? Afraid she'd end up working with the mages? *Had she known what it would do to me?*

There was the sound of someone on the stairs and Sofija looked past Elitsa, the warmth disappearing from her face as her lips thinned in distaste. "Come see me soon, dear," Sofija said, her cool voice at odds with her words.

"I will." Elitsa stepped back so Sofija could pass and saw who was waiting in the stairwell. It was Pipene. Her friend smiled politely, but Sofija squeezed past her without so much as a glance.

Sighing, Pipene stepped up onto the landing and rested a hand on her hip. "I might actually prefer her backhanded insults to pretending she can't see me."

Elitsa frowned in understanding. Though Sofija had always been kind to her and Orson, she'd never liked Pipene; something they hadn't understood until recently. Pipene had lived with her stepmother for several years before her father's death, then quickly moved out to live with Solveiga. It was there she'd learned about Sofija's long-held jealousy for her late mother, who her father had married first.

Usually, Pipene brushed off the woman's coolness, but today she looked pale and worried.

"Are you all right?" Elitsa asked, leading the way down the hall to her room, several doors down from Sofija's apartment. Pulling her key from her pocket, she unlocked her door and opened it, stepping inside. The hall was narrow and not a good place for conversation.

As Pipene followed her in and shut the door, Elitsa tugged on her scarf to loosen it then walked to the table, where she lit a thick candle. Pouring a glass of water from a chipped porcelain pitcher, she carried it back to Pipene, but her friend didn't seem to notice when she held out the cup. "Did something happen at work?" It seemed unlikely, as Solveiga did not tolerate misbehavior from guests at the House of Swans, no matter their wealth or station.

Pipene shook her head, fretting with the fall of hair over her shoulder. It was partially braided across the crown of her head, with a pale pink ribbon woven throughout the honeyed strands. "No, I'm sorry, seeing Sofija …" She shook her head. "It's Orson."

Orson was Sofija's son from her first marriage — to a cruel man who'd found his death one night by the docks — and, unlike his mother, adored Pipene. The three of them had played together as children, throwing dice in the narrow hall and chasing each other on the rooftop. As Orson was several years younger than Elitsa and Pipene, when they'd turned their focus from play to finding their place in the world, they'd stopped spending time together.

"Has something happened to him? Is he all right?" Whatever it was, Sofija didn't seem to know about it yet.

"He took a contract with the Tower."

Elitsa's heart skipped, and she lowered the cup abruptly, water splashing onto her hand. Had Orson found a mage to sponsor him as an agent? Would Vilis have—

No, that was unlikely. Orson must have taken a relic contract to farm. "Sofija said he'd taken extra shifts at the mill."

Pipene shook her head. "The seedbeetles have reduced the amount of good lumber. They're cutting everyone's hours." She crossed her arms, wrapping her cloak around her waist. "You know how much Orson adores his mother — cold shrew that she is — and with the pain in her hands she can't sew like she used to. He's determined to help her. If I'd known what he was thinking, I …" She winced, a look of apology in her eyes. "You've done all right working with the Tower, but Orson … he isn't you and I fear that … he won't be able to—" Pipene sighed, clearly unsure what she wanted to say. "You know I'm not judging your choices, but—"

"I understand. If I'd known this is what he was thinking, I'd have tried to change his mind." Elitsa's stomach churned, thoughts turning to Janso. Lots of people took contracts to gather essences for the Guild. If you knew where to look for the rarest ones, you could earn a good amount of money. At least you could before the seedbeetles' arrival and before overharvesting and depleted soil had thinned what you could find. What if Orson couldn't keep up with his payments to the Guild? "He'll be fine," Elitsa said, trying to assure herself as much as Pipene. If he'd already signed a contract, there wasn't anything she could do. "Orson is smart, and he's been going into the forest since he was a boy. If he's gathering—"

"No." Pipene shook her head. "He's going to sell to the Smoke Eyes."

Dread wove a knot inside her throat, and Elitsa turned back to the table, setting the cup down before she dropped it. "The Guild won't approve." An oversimplification of the rules Orson would have agreed to. Would they send her after him if they found out? She'd never collected a contract on a friend. But if she didn't, what if one of the other agents hurt him? Orson would run like the others.

Pipene walked to the window, staring out at the deepening sunset visible over the rooftop of the building across the court-yard, then she turned back around. "Is there any way his contract can be canceled? He only signed up yesterday. If he gives the relic back …"

"He must complete the term of his contract. They're only canceled when …" Elitsa cleared her throat, feeling helpless. "When they send an agent to collect. If you explain what will happen, maybe you can change his mind. You're his sister, regardless of what Sofija says."

Pipene shook her head. "You know she doesn't like me to interfere, and normally that wouldn't stop me, but I know Orson won't listen to my advice. He'll think I'm being overprotective. But you, you work for the Tower. You know the risks better than anyone, and if you tell him he can't risk selling to the Smoke Eyes, he might listen."

He wouldn't listen to her. Orson was stubborn, and if you challenged him, once he'd made up his mind, he'd dig in his heels to prove you wrong. "Pipene ..."

Reading her expression, Pipene pursed her lips. "What if you tell the Smoke Eyes to stay away from him? They won't want to anger an agent of the Tower, right?"

That's not how it works, Elitsa thought, though she didn't say it aloud. The gang would not be afraid of her. Everyone knew there were rogue mages within the Smoke Eyes, but every time the Tower tried to find them, to take their relics, they'd come up empty-handed. Even the city guards largely ignored the gang unless they publicly murdered someone in the street. The Smoke Eyes were everywhere in the city with ties to merchants, inns, laborers, and even the Hearth. They claimed to help the people, but anything they gave required steep payment. The only other place in Rivna where the Smoke Eyes didn't have a foothold, beyond the king's castle and the Tower, was the Aerie.

But impossible or not, Pipene was family and rarely asked for anything. Elitsa would do whatever she could to help. *If I stay in the open, I'll be fine.* "I'll talk to Orson. Do you know where he is?"

"He left half an hour ago for the Black Eyed Fish. I think he's going to try to meet with them today."

Dismay tightened her stomach. The tavern was a known hangout for the gang. It might already be too late. "I'll find him. I can't force him to come back with me, but I'll do my best."

Pipene nodded, hope chasing some of the worry from her face. Slightly taller than Elitsa, when Pipene grabbed her in a hug, her cheek pressed against Elitsa's temple. "Thank you. I'm sorry for asking you to leave so soon after getting home. I hope Orson knows how lucky he is having two wonderful women looking out for him."

Elitsa chuckled as Pipene drew back, smiling to hide her tiredness. "It's all right. I care about him too."

"Should I come with you?" Pipene bit her lip, brow furrowing. "Or maybe that'd put him on edge."

"It's probably better if I go alone." And safer too. It could be dangerous going into Smoke Eye territory tonight. She needed to be alert. Shaking off the exhaustion that settled on her when she glanced at her bed, Elitsa checked the essences stored in her earrings. She was prepared as much as she could be, and it wasn't so late that the streets would be empty.

Elitsa touched Pipene's arm. "Go home. I'll come by later, or talk to you in the morning. There's no point worrying here. As you've pointed out, I don't have any chairs."

Pipene's brow smoothed as she laughed. "You could at least get a few floor pillows or something."

"And risk more visitors? No, thank you." Lips curving at the corners as Pipene laughed a second time, Elitsa opened the door and stepped into the hall. She ran a hand through her hair as Pipene slipped past her, then shut and relocked her door.

Ignoring the ache in her feet, Elitsa led the way down the stairs and out into the empty courtyard in front. It was colder now, within the shadow of the building, and a chilled wind tugged at their hair and clothing. Golden leaves, shaken free from the cluster of trees by the wall to their left, spiraled past them. Across from them were two more dark gray buildings, both housing for those who lived in the Aerie.

"Be safe," Pipene said, adjusting Elitsa's scarf at her throat, like an older sister, before giving her another tight hug.

"I will. Now go home. That dress of yours looks like it's about as warm as a handkerchief."

"Yes, *Mother*." Laugh ringing like a bell, Pipene gripped the edges of her cloak, pulling it closed over her finespun dress, and broke into a run. Cutting right at the corner of the building, she disappeared in a flash of white feathers.

Smile fading, Elitsa followed after her at a slower pace across the dusky courtyard to the end of the building, but instead of turning, she continued straight. Unlike the majority of the Peoples' Suburb east of her, the Aerie was mainly stone. The buildings here were not as large or lavish as those within the Hearth and Moon Court, but the House of Swans, and the apartments Elitsa lived in, were inside an old estate that'd once served as a cloister for a goddess no one remembered. The outer walls had been partially torn down, save the small walled garden off the back of Solveiga's establishment, but the buildings still held traces of their former life — small, winged embellishments along the roofline and within shadowed corners. The wooden floors, unlike the lighter planks found in the rest of the city, were made from dark, onyx-black wood.

Elitsa pushed away her exhaustion, focusing on her worry for Orson. This week should have been easy, a few jobs, and then a break to clear her mind. Instead, she'd stumbled into something she knew would not lead anywhere good, but the questions wouldn't leave her mind. Who had killed Aleks and the others, and why wasn't the Tower concerned? Was she in danger if she left? Danger from who?

And now Orson was mixed up with it, tied to the Tower like she was. She couldn't fault him for wanting to help his mother. Elitsa had believed the Guild would improve her life too, not drain her. Not twist her into something she didn't recognize. Reclamations should have been a rewarding adventure, a noble and profitable way to chase criminals.

The king's party on the Tower's lawn popped into her head, and Elitsa curled her lip. Why wasn't he doing more? Casekraia was in crisis, people were starving, and he acted like the host of some unending party, letting the Guild rule. She'd thought the new queen might be able to reign him in — she'd seemed capable and serious when Elitsa had glimpsed her during their wedding — but after a year, it appeared she'd already given up. The Guild remained unchallenged, and though it unsettled her stomach, Elitsa knew it was impossible to fight back.

Following a black, tiled walkway past an oak tree, Elitsa glanced at the Aerie's fountain. It was dry like the one in the Lady's Square. The broken statue looked eerie in the fading light, a winged horse missing its head and the tip of one wing. Could the hints of winged creatures in the Aerie be associated with Mother Moon in some way?

Passing the old guard house — now a roost for Solveiga's messenger doves — Elitsa stepped through the open gate and turned east. The sun had set, taking its warmth with it, and Elitsa shivered as the wind brushed her cheeks, catching her hair in her earrings. She'd forgotten her gloves in her room. Pulling her scarf up over her head and lower face, she stuck her hands deep into her pockets. Her split skirt tangled around her legs as she strode down the street.

Lights glowed in frosted windows, and she passed a woman lighting the oil lanterns that marked the main road. They did not have lightprisms here like in the Tower and the wealthy neighborhoods by the king's castle. Leaving the Aerie, Elitsa crossed a bridge into the Peoples' Suburb and passed the school where the merchants' children learned about the intricacies of trade with the rest of Cerana. She'd always wondered what they were taught when the Guild painted the other nations' use of magic as foolishly dangerous.

Turning left, she skirted a parked carriage — the waiting driver brushing his dark brown horses — and headed towards a second bridge to the River District north of them. As she crossed the dark water and set foot on the other side, the city seemed to close in on her. The scent of woodsmoke thickened, spiced with charcoal and drying fish, and an occasional nose-wrinkling whiff from the tanneries to the north.

If the Aerie was a nest, the tradesmen district was a warren of alleys and wide, lumbering buildings covered in soot and grime.

It was easy to get lost in or to hide. She passed a few people, workers wearing dark clothes. Most ignored her, lost in their thoughts as they headed home, but occasionally she'd get a look of suspicion. Despite being fairly unobtrusive, not many young female agents worked for the Tower, which meant Elitsa was recognized more often than she wished. Today, it bothered her more than it had in the past.

As Elitsa wove through the darkening streets, she felt eyes on her back. She glanced over her shoulder, glimpsing a small girl wearing dark skirts with a cap over her hair before she ducked into a shadowed alley. *Probably one of Solveiga's cygnets,* Elitsa thought. Solveiga liked to know what was going on in Rivna, and the kids who worked for her — usually orphans who'd lost their parents — acted as her eyes and ears in the city. In return, Solveiga ensured they were fed and educated. It was also possible the girl was a nightjar, a street child who performed a similar job for the Smoke Eyes, but then you could usually count on them trying to pick your pockets.

The girl following her wouldn't be able to help if Elitsa ran into trouble, but they would alert her to danger with a sharp birdcall. If she disappeared completely, well, then that meant she was one of the Smoke Eyes. It was generally safe to walk Rivna's streets, but Elitsa had noticed new desperation in the eyes of some of the people in the city. Thefts were on the rise. With the king's guard and the mage guild largely leaving the River District alone, the Smoke Eyes had become stronger. As crooked as they could be, she wondered how much worse the streets would become without the threat of their interference. *A bear to keep the wolves in line*, Elitsa thought.

Walking past several dark warehouses, Elitsa headed towards the lantern light outside a small barn-like structure. There was no posted sign, just a green fish painted above the doorway, its bulbous black eye glimmering as light reflected in a shard of glass embedded in the wood. The door was propped open, the sound of talking and music spilling outside. A large man in a heavy wool coat and dark green hat watched as she approached, his whiskered face cast in shadow. Giving him a confident nod, Elitsa strode inside.

The Black Eyed Fish was brightly lit with lanterns hanging from the beams above and smelled of boiled potatoes and cinnamon-baked apples. Long wooden tables filled the room, and sawdust covered the floor. Men in rough wool trousers, collared linen shirts, and vests or coats sat at the tables drinking and talking. There were a handful of women, some similarly dressed like the men for heavy work, and others wearing traditional skirts with embroidered blouses and colored scarves over their hair. Sitting atop one of the tables, a bearded man played a domra, the rounded instrument resting against his thigh as his fingers teased a melody from the strings.

A slab of wood, propped atop old barrels, made up the bar at the back of the room where a small, red-haired woman filled glasses and directed the serving staff. Above the bar was a loft, accessible by stairs against the far wall, and Elitsa could see several people playing cards around a low table on the other side of the wooden railing. The skin prickled on the back of her neck as one of them, a woman in dark gray with short brown hair, slammed a knife into the table with a raucous laugh. Smoke Eyes.

Elitsa glanced around the room. If Orson was seeking the Smoke Eyes, then this was the safest place to find them. Walking towards the bar, she caught sight of Orson's dark hair at the end of one of the tables in the far corner. He was sitting alone with a long gap between him and the men farther down the bench. A wooden mug sat in front of him. He looked nervous, continuously picking at the edge of his sleeve.

Elitsa angled towards him. Keeping an eye on the crowd and the Smoke Eyes in the loft, she walked behind Orson's back and slid onto the bench opposite him. He flinched in surprise, blue eyes widening.

"Elitsa! What are you doing here?" Orson glanced past her towards the loft then leaned forward. "Is my mother all right?" He looked like Sofija, with the same long nose and pointed chin. His dark brown coat, similar in style to her own, hung open, revealing a crisp white shirt, and Elitsa could see Sofija's intricate embroidery in a thick stripe down his chest, hints of flowers visible inside the interlocking diamonds.

"Yes, she's fine." Elitsa's chest tightened. Had it really been so long since they'd spoken that Orson would immediately think something was wrong? They'd never been as close as him and Pipene, but he was part of her childhood. She studied his face, unaware of how to persuade him to abandon his plan. The last time she'd convinced Orson to do something, they'd both been children. "Pipene and I are worried about you."

Orson frowned, understanding passing like a cloud across his face, and he looked back towards the loft. "I'm fine, Elitsa. I know what I'm doing." He hunched forward and gave an incredulous shake of his head. "I can't believe she sent you after me. How did she even …?" He shook his head again, and took a drink from his mug.

Elitsa grimaced and laced her fingers on the table. "Orson, I … I don't think …" She trailed off. If someone had told her not to hunt her mother's killer or that she shouldn't join the Guild, she would have angrily blown them off. "Pipene told me what you plan to do." Elitsa lowered her voice. "I know you want to help your mother, but you shouldn't go against the Guild."

Orson glanced at her, irritation sparking in his eyes.

She knew what he was feeling and the argument brewing on his lips. "You know what I am, what I do," she said before he could argue. "And if you sell to them and the Tower finds out, they'll sever your contract."

"You'd tell them about me?" he demanded in a harsh whisper.

Elitsa leaned forward, narrowing her eyes. "Of course not, Orson, but I can't protect you. People have *died* during relic retrieval. If you get hurt or killed, how will you help Sofija then? Who will take care of her?"

Orson glared at her. "You know she can't sew anymore. I've been doing what I can at the mill, but there are fewer shifts and ... I can do this, Elitsa. A friend of mine knows where to find gadra root, whole fields of it. And how will the Guild find out? If you don't tell them, they won't learn it from the Smoke Eyes."

"It's not worth the risk. Orson, people who've had contracts for years, are unable to make their payments. You should have ..." She rubbed her forehead, an ache beginning behind her eyes. It would not help to tell him what he'd done wrong. He'd already taken a contract. "I'm not telling you to avoid gathering essence, but you don't want to—"

"I'm not stupid, Elitsa," Orson said, cutting her off. "I know the risks, but it's a lot better than starving."

"If you need money—"

"What, you're going to save us? Don't pretend you care what happens to us, Elitsa. Besides, it's not your problem. *I* will help my mother."

Elitsa glowered at him, torn between aggravation at his accusations and the guilty feeling that he was right. Of course, she cared; how dare he suggest she didn't? But she hadn't exactly visited them much either. She hadn't wanted to be a burden, not after Sofija had helped her. She'd been capable of taking care of herself, so she'd focused on that. And with the tension between Pipene and Sofija, it'd just been easier not to have to pick sides. *Maybe if I'd checked in with them, I could have stopped this.*

She was so caught up in wondering what to say that Elitsa stiffened in surprise as a man sat down beside her. She'd stopped paying attention to the room. *Sloppy,* she chided herself. A woman sat beside Orson, then two more men, wearing rough work clothes and carrying mugs of beer, sat in the space between them and the group down the table, who cast nervous looks their way but continued their conversation.

Elitsa eyed the man on her left, noting the glint of a chain around his neck. She'd bet on her life that he was wearing mage-silver. Lean with black hair and a narrow, bearded face, he sat with loose carelessness, but Elitsa could see sharp intelligence in his hooded gray eyes. Though he wasn't dressed differently than the other men in the room, Elitsa knew he was a Smoke Eye. She'd also bet the other two men, who'd started playing a dice game, were as well, despite their feigned indifference about her end of the table.

The woman, though, Elitsa wasn't sure what to make of her. Tall with an athletic build, she wore her brown hair braided and pinned at the base of her neck. There was something decidedly fox-like about her in how she held herself and the bright look of her brown-gold eyes. She wore a buttoned coat and split skirt over trousers, like Elitsa, though her charcoal gray shirt buttoned up around her throat and bore only the faintest hint of decorative stitching around the buttons. The woman was dressed to work outside, but the hand she placed on the table was not scarred or callused. Based on her hands alone, Elitsa would have guessed she was a scholar or worked indoors.

"Friends of yours, Orson?" Elitsa asked, trying to appear calm. Her heart thumped in her chest, but she kept her hands loose on the table. There was hardly any space between her and the man beside her, but she didn't slide away.

"I'll talk to you later," Orson said quickly, eyes jumping between the man and woman. "It was good to see you."

The gray-eyed man turned towards Elitsa and smiled, leaning on his arm. "There's no need to run off, Agent Serlov," he drawled.

Elitsa caught her breath, dread pooling in her belly.

CHAPTER 6

"I didn't tell them," Orson blurted, reaching across the table like he might grab Elitsa's arm. "I swear, I—"

"We don't want to hurt you," the woman said. Her voice was low and measured, and she gave Elitsa a look she obviously intended to be reassuring.

Says the woman with three bodyguards, Elitsa thought sourly. She glanced at the man's hands, prepared to grab the essences in her earrings. If they attacked her, she had no idea how she'd get away with Orson, surrounded as they were. If she set fire to the floor or table, she risked endangering the lives of everyone in the room.

"We just want to talk." The woman's eyes glittered as though she could hear Elitsa's thoughts.

Orson cleared his throat. "I'm the one who asked to speak with you. She wasn't even supposed to be here."

The woman smiled at him, then looked at the man beside Elitsa. "Ivo, why don't you take Orson to the bar."

The man's eyes narrowed slightly, and then he inclined his head, giving Elitsa a long look as he stood up and moved to the other side of the table. "Come," he said, clapping Orson on the shoulder.

Elitsa looked at the woman and then sideways at the men playing dice. She could feel their attention on her and Orson, though neither looked their way. Why did the Smoke Eyes want to talk to her? Were they hoping to get an inside woman in the Tower? Curiosity warred with the desire to get away. Catching Orson's eyes, she gave a little nod. She could handle herself.

Rising, Orson gave her a confused, uncertain look, then followed Ivo to the bar.

Elitsa eyed the stranger. She could see no visible relics, though that didn't mean the woman didn't have any. "Who are you, and what do you want with me?"

"My name is Verka. I'm an essence procurer."

Elitsa resisted the urge to look around. Verka didn't look worried about being overheard, but a statement like that could be dangerous if a Guild mage were in the bar. *And why risk telling me?* "If you're working with the Smoke Eyes you're either unlicensed or very brave."

Verka smiled, eyes gleaming. "It's not illegal to purchase essences."

It wasn't; that was true. There was even an essence market in the Kurdaima, though Elitsa guessed they'd be out of business soon. It was hard to compete with the Guild. Technically, anyone could own a relic, but if you broke the king's law while using one, the Tower would take it away from you. Of course, proof wasn't really required anymore. "I'm not going to help the Smoke Eyes," Elitsa said warily, trying to decide what Verka wanted. She was not going to risk her life giving her relics or essences.

"I don't want you to."

"No?"

"At least not in the way you think. I work with their organization and use their resources to find and sell essences, but I do not belong to it. My employer is someone whose utmost concern is the welfare of the people."

Who would work with the Smoke Eyes? *Probably someone rich who isn't concerned with angering the Guild.* "Who is your employer?"

Verka pursed her lips and ran her fingers over a silver ring on her right hand. "They wish to remain anonymous, but they've seen the Guild's lack of sympathy for the community. The Tower has forgotten why they were created in the first place. You've been chasing more contracts than ever, yes? Tasked to find people who cannot meet the terms of their deal? People who are your neighbors, friends."

What did Verka know about her or her neighborhood? Despite this woman's presence here among the workers, she seemed out of place — a rich woman perhaps, who would return to her warm bed and Guild-grown food. Someone with the luxury to *care.* "I do my job," Elitsa said flatly.

"Yes, you do. You are surviving like everyone else, but what if people could earn more? If *you* could earn more? I, through my employer, am in a position to pay twice what the Guild does per essence. The Tower *could* give more, but they choose not to. Despite all your hard work, even your salary is a fraction of what the lowest mage receives. And what does the Guild do with the essences? They lock them in their storerooms."

"And your employer? What do they do with the essences they acquire?"

"Help the people; ensure there is food in the markets, and medicine for the doctors. I won't pretend everything goes back into the community, some profit must be made, but we care about the citizens. We care about Rivna more than the Guild does, and we are the reason there is still food for the farmers to bring into the city."

A pretty speech, but that was probably all it was. "Why work with the Smoke Eyes? You can purchase essences through the market, same as anyone. Why risk the Guild's ire? Why align yourself with …" Elitsa lowered her voice. "With criminals?"

Verka smiled. "The market's prices are set by the Guild. We could purchase essences there, it's true, but then we would not be helping Rivna. Essence farmers cannot afford to sell there, only those bonded to the merchants."

Elitsa stared at her, trying to read what was behind Verka's eyes. Helping people couldn't be her sole motivation. No one was truly altruistic, especially not someone with money. If Verka could pay more than the Tower, it made sense people were willing to sell to her. And if it meant more people could afford to feed their families, why did it matter if the Smoke Eyes got a few extra essences on the side?

She glanced towards the bar looking for Orson. Why hadn't the Tower done more to stop the Smoke Eyes? They knew people, like Janso, were selling to the gang. They'd terminated his contract, sent Elitsa after him. And yet, here she was talking to Verka. There were no raids, no Guild mages tearing apart the River District. Were they afraid of starting a war? Or did they think it was not worth the effort to hunt them down?

"Have you decided what you're going to do once you finish your contract?" Verka asked abruptly. "This is your final week, isn't it?"

Elitsa blinked, caught off guard. How did she know about that? She didn't think Orson had told her, as he'd seemed surprised they'd even known who Elitsa was. Did Verka have connections in the Tower? Was she trying to catch Elitsa breaking her contract? She narrowed her eyes, distrust coating her tongue. She'd never seen Verka before, but there were a lot of people associated with the Guild. *Are they testing me?*

"I haven't decided." Anger that someone was trying to trick her threatened to cloud her mind, and Elitsa took a careful breath. Something didn't add up. She couldn't see the Guild mages willingly working with the Smoke Eyes. What would the gang get from helping the Tower weed out corruptible agents? If anything, it would be better for them if the agents weren't doing their jobs properly.

Verka folded her hands, and Elitsa thought again about how much she reminded her of a fox. "You've been asking a lot of questions recently. Scratching at the Guild's secrets."

Alarm hummed across Elitsa's skin. Questions? Was Verka talking about the messages she'd sent that morning? "You've been following me." Verka, or someone who worked for her, must have seen her at the messenger tower. Elitsa's stomach roiled. Someone had been watching her, and she hadn't even noticed. "If you're trying to recruit me, this is an odd way to go about it. I don't like being followed."

"They're dead, you know. If you keep looking, you won't find any retired agents. I've always thought it odd that no one has noticed. Do you care so little for each other?"

Heat flushed across Elitsa's cheeks. "You don't know what it's like, who I am."

"It's curious how easily obedience is obtained. Do you know what people call you? Ferrets." Verka's smile was sharp. "Though I think you're more like hounds, happily chasing your master's boots for scraps."

Rage slithered up Elitsa's throat and she clenched her fist, her nails scraping across the table.

"The payout they promised you, the bonus after eight years? You won't live to enjoy it."

Elitsa tensed, forcing the rage away so she could think. Verka was baiting her, threatening her. Why? Her tongue was sharp, cruel, but she hadn't made any physical move against her. It was like she wanted to see how Elitsa would react.

Verka smoothed her fingers over the ring again. It wasn't magesilver, and Elitsa wasn't sure she was aware of how often she touched it. "They won't let you become a mage, but I'd bet you've become quite skilled, using the essences and relics they gave you. What might you do when you're no longer tied to the Tower?"

Why did it matter what she'd do? Was Verka implying she was a threat? To who, the Guild? "You're suggesting that the Guild kills their agents." Though Elitsa meant the words to be sarcastic, disbelieving, she felt a prickle of ice across her skin. Was it possible? "Their deaths were accidental, random."

"I can see in your eyes, Agent Serlov, that you don't believe that. You've survived this long …" She smiled as Elitsa's scowl deepened. "However valuable you've been, they will use and discard you like everyone else." Verka gestured towards the bar. "Your friend, Orson, seems like a nice boy. Do you think the Guild cares about him or his mother?"

"Don't you dare threaten him," Elitsa growled, reaching for the essences in her earrings. She saw the crystalline shape of ice in her mind as water and wind combined. The air chilled.

"I have no intention of harming him," Verka said smoothly. She must have recognized Elitsa was holding her essences, but she made no move to call her own. "I want to help him. My associates may be criminals, as you put it, but they don't hide what they are, nor do they lack all honor. Orson will be paid well for his service."

Pipene's worried eyes came to Elitsa's mind. "I don't want you to work with him. Send him home."

"I'm afraid I can't do that, Agent Serlov. He's already made a deal with Ivo and the Smoke Eyes." Verka nodded past Elitsa. "They take care of their own, but I would not cross them."

Twisting in her seat, Elitsa saw Ivo and Orson by the bar. They were talking, Orson nodding earnestly. Heart sinking, she turned back to Verka. She'd failed. A rush of self-loathing stole Elitsa's breath.

"He is a man, is he not?" Verka said. "We cannot tell him what he can or cannot do. He makes his own decisions. Would you take that away from him?"

There was something in Verka's cunning gaze. "Is that what this was? A distraction?" Had she been so easily manipulated? "Surely Orson can't be that important to you."

Verka arched an eyebrow.

No, this couldn't just be about him. Why talk to Elitsa at all? Why mention Orson's safety and offer assurances? "You want my help with something in exchange for keeping Orson safe."

Verka laced her hands together, her lips curving. "I had hoped that concern for your future would be enough, but yes. Working with the Smoke Eyes can be dangerous. I'll promise to look out for him."

"In exchange for what?"

"There is a small guildhall in Kirtara. They have a stash of relics there. I need to know the movement of their guards in the evening."

"You're going to steal *relics* from the Guild?" Elitsa hissed, leaning forward. "That seems unwise." And needlessly dangerous. She doubted the Tower would continue to ignore them if there was even a hint of their involvement. It'd mark the Guild as vulnerable.

"All I need from you is information. As an agent, you can pass through the hall without notice. I'm not asking you to take anything, or do anything else; just tell me what you see."

"And you don't think it will look suspicious if I travel to Kirtara and the next day there's a theft?"

"There's a contract through the merchant guild that will take you there. You will hardly be the only person in town, and we will not make a move until after you've left. They will not suspect you."

Elitsa frowned. It was not uncommon for agents to travel throughout Casekraia, but what if the Guild was watching her? They were aware her contract was ending, but they likely believed she intended to sign another. Most agents did. *If Verka knows, the Guild may know too.* And now here she was, sitting down with Smoke Eyes in their territory. A chill brushed against Elitsa's neck. *She's put a target on my back.* "And if I'm not interested?"

Verka smoothed her sleeve, then refolded her hands. "It wasn't that hard to figure out what you were up to. If the Tower believed your unquestioning devotion, I doubt they will for much longer. Stay or go; at some point, they'll decide you're no longer useful, and they'll either kill you or cut you loose. Are you prepared to survive on your own? This winter will be hard on all of us, even you. If you work with me, I can pay you enough to give you options."

Elitsa glanced at Orson and Ivo. This wasn't her problem; Orson was old enough to make his own choices, as Verka had pointed out, and yet ... she couldn't go back and look Pipene or Sofija in the eye if Orson got himself killed, or if the Tower sent her after him. But it wasn't just about them. She had to fix this somehow, to save his heart, his goodness, or the guilt gaining strength inside her chest would devour her.

And Verka was right. Elitsa barely had any money saved. If she had to run, she wouldn't get very far. She tried to be loyal, but she owed the Guild nothing, and if they intended to shoot her in the back, better she left before they got the chance.

As if reading the thread of Elitsa's thoughts, Verka leaned forward. The gold in her eyes gleamed. "I'll give you ten silver."

Elitsa raised an eyebrow, her palms feeling clammy. That was enough to feed herself for several weeks. "All that for information?"

"Yes. Do we have a deal?"

It was just information. Elitsa wasn't *helping* them steal from the Guild. And if she didn't give Verka what she wanted, she'd probably go to someone else, like Cas. Cas would have no issue accepting Verka's offer.

And Vilis? What will he think of this? Elitsa felt a surge of guilt, but she shrugged it off. This wouldn't affect him. He had the luxury of keeping his hands clean. Despite their years together, he had made it clear that she had to make it on her own. The Guild wouldn't miss a few relics, and she couldn't leave Orson in the Smoke Eyes' hands alone.

"Fine." Elitsa narrowed her eyes, filling her voice with menace. "But if anything happens to Orson, you'll wish you never learned my name."

Verka smiled. "I look forward to working together."

CHAPTER 7

E litsa sat on the stone wall and stared at the ducks on the water, the sweet bread cooling in her hand. To her left, on the other side of a large lawn, behind a screen of trees, was the bridge that led to the tall stone castle of Rivna's king. She hadn't slept well. Orson had begged her not to tell Pipene or Sofija about his deal with the Smoke Eyes, and she'd agreed … at least temporarily. What could she say anyway after she'd involved herself with the gang?

Elitsa had seen Orson home, then sent Pipene a message that she'd taken care of it and would make sure he was safe. She knew that wouldn't satisfy her, but she wasn't ready to offer assurances that felt hollow or discuss what she'd agreed to. Pipene had never liked the Smoke Eyes, and often spoke of how they preyed on innocent people. Would she be angry about what Elitsa had done? Or disappointed? She wasn't sure which was worse.

The wind shifted, blowing Elitsa's hair across her cheek and filling her nose with the scent of cedarwood and apricot oil. She knew it was Vilis even before she heard his footsteps. She suspected he manipulated the wind, as it always seemed to move differently around him, but for some reason, she could never smell the essence he'd have to use, a sure sign he was accessing his magesilver.

Turning her head, Elitsa met the mage's somber brown eyes. "Good morning, Master Vilis," she said, inclining her head respectfully.

"Elitsa, you look well." Broad-shouldered with a boxer's broad chest, Vilis had shoulder-length brown hair threaded with silver. His mouth was framed by a carefully trimmed mustache and beard. Dressed in a dark green tunic — the magesilver buckles prominently displayed — and charcoal trousers, he'd chosen a heavy blue coat with fur along the collar and sleeves. One might think he was displeased to see her from the grave look on his face, but Elitsa had never seen him smile.

She handed him a sweet bread and cup of cider she'd purchased from the stand on the graveled path behind them. Taking the food, Vilis sat beside her on the stone wall, somehow making the sweep of his long coat look regal. Though she wouldn't say he'd been like a father to her, Elitsa had certainly spent more time with him than her own. He'd kept an eye on her after her mother's death, and he was the reason she'd made it into the Guild's service at all.

Vilis brought the cider beneath his nose and inhaled, staring out at the lake. He preferred to sit in silence, not brooding so much as thoughtful. He was always watching and listening to what was around him, a quiet, solid presence like a bear. Elitsa usually found it comforting, dependable, but now her thoughts hummed like a disturbed nest of bees as she wondered what the mage had kept from her. *What secrets of the Tower has he hidden behind those eyes?* Did he know the Guild was killing their agents? But if he did, wouldn't he have warned her or stopped her from joining? Elitsa wanted to flat out ask him, but she knew he was loyal to the Guild above everything. What if she didn't like his answers? Would it hurt more to know or to wonder?

Vilis looked at her, catching her staring at his profile, and raised a thick brow.

"My contract ends soon," Elitsa said abruptly, her fingers flattening the flaky bread in her hand. "At the end of the week."

His eyes were unreadable. "Yes. You've become quite proficient over the years. You've exceeded my expectations for you."

Elitsa nodded, momentarily caught off guard by his praise. It was rare for Vilis to congratulate her on a job well done. "Thank you for your confidence in me, Master Vilis. I've … I've been thinking about what I want to do when my contract is over." She held his gaze, trying to read him, but Vilis merely blinked and looked back at the lake, taking a leisurely sip of cider. After a moment, he lowered the cup and spoke, still looking away from her.

"You are considering moving on from the Tower." He said it as a statement, not a question, and Elitsa felt a prickle of unease. Was *everyone* watching her? "There are many paths you could take with what you've learned in service."

No warning to reconsider? "I thought I might travel for a while before I decide, start in Broceia." His face was as readable as a stone, and Elitsa tensed with frustration. "A retired agent, Aleks, was going to open an inn there, but he died shortly after he arrived."

"Death comes for us all eventually," Vilis said.

Was *that* a warning? A headache began between her brows, and Elitsa looked out at the water, following his gaze. She forced herself to take a bite of the sweet bread, though she could hardly taste it. *He probably knows about my visit to the messenger tower.* She could be direct. "I thought I might talk to some of the other agents who've retired to help decide what I want to do, but I couldn't find any who are still alive." Elitsa shot a glance at Vilis and saw he'd lowered his cup. "None came back here, to Rivna, and everyone I was able to track down is dead."

"There are certain dangers for anyone with a connection to the Tower." Vilis' voice was even.

"From rogues." Elitsa thought of his words after her mother died.

Vilis inclined his head. "It is a risk I warned you of when you asked for my help to obtain a contract. If you're not careful and make enemies over the course of your job, those consequences follow you."

"Yes," Elitsa said slowly. Was Vilis suggesting that everyone had died by accident or by rogues? Didn't he think it strange that no one survived after leaving? Some of the agents were more careless than others and likely had run afoul of various criminal elements, such as the Smoke Eyes, but surely the majority of them wouldn't be targeted without their relics. What was the point? They had nothing to steal. Rogues did occasionally attack and try to take the relics from agents, but usually they didn't kill the person. "It just seems questionable that I can't find anyone." Elitsa didn't know Verka, but she did know Vilis, and his mind was sharp. *He's hiding something. Why?*

"If you're worried about your safety, Elitsa, perhaps you should stay here, in Rivna, or travel with a merchant. You've proven you're capable of taking care of yourself, but a caravan would afford additional protection." He looked at her, and she thought she saw a hint of disappointment in his dark eyes. "I am surprised you would leave out of fear. I expected you would sign another contract."

Anger spiked across Elitsa's chest. Was Vilis implying she was a coward? He knew what she was capable of, knew what she'd done all these years! She took a careful breath and forced herself not to snap back a response. He was trying to get a rise out of her, see if she'd let herself be ruled by her emotions. *I'm not a little girl anymore*, she thought, sipping at her cider. She could control herself. "I'm undecided." She set her cup on the wall between them. "The fountains are dry early this year."

Vilis looked at her with the same enigmatic expression. "Speak what is on your mind, Elitsa. You're dancing around something."

"I …" Elitsa grimaced at the bread in her hands. She was tired of worrying about her words, of being careful around the mages, but Vilis was like family. *I should be able to be honest.* Straightening, she met his eyes. "The Guild doesn't seem very concerned with helping people, not like they used to. We're collecting more contracts than ever; essence prices are low — lower than they need to be — people are starving, and with the seedbeetles and everything, it just seems … it seems like the Tower should be doing more. *Can* be doing more. That's why they're here, isn't it? What is the point of protecting Casekraia if they let everything die around them?"

Vilis gave her a thoughtful look. "Is it an eagle's job to care for bees on the ground? Or a wolf to put food in the mouths of hares? The Guild ensures the protection of the realm from threats that the people cannot see or are equipped to face. Our purpose is not to make life easier or to perform tasks they can do themselves."

So because they were focused on bigger problems, the Guild could ignore everything else? There'd been no sign of the frost wyrms since the Winter War. Whether or not the Guild was waiting for their unlikely return, there was so much they could do for Casekraia now. "But without the hares, the wolves don't eat. And if the bees succumb to plague or famine, and the flowers die, then the small animals the eagles hunt might starve. What would they feast on then? It's connected." Elitsa waved the sticky bun towards the city behind them. "I'm not suggesting that the Guild do everything, but if they'd help grow food or pay more for essences so people can meet their contracts then doesn't it benefit the Tower? If none of the essence farmers can afford to work, then who will fill the Guild's stores?"

"You sound like your mother."

Elitsa blinked. Her mother? She had never heard her mother talk about the Tower's involvement in Rivna. Why had Vilis brought her up now?

"Where has all this fresh concern for the plight of others come from? Most of the people here would leave you in the street if they found you bleeding."

He wasn't wrong. If not for Solveiga, there would be no place for her in the Peoples' Suburb. Still, life didn't have to be that way, did it? There were good people here, people like Pipene, who was always giving away clothes and food. *We are capable of more than our instincts for survival. Maybe I can be part of something good for a change.* Maybe Verka and her employer truly did want to make a difference, and they could get more relics and essences into the hands of people who needed them.

"I suppose," Elitsa said, "that not knowing what I'm going to do next has made me think of things differently."

"Don't forget, little bird, the only person you can truly depend on is yourself. The people you seem so concerned with now follow the same principle. They'll save their own skin over yours if the choice must be made."

There was no callousness in his tone or face, just practicality. This is what he'd taught her, after all, had encouraged persever-ance and self-reliance. "And the Guild?" Elitsa asked, not missing the sharpening of Vilis's gaze.

"The Guild does what it must."

A careful answer. If Vilis ever questioned his loyalty to the Tower, he wouldn't share it with her. *I have to look out for myself,* Elitsa thought. She wasn't important to the Guild, not like Vilis. She had to be ready. Whatever was going on, he'd expect her to figure it out herself.

If Vilis recognized the thoughts moving through Elitsa's eyes, he didn't show it. "Headed out on a job?" he asked, nodding at the pack at her feet.

Elitsa's heartbeat quickened. "Yes," she said, afraid she'd

somehow give away her plans. "I have a contract from the merchant's guild."

"To Broceia?"

"Kirtara."

"Mmm. I'll let you get on your way then. Fair travels, little bird." Vilis stood up. Somehow he'd managed to avoid getting any breadcrumbs on his clothing.

"Thank you, Master Vilis. Good day to you."

Vilis returned his empty mug to the cider stand, then headed south down the gravel path towards the city.

Elitsa looked at the crushed bread in her hands, considering their conversation. Vilis hadn't seemed surprised by the dead agents or upset when she'd criticized the Guild. Had his reminders that she could only depend on herself been warnings to be careful? He'd seemed disappointed that she wanted to move on. Was he protecting her, or was he protecting the Guild? Vilis had never been outwardly affectionate, but she'd always thought he had her best interests at heart. Was that still true? It was becoming increasingly evident that she needed to put some distance between her and the city. She didn't feel safe here anymore, and as much as the thought pained her, she couldn't trust Vilis.

Elitsa tossed the bread away from her onto the grass then hopped off the wall. She brushed crumbs from her clothes, watching as a flock of small birds descended in a noisy flurry of feathers. In seconds, everything was gone.

Frowning, Elitsa picked up her pack and drained the last of her cider. She needed to meet with the merchant to confirm the terms of her contract in Kirtara. It was time to go.

CHAPTER 8

The road to Kirtara was wide and pleasant, and Elitsa made good time on foot descending from the mountains around Rivna. It would have been faster to rent a horse or carriage, but it'd been a long time since she'd allowed herself to enjoy the countryside, and Elitsa wanted the distraction. Though the wind was cool, the sun was warm overhead. The grassy hills and scattered forest were bright and open, and without the threat of easy ambush — there was hardly anywhere to hide close to the road — Elitsa could relax and pretend that life was no more complicated than walking from one place to another.

As she crossed a stone bridge over the Kalien — a broad river that wandered south from the mountains west of Rivna all the way to the Moon Sea — Elitsa glanced at the slow-moving water. It looked low, the current too weak to power the watermills on the opposite bank. Her peace cracked and disappeared, and Elitsa increased her pace as she left the deserted flour mills behind.

Turning left at a fork in the road, she continued south. She planned to stop at the Golden Horse for the night, an inn where the road branched again, giving the option to turn northwest towards Velasa on the western coast. Disquieted by the river, Elitsa barely noticed her surroundings as she left the bridge behind, her eyes focused on the dusty road before her.

She reached the inn around dinnertime, feeling a flicker of surprise when she caught sight of the large building's amber shingles through a wall of thin white trees with golden leaves. Somehow the day's journey had passed quickly. The knot in her chest, that'd grown ever-tangled with every step, eased, and Elitsa finally felt the soreness in her back and legs from her unrelenting pace. Adjusting her pack on her shoulders, she turned towards the trees.

The Golden Horse was a good place along the road to get a bite to eat, or if you had the means, hire a horse. There was no town here, just the inn, its stable, a small bakery — run by the innkeeper's sister — and an old stone shrine to Father Sun, a rearing horse of white marble with golden hooves. Though night had not yet fallen, they'd lit the lanterns along the road leading the way to the front steps with welcoming light. In the garden, white pumpkins and orange-red roses decorated the base of the shrine.

As Elitsa stepped up onto the porch of the two-story inn, a cold breeze ruffled her hair and sent the sign hanging overhead creaking. She shot a glance at the road, a shiver dancing across her neck, but saw nothing in the fading light.

Stepping inside, she scanned the room, finding it much as she remembered from her last trip along this route. The exposed beams overhead were painted gold, as was the bartop to her left, where several weather-beaten travelers nursed drinks on tall wooden stools. Buying a meal and room for the night from the innkeeper — a tall, bearded man who thankfully didn't attempt to trap her in conversation — Elitsa quickly ate by the fire, then retired to her room.

Head aching dully when she woke the next morning, Elitsa left while mist still lingered over the cleared farmlands along the road. She'd dreamed of her mother, and the unease she'd felt on the inn's front porch followed her as she walked, her mouth settling into a tight line. *Who are you, Elitsa?* her mother had asked, her narrowed eyes cold. *Who are you?*

Unlike the day before, Elitsa watched the fields closely. She felt tense, unable to relax the muscles in her jaw. The farmland was drier than it should be, and it was clear some of the farmers had been forced to harvest early. Someone had abandoned a wagon alongside the road, and as she skirted it warily, she saw a large hole in its side. The day warmed by the time she reached the forest, and though the trees that edged her path were lovely to look at, the ground awash with fallen leaves in red and gold, she could see signs of the seedbeetles farther in, rotted trunks toppling over moss-capped stone. When Elitsa came out the other side, she caught her first glimpse of Kirtara.

The town was in a large grassy plain, flat save the tree-topped hill where the guildhall perched above it. The buildings were not as tall as in Rivna and had the same gently sloped roofs as the inn. When it snowed here, it was barely more than a dusting across the ground. A cluster of grain silos, looking like three silver pillars, marked the eastern edge of town, and there was an air of neglect to them that she didn't remember.

Rubbing her left temple — her headache had moved behind her eyes — Elitsa walked beneath an old stone archway, its carvings of spirits and twining vines worn down by wind and time. She'd seen many similar etchings throughout the kingdom on her travels, left behind on crumbling towers and root-claimed stones. They were remnants of an earlier age when essences were thought to be the souls of gods.

Elitsa followed the main street, passing several shops and open stalls. The wind was often strong here in the flatland, and the stalls had heavy curtains that could be tied shut against the dust-filled gusts of air. By a stand of mealy apples, the crates mostly picked over, a woman in a worn blue dress haggled over prices with the stall's owner, while a hungry-eyed child peered at Elitsa from around her skirt. Elitsa smiled, and the child quickly hid their face.

As the seller picked up one of the crates, the memory of the shiny apple on Guild Mistress Astraia's desk rose in Elitsa's mind. *Why won't the Guild do more?* she thought, a tight pain inside her chest. The Tower could afford to share, or at the least, offer their mages' magic in the fields. How could they let children go hungry?

Hunching her shoulders, Elitsa passed an old shrine with a gnarled oak growing in the yard. Faded yellow ribbons, threaded with bits of glass hung from its branches, prayers to Father Sun. She thought about Vilis and their conversation in the park. He'd said she'd sounded like her mother after suggesting the Guild could help grow food. *Would she approve of Verka's plan? Of my decision?* Whether or not she sympathized — her mother had been kind — Branka had also taught Elitsa about honesty and responsibility and to always keep her word. But integrity could not be one-sided. *Devotion should be earned.* Solveiga had the Aerie's loyalty because of her actions, not what she owned.

Ahead, Elitsa saw the town's inn and stables, a tall, two-story building painted white. Her stomach grumbled unexpectedly, but her hunger faded as she thought of the child's hollow gaze. Glancing back, she considered giving the child's mother some of her own meager coin, but they were already gone. *She probably wouldn't have accepted anyway,* she thought. *I wouldn't have.*

Feeling overwhelmingly weary, Elitsa turned onto a street between the shrine and a cooper's workshop, catching sight of the Tower's emblem on a marker hanging from the building's eaves. She'd been here before, so she didn't need it to find her way. She wanted to wash off the dust from the road, but first she had to stop at the guildhall. It was considered customary for any agents passing through and was why she was here in the first place. Following the road up a steep hill, Elitsa left the town's wooden buildings behind.

On the other side of a small grove of twisted oak and standing stones, Elitsa caught sight of the guildhall's peaked roof and increased her pace. Though it was only midday, the sun had disappeared, and the sky was dark with clouds; the wind felt cold within their shadows.

More a large house than a tower, the architect who'd built Kirtara's guildhall had favored the same blood-colored stone used in Rivna, but Elitsa thought it looked more ominous here, like a stain on the golden fields around them. Tall windows glittered with the constant glow from lightprisms and kept the hall bright during the day. It certainly wasn't as defensible as the Tower, but the large, double oak doors seemed strong enough. Hedges of brambles grew wild beneath the bottom row of windows. They appeared to have been trimmed in the past and then left to run wild. The whole structure had a slightly unkempt look, like something old and forgotten.

The last time Elitsa had visited, there'd been a guard stationed by the door, but there was no one standing on the porch now. Frowning, she hurried up the steps and grabbed the door handle, pulling it open. She winced as the heavy door squealed. Slipping quickly inside, she glanced in both directions, but the long gallery was empty of people. It was also only marginally warmer than outside, the fireplace in the opposite wall cold. Carved wooden furniture cast shadows across the floor. To her left, marble plinths held the busts of the four mages who founded the Tower, sculpted from red-veined stone. Supposedly they had been around during the Winter War, though Elitsa wasn't sure she believed that. That would have made the mages nearly two hundred years old when the Guild was formed, and as far as she knew, no one was that long-lived.

A few steps down the hall to her right, a door was cracked open, spilling out light and the faint hum of conversation. The missing guards, perhaps? *This place has even less security than it did before*, Elitsa thought, unsettled by the Guild's lack of concern. Despite the creak of the door and the echo of her footsteps, no one had yet come to investigate. Verka's people would have no problem sneaking inside.

The collections office appeared closed. It was several doors down from the open room, and no light shone beneath the red-painted wood. High Mage Bojan, the Guildhall Master here, a spindly old man with a pouf of white hair, liked to keep morning hours so was likely already away on an extended lunch. Elitsa stood motionless in the entryway, her heartbeat thumping more quickly as the silence stretched. The air smelled stale, and she loosed the scarf at her throat.

What she should do is announce herself, but the quietness of the hall offered an opportunity. She'd never wandered any farther than the main gallery on her visits and had only been up on the second floor once, a year ago, to deliver a message for Vilis to a Guild researcher named Freythen. She'd been accompanied then and hadn't made it past the stairs. *I might not get this chance again.*

Careful to keep her steps soft, Elitsa turned away from the sound and light and headed down the opposite hall. She eyed the closed doors opposite the windows, convinced someone would open one and demand to know what she was doing, but she made it to the end without incident. Senses heightened by the precariousness of her unauthorized search, Elitsa rested her fingertips against the wall as she filled her lungs, then headed up the winding stairs.

Exiting onto the second floor, Elitsa saw the hall stretched the length of the building like below, with doors to what was presumably the mages' quarters on her left. Unlike the Tower, she knew only a few mages had their residence here in Kirtara. Dark wood tables and overstuffed leather chairs with tall backs were arranged in small groups in front of the massive windows to her right, offering a view of the trees and standing stones and the rooftops of the town below the hill. The chairs appeared to be empty, but to make sure, Elitsa stood silently by the stairs for several moments listening to the natural sounds of the hall.

Taking a careful step forward, she was relieved the floor didn't creak beneath her feet — a problem with older buildings like this one. The relics would likely be stored close to the research room, which Elitsa was reasonably sure was up here by the mages. She studied the doors as she passed, looking for identification, but they were all plain wood, nothing to differentiate one from another. Light leaked from beneath the door of one ahead, but when Elitsa stopped to listen, she didn't hear voices or movement inside.

Elitsa knew she needed to hurry and was relieved when she saw the Guild's insignia etched into the door three down from the end of the hall. Instead of just the gauntlet and flame, the gold-painted hand was surrounded by the five elemental symbols — fire, earth, water, wind, and spirit. She stepped closer, glancing at the floor but saw no hint of light. Looking back to ensure no one had come up the stairs, Elitsa turned her cheek and leaned towards the door. She wanted to use her essences to sense if the room was occupied, but it was already risky enough being upstairs without permission. Getting caught using magic would be difficult to explain and result in attention she did not need.

Confident she couldn't hear anything on the other side of the door, Elitsa reached for the handle and slowly pulled it open. She peeked inside, finding a darkened room filled with tables and the occasional chair tucked beneath it. Vials and various bowls covered the tables along the walls, and she saw the unmistakable glow of essence — the green vine-like form of a plant, which she couldn't identify unless touching it, and the warm orange-red of fire. There was water as well as several essences Elitsa recognized from insects.

Her heartbeat quickened, this time from excitement, and

Elitsa stepped inside and closed the door. She allowed her eyes to adjust to the shadowed room, then began to walk around the tables. There were no windows, but the stored essences softened the darkness. Someone had left a large book open filled with notes and what looked like a drawing of a wing-shaped relic. *This has to be the research room.*

Feeling hopeful, Elitsa wandered to the back wall and around a pair of tall bookshelves that created a secluded nook in one corner. She stopped to read several of the titles — attention snagging on the worn spines that were in desperate need of a binder's service. One was *The Intuitive Nature of Magick - Its Risks and Practice*, and another *Energy Transfer Between Man and Beast*. Elitsa raised her eyebrows curiously, wishing she had time to read, but instead turned away towards the wall. There was a door here, hidden by the shelves. *A storage closet, perhaps?*

Startling a pale brown paper moth as she opened the door, Elitsa withdrew a weak fire essence from her left earring and shaped a small ribbon of light above her palm. She leaned inside, raising her hand and illuminating rows of shelving. Magesilver glinted in her flamelight. Most of the relics were small, medallions and brooches, but she could see a gauntlet partially wrapped in white fabric and a case of slim daggers. Elitsa's eyes widened. She'd expected a few relics, but not the hundred or so carefully placed on each shelf. Some were tagged with slips of paper, and others, on the lower shelves, were dusty as though they hadn't been touched in a while. This was a small fortune.

Why did the Guild act as though the relics were too precious to share? If they rented these out at a fair price, not only would they get more essences, but more people would have a way to support themselves. Why did they insist on limiting rental contracts to two years? Anger settled in the pit of her stomach, bringing back her frustration with the Guild's apathy towards the people they were meant to serve.

A small cuff bracelet caught her eye, the metal hammered into the curving shape of a dragonfly's wing. It was covered in dust and didn't have a tag tied to it. Would they even notice if it was gone? Elitsa's stomach twisted, horrified by how quickly her thoughts had turned from criticizing the Guild to self-absorption. *This is not who I want to be, heedless of honor or consequence.*

A door opened behind her, the sound of footsteps giving her only a moment to yank herself backward out of the relics' room.

CHAPTER 9

A figure stood in the doorway, backlit by the soft light from the hall. "Annika?" The voice was reedy and uncertain. They raised the magelit lamp in their hand, illuminating a narrow face with a thick white beard, wild eyebrows, and a long pointed nose. Blue eyes squinted in her direction. "Is that you? What are you doing in the dark?"

Heart hammering in her chest, Elitsa took a confident step forward. It was Freythen. Sister Luck, it seemed, was on her side, at least if she could come up with a convincing reason for her presence. Mind spinning, she released the fire essence in her hand, letting it dissipate into the air. Once drawn, an essence could not be put back into magesilver, just like blowing out a breath of air into the wind could not be returned. She'd need to replenish her fire essences soon.

Freythen frowned, approaching her. "Apologies, who are—" He blinked, raising his lamp towards her face. "We've met before, haven't we? I'm not always good with faces ..."

"I was looking for you," Elitsa blurted. She straightened her shoulders, projecting an air of what she hoped was calm confidence.

"Well, you've found me. Miss ...?"

"High Mage Vilis sent me." Elitsa crossed her arms and leaned a hip against one of the tables. "There was no one to greet me so I came up here to look for you."

Freythen's confusion darkened to irritation, and he looked back towards the door. "I've told them they're too lax down there," he grumbled. "Why, when Iliona was Head Mage ..." He blinked, mood shifting yet again, as he looked back at Elitsa. "Vilis sent you?" The hand holding the lantern shook, and he set it down on the table. He clasped his hands, then separated them again, shoving one into a pocket on his robe. It looked to be heavy, with long bell-like sleeves and a hem that dragged the floor. Beneath, his thigh-length tunic looked rumpled, the floral embroidery down the middle of his chest beginning to fray. His pants had also seen better days and bore traces of ink.

Elitsa watched him curiously. He was nervous about Vilis? Was it related to the message she'd delivered last summer? She still didn't know what it'd been about. Certainly hadn't been curious enough to break the seal on the letter. Could she use this somehow? His uncertainty? Were they working together on a project, or did Freythen owe Vilis something? She had to be careful what she said, or he'd realize she didn't know what business the mages had together. "He did." She gave him an expectant look. When confronted with silence, nervous people often felt compelled to fill it with talking. It all came down to confidence.

Freythen licked his lips. "He's told you about ...?"

"He wants an update," Elitsa interrupted.

"Of course, forgive me. There have been a few, uh, difficulties, but I'm confident I can work through them."

Difficulties? Elitsa raised an eyebrow, hiding her surprise. No mage had ever apologized to her before. Reclamation agents weren't highly regarded inside the Tower, despite their retrieval of the relics the mages relied on.

"I just need a little more time."

What was he talking about? Curiosity needled her, but Elitsa swallowed her questions. "I will relay your confidence," she said, though she had no intention of telling Vilis she'd spoken with Freythen. That would bring up more questions than she could talk her way out of. This might come back to haunt her, but if her luck held, they wouldn't communicate before she was gone. In four days, her contract would be over, and she'd be on her way to … well, somewhere. If Verka was right and agents were being killed, Broceia would not be far enough away. Maybe it was time to travel beyond the continent as her father had. Home was starting to seem just as dangerous as the risks beyond their shores.

Elitsa straightened, mentally chastising herself for getting distracted. She couldn't worry about that now. She needed to keep her mind on the job, finish here, and go to the inn.

"Yes. Good." Freythen nodded, but it looked like his thoughts had moved past her, his eyes fixed on one of the tables.

"I'll show myself out." Pulse quickening, Elitsa strode past the Guild mage and out the door, turning right. The skin on her neck prickled. Surely Freythen was going to yell after her, realizing she wasn't supposed to be there. When she made it to the stairs, she rushed down, taking them two at a time until she was at the bottom. She wanted to hurry out the door, get away from the guildhall, but she couldn't leave without checking in with the reclamation branch.

Sighing, she strode to the open door and, pulling on the handle, stuck her head inside. Two guards — coats unbuttoned and hats hanging from the backs of their chairs — were sitting around a table along with a portly man with reddened cheeks and long silver hair. They were drinking and playing cards and didn't notice her in the doorway. The room reeked of alcohol, and Elitsa wrinkled her nose as she scanned the stuffy chamber. Tacked to the wall behind them was a large map of Casekraia with illustrations of ice wyrms churning in the Crystal Sea. To its right, a magelit lantern and a plant that had long ago perished sat atop a tall bookcase filled with dust-covered record books. The only other furniture was a weapon rack from which three iron birch truncheons hung from leather straps. One of the men burped, and Elitsa resisted the urge to plug her nose.

Tension draining from her body, Elitsa stepped inside the room and loudly cleared her throat. The guards' eyes swung her way, cards still carefully shielded from each other. They didn't seem alarmed, more inconvenienced than anything. *They're lucky I'm not an envoy from the Tower*, she thought, as she flipped her collar to show her Guild pin. "I'm Agent Serlov. Is the Guild master of reclamation here? I'm carrying out a merchant contract in Kirtara."

The red-cheeked man narrowed his eyes at her. "I'm Master Kalnin."

Elitsa didn't recognize him. Had the previous master died or been reassigned?

"You're a reclamation agent?" the guard closest to her asked, rough voice filled with incredulous laughter. A card slipped out of his hand and he cursed, almost falling out of his chair as he reached down to pick it up off the floor.

Elitsa's lips thinned. "As I said." She looked back at Kalnin, noting the cloudiness in the man's eyes. "Are there any unassigned contracts to pick up?" She wasn't entirely confident he'd be able to remember if there were.

"No, no new contracts from the Tower." Master Kalnin looked back at the cards in his hand then laid one down on the growing pile in the center of the table.

That simplified things. She'd rather not be stuck in Kirtara longer than was necessary. She glanced at the plates of half-eaten food. Where was the staff? "It's quiet here today."

The second guard, a broad man in his fifties with thinning red hair, held his cards close to his eyes as though having trouble focusing. "The Hall Master is away," he said distractedly.

Master Kalnin squinted at him, lip curling. "Stop jabbering and play the game, Martial."

Elitsa watched the men play. It was only midday, and yet they'd clearly been drinking for a while. She doubted they'd be conscious by dusk. She needed to get a look at the rest of the downstairs hall and find out who else was on duty at this hour. Even if the guards were away from the door here — and she had suspicions this was a routine game — a maid gathering the mages' laundry could easily interfere with Verka's plan. "Do you mind if I stop in the kitchen? It was a long walk from Rivna, and I'd appreciate some water."

Master Kalnin grunted, slapping another card on the table. "The town inn serves food."

"Yes, Master Kalnin. I just thought that since I was here ..." She coughed and cleared her throat, wincing apologetically when he scowled at her.

"She just wants a drink of water, you old donkey," the older guard said.

Master Kalnin shifted his glare to him, though he seemed to be used to the familiarity. "Fine. Just water. The hall isn't paying for your meals, Agent Serlov."

"Of course, thank you, Master Kalnin." Elitsa cleared her throat again and gave what she hoped was a grateful smile. "I'll leave you to your game." She nodded at them and then backed out into the hall, thankful that Master Kalnin's disapproving glare had shifted back to his cards. He seemed suspicious of her, but perhaps it was more irritation at the interruption and his men being free with information about the Hall Master.

Continuing down the hall, Elitsa rounded the corner and found a small dining room and the kitchen beyond. It was warm and cozy and filled with the scent of baked bread and roasted meat. Windows looked out onto a tidy vegetable garden protected by a roundpole fence of split spruce. A middle-aged woman — presumably the cook — with pale pink skin and brown hair looked up from where she was folding linens at the large table in the center of the room, and a young girl, who Elitsa guessed was the woman's daughter, was drying dishes by a basin of soapy water. They both wore white dresses with blue flowers embroidered in bands around the upper arms and long red aprons.

"Can I help you, Miss?" the woman asked, eyes taking in Elitsa's clothes as if she were trying to decide who she was.

"Good afternoon. Yes, a cup of water please?"

"Of course." She made a move to stand up, but Elitsa waved a hand at her.

"Please don't get up on my account. I can get it. Over here?" She walked towards the counter the woman had glanced at and grabbed a cup beside a ceramic jug of water with a metal spigot.

The girl drying dishes glanced curiously over her shoulder. "You're a mage?" she asked, wonder in her voice.

"Mila!" the older woman said chastisingly. "Forgive her curiosity, Miss."

Elitsa, having finished filling her cup with water, turned back around smiling. "Oh, it's fine. I'm not, actually. I'm a reclamation agent." She showed the girl her pin.

"Oh! That must be exciting work. Getting to travel all sorts of places. Is it dangerous?"

"Mila!" Her mother gave an exasperated sigh and resumed folding.

Elitsa hid a smile as she sipped her water. She'd once romanticized the profession herself. *I wasn't prepared*, she thought, mood darkening, as she recalled the last few years. "It can be." She glanced at the doorway, though she didn't expect Master Kalnin to chase her in here. They'd likely already forgotten about her, considering how far they were into their cups. "It's quiet here today. The Hall Master is out of town?"

"Yes, left on Guild business this morning."

"Won't be back until Sunday," Mila offered. "I think it gets quite dull around here when he leaves on his trips with the other resident mages, but Mama says she likes the quiet."

The woman glanced towards her daughter with her brow furrowed but didn't say anything. Elitsa could see that she thought her daughter should be careful about what she said about the mages.

Elitsa needed to get on her way. If the cook was interrogated, she didn't want the woman to remember her asking too many questions or seeming interested in the absence of the Hall Master and mages. "Thank you for the water." Elitsa took the cup back to the counter where Mila had been washing dishes.

"Of course," the cook said. "Blessings to you."

"And to you," Elitsa said. Smiling at Mila, who turned to wave at her with the dishtowel, Elitsa headed back into the main hall. She passed the guard room and heard the men still talking. It seemed that if Verka wanted to sneak inside, her people wouldn't have much resistance the latter half of the day.

It seems much too easy, Elitsa thought as she opened the front door. In her experience, something always went wrong.

The cold wind brushed across her face, and Elitsa shivered, tugging up the collar of her coat. It was hours still until nightfall, but the sun was nowhere in sight in the dark gray sky. She rewound the scarf to cover the bottom half of her face and was tempted to burn one of her fire essences for a little extra warmth, though that would require her to keep her hand out of her coat. As she tugged on her gloves and stuck her hands into her pockets, she glanced back at the upper windows where she'd left Freythen and the relic room. She could still decide not to help Verka, to complete her merchant contract and go home. So far, she'd only asked questions, and if the Guild axed every agent who visited the Black Eyed Fish for a drink, then they'd have no one to perform reclamations.

Elitsa bit the inside of her cheek, thinking about Orson. Even if Verka hadn't lied about looking out for him, there was no way he'd come out of this unscathed. She couldn't leave him at the mercy of the Smoke Eyes or the Tower. She'd never forgive herself if he got hurt. Would never be able to look at Pipene or Sofija without shame. *Protecting him must be more important than my contract with the Guild.*

She glanced down as a stick snapped beneath her foot and saw the tiny bones of a mouse in the dying grass. The Guild had brought this on themselves. They could hardly be surprised that people like Verka were beginning to fight back. For all their money and power, they'd let Casekraia suffer; they'd hardly done anything to stop the spread of the seedbeetles. *What is the point of their magic if they cannot do more?* Their researchers had to be capable of devising a way to help the crops grow, yet the Guild offered nothing more than vague platitudes. If the king, the one person who could apply pressure, continued to do nothing, someone had to intervene.

Following the path through the trees, Elitsa realized she no longer felt conflicted about helping Verka. A theft like this, it didn't even matter. The true thief was the Guild, stealing lives and hope, destroying the very people who'd raised it in the first place. The Tower had earned any advances made against them, and she couldn't muster up an ounce of sympathy. Besides, she wasn't participating in a revolt or getting involved in a war. *I'm only looking the other way.*

CHAPTER 10

Elitsa curled her cold fingers around the bowl of beetroot soup and inhaled the sweet and earthy scent with an appreciative sigh. The red soup was a favorite of hers, and she couldn't help smiling at the dollop of sour cream melting into the warm broth. Giving the room another glance over a big spoonful of beets, cabbage, and potatoes, Elitsa took a big bite. No one seemed to be giving her extra attention, but she'd been keeping an eye on the stairs and door as she waited for Verka's contacts.

The soup was good, though not as wonderful as her mother's. The familiar creep of sadness unfurled inside her chest, and she shoved it aside as she reached for one of the fresh-baked garlic buns piled on a plate in the center of the table. She couldn't sink inside her misery here; she had to pay attention. If the Guild was watching her, then she'd rather see them first. There was nothing worse than being surprised or backed into a corner.

Elitsa watched a serving woman chase a black cat off one of the tables, then head back into the kitchen. Perhaps Aleks had had the right idea wanting to open an inn. It wouldn't be a bad life surrounded by the scent of fresh bread and simmering stew.

Though as appealing as the idea was if she stopped to settle down, the Tower would have no problem tracking her.

Her appetite waned, and Elitsa's lips pinched as she eyed the half-eaten bun between her fingers. Her final week wasn't supposed to be confusing, nor her future unclear. As much as she wished she could simply leave, take the vacation she'd talked about with Pipene, she didn't want to spend the next few months constantly looking over her shoulder, worried someone wanted to kill her. She could continue in the Guild's employ and pretend she didn't know what they were up to, but the thought of signing another contract tore holes in her stomach.

Elitsa knew the Tower was dangerous, but that didn't mean they were murdering every agent who left. She couldn't believe that every arch-mage on the council would sanction such an action. *I need proof,* she thought. She couldn't simply take Verka at her word. The woman had an agenda, a need to convince Elitsa to help her. But evidence would be complicated to obtain. Disappearing was sounding more and more like the best and easiest course of action. Let someone else worry about this mess.

Elitsa leaned back, flexing her feet under the table. She couldn't disappear without a word. Pipene would never forgive her. *Can I convince her to leave with me?* But how was that fair? Pipene might be in danger just being near her.

A woman was eyeing her from the stairs. Pulse spiking, Elitsa gave her a passing glance, then let her gaze wander as if she were merely looking around the room. She took a bite of the bread in her hand. The stranger was dressed much like the guildhall's cook in a dark blue skirt with a red apron and white shirt, floral embroidery on the sleeves, and neckline. An orange and black scarf covered her hair, though several black strands had escaped, brushing her cheeks. Something about the focus with which she watched Elitsa made her think that she was not a local village woman coming for a bite of food after a long day of work.

On the woman's heels was a young man with brown hair, a

square, boyish face, and narrow shoulders. He was dressed like a stablehand, and his eyes kept flicking in Elitsa's direction like the woman's. They didn't seem tense, like people expecting violence — which eased her nerves somewhat — and she'd bet a garlic bun that they recognized her. *Either they're Verka's*, Elitsa thought, *or the Tower has decided to start tracking me.* It would have been easier if Verka had shared her contacts' descriptions instead of telling Elitsa they'd know who she was.

The strangers stopped by the bar, perhaps to order food, and Elitsa watched them talk to the innkeeper. The man laughed at something, seeming at ease. No, these people did not belong to the Tower. *What do they intend to do with the relics?* she wondered, looking them over. She hadn't questioned Verka very thoroughly about their plans. She hadn't wanted to know more, but that was reckless. However small her role was, she was still involved.

What she'd seen in the guildhall's storeroom before Freythen's interruption wouldn't be enough for an assault on the Tower or the king, but the Smoke Eyes could still hurt people. Did Verka have as much control as she claimed, or was Elitsa helping arm rogues? *Like the one who killed my mother.* She dropped a hand into her lap, fingers curling into a tight fist. She no longer believed every person with an unlicensed relic intended to do harm, but Elitsa had seen enough to know the damage someone could do. Still, the Smoke Eyes weren't trying to destroy the city or terrorize the people. They just had rules they weren't above using violence to reinforce.

They were heading towards her now on a surreptitious route around the perimeter of the room, and Elitsa forced her fingers to relax. Reaching her table, the woman met her stare with a smile. She was holding a glass of what looked like mulled wine in one hand. "May I sit here?" she asked pleasantly.

The man stopped at the woman's elbow and smiled, raising his stein as though in a toast.

"Sure." Elitsa gestured permission with a garlic bun. Her gut was telling her they were safe enough, so she studied them as they sat across from her. She saw no relics, but they were easy enough to hide.

"Traveling through?" the man asked.

Good, they are also cautious. "Yes, here for business. And you?" Elitsa slid a glance past him towards the door. As innocent as their conversation appeared, she still had to keep an eye on the room.

"I work in town."

"Horses, right?"

He grinned, seeming surprised and pleased. "Yes! How can you tell?"

"Because you stink of the stable," the woman said dryly.

The man sniffed at his sleeve and laughed. "Ah. I hardly notice it anymore. I'm Artem."

Elitsa smiled, deciding not to point out that there were horse hairs on his vest. "Elitsa."

"This is my sister, Galyna." Artem nodded at the woman. "Different fathers."

Galyna rolled her eyes. "She wasn't going to ask."

Two serving girls approached from the kitchen, one setting down two bowls of soup, while the other added another plate of bread rolls to the table. They quickly moved off in different directions, responding to calls for drink refills.

"I assume you know who I am," Elitsa said after watching Artem gleefully dig into his soup. "You recognize me."

Galyna smiled. "Yes, our mutual friend gave us your description." She picked up a roll and glanced at the nearby table where a tired-looking man and woman were absorbed in their meal. "Have you been to the hall?"

"I have." Elitsa took a sip from her cup of cider. Were the siblings Smoke Eyes, or did they work for Verka? They seemed friendly and easygoing, not at all like the more cutthroat gang members that prowled the River District. *What drove them to*

89

become professional thieves? Are they here because of some noble goal or for money?

"It's quiet, right?" Artem said, unaware of the storm of questions in Elitsa's mind. "We've been keeping an eye on it, and—" He cut off as someone walked past the table.

Elitsa tracked the man as he wandered towards the door, shoving a hat on his head. He didn't seem interested in them at all. "What are you going to use the relics for?" she asked quietly, looking back at the siblings' faces. She was crossing a line, entangling herself more firmly than she wanted, but she couldn't pretend it didn't matter.

"They'll be given to Verka," Galyna said.

"And then?" Elitsa held the woman's eyes. "I'd like to know if I'm becoming involved in some kind of coup."

"We have no intention of starting a civil war if that's what you're asking."

Artem grinned. "Think of it as a slight shift in power. Not enough to tip the scales, mind you, just enough to keep the wolves from ransacking the henhouse."

So it's not just about money, but the balance of power in Rivna. The Smoke Eyes were already largely left alone in their territory, but the Guild still controlled their relics and essences, at least what they could use openly. *Are they trying to change that?*

"Do you really want to know more?" Galyna asked, raising an eyebrow. "Are you intending to join us? I'm sure our friend would—"

"No." Elitsa shook her head. Increasing tension between the gang and Tower was even more of a reason to leave. She did not want to be caught in the middle of that. She still thought they deserved whatever was coming, but she didn't want to get involved any deeper. *I don't have to be a hero, just a decent person.*

"Do you have the money?" Her stomach churned as she took a bite of a garlic bun, mostly to give herself something to do. *Think of Orson*, she reminded herself. She'd never taken a bribe before. Never even considered it, and yet here she was.

Galyna passed something to Artem, and Elitsa felt a soft tap on her knee. She didn't jump, thank the Mother. Elitsa reached blindly under the table, her fingers brushing something soft, and then she felt a pouch pushed into her hand. Confirming the rounded edges of coins with her fingertips, she tucked the bag into her pocket.

"Half now, as agreed," Galyna murmured. "Verka will arrange final payment once you return to Rivna and the job is done."

Elitsa nodded and wiped her fingers on a napkin. "There are guards inside, but they don't seem to be very cautious." She eyed them, wondering if she was making a mistake in helping them.

"And their placement?" Galyna asked quietly.

"I can't say with certainty that this is a daily occurrence, but when I arrived, they were down the hall to the right, towards the kitchen, playing cards." Elitsa took a bite of soup as a serving girl rushed past, and cast another look around the room. "I was able to walk inside and go upstairs without anyone noticing, and I imagine they'll be even less attentive the later it gets. They'll definitely be nursing hangovers tomorrow."

"And the relics?" Artem asked. He was watching a table to Elitsa's left.

"Upstairs, inside—" Elitsa cut off and plastered a smile on her face. She chuckled as though Artem had said something funny. A man behind him and Galyna had turned his face slightly towards them.

Galyna's eyes narrowed slightly, seeming to catch on. "And that is the last time I let my brother here bake bread!" she said.

Elitsa laughed, and Artem made an offended noise. The man behind them stood up, without looking at them, and headed towards the bar, leaving an empty bowl and cup behind. "They're inside a room with the Guild insignia on the door," she continued quietly, "close to the far end of the hall. You should be quick.

There is at least one Guild mage there. I ran into him in the research room."

Galyna nodded, looking over her shoulder. She didn't look as nervous as Elitsa expected.

If Freythen discovered them, would they run or fight? *Will they give me up to save themselves?* Her heartbeat quickened, and Elitsa felt another wave of indecision. "What will you do if someone tries to stop you?"

Galyna eyed her. "Do you really want to know the answer to that question?"

"We're not intending on hurting anyone," Artem said, eyes earnest. "We're quite stealthy, you know. They won't know we're there. Especially with the Hall Master gone."

Surely Verka wouldn't send them if she didn't think there was a high chance of success. "The only other people I saw were the cook and her daughter, and they were in the kitchen."

Galyna nodded and exchanged a look with Artem. "Less of a chance we'll encounter one of the staff in the hall. Artem has been there a few times in the stable, and no one noticed."

"Don't suppose you'd loan us your agent badge," Artem said.

He seemed to be teasing, but Elitsa stiffened. She swept the room again, skin prickling on the back of her neck. No one here knew she was an agent, and she wanted to keep it that way. "Won't do you any good. They'll know you're not an agent. I'm not supposed to be near the relics anyway, so it's not a free pass to the second floor."

"But they gave you some," Artem said. His eyes glittered curiously. "Good ones, right?"

"Careful, Artem," Galyna murmured, watching the room.

Elitsa started to raise a hand to touch her earrings but reached for her cup instead. "Yes, which I'm expected to return at the end of my contract." It'd be strange to be without the magesilver. To be unable to feel or use magic anymore. She knew the relics didn't belong to her, not really, but after one year had turned into two, into four, and they'd become a part of her, she hadn't stopped to consider the day when she'd have to give them back.

She'd put off thinking about what she'd do if she weren't an agent anymore, and now that the end was looming, and the money she'd been expecting to carry her over was uncertain … what was she supposed to do with that? Working for the Guild should have brought freedom, autonomy. Instead, it seemed, despite her loyalty and hard work, that everything could disappear as easily as smoke. She was no better off than when she'd started.

If I have to run, why bother returning the earrings at all? How could she protect herself without the relics if they wanted her dead?

"How much time do you have left, if you don't mind me asking?" Artem said, scooping up several red-stained potatoes in his spoon.

Elitsa narrowed her eyes, focusing on her companions. What had Verka told them? "Time?"

"Your contract. I assume it's ending? Why else risk—"

"Don't be nosy, Artem," Galyna murmured, giving him a pointed look. "Her reasons are her own."

"Right, just curious." Artem smiled apologetically and continued eating his soup.

Elitsa pushed back her finished bowl. No matter how confused and unsettled she was, she'd learned early on to eat when she had food. "I must take my leave. I have a contract to collect tomorrow. I suggest whatever you plan to do, you do tomorrow evening, or time around their meals."

Galyna nodded and raised her cup. "Mother's Blessings to you, Elitsa."

"And you."

Artem kissed his fingers and traced the shape of a wheel on the table. "And may Sister Luck be with us all."

CHAPTER 11

E litsa winced in the bright morning light and wished she had a hat to block the sun. She hadn't slept well. Unease had twisted her dreams, and when she'd dragged herself from bed to head to the market, she couldn't shake the feeling that she'd made another error in judgment. *Would I even know if my internal moral compass is corrupted?* She was now complicit in theft against the Tower, and if the Guild ever found out she was involved, she doubted she'd get a simple slap on the wrist.

Following the street away from the inn, Elitsa kept an eye on the shadowed alleys, though she couldn't see much beyond vague shapes with the harsh sunlight. She kept waiting for an attack or a summons from the Guild, but the day was quiet, and it was making her jumpy.

It can't always be wrong to fight back, she thought, watching a cat chase another across the dirt road in front of her. If laws no longer protected the people they were meant to serve, then sometimes order had to be broken to bring change. Life was rarely black and white. *All we can do is choose, and live with the consequences.*

Something moved in a window to her right, and Elitsa glanced sideways, ready to draw on her essences, but it was only someone passing through the room. She tensed her jaw, looking forward. This would all be easier if she felt anger and outrage at the Guild, but that required energy she didn't have. In truth, she wasn't surprised with Verka's accusation that the Tower's ruthlessness extended to their agents. *I should have expected this,* she thought, moving around two young girls talking in the center of the street. *A betrayal on some level.* But she'd been so focused on solving her mother's murder that all she'd seen was an opportunity, seemingly offered up by Sister Luck herself.

Elitsa loosened her scarf, fingertips pausing on her hidden pin. Disregarding the Tower's capacity for cruel artifice, she didn't understand why. *Why kill someone who's been useful to you?* The Guild couldn't honestly believe that everyone who left their service would turn around and attack them. They weren't killing essence farmers after their two-year terms. *Why focus on the agents? Does it have something to do with time spent using Guild relics, and they believe they're protecting themselves? But from what?*

Elitsa turned a corner, following the smells of smoked meat and fried potato pancakes. She couldn't rival a mage's power. She lacked their training and money. Everything she'd learned beyond her training with Lelja had been through experimentation on the job and from observing the contract-breakers. Some of them had picked up useful tricks, figured out interesting essence combinations. *Is that what worries the Guild?*

She rubbed her forehead, hoping the headache that was starting wouldn't haunt her all morning. The Tower was rotten, but she didn't know for sure if they were responsible for the deaths. It could just as easily be someone who wanted to strike at the Guild but didn't want to risk reprisal. The Guild's fighting branch, the Flame, would protect the mages and the Tower but wouldn't go out of their way for the agents.

Elitsa frowned. She'd reached the market. The harsh wind

was absent today, and Kirtara's residents were out enjoying the warm sunshine, laughing and talking as they shopped. They seemed happier somehow than the people in Rivna, though Elitsa could see from their clothing and wares that hardship had touched them even here.

I shouldn't feel bad about helping Verka. As much as it pained her, there was no honor in her profession, no loyalty, but Elitsa had always tried to stay on the side of the law. Part of her wanted to call it off, to keep her head down and just keep moving forward like everyone else, but she didn't know where Galyna and Artem were, and she certainly couldn't show up at the guild-hall on the day they were planning on sneaking in.

She watched a man lift a small child onto his shoulders with a belly-shaking laugh. *All I can do is go about my day as usual.* Complete her merchant contract and go back home before the Guild realized anything had happened. Maybe that was naive, but there was no point wearing herself out by assuming the worst had already happened.

Wandering the stalls and shops around the market's edge, Elitsa focused on her task. She was here to retrieve Merchant Melenska's stolen documents from a reportedly unscrupulous usurer who worked out of the square. On another day, she might have been distracted by the good smells and the townsfolk's cheer, but today she felt an undercurrent of desperation as if they were saving up good moments to carry them through the end of the year.

Elitsa found the usurer, Master Spiva, between a tailor's shop and an apothecary. The lower floor of his building had a sturdy oak door and narrow windows set with glass, while the upper had large windows that undoubtedly offered an excellent view of the courtyard below. *What must that have cost?* she wondered, shocked by the display of wealth.

A man with a brown cap and long gray coat was loitering outside, leaning against the wall beside Spiva's door. Though he was affecting an air of boredom, Elitsa could see that he was covertly watching everyone who passed. A young girl ran past him, slowing for a moment, and Elitsa saw her slip him a piece of paper before she disappeared back into the crowd. *So, Spiva's using the local youth to spy for him.*

Purchasing a mug of cider from an apple cart, Elitsa walked to the round stone well that gave her a view of the lender's front door. She sat on a nearby bench, draped with a cozy reindeer fur, and considered her options. The shops in the center of the square offered her some cover from the man by the door, so she was reasonably confident that he wouldn't notice her scrutiny.

A shadow passed in front of her, and Elitsa leaned back, eyes rising from a man's buckled vest to Cas's familiar face, mouth lifted into a pleased smile. Her heart skipped, thoughts flying to Galyna and Artem. "What are you doing here?" she asked, stunned confusion shifting to irritation at the rakish light in his eyes.

Plucking the mug from her fingers, Cas sat beside her on the bench and took a long drink, ignoring the glare Elitsa gave him.

"Delicious," Cas said, putting the mug back into her hand. "They always have the best cider."

Elitsa grimaced at the mug then at Cas before lowering it to rest on her knee. "You have a contract here?" There hadn't been any other contracts from the merchants' guild in Kirtara, but the Tower or another guild's contract might have sent him this way. Whatever the reason was, it was bad luck. Had he already been to the guildhall, or had he yet to check in?

"Nearby." Cas grinned at the crowd, his dark hair falling over his cheek. He shoved it back and glanced sideways at her. "You're watching that man over there, aren't you. What'd he do?"

"You're nosy."

"Your contract is up soon, isn't it? End of the week? Why aren't you taking it easy? I would." He pursed his lips, then grinned. "You're trying to make a good impression to negotiate your next contract, aren't you!"

"The Guild is already impressed with my work," Elitsa said. She glanced at the man guarding the door, then back at Cas, brow furrowed. Was it mere coincidence he was here? "Shouldn't you go do whatever it is you're here for?"

Cas leaned back and crossed his legs, lacing his fingers over one knee. "I have a couple hours. Thought I'd do some shopping."

Elitsa raised an eyebrow. He had no packages with him, though it was possible he'd purchased something small enough to fit inside his coat.

"I need to check in with the guildhall, but I've been putting it off. High Mage Bojan is about as interesting as a sun-drunk turtle, and he always insists on forcing me to have tea with him. Can't get anyone else to sit through his stories, I suppose!"

Elitsa's heart sped up again, and she forced herself not to stiffen. Cas didn't seem to know Bojan was out of town.

"And Master Kalnin," Cas continued, "looks at me like I'm a stray dog tracking mud across his doorstep. Not that Vevere was any better." He shook his head, tracking a ruby-crowned kinglet as the small bird dove for crumbs on the dusty beige cobblestones. "You'd think that with all the work we do for them, they'd show us at least a modicum of respect."

"You know there's a nice inn out that way with servers who'd *love* to listen to your chatter."

Cas looked sideways at her, eyes teasing. "Come on, I know it bothers you. They certainly don't pay us enough."

She frowned, uncertain what reaction he wanted from her. "So why do it then?"

"Well it's better than the mill, isn't it, and it's certainly not boring. Still … sometimes I think about boarding a boat to Xiltarma and trying my hand at piracy." He grinned. "Think I'd make a good pirate?"

Elitsa studied him surreptitiously, suspicion tightening her fingers on the mug of cider. Why speak to her about leaving Casekraia? His criticism of the Guild wasn't exactly new, but why bring it up now? The timing felt too coincidental. *Does he suspect I might leave?* "You're certainly untrustworthy enough." She leaned towards him and wrinkled her nose. "And smelly enough."

"Ah, Eli. You wound me!"

"I doubt that." She looked back towards the usurer's building. If the man was guarding the place, then it likely meant Spiva was there. She'd caught some movement in the upper windows but had no way of knowing for sure unless she went and announced herself. She wanted Cas to leave, but he had plans to go to the guildhall. What if he encountered Galyna and Artem? Would he stop them? Would they kill him? As irritating as he was sometimes, she didn't want him to die, and she certainly didn't want him to discover her involvement. She had no doubt that he'd sell her out the first chance he got. Cas's priorities seemed to revolve around money, risky contracts, and flirting.

Suppressing a sigh, Elitsa gave Cas a calculating look. "Though I'm undoubtedly going to regret this, I could use you if you're really as bored as you say."

"Oh?" Cas raised his eyebrows. "You want *my* help?"

"Want, no, but I'm not sure what I'm going to be walking into here. I pulled a muscle in my leg during my last job, and if things go sideways, it'd be nice to have backup."

"Expecting trouble?" His face brightened as Cas looked towards the man by the door. "A retrieval job?"

"Yes. Spiva stole a trade document, and I'm paying the ransom. There's a high possibility he'll attempt to renegotiate." Which meant it could get violent.

"Hmm." Cas tilted his head, eyes on the door. "I don't know, seems like a poor use of my time. Look at that guy. I doubt he'd make a good fight, all speed but no skill."

"Yes, you seem quite busy," Elitsa said dryly. She hid another grimace by drinking from her mug. "You'd be doing me a favor. I don't want retrieval to drag into tomorrow. Aren't you always prattling on about wishing we worked more together?"

"I believe I asked you to stop getting in my way."

"I'll pay you."

Cas glanced at her, eyes glittering like a magpie's. "Half."

Elitsa barked a laugh. "I don't want you that badly."

Cas arched an eyebrow, his grin widening.

"Your *help*, Cas. Gods above, not everyone wants in your pants."

"These happen to be exceptionally comfortable," Cas said, stretching one leg out across the ground.

"One silver."

"Two, but only because I like you."

"Fine," Elitsa growled.

"You must really want to get back to Rivna." Cas narrowed his eyes playfully. "Got a lover stashed at home?"

She flushed. "I just don't want to waste this week."

Cas tilted his head, studying her.

"Let's go." Elitsa stood up, afraid he'd glean something from her face. He could, on occasion, be incredibly perceptive.

Uncrossing his legs, Cas rose beside her. He stretched, body arching in a cat-like manner, then scratched the back of his head. "What's the plan? Are we going to sneak in? Drop down from the eaves? Pose as a poor housewife and her delicious husband?"

"We'll go in the front door. Like I said, I want to take care of this quickly." She glanced at his shirt, where Cas hid a magesilver pendant shaped like a beetle wing, in addition to the rings on his hand. "You stashed up?"

"Always. Lead on, Serlov. You promised me action."

Hoping she wouldn't regret bringing Cas along, Elitsa wove back through the crowd to the cider seller and returned the mug. She purchased a bag of toasted walnuts and put them in her pocket. If she had to use her relics, she'd need to replenish her energy.

Adjusting her scarf, so her reclamation pin was visible, Elitsa straightened her shoulders and marched towards the man on duty. His dark brown eyes caught hers, though he retained his careless slouch against the wall, watching as she approached with Cas in tow. "I want to speak to Master Spiva."

The man looked at the pin on Elitsa's collar and then glanced at Cas.

"Greetings," Cas said goodnaturedly. His tower pin was hidden, and he seemed to enjoy the man's assessment. He crossed his arms, one hand resting loosely on the other, so the magesilver rings on his hand were visible.

In Elitsa's opinion, it was better to keep your relics hidden. The man would assume she had one, as she was of the Tower, but if he didn't know where it was on her body, he might not try to grab it in a fight, as dangerous as that was. Her hair, covering her earrings, brushed against her cheek as a soft wind blew through the square. She inhaled automatically, sensing the strength of the essence inside it. It was weaker than it should be, and Elitsa felt a moment of disquiet.

"Do you have an appointment?" the man drawled. "Master Spiva is a busy man."

Elitsa smiled thinly. "I don't need one."

"We won't take up too much time," Cas said. "Just want to have a friendly chat, is all."

Considering that a Tower agent wanted to speak to Master Spiva, the man probably didn't believe that at all, but still, it was generally not a good idea to turn them away. Leaning sideways, the man banged on the door with the back of his fist, then crossed his arms and resumed his original position. "Go ahead."

Nodding, Elitsa reached for the door and pulled it open. A small entryway greeted her with space enough for two people, if they squeezed together, at the base of a steep staircase. The wooden stairs were narrow and worn, the steps scuffed from numerous feet, but the walls showed Spiva's wealth — pale green wallpaper overlaid with a diamond pattern in soft silver. Glancing back at Cas, who was also admiring the walls, Elitsa started up the stairs.

The sound of their ascent was loud, and by the time they reached the top, Elitsa wasn't surprised to find two large men waiting by the doorway. *Spiva must believe he needs protection*, Elitsa thought, looking them over. The man on the right reminded her of a bear with a thick black beard and shaggy hair. He was dressed in well-made clothing, but the scars on his hands had likely come from either timberwork or punching people in the face. The top of a knife showed in his calf-high boot, and Elitsa had no doubt he had more inside his vest.

The second man was tall like an oak tree with a weasel-shaped face and mean brown eyes. His light green tunic, belted over loose striped pants, bore several stains that looked suspiciously like dried blood.

Taking a step inside so Cas could enter behind her, Elitsa glanced past the bodyguards and quickly surveyed the large room. If Spiva had hired thugs, he might have other safeguards in place. Padded wooden couches, the polished wood carved into various depictions of Mother Moon and Father Sun, sat around the room atop a dark red Xiltarman rug. The walls were covered in the same wallpaper from the stairwell, so it was impossible to tell if someone hid behind them.

To her right, large windows looked out over the square with a heavy paneled desk set in front. A man sat behind it, watching her, and she assumed he either had a weapon trained on her or one within reach. Mustached and curly-haired, Spiva was dressed entirely in green with gold stitching across the neck and shoulders. If he was experiencing any financial hardship this year, it was not evident.

A woman in a black dress with red and gold flowers sat in a chair to Spiva's left doing embroidery. Her blonde hair was braided in a crown around her head and adorned with small emerald pins — likely from Xiltarma like Spiva's expensive rug. Her eyes flicked up to Elitsa and Cas with a disinterested look, then back down to the sewing in her hands.

"Mother's Blessings to you, Agent Serlov," Spiva said, writing something on a sheaf of papers. "I've been expecting you. If you wanted to sample Kirtara's cider, I would have happily offered you a cup." He glanced up, his mustache shifting as he smiled.

So, he noticed me watching from the bench outside. Elitsa wasn't surprised. People in his position often kept an eye on everything that happened around them.

"Who's your friend?" Spiva asked, glancing at Cas.

"No one important."

Cas shifted, perhaps annoyed by her dismissal, but he merely smiled and tucked his thumbs into his belt. "What she said."

Spiva raised an eyebrow, then set down his pen. "I can't say I'm surprised that Melenska didn't come himself. He sent you with the money?"

Though it should have seemed odd that they were discussing extortion so openly, Melenska had told Elitsa that the local constabulary refused to get involved. It wasn't unusual, unfortunately. Though no one would admit it aloud, everyone knew that the Guild was the true power in Casekraia, and King Dmitrei did not often extend his authority into the towns outside of Rivna. Elitsa could expect no help from the local guards here.

Shoulders itching with the men at her back, Elitsa inclined her head. "Show me the document."

Spiva opened a drawer in his desk and removed a rolled parchment. He turned it so Elitsa could see the seal. It'd obviously been broken, but she recognized it as Melenska's.

"Open it," she said.

Lips pursing, Spiva unfolded the document and held it up.

Elitsa approached the desk, trusting Cas to keep an eye on the men at their back. She scanned the text, recognizing Melenksa's handwriting. It was indeed an agreement between the merchant and the port master in Kreanos. Times like this made her grateful for her former apprenticeship to Master Davor.

Spiva rolled the document back up and tapped it against his palm. "You have payment?"

"Yes, a banknote as agreed."

Spiva smiled and turned his head a fraction towards the woman in the chair. *Curious,* Elitsa thought. Attuned to every move and glance Spiva and his companion made, Elitsa saw the woman raise two fingers over her embroidery. "On second thought," Spiva said, "I've decided to double the amount."

Elitsa's heartbeat skipped, energy moving through her body. She'd expected this when she'd seen Spiva's hired muscle. He likely never intended to accept anything from her, planning to send her back to Rivna empty-handed. She sensed Cas move beside her. "This isn't a negotiation," she said. "I have the payment you agreed upon with Melenska, nothing more."

"Well, that is unfortunate, but—"

She was wasting time indulging this facade. Elitsa turned away from Spiva and looked at the woman in the chair. She was still pretending she wasn't paying attention, but her sewing had slowed several times. The gesture with her fingers had been her signaling Spiva. *She* had changed the price. "Mistress Spiva, I am here to fulfill my contract, and whether or not you want to change the terms of your deal, I will be leaving with the document today."

The woman looked up; her green eyes chilled despite her smile. "Mistress Hengar," she said with a cool, clipped voice. "*Not* Spiva."

Spiva had fallen silent and leaned back in his chair. Though he was still smiling, his face had tightened as though confronted with an unpleasant smell. He tapped the document against the palm of his other hand.

Elitsa's mirrored Hengar's thin-lipped smile. "As I said, I'm leaving with the document. You're welcome to discuss additional payment with Melenska."

"You're confident," Hengar said, eyes narrowing, "which I appreciate in a woman, but I fear you've underestimated me."

Cas laughed suddenly, drawing everyone's eyes. "Underestimated you? You have two Tower agents in your office."

Hengar didn't look surprised and carefully set her sewing down in her lap. She laced her fingers. "You assume you are the only ones in this room with relics."

The door slammed shut, and Elitsa smelled the scent of a bonfire as someone behind her drew an essence. It was a mistake, a show of strength, but ultimately impractical in a building made out of wood. Elitsa was also standing in between the guards and the people they were supposed to protect.

Elitsa lunged forward. As close as she was to Hengar, the guards couldn't risk attacking her. Hengar's eyes flared, her sewing tumbling from her lap as Elitsa grabbed her shoulder. Clenching her fingers in the fabric of the woman's dress, Elitsa spun around the back of the chair to bring the others into view. Hengar grabbed at her hand with strong fingers, trying to pry her free, but Elitsa had used their surprise to pull a knife from her coat, and she pressed it against the side of Hengar's neck.

"Nobody move!" Elitsa bellowed. Heart pounding, breath quick, she swiftly took in the room.

Cas — with a near-feral grin — was halfway around the desk to Spiva, who was standing with a letter opener clutched in his fist.

The men by the door had crossed half the room and were standing in the center of the rug. The weasel-faced man held a knife, poised to throw, and the bearded one had a relic in his hand. Their faces were tense, their attention on Elitsa and Hengar.

"Don't just stand there!" Hengar growled.

"Careful!" Cas said, eyes silvering for a moment as the scent of sea and brine filled the room. He grinned at the knife-holder and shook his head. "I suggest you don't try to out-throw Serlov here. She's got fast hands." Spiva shifted, and Cas made a tsking sound.

Elitsa moved the knife on Hengar's neck, careful not to draw blood. "All we want is the document. Give it to me and—"

A stab of pain shot through her hand as Hengar drove a knitting needle between her fingers. Swearing, Elitsa released her grip on the woman's shirt. She had to immediately throw her head back as Hengar stabbed over her shoulder, this time nearly driving it into Elitsa's eye. A burning sensation crossed her cheek as the needle scraped over her skin.

Hengar's hand clamped on hers again, prying at her fingers as she twisted. Elitsa felt her knife cut and immediately loosened her grip, allowing the woman to throw herself sideways out of the chair. Mindless of the blood running down her throat, Hengar clamped a hand across it and glared at her guards. "Do something, you worthless thugs!"

The bearded man's face tightened in concentration, the scent of fire replaced by a lightning-scented windstorm. Relying on speed versus her essences, Elitsa threw herself sideways in the direction of Hengar as a blast of air hit the chair. It flipped, splinters filling the air as a chunk of wood tore free.

Cas grabbed Spiva's arm and slammed his hand into the desk, hard enough that the man shrieked and let go of the knife. Then Cas raised his ringed hand, sending wind back at the bearded wielder. It knocked the man off his feet into the wall, his head cracking against it hard enough that he stumbled.

Rolling up onto one knee, Elitsa saw the knife-wielder lunge towards Cas. She grabbed wind and water, icing the floor beneath his feet. Foot slipping, he stabbed wide, allowing Cas to get out of the way and kick the man's knee.

A hand clamped on Elitsa's calf, and she looked back at Hengar, who was casting about for another knitting needle. Shaking her off, she lurched for the desk.

The scent of a windstorm filled the air again, and she saw Cas's eyes widen, but she was already halfway up onto the desk. Before Elitsa could continue the motion, he grabbed her around the waist, spinning her sideways.

Spiva screamed and ducked, and the large window behind him exploded from the concentrated blast of air, glass and wood showering the square below. Screams and shouts drifted up from the market.

As Cas pulled her around the side of Spiva's desk, Elitsa spun free from his arms, pushing off his chest with one hand. Grabbing the document off the desk, she elbowed Spiva in the collarbone as he struggled to stand, then, catching Cas's eye again, hurled herself out the broken window.

CHAPTER 12

Elitsa hit a stall's fabric-covered roof, gasping as the air was knocked from her lungs. Before she could recover, the canvas dipped, rolling her sideways. Stomach tightening as she dropped off the side, Elitsa landed on her feet, pain lancing up both legs. She heard a crash from somewhere to her left.

Shoving the document into her coat, Elitsa staggered around a woman picking up her jewelry from the broken remains of her stand. Glass and splintered wood from Spiva's window littered the ground. It was chaos as people tried to figure out what happened.

"Are you all right?" the jeweler asked, a necklace dangling from her hand. Her eyes were wide as she looked from Elitsa to Spiva's building.

"Yes. Fine," Elitsa said, hurrying past. She sidestepped a child, a half-eaten apple forgotten in their hand. Someone yelled for the town guard.

"Time to go!" Cas whirled around her, appearing from between a honey stand and a tent that sold candles. His grin was as wide as she'd ever seen, his eyes sparkling as he jogged south away from the market.

Sparing a look towards Spiva's broken window, Elitsa caught sight of Hengar's angry face, then she took off after Cas, not wanting to have to explain what happened to the town's guards.

Catching up to him on the eastern edge of town, they took refuge behind a large gray barn that looked in need of some care. Cas bent over laughing as Elitsa shook glass from her clothes and tried to straighten her hair. There was blood on her hand from when Hengar had stabbed her. She'd also taken a cut to her forearm, but it had already stopped bleeding.

"Oh Eli, that was spectacular! You know how to have a good time." Cas grinned at her, and Elitsa's stomach flipped. Somehow, despite falling from a window, his clothes barely looked to have been rumpled. There was a bruise beginning on his cheek, but he'd made it out unbloodied. His magesilver pendant swung free around his neck, and as he straightened, he tucked it back inside his shirt. "You got it, I take it?"

"Wouldn't have dove through a window if I hadn't." Elitsa pulled the document from her pocket, then, opening her coat, slipped it into her vest. While traveling, she often wore the extra piece of clothing for additional protection, the stiff fabric tough enough to turn aside small blades.

"We should team up more often! If I'd known this was how you get things done …" Cas chuckled and leaned against the barn, crossing his arms. He looked good in the sunlight with laughter in his eyes.

Her traitorous stomach pitched again, and Elitsa clenched her jaw. Was she actually *admiring* him right now? "Sadly, there won't be much opportunity for that," Elitsa said glibly.

Cas's eyes took on an interested sheen, and Elitsa cursed silently. "You're not going to sign a new contract, are you?"

Elitsa didn't answer, bending down to retie her boots.

"I'm surprised. Why stop now?"

"I thought I might try something else." She didn't bother denying it. Cas was like a fox with a hare.

"Something else? You'd give up your relics to do what, guard a merchant's wagon?"

"Not all contracts belong to the Tower."

"No, but the magesilver does." Cas shoved his hair back from his forehead. "What are you going to do?"

"Travel for a bit. Take a vacation."

Cas gave her an amused look, which made Elitsa glower. How dare he judge her? He had the morality of an egg-stealing spearwing.

"And you?" Elitsa demanded. "You're going to remain a reclamation agent until you die on the job?"

"Maybe."

"And how will you spend your money then?"

"No one lives forever. I intend to live as well as I can until then."

Elitsa straightened and studied him. Was it possible he knew what the Tower was doing? "Don't you think it's odd that there are no agents in retirement?"

Cas raised an eyebrow. "Of course there are. Our work can be risky, which we knew when we signed up, but it's rarely deadly. Sometimes I wish there was more excitement." He sighed, bracing his hands on his hips. "More often than not, I'm chasing farmers instead of mercenaries."

"Yes, that's my point. A farmer can still get a lucky shot in, but most bounties don't turn violent, at least not to the point where we can't handle it. There should be more of us. Do you remember Aleks? He retired last year, was going to open an inn."

"All right."

"He's dead. And Minna, remember her? Also dead."

"So?"

"Every agent who left the Tower, who received their final

payment, died before they could use it. I can't find a single living agent who has retired anywhere."

Cas gave her a skeptical look. "Well, it's hard not to make enemies with this job. Look what the local guards think of us. I bet even in the Aerie, not every glance you get is friendly."

True, but none of my neighbors have tried to murder me. "Come on, Cas. You're smart. This doesn't add up. The likelihood that *no one* is still alive is low. Why have none of them stayed in Rivna? It's a nice enough city."

"So what, you think someone is killing agents after they retire?" Cas narrowed his eyes. "You think the Tower involved?"

"I don't know who is behind it," Elitsa said quickly, "or why they'd want to kill us, but I need to find out." She did not want to spend the rest of her life feeling hunted.

"And you're still planning on leaving the Tower. You think you're putting yourself in danger." Cas grinned suddenly. "You're a tough woman, Elitsa. I'll give you that. Never one to run from a fight."

Elitsa suppressed a sigh. That's what he took from this? She couldn't risk pushing him on it further. She doubted he'd inform on her to the Guild, but a comment made in passing could be just as damning. *Do I leave, or do I stay?* Despite her earlier decision, leaving might be the more dangerous option. *And if the Tower already knows I'm asking questions …*

Cas tilted his head, staring at her.

"What? Is there something on my face?"

He reached forward, and when she didn't pull back, he brushed his fingertips across her left cheek. "Was this from a knitting needle?" His lips quirked, then he dropped his hand. "Have to admire the woman's tenacity. Maybe the two of you should be friends."

Elitsa rolled her eyes. "Yes, this is how I meet all my friends."

It annoyed her how pleased Cas's grin made her, and she looked away from him. "You should steer clear of Kirtara for a while."

"Yes." Cas looked back towards the center of town. "I'd rather not spend the afternoon in jail. Might need to give them a few days to cool off."

Elitsa felt some of her tension ease. If Cas left, she didn't have to worry about him running into Galyna and Artem. She needed to get back home herself. She couldn't risk being connected to whatever they did at the guildhall.

"So," Cas said, unbuttoning the top of his coat, "are we going to split the ransom?"

"What?"

"From the merchant. You got the document, so who's to say you didn't pay him?"

Elitsa gave him a disgusted look and shook her head. "You are unbelievable. I'm not keeping it."

"Come on! It's a victimless crime. Merchants pay ransoms all the time. I bet he's already written the payment off."

"Victimless? I ..." She pinched the bridge of her nose. "I'm not certain how you've lived this long. If the Guild—"

"Eh, they're not as scary as you think."

What made someone disregard their safety and wellbeing so easily? "I'm returning it, Cas."

"All right." He raised his hands in a conciliatory gesture. "Until next time?"

Elitsa rolled her eyes, sending a plea to Sister Luck that there would be no next time, as they exchanged their goodbyes. They headed in opposite directions — Cas on the eastern road towards Luark or Tristi, and Elitsa north, back towards Rivna. She glanced after him several times until the fields turned to trees, blocking her view. There was no reason Cas should double back, but if he chose to now, she couldn't spare the time to follow him.

Leaving the road to enter a thicket of trees, Elitsa uncovered her pack beneath the moss-covered roots of an old tree, relieved to find it untouched. She'd gotten in the habit of leaving her pack outside of town before she started a job. This wasn't the first time she'd had to make a quick exit, and she couldn't afford to leave anything behind.

The day was cool, but the sun had returned from behind scattered clouds, its warmth on her head a welcome distraction from her concerns. After the excitement in the market, she needed to let her body unwind. *If the Tower is going to grab me, they'll do it Rivna.* The field to her left became forest, the trees on either side casting shadows over the packed dirt road. Elitsa watched them, less out of concern of ambush and more admiration of the fall colors. Insects buzzed, and squirrels chittered from high branches. Somewhere overhead, a raven called, drawing her eyes up to a pale blue sky.

Climbing a short rise, Elitsa heard voices. As she reached the top, the road ahead opened up to her, and she saw a slim, black-haired figure in what looked like a Guild mage coat, facing off against four others in worn clothing. One of the assailants, a blond-haired man in dark blue, held the mage's wrist, perhaps to prevent their use of a relic.

"Hey!" Elitsa yelled, her heart thumping in anticipation. "What are you doing?" She should know by now not to involve herself in dangerous situations, but seeing a group trying to overpower another always set her blood boiling.

Two of the men glanced at her. "On your way, girl!" the taller one called, as the other — bald and bearded — laughed dismissively. The man who'd spoken was lean with bright red hair and a dagger on his hip.

"Unhand me!" the mage yelled, still struggling. Compared to those in the upper echelon, they looked young, perhaps five or so years older than she was.

Girl, was it? Her lip curled in distaste. Dropping her pack, Elitsa sprinted forward. She didn't know what to do about the Guild, about her future, but this? This felt familiar.

The redhead's face showed surprise, and then he turned to face her fully, grinning. He didn't reach for the dagger; instead, he sunk his hand into his pocket.

Rogue! The ground trembled. Elitsa twisted sideways, throwing herself into an awkward jump as the dirt ripped apart beneath her feet. Landing with a wince, she seized the essences of water and air from her magesilver and released an ice-edged gust of wind. It wasn't the strongest attack she could manage, but she couldn't risk injuring the mage. She felt a spike of irritation as he struggled to free himself. How had he gotten into this situation in the first place?

The redhead rocked backward, shielding his face, but the bald man sunk into a crouch. He glared at her balefully, clutching a chain around his neck.

Elitsa held out a hand. "I'm a reclamation—"

A blast of fire spiraled towards her, a bead of metal at its center. Elitsa ducked right. Before she could straighten, a gust of wind blew her onto her backside. She spared a glance at the mage, who'd finally wrenched himself free and seized his medallion, burning the blond man holding him.

"Need help, Amos?" the fourth man asked, torn between joining the others against Elitsa or helping the cursing blond with the mage. He was wearing a red jacket that appeared several sizes too small, his stringy black hair hanging into his eyes.

"No!" The redhead gestured angrily at the mage. "Get his relic!" He made a sharp gesture at the ground in Elitsa's direction, kicking up a spray of gravel.

Throwing an arm up to protect her eyes, Elitsa smelled fire and immediately rolled left, scraping her elbows but avoiding the attack. She seized another air essence, a strong one, and blew the fire-wielder off his feet into a tree, showering the ground with leaves and sending a raven into the air with an irritated caw.

"Cease your attack immediately!" the mage yelled at his attackers, fire sparking across his fingers.

The blond, sleeve burned and forearm blistered, started to pull his sword.

The mage lunged forward, releasing a burst of fire that slammed into the man's chest, hungry flames exploding in all directions and setting his shirt alight. The blond man screamed. "Agent!" the mage yelled. "To me!"

Distracted as she stood, Elitsa didn't see the redhead until a stone smashed into her shoulder. She fell painfully, instinct making her roll left as his foot smashed down to kick her. Grabbing his ankle, she seized another essence and tossed embers into his face.

Ignoring his shriek, Elitsa scrambled to the mage's side and assessed their situation. The black-haired man writhed on the ground, clawing at his eyes. The redhead and the blond were both on fire, though the blond had fared far worse, and the bald fire-wielder was headed towards them with murder in his eyes.

The mage's blue gaze flicked to hers, and then he reached down into his boot and removed a palm-sized relic shaped like a shield. Elitsa caught her breath. Could that be the relic the girl had described at the seamstress's shop? *She saw a Guild mage!*

Before Elitsa could examine it further, the mage flung out his hand, relic towards the men. The scent of ozone and storm filled her nose, and she heard a loud clap of thunder as a shockwave blew the rogues off their feet. A repelling spell! The mage lowered his hand, chest heaving, glaring at the men as they rolled and groaned in the dirt. "Leave, now! Or my next attack will not be so gentle!"

Elitsa's curiosity reared up, overwhelming her suspicions as she stared at the mage's long-fingered hand. *Would the relic have rebuffed the rogues' essence attacks? Why didn't he pull it out earlier? What essences did he use?* The execution had been so quick too. *Does it hold a single charge, or does he have more?*

The bald man, eyelids red and puffy, crawled blindly towards the others, getting help from the red-haired man to stand. The rogues were battered and bloodied, and though hatred shone in all their faces, they seemed to have had enough, unwilling to go against the mage again. Like Elitsa, they must be wondering what else he was capable of and why he'd held back.

Elitsa and the mage watched them until they limped away into the trees. When they'd disappeared, he slipped the relic into his coat instead of his boot. He grumbled something, slapping dirt and wrinkles from his clothes before turning a suspicious eye on Elitsa. "I'm grateful for your assistance, but who are you? I hope you have a contract for the relic you're carrying." The wind chose that moment to blow his tangled black curls into his mouth, and he grabbed at them, spitting, losing some of his authoritative posturing.

Straightening, Elitsa brushed gravel off her chest and collar and showed him her pin. "Agent Serlov, sir. I'm returning from a contract in Kirtara." Could he be the person she'd seen outside the seamstress's shop?

"Ah." The mage rubbed a hand over his jaw. There was surprise in his eyes, but his attitude seemed to warm slightly. "I'm glad you happened this way, Agent. I'm Mage Melnyk, of the Scholars."

Mage, so not a high mage. Would he have been able to hold the rogues off if they hadn't retreated? "That relic ..." Elitsa said casually. "I haven't seen one like it before." Melnyk had similarly fine features to the person she'd glimpsed, but his mouth looked wider, his chin more square. And, unless she remembered incorrectly, he was too tall. *Could he have loaned it to someone, or is there more than one relic like his?*

"Ah, yes, it's a standard protection item for Tower mages. Everyone has them, well, except for the acolytes." Melnyk looked back at the trees. "We don't often need to use them, but it seems there are more desperate men of late."

Elitsa's heart sped up. *So, a Guild mage is involved.* She frowned, recalling what the witness had said. The person Neci had seen had come *after* the seamstress had died from the Night Sickness. Had they killed her earlier and then came back for some reason, maybe to see if they'd left something behind? Or had someone else killed her … someone they knew. *Another mage.* If the killer or killers were part of the Tower, that explained why they hadn't caught them. *Unless they are allowing it for some reason?*

She blinked, realizing Melnyk was staring at her curiously. "Hmm. I can see how it would be handy."

"Yes, I don't know why they don't give them to you." He gestured. "Agents, I mean. You deal with violence much more than the rest of us." He turned around distractedly, looking at the ground.

"Did you lose something, Mage Melnyk?"

"There!" Melnyk limped over to the road, bending over a pack on the ground. Several items had spilled out of it, including a thick book, and Elitsa helped him gather everything up before going to retrieve her own pack at the top of the hill.

When she walked back down, stepping over the torn earth the red-haired rogue had left behind, she found Melnyk waiting for her. He smiled hopefully, reminding her of a golden-haired dog Pipene had rescued several years ago. "You're heading to Rivna, yes? I thought we might walk together." He glanced at the woods, fiddling with the strap of his bag on his shoulder.

"You're headed that way?" Elitsa started walking, hiding a smile as the mage quickly fell into step beside her. He reminded her of Orson when he was younger.

"Yes. I was in Ravisti. The seedbeetles have been devastating there. Have you been? They've destroyed all the birch." He shook his head regretfully.

"Oh, that's unfortunate. I've always thought the trees there were quite beautiful." She glanced at him. Why was he on foot? It seemed an unnecessary risk for someone who had the money to travel well. "Why not hire a carriage? If you don't mind me asking."

"Ah, well." Melnyk blushed. "I had, to Kirtara, and then I thought it'd be fun to walk. I uh … I didn't remember how far it was between town and the Golden Horse. The inn where the road branches ahead?"

Elitsa nodded. "I'm staying there tonight."

"Yes! Of course." Melnyk squinted up at the sky. "I suppose we will reach the inn by the evening. Anyway, the rogues surprised me and …" He cleared his throat. "I will tell the Tower of your service to me today."

"No need," Elitsa said, perhaps a touch too quickly, but Melnyk didn't seem to notice. She doubted the Guild would do much beyond thanking her, and she didn't want them to spend any more time thinking about her or Kirtara than they did already.

"You're quite skilled."

"What?"

"Fighting, with essences. You were fast. This was the first fight I've been in." He laughed awkwardly.

That explained how he'd gotten surrounded in the first place. "Yes, I've picked up a thing or two," Elitsa said.

"Yes, I imagine so. I've always wondered why they don't let you join the Flame when your service is done." The mage's voice sounded thoughtful, and Elitsa gave him a sharp look. "You don't have the training, but you clearly learn how to use your relics. It seems like a waste of potential."

"You think agents should be allowed to become mages?"

Melnyk blinked and looked at her. He grimaced and shifted his bag against his hip. "Well, it's not up to me."

Elitsa wanted to ask him about the dead agents, but how could she phrase it in a way that he'd answer? He seemed to realize he was talking about something he shouldn't.

Melnyk cocked his head, narrowing his eyes on her face. "Wait a minute, what was your name again? Serlov … you're the girl High Mage Vilis sponsored!"

Elitsa's stomach dropped. She smiled, trying to keep her sudden tension from her face. "Yes, that's me."

"Ah! Yes, there was some talk about it. You weren't from the ..." He cleared his throat. "Um ..."

"Right neighborhoods?"

"Yes, well, you seem to have done well for yourself."

Elitsa raised an eyebrow. Based on what? Her clothes didn't exactly scream money, and she had a feeling that Melnyk had no idea what her closure rate was. "How do you know High Mage Vilis?" He was of the Hunters, the mages who explored and searched for relics, though she hadn't seen him leave Rivna much the past few years. Honestly, she didn't really know what Vilis spent his time doing.

"We sometimes talk about my projects," Melnyk said. "He has a very keen mind. I've asked Vilis why he doesn't move to the Scholars, but he likes traveling. Doesn't like being stuck indoors, I suppose."

What part of Melnyk's research was Vilis interested in, and why? "You're out and about," Elitsa said, gesturing at the sky. They had left the trees and were walking through a field of tall, golden grass. She guessed that they were no more than an hour away from the Golden Horse. This was the most casual conversation she'd ever had with a mage before, but Melnyk seemed like he wanted to talk. Perhaps he thought they'd bonded during his near-death experience.

"Yes, though, as you probably guessed, this does not happen often. I've been studying the seedbeetles, and I thought I'd found a way to stop them."

"You're studying them?" Based on what she'd seen, Elitsa had started to believe that the Tower wasn't really doing anything at all about the problem, despite the devastating toll the beetles had taken on the crops and trees.

"Yes, they're stronger than they should be."

"Stronger?"

Melnyk gestured at the grass growing alongside the road. "Every living thing has essence, right? Some are stronger than others. Usually, it's based on the size or intelligence of something ... humans and bears, for example, have a stronger essence than that grass or this breeze." He wiggled his fingers in the air. "Ravens, too. If you try to harvest an essence from a large animal or another human, the chance that you will lose is high. That your essence will be absorbed by theirs."

Elitsa held her breath, not wanting to interrupt him. It was considered abhorrent to harvest an essence from anything larger than an insect, which the Tower upheld. Animals were never harvested from, at least no one was supposed to. And a human? That resulted in execution. She hadn't heard of anyone being brought before the Tower for that though, for over a century.

"Essences have been growing progressively weaker the past few years," Melnyk continued. "The wind, the trees ... The collective energy in the natural world does wax and wane, shifting as some things flourish and others weaken, but right now, there is an imbalance, a significant one. It's like if you overdraw on a spring, and it starts to—" He cut off, his light brown cheeks paling. Clearing his throat, Melnyk snapped his hand into a fist. "The uh, seedbeetles are stronger than they should be, which is why they've been so devastating this year." He pressed his lips together, falling silent.

Elitsa glanced at him. She'd thought that essences had felt weaker than before but assumed they were just having a difficult year. *Does Melnyk think something specific is causing it? But what? Could it have a connection to whatever Freythen and Vilis are working on?* "So you know how to stop them? The seedbeetles?"

Some of the tension left Melnyk's face as he sighed and shook his head. "No. They are susceptible to fire, of course, but I'd hoped to interrupt their growth cycle." He made a thin smile. "Back to the research rooms for me."

Elitsa tried to rouse Melnyk into further conversation as they walked, but the mage seemed to have sunk into his thoughts, his earlier enthusiasm gone. When they reached the Golden Horse, he insisted on buying her a meal and renting a horse for her when she left in the morning, as thanks for her assistance on the road. Over soup in the common room, they talked about idle things — music and books and favorite children's stories about Mother Moon — and then separated for the night, Melnyk retiring to one of the nicer rooms on the second floor.

Elitsa left at first light, grabbing a quick breakfast from the cook on her way out the door. Melnyk was nowhere to be seen, so she assumed he was still sleeping. The stablemaster, saddling a sturdy brown mare named Agnia, warned her that wolves were approaching the road — typically an infrequent occurrence — but Elitsa saw nothing beyond a fox and several deer once she got on her way.

As she followed the road, Elitsa thought about Melnyk's shield and the Tower's connection to the Night Sickness deaths. She still didn't understand what connected the victims to each other and the Guild. The only mage she'd ever seen her mother with was Vilis. *Is that why she was targeted?* But if they were going after people he seemed close to, why had no one attacked Elitsa? She'd experienced her fair share of fights, but they'd all been connected to relic retrievals.

Vilis doesn't explain the other deaths, Elitsa thought. She doubted he was the thread that bound everyone who had died. He was a skilled high mage, but there were many above him with more influential positions. Whatever Vilis might be able to offer if threatened, couldn't be worth killing multiple people.

Elitsa needed to talk to the witness again, see if Neci remembered anything more about the person she'd seen. The horse stumbled, and Elitsa tightened her fingers on the saddle, foreboding unsettling her stomach. If the Tower was covering up the deaths, or a mage was involved, the girl might not be safe.

CHAPTER 13

Elitsa reached Rivna's southern gate at midday, passing a
farmer transporting pumpkins — the bright orange
and yellow vegetables mounded high in the back of his
wagon. She rode Agnia to the Travelers' stable, a large barn near
the southern wall that worked with the Golden Horse. The mare
would eventually make her way back home when a stablehand or
another traveler headed south. Dismounting, Elitsa gave the
horse a friendly pat on the neck and handed her off to a boy with
copious red-gold freckles across his face, then headed on foot
towards the River District.

Elitsa winced as she walked. It'd been a while since she'd
ridden a horse, and she knew she'd feel stiff the following day.
Still, it'd been worth reaching Rivna so quickly. She wanted to
talk to Neci, grab lunch and freshen up, and then find out if
Verka had received any messages from Galyna and Artem. With
the messenger towers, they might have already checked in.

Crossing one of the bridges into the River District, Elitsa
headed to the fountain near the weavers' warehouses. That was
where Neci would most likely be, as it was a popular hangout for
the street kids who worked in the Smoke Eyes' territory.

The fountain was dry, a simple basin with a broad rim and a chipped statue of a woman holding a hammer in its center. A boy was perched on the small pedestal beneath the statue's feet, legs swinging. The kids sitting and standing by the fountain's edge eyed Elitsa as she approached but made no move to run away. They considered this their place, and she saw more than one raised chin and confident swagger.

"What do you want, ferret?" a red-haired girl called out, arms crossed across her chest. Several sizes too big, her coat was belted tightly around her waist, the cuffs long enough to cover her fingers.

"Neci, is she here?"

The girl narrowed her eyes suspiciously, likely to object to knowing anyone by that name.

"She did a job for me," Elitsa said, thinking quickly. "But never collected her payment."

Eyes lighting up, the girl hopped off the wall, then tried to hide her interest by examining her dirty fingernails with a bored expression. "How 'bout you give the payment to me? I'll see she gets it."

Elitsa smiled flatly. "Thank you, but I need to speak with her. I will give you a copper if you can tell me where I can find her."

"Don't be beastly, Agra." A young boy stepped up beside her, the skin yellowed beneath his eyes. He was small with thick brown hair and large ears that stuck out from beneath a worn cap. "Neci is dead, Mistress. I'm sorry."

Elitsa blinked, the dread she'd felt on her ride to Rivna like ice across her back. "She's dead?"

Agra, glaring at the boy, crossed her arms and slouched back against the fountain. "I was going to tell her," she grumbled.

The boy pursed his lips. "She drowned in the river."

Drowned. Elitsa studied the children's faces. Neci certainly wouldn't be the first to disappear into the cold water, but the timing seemed suspect. It couldn't be a coincidence that the one person who could tie the sickness to the Tower was dead. "Do you know how it happened?"

"The grebes …" The boy paused, cheek dimpling. "That's what we call the guards, Mistress, because of how they strut around. They think she slipped and hit her head. Neci never cared much for water, though; I think she was afraid of it."

"Thank you …"

The boy's smile widened. "Miros."

"Thank you, Miros. Here." Elitsa fished several coppers from the lining of her coat pocket and held it out.

Agra's eyes narrowed as Miros took the coins, and considering the look she gave him, Elitsa hoped he'd get to spend it.

"You look distressed, Mistress," Miros said, moving closer.

"Yes." Guilt knifed through Elitsa's stomach. She knew it wasn't rational, but she felt responsible for Neci's death. Could she have prevented it? She knew now the Guild or a Guild mage was involved somehow, with the Night Sickness, but had that put her any closer to her mother's killer? She didn't know what mage Neci had seen. *Am I going to start questioning the hundreds of mages inside the Tower?* That was a surefire way to get a knife in the back.

"Does it have something to do with the seamstress?" Miros asked.

Elitsa started, looking at him closely. "You know about that?"

"Neci said she was there."

"What are you talking about?" Agra asked suspiciously, stepping closer.

The other children at the fountain seemed to be ignoring them, resuming a dice game on the ground.

Miros frowned, forehead furrowing. "Do you think she was killed?"

"I have suspicions."

"By who?" Agra demanded, propping her hands on her hips.

"I don't know." Elitsa would not risk sending the kids after the

Tower. She had no idea what they might try to do if they got it into their heads to avenge their friend. *Can they still assist me?* "Maybe you could help me."

Agra's eyes narrowed. "Doing what? Something that might get us killed?"

"No." Elitsa's chest tightened. *Am I making a mistake involving them?* This was probably less dangerous than what they already dealt with daily on the streets. "I want you to tell me if there is another death from the Night Sickness, as soon as it happens. That's it, no investigating, just come find me. I'll pay you a copper for the information." Maybe she could catch the mage this time and finally find out what was going on. If she had proof, something that tied the Guild to the deaths, then she could talk to Vilis. He could question people in the Tower.

"I can do that," Miros said, nodding seriously.

Agra puffed out her chest, jaw set. "And me! But you pay both of us when we deliver the message. Not going to let Skinny here run around without protection."

Miros rolled his eyes but gave Agra a bright smile.

"Thank you. Remember, just tell me when and where. My name is Elitsa. I travel a lot outside the city, so bring your news to my friend Pipene at the House of Swans."

Miros brightened. "The Swans? The cook always feeds me muffins there."

"You have yourself a deal, ferret," Agra said.

HEAD ACHING, ELITSA CLIMBED THE STAIRS TO HER FLOOR. Between Kirtara, the fight with Melnyk, and Neci's death, she felt worn. She had no idea what she should do. Or if the decisions she'd made so far were sound. *I can't keep questioning my own motives,* Elitsa thought. She had to trust herself again. She was trying, wasn't she? To make the world better, to atone, in whatever way she could.

But as much as Elitsa wanted to distance herself from the Guild and make them pay, she was still just a reclamation agent, and only for two more days. Her resources were limited, and if she voiced any suspicion that the Guild was involved in something nefarious, she doubted she'd even make it to Velasa, let alone board a ship.

Looking up, Elitsa saw a boulder of a man standing in front of her door, arms crossed over his chest. She paused, heartbeat jumping like a startled horse. The soft light from the hall illuminated his face as he glanced towards her. He was Solveiga's man, one of the bouncers who watched the doors at the House of Swans. *What's his name? K something?*

"Karel? What are you doing here?"

Karel inclined his head in greeting, mouth hidden beneath a thick beard. "Solveiga wants to see you."

"What, why?" Elitsa couldn't recall a single time Solveiga had asked her to visit.

"Someone broke into your room. Pipene was hurt."

"What?" Fear thrust its hands into her chest. Elitsa studied her door but saw no damage to the pale wood or the keyhole. Her thoughts chased a hundred horrible possibilities, and she clenched her fist. *Calm down. If she was dead, he would have told me.* "Is she all right?"

Karel made a gruff sound of confirmation.

"Who broke in?"

The big man shrugged, staring at the opposite wall. "Talk to Solveiga."

Elitsa looked back at the door, torn between wanting to see Pipene and what had happened inside her room. Giving Karel another look, she reached for the handle. The door opened, unlocked. No one had a spare key to her room, not even Pipene. How had they gotten in?

Dropping her bag on the floor as she stepped inside, Elitsa released the door, letting it swing shut behind her. Her eyes swept the room as she walked to the table and lit a candle. Her chest tightened. There was blood on the floor. Not enough for a mortal wound, but it was clear someone had been injured. *Pipene.* Nothing else seemed out of place, nothing but …

Elitsa rushed towards her bed. She dropped to her knees, looking beneath it. The floorboards were pried open, the hollow beneath empty. Her stash of essences was gone.

Swearing, Elitsa rocked back onto her heels. No one had known what she'd hidden there, and no simple thief would have found it. *A mage.* A mage had been in her room. Thefts were common in other areas in the city, but never the Aerie. Solveiga was too respected. It couldn't be someone from a gang inside the city; they'd never risk making her angry. Elitsa wasn't sure why, but the Smoke Eyes were wary of her.

Alarm sent a rush of cold through Elitsa's skin. The Guild wasn't afraid of Solveiga. *They know I met with Verka.* Which meant they might already know about Kirtara. She focused on her earrings, delving the essences inside the magesilver chains and hoops piercing her skin. She was running low but still had several fire and water and—

Someone was behind her.

Dropping her right knee forward, Elitsa spun sideways, attempting to spring up into a standing position, but as she turned, she saw a blade driving towards her. She threw her upper body backward, grabbing the person's wrist as they stabbed past her face, and pulling down and to the right. Her attacker, off-balance now from their lunge, fell face-first into the side of the bed. Elitsa shoved them again, pushing off their back to put space between them.

The person was taller than she was and dressed all in black. Recovering quickly, they spun around, and she saw a masked face and determined brown-gold eyes. Another knife streaked towards her. Gasping, Elitsa threw herself back, arm raising, and felt the blade cut a thin slit in the fabric of her sleeve as it passed, thumping into the far wall.

The door opened, and Karel stuck his head in. "Serlov?" His eyes widened as the figure straightened by the bed.

Pulse racing, Elitsa raised her hand, reaching for an essence of air. She was too slow. Her blast hit the person's arm, but the knife had already left their hand. As the assassin regained their balance, the silver handled blade embedded deep into Karel's right eye with a horrible thunk. He cried out, surprised, then toppled forward.

Horror rose in Elitsa's throat. The assassin was too fast, their movements clearly enhanced by essence. She couldn't hold back or risk a drawn-out fight. They were stronger, faster. She pulled a water essence from her magesilver, the strongest she had, and channeled a spray of water across the person's boots and pants, drenching them and the floor beneath.

The assassin jumped back, eyeing the puddle under their feet, then their eyes crinkled at the corners. They slowly pulled another dagger from a sheath against their ribs, the hilts of several others glinting as they moved.

Sweeping her fingers up in front of her as though gathering the air, Elitsa seized the single essence of a sparkwyrm and threw it towards the puddle of water. The jagged line of light sizzled as it struck the assassin's boot, and they convulsed with a harsh gasp, fingers clenching around the blade in their hand.

Elitsa had no time to marvel that it'd worked. The sparkwyrm's essence was sharp and painful, but it could do no more than momentarily stun. Pulling her knife from her boot, she sprinted forward. Her momentum carried her within the assassin's arms, and before they could redirect their knife into her side, she slammed hers into their neck between their mask and collar. Three more thrusts, faster than the thunderous dash of her heartbeat, and then she danced backward into a defensive stance.

The assassin grabbed at her, fingers slipping off the heavy

fabric of her coat. Their hood was growing wet with blood around their throat. They took a step, raising the knife, then fell onto their knees.

"Who are you!" Elitsa demanded, brandishing her bloodied knife. She ignored the red on her hand and the metallic scent filling the air, overpowering the lingering traces of her used essences.

The assassin only blinked, eyes dulling, and then they slumped onto their side.

Elitsa darted a glance at Karel, but the man was dead and beyond her help. Anger and confusion lanced through her, making her fingers shake, then she set her jaw and cautiously moved forward. Still holding the knife, she pulled up her attacker's mask. It was a man with a sharp nose and beardless face. He looked vaguely familiar, but she couldn't say with certainty if she'd seen him before or where.

Convinced he wouldn't be moving again, Elitsa searched his clothing, unearthing a magesilver coin with a tower on one side and a knife on the other. *A Tower assassin!* She'd thought they'd been retired. The assassins were a former elite division of the Flame — the Guild branch of mages trained in fighting and the knights that protected the Tower — that had previously been sent on missions for king and country to the lands beyond. Casekraia had had relative peace with the other nations of Cerana for the last eighty years, a time of trade. What was one doing here on the floor of her room?

Fear and anger swirled inside Elitsa's chest, and she dropped the coin, gripping her knife tightly. The assassin had been waiting for her. Had this man attacked Pipene, then come back? *He must have had an ebonweaver's essence.* That had to be why neither Karel nor Elitsa had seen him.

She stared at the body, her heart still beating too fast. *The Tower is trying to silence me.* She'd expected censure or maybe imprisonment, but sending a Guild assassin seemed like an over-reaction for what she'd done. *Maybe this has nothing to do with Kirtara but Neci and the seamstress.* Maybe the Guild was afraid of what Elitsa had uncovered or where her questions might lead her next. *This is probably how they killed the retired agents.*

Pipene. Would she be safe at Solveiga's? *I need to get away from the city.* Away from the people she cared about, before the Tower tried again, but first she had to make sure Pipene was all right. Grimacing at the bloodied knife in her hand, Elitsa quickly wiped it on the assassin's coat, then pushed it back into her boot. She recovered her pack from near the door and then carried it over to the chest that held her clothing and a handful of her mother's books. Stuffing several outfits inside her bag, Elitsa added a book of old stories with a soft green cover, her grand-mother's handkerchiefs, and a small wooden carving of a winged bear — the only possession she had from her father. She retrieved her mother's bracelet from the trunk's lining — a circle of painted beads — and slid it onto her wrist. Regretfully, Elitsa ran her fingers over the books she'd have to leave behind and then closed the chest's lid. If she had to run, she wasn't sure when or if she could come back.

She needed to send a message to Orson and Sofija. The king's guards would eventually come sniffing around, but hopefully, they would think Karel and the assassin had killed each other. More likely, the Tower would recover the assassin first, before the city watch was notified, and Elitsa needed to be as far away from here as she could before that happened.

She glanced back at the body. If she had more time, she could take whatever essences the assassin had left, but she couldn't risk lingering here any longer. Stepping out into the hall, Elitsa looked in both directions as she closed the door. If anyone had heard the noise, they'd decided it wasn't worth their inquiry and stayed inside their rooms. Taking the stairs, Elitsa exited into the courtyard. She walked the length of the long building and turned the corner, stepping from the darkness into the warm glow that surrounded the gilded doors of the House of Swans.

To the right of the door, a muscular woman sat knitting on a stool. Her thick black hair was braided into a crest across the top of her skull, and specks of gold dusted her warm brown cheeks. She was dressed in a soft gray jacket, buttoned up to her neck against the chill, and sage green trousers with white flowers embroidered from hem to knees. Her thick fingers deftly worked the wooden needles, and she glanced up as Elitsa approached.

"Evening, Dace," Elitsa said, stomach twisting as she forced herself to smile. Dace was one of four guards, including the now deceased Karel, who kept the peace at the House of Swans. She didn't know if they'd been close, but she had to tell Solveiga what had happened first.

Dace dipped her head, pale blue eyes dropping back to her knitting. "Serlov."

Elitsa grabbed one of the polished copper handles, shaped like a swan's curving neck, and opened the door. Music and laughter spilled out to envelop her. Giving Dace another quick look, she stepped into the large parlor. The House of Swans was an oasis in the city. People lounged on plush couches, laughing and whispering to each other, separated by wooden screens and surrounded by plants. Solveiga's wife, Irusya, was the magic behind the lush greenery. Somehow she'd managed to keep these plants alive and thriving despite the difficult season they'd had and the approach of fall.

The Swans, identifiable by their beautiful cloaks of white feathers, moved around the room with drinks or entertained their guests. To Elitsa's left, in a cozy alcove where several people lounged together, a voluptuous figure danced behind a silvery screen, the movement of their silhouette reminding her of a snake's sinuous motion.

Searching the room for Pipene's blonde hair, Elitsa hurried to the staircase in the back of the room. She'd visited Pipene often enough that no one moved to stop her as she headed up to the second floor. Guests were usually entertained downstairs in the parlor and adjoining rooms, but upstairs was where the Swans lived, as well as Solveiga and Irusya. Finding Pipene's corner room empty, Elitsa immediately headed to the opposite side of the building and rapped her knuckles on Solveiga and Irusya's door.

CHAPTER 14

Solveiga's rooms were as Elitsa remembered, less lavish than downstairs but still elegant and comfortable. She'd only been inside once, shortly after her mother died when the Mistress of the House of Swans had told her to come to her if Elitsa ever needed help. Though they'd lived in one of her buildings, she hadn't known Solveiga was friends with her mother or understood why the woman had cared about her wellbeing. Elitsa was older than most of the street kids Solveiga took in and had already received an education through her mother and Master Davor, so she'd been confident she could do just fine on her own.

Elitsa had never taken Solveiga up on her offer, even when she'd lost her apprenticeship. Instead she'd found work in an inn's kitchens in the Kurdaima before she'd convinced Vilis to sponsor her to agent. After Pipene started working at the House of Swans, Solveiga had become more of a casual acquaintance than a stranger.

The pair of them were at the foot of Solveiga and Irusya's canopied bed, Pipene reclining on the peach-toned chaise, and Solveiga standing beside her. The Swans' proprietress was a striking woman, her presence like the moon's pull on the tide, but Elitsa immediately focused on Pipene. Her friend's left eye was swollen shut, and there was a dark red bruise beneath the bag of ice she held against her cheek and jaw. Her arm was wrapped in a sling, and as she started to smile, she winced, likely feeling pain from her split lip. Something had hit her with force.

"Pipene!" Elitsa gasped, rushing forward.

"I'm all right." Pipene lowered the bag of ice as Elitsa dropped into a crouch in front of her. She tried to smile again then immediately winced, touching her fingertips to her swollen mouth.

"What happened? Who did this to you?" Elitsa thought about the assassin dead on her floor. "Was he masked?"

"So forceful with your questions," Solveiga said, arching an eyebrow. If a voice could contain the lazy heat of a summer day, it'd belong to Solveiga, the honeyed tones of her words somehow still alluring despite their obvious chastisement.

Elitsa flushed and made a move to stand, but Pipene caught her hand.

"It's not your fault, Elitsa." Her brow furrowed, regret crossing her face. "I'm sorry about your essence stash. I tried to stop him."

Elitsa shook her head, sparing a quick thought to wonder if Pipene felt hurt that she'd never told her about her reserve. She wasn't sure why she'd kept it secret exactly, but it didn't matter now. It'd still been found. Elitsa frowned. The assassin hadn't taken her essences; the bottles she'd used for storage were gone. *There was a second person.*

"Was it the Smoke Eyes?" she asked, though that didn't ring true. Why would they try to steal from her when she'd been helping them? She glanced at Solveiga. *No, a Smoke Eye wouldn't dare set foot in the Aerie unless they were visiting the House of Swans as a guest.* "Or a rogue?"

Pipene hesitated. "He was a Guild mage, Elitsa. The Tower's symbol was sewn into his clothes."

Solveiga shifted, her long dress whispering against her bare legs as she crossed her arms and made an irritated noise.

Elitsa's stomach hollowed. How could the Tower disregard her years of service so hastily? No one had sought to question her or ask about her intentions. Why move so quickly to kill? *Does Vilis know?*

Pipene moved the ice on her face. "I was on my way to see Faena and saw your door was open. I thought you were home, but when I poked my head in, there was a man pulling bottles from under your bed. I yelled at him, and I ..." She glanced at Solveiga, who was looking out the window. "I thought he was a rogue, so I pulled out my relic."

Elitsa frowned, thinking about the Guild.

"I'm sorry I didn't tell you, Elitsa," Pipene said quickly. "I trust you, of course, but with your job I, I didn't want you to have to lie for me."

Elitsa forced a smile. "You don't have to apologize. I suspected you had one." It still stung to have it confirmed, but she could hardly fault Pipene for keeping secrets. *I have enough of my own.*

Solveiga turned her head and gave Elitsa a considering look, which she ignored. Elitsa had seen a few of the Swans with relics, but she'd never confronted anyone. In contrast with the Smoke Eyes, she thought they were honorable, using what they had to protect themselves and the community. The Aerie was a safe place because of it. She'd never considered turning them in or telling anyone about it. Perhaps she would have been conflicted when she'd first become an agent and thought the Guild was protecting the people, but her trust in their mission had not lasted long. Elitsa suspected Solveiga had helped the Swans obtain their relics, but she certainly wouldn't say that aloud. The less she knew, the better.

She chewed on the inside of her cheek. If Pipene had shown her relic, that explained why a Guild mage attacked her. "Did you draw on an essence?"

"No," Pipene said, "at least not at first. When I realized he was from the Guild, I just stood there. I was going to run, I know it's illegal to have a relic, but then he said, 'You should have stayed in the pond, little bird' and then he moved to take it and I … I reacted, but I wasn't fast enough."

Elitsa's face went cold, and her fingers tightened on Pipene's hand. "What did he look like?" she asked, a growing dread filling her chest.

"Tall, brown hair turning silver, brown eyes. He had a beard … and he smelled like apricots."

Elitsa stood up, her heartbeat quickening. Confusion furrowed her brow. Vilis had broken into her room, had hurt Pipene. *Why? How did he know about my essences, and why did he take them? Did he find out about Kirtara?* She thought back to their conversation in the park. She'd asked him about the dead agents. Had she said she was going to leave the Guild? Was that what this was about? *He thought I was leaving, and what … he wanted to make sure I couldn't fight?* His betrayal felt like a physical blow. He was connected to the assassin somehow. He had to be.

"Elitsa, are you all right?" Pipene touched her arm. "Do you know him?"

"It's nothing," Elitsa said quickly, ignoring Solveiga's sharp stare. As far as she knew, Vilis had never visited the House of Swans, but that didn't mean Solveiga had never met him before. She needed to talk to him before Solveiga did; demand an explanation.

Elitsa hugged Pipene suddenly, inhaling her friend's scent of vanilla and lavender. She was the only person she trusted, despite their secrets. Elitsa had thought Vilis was on her side, but she'd always known he belonged more to the Tower than her. Had he expected this when she'd shown up at his door all those years ago? That one day he'd betray her? *Can I trust anything he's ever said to me?*

She felt like she should cry, but instead, she felt cold, her anger like the winter snow. Her fingers tightened on Pipene's dress. Vilis had hurt her, the only true friend Elitsa had. If she'd been killed ... No, she wouldn't let her mind go there.

"Karel is dead," Elitsa blurted, pulling back.

Pipene gasped, looking up at Solveiga.

"How?" Solveiga demanded. Her bright blue eyes glittered dangerously, her sensual grace sharpening somehow, giving Elitsa the impression that a snow leopard was staring her down.

Elitsa hesitated. She hadn't told them about the assassin yet, but she couldn't exactly hide it. She had a sinking feeling that the more Pipene knew about the Tower, the more danger she'd be in. Pipene would want to help, but Elitsa needed to take care of this on her own.

"What happened, Elitsa?" The room seemed to chill with the tone of Solveiga's voice.

If she didn't tell them, Solveiga might assume she'd killed Karel herself, and Elitsa did not need any more enemies. "There was a Guild assassin in my room, hiding in the shadows. I killed him, but not before—" Guilt tightened her stomach. She could have prevented his death if she'd been faster. If she hadn't been so distracted by her fear. "The bodies are still there. I don't know if anyone heard, and the city watch will—"

"I'll take care of it." Solveiga looked displeased, and Elitsa wasn't certain if she felt any grief over Karel's death or not, but when Pipene reached for the woman's hand, she took it. "You are certain he was an assassin?"

Elitsa nodded. "Yes."

Pipene looked back at Elitsa, tearful eyes wide with shock. "I don't understand. Why would the Tower try to kill you?"

Elitsa stood and crossed her arms over her chest, looking past them at the bed frame, the carved wood posts like the enfolding branches of trees. She'd forgotten that Pipene didn't know about the dead agents. *It's too late now.* She couldn't risk Pipene or Solveiga knowing about her deal with Verka. If that had any connection to the assassin, Elitsa couldn't let the Guild think they were somehow involved. She needed to get moving.

"You can't go home," Solveiga said. "I'll hide the body. If the Guild thinks the assassin is still alive, they may wait before trying again. It is good it wasn't another agent; that may mean there is no official contract out on you. You may not need to run from the city just yet."

Elitsa's stomach dropped, thinking of Guild Mistress Astraia signing a contract retrieval notice with her name. What reason would they list? Her contract was not yet over. A rush of anger tightened her skin. The essences Vilis had stolen. Would they try to claim that she had sold to the Smoke Eyes like Janso, the farmer? *I will not let them drive me from the city without knowing why.* She needed to talk to Verka and get paid, then acquire more essences. She was now one of the hunted.

"You'll stay in the Aerie, won't you, Pippe?" Elitsa asked.

Pipene frowned. "What are you going to do?"

"I have business in the River District."

"Is this really a good time to be roaming the streets?"

"As Solveiga said, they're probably waiting to hear from their assassin." Elitsa refastened her coat, fingers pausing on a spot of dried blood. "I'll be safe enough. You know I'm not one to hide."

Pipene's eyes narrowed, but whatever she was going to say was interrupted by Irusya entering the room.

A full head higher than Solveiga, who already rivaled the tallest Casekraians in the city, Irusya was a generous woman with curly black hair and warm brown skin. She had the height and complexion of a Xiltarman, but if that had been her home, Elitsa didn't know how she'd ended up settling here in Casekraia. Though the two countries traded freely, Caskeraian merchants — funded by the Tower and king — were always carrying back stories of how dangerous the other continent was and their applications of magic. Elitsa hadn't spent much time thinking about their warnings. The other lands were far away, so she couldn't see how anything Xiltarma or the other nations did would have much effect on Casekraia.

Dressed less glamorously than Solveiga, Irusya's green skirt and high-collared white blouse were embroidered with red and green flowers. Layered necklaces of orange-red beads hung around her neck and another of silver coins and tiny bells that chimed as she walked. As Irusya turned around from shutting the door, Elitsa saw she had a bowl balanced against her hip.

"Elitsa!" Irusya said, her lilting voice surprised. "I am glad you are well. We were worried." Her brown eyes moved to Solveiga, some unspoken communication passing between them.

"Yes, thank you for caring for Pipene. I was just on my way out." Irusya was a skilled healer and was often the first person everyone went to before seeking one of the doctors in the city. Elitsa wasn't any closer to the woman than she was to Solveiga, but Irusya had always been kind and welcoming.

"Of course." Irusya went to stand by Solveiga, who put an arm around her waist and rested her chin against her shoulder. Smiling, Irusya looked back at Elitsa, eyes dropping from her face to her sleeve.

Elitsa followed her gaze and found the cut the assassin's knife had left behind. She put her fingers over the tear, some of the energy she'd felt in the heat of battle returning for a moment and sending chills down her arms.

"Where will you be staying?" Irusya asked.

"Yes, Elitsa," Pipene said, "I hope you're not planning to curl up upon someone's doorway like a cat tonight."

Elitsa smiled. "No, Pippe." She glanced at Solveiga, gauging her expression. She seemed more at ease with Irusya beside her. *Do I dare ask for more help?* She didn't like requiring assistance — it was never good to owe favors — but she needed somewhere to lie low. "Is there somewhere I can sleep tonight? Not here, of course; I don't want to put you at risk if they come looking for me again."

Solveiga straightened and braced her hand against her hip. "I own the room above Mistress Moon's. She's already closed for the day. You'll be safe there. Listen for the cygnets. They'll let you know if anyone wanders the Aerie tonight that shouldn't. There's a key beneath the bottom of the spirit house in the window."

Elitsa nodded. The small bakery was along the road south of them that led to the Green Gate. It was a warm and cozy place where she occasionally purchased sugar-dusted honey cakes. She hadn't known there was a room upstairs.

"Be careful, Eli," Pipene said.

"I will. I'll come back in the morning." Elitsa nodded at Solveiga and Irusya, then turned and strode from the room. She hurried back downstairs, exiting through the kitchens into a small walled garden where Solveiga kept goats and chickens. Slipping through a small door onto the street, she headed towards the river and the Black Eyed Fish.

CHAPTER 15

"What happened?" Elitsa asked, wasting no time as Verka sat down across from her. She was wearing a pine-green coat with a high collar, trimmed in black wool. Dressed as she was, Verka would be hard to spot in the darkened streets. The essence procurer hadn't been at the tavern when Elitsa arrived. Gambling that the bartender would know how to contact her — the Smoke Eyes owned this building after all — she'd purchased a mug of cider and sat down to wait.

Verka eyed her from beneath the brim of a black cap, several tendrils of her hair curling against her neck. It was unclear what she was thinking, though she didn't appear worried or nervous as she raised her mug to her lips, inhaling the apple-scented steam. "There was no need to come in person," she murmured as she lowered the polished wood cup. "I intended to send payment via runner." She cocked her head to the side. "Are you worried about your friend? He is safe, as promised."

In truth, Elitsa hadn't spared much thought for Orson since her adventurous day in Kirtara with Cas. She pushed away her guilt. There were bigger problems now that needed addressing. The door opened, making her heart spasm in her chest, but it was only a worker heading wearily to a table. "Someone entered my home and injured my friend." She narrowed her eyes at Verka, deciding not to tell her about the assassin, not yet. "Did anything go wrong?"

Understanding crossed Verka's face, and she shook her head. "The job was completed without incident, though I do expect the anthill to begin seething soon. That is why I suggested waiting for me to contact you." She inclined her head at the room, though no one appeared to be paying them any particular attention. The tavern was busy for the night. "Your presence here may encourage questions."

"No one came here looking for me?"

"For you? Why would they?"

Elitsa picked up her mug, mind spinning. If the Guild didn't know about Verka and Kirtara, then either Vilis had betrayed her because of her questions about the agents, or the Tower had singled her out. The only other people who'd known she might not stay in Rivna were Pipene and Cas. She pictured Cas's lanky form leaning against the barn, grinning at her after their fight with Spiva. Could he have already returned to the city? Suspicion and anger clawed across her skin, but she shook it off. She doubted their conversation had warranted a rushed missive to the Tower. It didn't make sense.

And Vilis ... why would he try to kill her? She wasn't a threat to him. *This must have something to do with the agents and the Night Sickness.* Had Vilis lied about her mother? Could he know who had killed her and why? *What is the Guild so afraid of?*

A knowing look came into Verka's eyes, and she leaned forward on her elbows. "You believe me now, don't you. They've betrayed you. You think they broke into your room. Did they take something?"

Elitsa frowned. Why would Verka think they'd taken something? "Yes."

Verka nodded, casting a look towards the door. "You need to

be careful, Agent Serlov. Maybe consider leaving town."

Elitsa bristled, irritation like a hot iron against her skin. Why was everyone telling her to run? Turn your back on a wolf, and it will give chase. She'd never run from a fight before, and she wouldn't start now.

"A word of advice," Verka said, eyes sly beneath the rim of her cap. "Take care what you tell your mentor."

Startled, Elitsa leaned forward, her mug thumping against the table. "What do you mean?"

"You know what he does, don't you?"

"He's a Hunter."

"Yes, but not for what you think."

Elitsa narrowed her eyes, a shiver of forewarning across the back of her neck. "Speak plainly, Verka. What does Vilis hunt?"

"Threats. Your mage identifies threats to the Tower."

A rift opened up inside her chest, and Elitsa lowered her eyes to the buttons on Verka's coat. Understanding brought anger and confusion and the void-deep sting of grief. It was too much, and the desire to force it all away, to lock it deep inside herself, taunted her. Vilis was the reason she'd turned her eyes to the Tower, the reason she'd endured the distrust and scorn of her neighbors. He had filled her with anger and set her hunting rogues. Had it all been a lie? Had he been the mage that'd cleaned up her mother's death for the Guild?

"They'll come after you again," Verka said.

Elitsa's anger surged, drowning the hurt with an overpowering thirst for vengeance. She'd earned every coin the Guild had promised her and more. She'd never asked them for anything, never complained, never challenged them. They deserved whatever Verka had planned for them. They deserved to be hunted. Their greed and arrogance had corrupted the service and protection they'd once provided. The Tower needed to *burn*.

"I'm not going to run from them," Elitsa snarled, cider spilling from her cup onto the table.

"Good." Verka leaned forward abruptly, her brown-gold eyes hungry. "They should be afraid, not you. The Guild has wallowed in their stolen power for too long. Balance must be restored to Rivna, to Casekraia."

It was tempting to revel in the heat of her anger, but the fervor in Verka's voice gave Elitsa pause. What was she planning with the Smoke Eyes? Elitsa had never wanted to be part of a revolution. Angry or not, she hadn't lost her senses. She took a deep breath, forcing herself to calm down. "Are you going to attack them?"

Verka pursed her lips and leaned back. "Not attack, no. My employer and I don't want war in the streets. The cost would be too high."

Elitsa thought back to what Artem had said about a shift in power. "Does this all come down to rattling swords? A show of strength?"

"The Guild's power largely stems from what they have in their possession. They would like everyone to believe their training is superior, but you yourself have learned how to cast spells and harvest essence. We don't need the Tower, but they need us."

Elitsa glanced up at the loft, catching sight of Ivo leaning with his back against the railing. Verka's mysterious employer might not desire to fight, but could the gang have different plans? They never shied away from using force to get what they wanted.

And the Guild, Verka was gambling that they wouldn't fight back. "How can you be so confident that they'll back down instead of trying to wipe you out?" Elitsa narrowed her eyes. "If history is to be believed, they destroyed the frost wyrms and ended the Winter War, saving Casekraia. They have powerful magic."

"They do, but not like they did then. Much has changed over the centuries, and when the Tower split, knowledge was lost, and relics disappeared. The Guild loves their wealth and position more than anything, their ability to influence policy, to control trade. They can't risk appearing like they're outside the king's power."

"Aren't they? Everyone knows the king does nothing."

Verka's lips tightened as though offended by Elitsa's words. "Appearances are deceiving, but either way, if the Guild appears to break free and overthrow the monarchy, they'll draw the attention of the other nations. We'd be open to invasion. As much as the Tower loves their autonomy, they wouldn't risk losing Casekraia completely."

Invasion, Elitsa had never considered that as a possibility. She looked down into her mug, unsettled. This was all so much bigger than her. All she desired was justice for her mother and to live long enough to figure out what she wanted to do. *Who am I with all this stripped away?*

Without Vilis, Elitsa had no power to force the Guild to admit their involvement in the Night Sickness or their killing of retired agents. *Can Verka with the Smoke Eyes backing her?* How many relics and essences would they need to tip the scale? To be feared?

"How close are you?" Elitsa asked, thinking about Kirtara.

Verka gave her a sly look. "Close. We've been working towards this for years. My employer has many friends and resources." She steepled her fingers. "We must move swiftly now. Our recent movements will not go unnoticed. Help me again, and I will make it worth your while. You want revenge? Money? I can give you both."

"You're not concerned I might take what I learn from you to recover my place in the Guild?" It was dangerous voicing those words aloud, but Elitsa needed to know how Verka would respond.

Verka's smile remained unconcerned, though she flicked her gaze up towards Ivo in the loft as though to draw Elitsa's attention there. "I don't believe they have your loyalty any longer. You have seen them for what they are. No, I think you will do whatever it takes to protect those closest to you. Your friend and his mother." Her eyes glittered. "And Mistress Skliar at the House of Swans."

Pipene. Elitsa's face tightened, and Verka held up a calming hand.

"As I said before, I would never try to force you into anything. I am merely informed about who you spend your time with. I have to know who I can trust, which I'm sure you can understand. The Guild wants you to disappear, and if they can't find you …" She let her words hang in the air, the implication clear.

"And the Smoke Eyes?" Elitsa growled.

"They don't care about your friends, but if you continue working with me, you will be working with them."

Elitsa glanced around the bar, picking out some of the gang's enforcers talking and drinking. There was no going back if she aligned herself with them. No return to the Guild, no reconciliation with Vilis, though she had little desire for that now. *He burned that bridge himself.* Despite her anger and frustration, running still felt appealing. Hope was risky, and there was no guarantee that Verka and her allies would actually succeed. They would need the people to stand behind them, and despite the dislike and distrust that many carried for the Guild, there was fear there too. Verka and the Smoke Eyes might not need the Tower, but the essence farmers did. *They're still starving*, Elitsa reminded herself, *despite their access to the Guild's relics.*

She straightened. She had to be pragmatic. The problems of the people were not hers to carry. Life was struggle and survival. Setting everything else aside, Elitsa needed money, and she certainly couldn't risk returning to the Guild for a new contract. She also needed time to decide what to do about Vilis, and she'd need essences to confront him. She had to be ready to defend herself. To fight.

Elitsa held Verka's gaze, steeling herself against the flutters in her stomach. "Consider me for hire."

CHAPTER 16

Elitsa inhaled the lingering scent of cinnamon and baked peaches as she climbed the narrow staircase from the kitchen to the room above Mistress Moon's. The bakery's key had been where Solveiga said, though she'd had to be careful not to drip wax on her hand from the candle burning inside the spirit house.

She unlocked the green door at the top of the stairs and stepped into a cozy room, long and narrow like the bakery. Lighting a nearby lantern with a match from a small glass jar, Elitsa scanned the room. It felt safe and warm, and she let her shoulders slump, unable to hold the tension in her body any longer. There was a window, covered by a decorative screen, that looked out onto the street and the apartments across the way, a bed with folded blankets, and a small bookcase. A handful of paperbacks leaned against each other on the lower shelf — a mix of stories meant for entertainment — and on the top was a bowl of apples and two crystal decanters, one filled with water and the other honey-spiced liquor. She could see traces of Solveiga's hand in the cream-colored wallpaper of swans taking to the air.

Shutting the door, Elitsa bolted it firmly then dumped her pack on the chair by the bed. She walked to the window and looked out at the street through the screen. She hadn't seen anyone follow her, but she stood watch for several minutes to be sure. Motion caught her eye, and Elitsa gripped the window screen as a small figure scurried up a drainpipe on the building across from her to the top of a low wall. They were dressed in dark colors, and as they settled into the shadows, she lost sight of them. A moment later, she heard the call of a bird. Solveiga was keeping an eye on her.

Shrugging off her jacket, Elitsa grabbed an apple from the bowl and forced herself to sit down on the bed. Verka was sending her to Talsa with two Smoke Eyes to liberate the Tower's relics at the guildhall there. Elitsa would meet them outside the Eastshore Gate in the hour before dawn. Verka had been light on the other details, telling her it was better she discussed the particulars with her crew after she'd left the city, just in case the Guild managed to find her during the night. Elitsa couldn't fault her logic, though now, locked into a room a short walk from her building, she felt restless and jumpy. She didn't do well with sitting still.

Is this what it felt like to be a contract-breaker? *I suppose that's what I am now.* Elitsa scowled as she felt the now-familiar twist of guilt and shame and brushed her fingers over the magesilver in her left ear. The Guild had broken their contract first. She would *not* feel like she was the dishonorable one. Working with Verka was a necessity, one they had forced on her. Emotions aside, she would be practical. She would get money, gather new essences, confront Vilis, and then decide if she was willing to walk away. This was the closest she'd ever been to finding her mother's killer, but she had a sinking feeling that some truths were beyond her reach.

Elitsa looked at her wrist, running her fingers over the

painted beads of her mother's bracelet. It'd belonged to her grandmother, another member of her family Elitsa had never gotten to know. She had no aunts or uncles, no cousins. Her only memories were of her mother, and those felt faded like a book left too long in the sun. As far as her father, she had no idea what kind of person he'd been or what he'd looked like. She'd been too young when he'd disappeared. Did she have his chin? His nose? Her dark brown hair and blue eyes were from her mother.

For a time, Elitsa had thought Vilis might be her father. Not because they looked like each other, but because she'd never understood why he'd taken such an interest in her. He could have just walked away as Orson's father had, but he didn't. And now … and now he'd stolen from her mere hours before the Tower tried to kill her. Had he truly believed her dangerous enough to threaten the Guild? It didn't make sense. She'd never expressed any radical ideas. *Did he help me all those years ago because of my mother, or because the Guild told him to?* But how much of a threat could a fourteen-year-old kid be?

Elitsa's anger had burned itself out as she'd walked back to the Aerie. She couldn't fault Vilis for doing what anyone would. Fondness for someone didn't matter much when faced with saving your own skin. She would let him explain himself. If Vilis was truly friends with her mother, then she owed him that much.

Elitsa stared at the floor, letting her eyes go softly out of focus. She pulled her awareness from the tangled thoughts and emotions rushing through her and focused on her breath, on the weight of her body as she leaned against the wall, making herself relax. She had to be ready for tomorrow and would not let herself get distracted by all the unanswered questions. Worry would dull her senses, and she needed to be sharp, prepared.

The candle flickered, and Elitsa became aware of a spider lowering itself on an unseen thread before her face, near-invisible in the darkness. She could feel it somehow, even before she saw it. Barely breathing, Elitsa slowly raised her hand beneath the descending spider. It landed with delicate feet, a tickle against the flat of her palm. Then, as though it knew she was watching, it turned around to face her.

Elitsa's heart pounded in her chest, awe stealing her breath. It was an ebonweaver, its body black as ink and near impossible to see. It looked like she held a knot of shadow in her palm instead of a living creature. This was how an assassin could disappear inside a room, hide in shadows. Elitsa couldn't even imagine how much the Guild would pay for such a rare essence.

"Sister Luck favors me today," Elitsa breathed. This essence just might save her life if she could figure out how to use it. At the very least, it was worth a lot of money. She could feel the spider's attention on her in a way she'd never experienced with something so small, its observation like a soft breath on the back of her neck. *Perhaps because my senses are heightened?*

Elitsa had never cared much for insects before, yet she felt almost regretful as she focused on the magesilver in her right ear, tuning into the emptiness of the relic. She imagined that space expanding out over her palm, like opening a door to invite someone in. The spider's essence became a visible thing, a core of heat as though she held a hot bead. It smelled like spice and dark nights and velvety linen.

A shiver whispered across Elitsa's skin, and she began to draw the ebonweaver's essence into the earring, a swirl of shadow taking shape in her mind. She felt no resistance from the spider, no hint of struggle as she took its life, which felt wrong somehow. As vile and illegal as it was, Elitsa had heard of rogues taking essences from animals, but she'd never had someone use one against her. The disgust she'd always felt to think of it felt more real now.

The spider sank in on itself, legs curling in death, as coldness replaced the warmth in Elitsa's palm. Her earring warmed, like the flare of a newly lit lantern, then softly faded into the back of her awareness. Sadness and exhaustion settled on her like heavy mist, and Elitsa carried the dead spider to the window sill. Laying it down in a diamond-shaped patch of moonlight, she returned to the bed and lay down. She had to sleep. She didn't have the luxury to mourn spiders and broken promises. She needed to be ready for whatever came next.

CHAPTER 17

I t was cold and drizzly when Elitsa left Rivna in the company of two strangers. The lake, to their left, looked dark as a raven's wing; the surface churned into small waves by a strong, rain-filled wind. Despite falling asleep quickly the night before — more worn out than she'd realized — Elitsa did not feel rested. If she hadn't been woken by the sound of Mistress Inna entering her kitchen downstairs, Elitsa might have missed her rendezvous with Verka's people.

There wasn't time to see Pipene before she left, so Elitsa sent her a message through one of Solveiga's cygnets, telling her she'd left town again for work without any of the details. She didn't want Pipene to get involved with Verka. Her friend was compassionate to a fault, and despite her distrust of the gang, Verka's aspirations might sway her to their cause. That was if Solveiga didn't catch wind of it. The Aerie's protector might actually be on the Smoke Eyes' side in this instance, but Elitsa couldn't see them working together.

Though uneasy about leaving while so much was unresolved, Elitsa had to admit that it felt good to put some distance between her and the Guild's assassins. She did not feel ready for another encounter.

Yure, the apparent leader of their group, set a quick pace, his long legs keeping him several steps ahead of Elitsa and Birtua, who were walking together. Talsa was a mountain town a day and a half from Rivna, or a day if they'd taken a carriage. Unfortunately, carriages were too expensive, and it didn't seem the brightest idea to rent one on the way to rob a guildhall. Records were kept of every trip and passenger.

Trying not to think about how much warmer and drier a carriage would be, Elitsa tugged her scarf higher up around her chin and studied the woman walking next to her. In her forties with thick blonde hair, a sun-tanned face, and a broad nose, the older woman looked more like one of Sofija's friends than a criminal.

A word I'm going to have to apply to myself now, Elitsa thought uncomfortably. "What's the plan?" she asked aloud. "When we reach Talsa."

Birtua glanced sideways at her. The cold had turned her nose and cheeks a rosy red.

"Take the relics," Yure answered without turning. His black hair, heavy from the mist-filled air, curled against the base of his neck.

Elitsa arched an eyebrow at his back. "Obviously, that's the goal, but you must have a strategy for doing so safely."

"You've been there before," Birtua said, more statement than question.

"I have. Did Verka tell you about me? What I am?"

Birtua nodded, a flicker of something akin to wariness in her eyes. "She did." It wasn't hard to guess she didn't trust her.

"You're wondering why I'd betray the Guild."

"I'd rather not guess," Birtua said mildly. "If Verka says you're on the job, then you're on the job."

Not exactly an endorsement, but it'd have to do. A lot could go sideways on a mission where she was the outsider. *I have to be careful.* Elitsa didn't doubt that if she were caught, she'd be on her own. She couldn't help wondering what conclusions Birtua and Yure had made about her. *Do they think I've betrayed the Guild before? That the promise of money can easily sway me?* Part of her wanted to convince them this was out of character, that she was honest and loyal and tried to do the right thing. But as uncomfortable as Elitsa felt, it didn't matter what they thought of her, and she couldn't let herself be distracted by it either.

"It's a well-fortified building," Elitsa said, forcing herself to move on. "Difficult to sneak into."

"It is," Birtua agreed. "Fortunately for us, there was a fire recently, and they were forced to move their relics into a separate building on the grounds."

Elitsa narrowed her eyes, studying the woman's bland expression. A fire? Did Verka have friends inside the Guild? "Was it suspicious? Because if the hall is on alert to sabotage—"

"No," Yure said over his shoulder. "The mages are arrogant and believe themselves impervious to deception. They don't even notice the faces of their staff."

"Whatever inattention they may have now will disappear as soon as the relics go missing." Elitsa kicked at a stone on the road. The Tower had to have heard about Kirtara by now. If they thought it was an isolated incident, that would change as soon as another guildhall was hit. "Is Verka targeting any other towns?"

"Why does that matter?" Birtua asked. Her voice sounded suspicious, and Elitsa hid a sigh.

"It doesn't." She frowned, recalling what she knew about the Talsan guildhall. She'd never bothered thinking about how one might break into the place or spent much time observing the guards. Their security had never mattered to her before. Like Kirtara, the hall was just outside of town on a hill overlooking the village. The rich, Elitsa found, seemed to prefer seclusion over community. Excellent for hiding their activities but also leaving them open to ingress. The only outbuilding Elitsa remembered was behind the large estate by the stables and thick forest.

The high mage managing Talsa's guildhall liked to keep an eye on things, and Elitsa had seen her on more than one occasion roaming the building with the air of a fox hunting rabbits. High Mage Chayka had likely put guards on the warehouse. "There will be guards."

"Yes," Yure said, slowing down so he could walk on Elitsa's left, "but no more than two or three. They won't be a problem."

"And if they're using relics?" Elitsa saw no obvious weapons on either of them, but she doubted they'd risk a fight with trained guards with no more than a knife or two between them.

"We'll strike first," Birtua said, "before they see us coming."

Yure inclined his head. "After their evening meal when their bellies are full and their minds slow."

"How will you incapacitate them without killing them?"

"An agent with an aversion to killing?" Birtua snorted. "That's a first."

Heat flushed Elitsa's cheeks as she glared. "I've never killed a contract-breaker." She had come close, but thankfully she had no one's death on her head. *No innocent death, that is.*

"No?"

"No, and I'm certainly not going to start now. The Guild will be angry enough when the relics go missing, but if someone dies? They'll send assassins after us." *Or in my case, maybe a whole squad.*

"They don't use assassins anymore," Birtua snorted.

"Yes, they do."

Yure gave Elitsa a long look. "We can't risk being identified, and I doubt we can get inside without the guards seeing us."

No, there has to be another way. A safer way. These guards were people with families and lives. They were just doing their jobs. "We don't need to kill them," Elitsa said firmly. "What essences do you have? And don't deny that you have any. I doubt Verka would send you against the Tower without at least one relic between you."

"Wood, water, fire," Yure said.

Birtua glanced at her, lips thinning. "Wood."

Elitsa nodded, chewing on the inside of her cheek. They were the most common essences and likely what the guards would have as well. They needed to overpower them somehow, knock them out quickly before they could raise the alarm. "Moon mushrooms, I need to find moon mushrooms." Elitsa glanced towards the forest.

"You want mushrooms?" Birtua said, raising an eyebrow.

Yure stopped and crossed his arms. "For food or harvest?" Unlike Birtua, whose thoughts and emotions occasionally bled into her face and voice, Yure was unreadable, his speech and mannerisms even and unruffled.

"They can be used to make a sedative," Elitsa said, studying the ground around the trees to their right.

"You want us to put it in their food?" Birtua pursed her lips. "That sounds more complicated than knocking them out."

"No, I'm going to make a mist. All we need them to do is breathe it in." Taking several steps into the forest, Elitsa stepped up onto a moss-covered rock. She spied a small hollow leading down away from the road, the foliage lush and damp against the hillside. "That way," she said, pointing.

⚜

Twenty minutes later — followed by Birtua's increasingly displeased sighs — Elitsa finally spotted the annoyingly elusive pale blue frills of moon mushrooms tucked beneath an old rotting log where dark green moss dripped like sodden hair. Careful to keep the relief from her face, she crouched down and brushed her fingers over the small caps.

"I hope it's worth it," Birtua said, wiping dirt from her pants.

"It is." Drawing on an empty magesilver hoop in her right ear, Elitsa slowly exhaled, then carefully pulled on the essences from one of the mushrooms. She smelled the scent of damp earth, and something sweet as the essence's shape appeared in her mind. It manifested as a small blue orb, tendrils unfurling from its base like branching vines. The mushroom paled as its essence left, the soft flesh drying and turning to powder.

After harvesting the entire cluster, Elitsa took a deep cleansing breath and rolled her shoulders. Her heart was beating quickly, her pulse slightly elevated like it always was after harvesting. She'd tensed unconsciously, and she winced at the sudden but fleeting pain of a cramping muscle in her back. Resisting the urge to rub the offending muscle, Elitsa moved several essences of fire and water into the earring with the moon mushrooms — the combination to create mist — and stood back up.

Birtua was looking at her with obvious discomfort while Yure stared off in the direction they'd come with his usual inscrutable expression. "Does it feel odd when you do that?" Birtua asked, gesturing at the now-dead mushrooms.

"Odd?" Brushing damp dirt off her knees, Elitsa readjusted her coat. "Have you never harvested before?"

"No. Never needed to."

Elitsa raised her eyebrows. Why carry a relic if you didn't harvest? Essences could be expensive, and she doubted the Smoke Eyes had enough money lying around to buy all they used. And with essences becoming weaker, they were harder to obtain. Even the most common elements like wind, water, and fire were no longer as dependable as they once were.

Yure glanced back at them. "Birtua is uncomfortable with harvesting souls."

"I just think we should be careful," Birtua said defensively, glaring at him.

"Ah," Elitsa said. There were people in Casekraia who still

followed the old ways. They believed that every living thing had a soul, even plants and insects, that Mother Moon had infused all life with a piece of her divinity. They didn't care much for relics, so it was surprising that Birtua would still be willing to use one. She glanced at Yure. "And you?"

"I stocked up before we left, but I can harvest." Yure nodded back in the direction of the road. "We should continue. I want to reach Talsa by midday tomorrow."

They headed back to the road, stopping to fill their canteens at a fresh spring in a hillside. By the time night fell, they had started their ascent into the mountains, giving them a broad look at Lake Odarka and the soft lights of Rivna below. They found several boulders near the road that offered some protection from the wind and made camp. Hearing the far-off howls of wolves, they were careful to keep their fire burning through the night.

In the morning, after a quick breakfast, Yure extinguished their fire by pulling the essence into whatever hidden relic he had, and they set off again to Talsa.

When they reached the mountain town's outer border, Yure turned off the road, leading them up what Elitsa thought was an old game trail. It was steep and narrow, and she was sweating despite the chill wind when they reached the top.

Crouching down within the treeline, they studied the back of the guildhall. The alpine trees were thicker here, appearing to have had some magical help in their growth to create a natural barrier around the cleared pasture where the guildhall sat. With a peaked roof that could withstand the heavy snow, the two-story building was made from interlocking logs of blue-painted pine with a covered balcony that ran around its length. It was a perfect place to keep watch over the grounds, and Elitsa's pulse spiked as she watched, worried someone would see them in the trees.

"They have a guard walk the perimeter every two hours," Yure said, nodding at the balcony as a figure appeared around the corner of the house.

Elitsa's breath caught, but she didn't have to worry. As the man strolled past, his gaze swept over their location without seeing them. He was tall in a high-necked green overcoat and wearing a fur hat. Elitsa couldn't see if he had a weapon, but she guessed he wore a truncheon on his belt based on her previous visits. She glanced at Yure who was watching the guard. "You've been watching the hall?"

"We've had eyes on it the past week." Yure nodded at a second building towards the right, which looked to Elitsa like a large barn. "The relics are there. There's a secondary road on the other side of it that winds down through the trees. Someone will meet us with a wagon tonight and take the relics back to Rivna."

Elitsa remembered an overgrown trail she'd seen fifteen minutes south of town. That must be where it rejoined the main road. "And the guards?" She couldn't see any from their position, but she doubted High Mage Chayka would leave the security of their relics to a passing glance from the guard on the second floor.

"Two at the door, sometimes three," Yure said. "The guard up on the balcony can only see them once he passes the side of the building. If we work within that time, we can get in and out before he comes back around."

Birtua plucked several green needles from the pine tree she hid behind, sticking them between her teeth. "You sure this mist of yours is going to work? We only have one chance to surprise them."

"It will work, especially at dusk when the light is fading." Elitsa studied their clothing. "We should buy some fabric, make masks for ourselves. Wind can be unpredictable, and as you said, we don't want to be recognized."

"Can't you control it?" Birtua asked, chewing on the needles.

"Yes, somewhat, but I'd rather not burn more essences than I have to." Better to anticipate that something was going to go wrong than be caught unprepared.

"Yes, good thinking," Yure said. "Go to town and find what you need. Take Birtua. I'll wait here."

"Good." Birtua laid a hand over her stomach, grinning. "My stomach's been grumbling the past hour. I could do with a little food."

"Fine, but be back before sunset," Yure said. "Make sure you're not seen on the main road. Especially you." He looked at Elitsa. "Last thing we need is for you to be seen here. You'll be no good to Verka then."

Yure was right. If the Tower learned she'd been present at two robberies, it wouldn't take much to put two and two together. *Considering the assassin, does it even matter?* They'd tried to kill her. With a start, Elitsa realized her contract had expired the night before. She was free. *Free and hunted.*

"Let's go," Elitsa said, rising from her crouch.

Birtua looked at Yure, her mouth pinching, then she stood and gestured at Elitsa to lead the way. Staying in the cover of the trees, they circled the property until they came to the main road. As they descended towards the town, the forest thinned, their pace further slowed by slick red-veined granite and broken boulders.

Twenty or so minutes later, they slid down an embankment behind the blacksmith forge. Not quite as large as Kirtara, Talsa was built in a circular pattern with businesses like the blacksmith and stables on the outside, followed by several rings of shops and homes with a large common space in the center called the Green. There they had a well, a small stage for gatherings, and an open-air market. Despite the chill in the air, Talsans loved to spend as much time as possible outdoors, and Elitsa had heard they kept the market open even through the snow.

Following a narrow street between several peak-roofed homes, Elitsa found the market in full swing. Autumn decorations were everywhere, with pine-cone guardians — handmade sculptures of winged beasts — standing guard around the open area. Harvest wreaths hung on every green-painted door that faced the Green. In addition to spirit houses, candles lit despite the daylight, moon-like orbs of glass dangled within the windows, framed by gold-painted shutters. Barrels of hay were set around the tent-covered tables, offering places to sit, and painted pumpkins were everywhere, gathered in clusters like large mushrooms. Though the Night of Souls was weeks away, Talsa seemed to have decided on a month-long celebration. Elitsa observed all the smiling faces, wistfully wishing she could simply disappear into the crowd.

"Is that an acting troupe?" Birtua asked, nodding towards a colorfully painted wagon parked by the stage.

Elitsa followed her gaze, catching sight of two robed figures hanging a curtain. One was dressed in white with their head covered, and the other in gold — a man with small horns jutting from his curly black hair. "Yes, that's the Mother's Masks. They're quite good." Pipene loved the troupe, and they'd always gone to see them together whenever they came to Rivna. Elitsa's breath caught. *Will we ever watch another show together?*

"Well," Birtua said, "you go find the fabric you need, and I'm off to get food." The older woman clapped her on the shoulder hard enough that Elitsa staggered, then moved off into the crowd.

Ignoring the hopeful grumble her stomach made, Elitsa turned in the opposite direction, eyes open for someone selling fabric. She paused by a stall to admire several beautifully painted eggs, then, unable to resist the scent of hot food, traded a coin for a cabbage roll from a woman carrying a tray. Wolfing it down, she was wiping off her fingers when she saw a clothing stall with an assortment of thick scarves. It wasn't exactly what she was looking for, but it could work.

A short woman with braided black hair and a kind smile came up to her. "Warm welcome, miss! Can I help you?"

"Yes, thank you. These are lovely." Elitsa touched her fingers to one of the scarves on the table.

The woman beamed, eyes nearly disappearing as she smiled. "Thank you, dear. That blue one would look beautiful on you!"

Elitsa smiled and gestured at the racks of clothing along the walls. "Do you sell any fabric? My sister loves to sew and wants to make new aprons."

"Oh! How lovely. Unfortunately, I don't have anything available today. I do have several aprons, though." She pointed towards the back of the tent.

Elitsa gave the woman an apologetic smile. "Thank you, but she really wants to make her own. I am thinking about buying some of these scarves, though."

"Oh!" Her face brightened. "The blue?"

"These dark green ones." Elitsa lifted a more simplistic scarf. "For my brothers."

"What a sweet sister you are. Yes! Those are twenty coppers each."

Elitsa's stomach flipped. Definitely more expensive than untreated fabric. *Maybe Verka will pay me back?* She haggled with the woman for a few minutes, getting the price down to fifteen, and then handed over the coins.

Another customer wandered into the tent. Elitsa nodded her thanks to the vendor, then shoved the scarves into her pack as the woman moved off to greet them. Turning to leave, she was thinking about where to find Birtua and found herself face to face with Cas.

CHAPTER 18

Elitsa cursed inside her head, forcing herself to smile despite the frantic thud of her heart against her ribs. "I'm starting to think you're following me, Cas."

Cas grinned, his eyes sparkling. He looked good, his cheeks slightly flushed from the cold and his hair curling out from beneath a fur-lined hat. "Flush with cash, Eli? Every time I run into you, you're shopping." He nodded at the clothing. "I would have expected to find you throwing knives or arm-wrestling the town's blacksmith." He'd left his dark gray overcoat open, and she could see the russet-colored vest beneath, the twisting silver embroidery across the stiff fabric reminding her of tumbling autumn leaves.

"I need clothes, same as everyone," Elitsa said defensively, wishing she had been shopping for knives. "Also, I didn't think it'd be fair to compete in the games. Why are you here?"

"For you, actually."

Elitsa's breath caught, her heart nearly stopping. She tensed, prepared to run. *Did the Tower send him?* "I think we've had enough sharing. Having trouble completing jobs on your own now?"

Cas laughed, bracing his hands on his hips. "Oh, please. You know I'm the better agent. No, this isn't my idea, actually."

Elitsa's face felt cold. "What idea?"

"I received a message in Pelisk from the Tower, told to go help you. I thought it'd take a while to track you down, but here you are! Second town I've checked." Cas beamed proudly. "Thanks to Sister Luck, the Guild was feeling charitable and paid for my carriage ride."

"Who sent the message?" *Was it Vilis or Guild Mistress Astraia? Who is worse?*

"I don't know. Message had the Tower seal. All I care about is that they're paying me." Cas ran a hand through his hair, shifting it out of his eyes. "Maybe they know you want out and want to make sure you don't run away with your relics." He wiggled his eyebrows, grinning at her.

Elitsa forced herself to hold his gaze, though every muscle in her body was telling her to run. "It's probably just Vilis being Vilis," she said, rolling her eyes, trying to appear unconcerned. Cas didn't seem to know her contract had ended.

"For being your mentor, or whatever he is, he sure doesn't seem to like you. No special treatment or anything!"

Elitsa glanced past Cas's shoulder, thinking furiously. She needed to get rid of him before Birtua found her. "Well, sorry to disappoint you, but I'm not executing any contracts right now. I'm on an errand for a friend."

"To buy clothes in Talsa? Your friend has very specific taste." Cas sighed, narrowing his eyes. "You're going to be boring, aren't you."

Elitsa shrugged, looking past him again at the people passing the stalls. She saw Birtua carrying something in her hand. The woman looked at Cas's back, then at Elitsa, her eyes narrowing.

Giving the barest shake of her head, Elitsa looked back at Cas. "Yep. You might as well go watch the hammer throwing or find someone to flirt with." She turned back to the tent, barely glancing at it as she pulled a dress off the closest rack. "I'm going to go try this on. See you later."

"Sure you don't need me?" Cas asked, winking as Elitsa looked for the dressing room. "I've been told I'm quite fashionable."

"I'm certain I'll survive without your commentary," Elitsa said over her shoulder as she walked to the back of the tent. Nodding at the woman she'd purchased the scarves from, Elitsa entered the dressing room and yanked the curtain closed.

She dropped the dress on a stool and faced the back of the tent, considering. She needed to get out of here without Cas following her. Eyeing the bottom of the tent — which was very securely pegged down — Elitsa was reaching for her dagger when she heard a soft tearing sound, and the tip of a knife appeared through the wall of the tent. She stepped back into a defensive position, uncertain whether to attack or cry out when the split widened, revealing Birtua. She gestured impatiently, and Elitsa hurried forward, squeezing through the rip as carefully and quietly as she could.

Turning away from the Green, Elitsa followed Biruta out of town. She looked back over her shoulder, but she thankfully didn't see Cas. Hopefully, the tent owner wouldn't notice the damage until they were well into the trees.

Once they were out of sight of the market, Birtua gave Elitsa a stern, suspicious look. "That boy of yours is still standing outside the tent waiting for you. Who is he? How did he know you were here?"

"He's an agent," Elitsa said, "and it was random chance. Best we get away from here before he starts looking for me."

"If he finds out what we're doing— "

"He won't." Annoyed by the distrustful look on Birtua's face, Elitsa hurried past her, leading the way back up the ridge to where they'd left Yure.

They arrived at the guards' shift change. Elitsa and Birtua quietly crawled up next to Yure, who had settled himself behind a tangle of rock and fallen branches on the north-facing side of the barn. From here, they could see the second road, which, lucky for them, was out of sight of the few windows on the second floor and balcony. They could also see the front of the barn, a covered space, where two guards stood at attention on either side of the door.

A broad-shouldered woman and a much shorter man with a heavy blond mustache took up the same positions as the departing guards, sharing laughter and words with them about their captain's foul mood.

Passing Yure a wrapped sandwich from her pocket, Birtua pursed her lips at the guards. "Why don't they just sit down on those barrels there?" She gestured at the makeshift chairs.

"Probably afraid of High Mage Chayka," Elitsa guessed aloud, studying the guards' posture. "You don't stand on ceremony for nothing."

"I agree," Yure said. "Perhaps I won't have to use this after all." He hefted his crossbow, removing it from the waterproof cloth it'd been wrapped in. Another of Verka's people had apparently left it for him in the woods behind the barn.

Elitsa nodded, feeling the whisper of anticipation humming beneath her skin. There would be no going back once she used her essences against the guards. No more pretending she was more principled than anyone else in Casekraia.

The sun set as they waited, the shadows deepening beneath the trees as the light disappeared behind the mountains. With the clouds overhead, darkness gathered quickly, and wisps of fog began to fold in around them. Though they continued to hold their posts, both guards seemed to lose some of their sharpness as time passed. The woman rolled her shoulders, and the man belched, then pressed his hand against his belly with a breathless laugh. Making a joke, he lit the lanterns hanging above the doors.

Removing the scarves from her pack, Elitsa handed them out then wound the third around her nose and mouth, hiding the bottom half of her face. It quickly warmed with her breath, drawn against her lips as she breathed.

The guard up on the walkway passed, nodding at the guards, then disappearing around the side of the building. Their two hours had just begun.

"Ready?" Yure asked.

Elitsa nodded, her stomach tightening nervously.

"Ready," Birtua said, staring at Elitsa. It was clear who she'd blame if something went wrong. As Birtua flexed her hands, Elitsa smelled the faint sweet scent of balsam — the essence of a black poplar tree.

Crawling forward, Elitsa moved as close to the edge of the grass as she dared. If one of the guards spotted her, Yure would use his crossbow, and there would be no way to avoid bloodshed. Taking a calming breath, Elitsa focused on the essences of the moon mushrooms, combining them with water and a touch of heat as she drew them out of the magesilver and into the air in front of her. She smelled earth and water, and the smoky scent of a campfire as their elemental forms manifested into a mist-like shimmer.

The taller guard wrinkled her nose, and as her head started to turn in Elitsa's direction, she quickly reached for wind and pushed the mist forward. The guard raised her hand, mouth opening, as the cloud washed over her. Eyes catching on Elitsa, she made a soft exhalation of protest — her warning never making it past her lips — then she reached for the truncheon at her waist, took two steps forward, and collapsed onto her knees.

The second guard looked up from adjusting his belt, eyes widening. "Sokolov?" Leaning down to put a hand on the fallen guard's shoulder, he pitched forward onto his face.

Elitsa waited for several heartbeats, hearing a soft rumbling snore, then slowly stood up.

"Well done," Yure said, clapping her on the shoulder. He

shifted his crossbow onto his back and started forward. "Let's get to work."

Elitsa caught his arm. "Hold your breath until you're inside. I'm not certain how well these scarves will work. Let the vapor disperse." It was tempting to relax with the relief that her plan had worked, but Elitsa forced herself to remain vigilant. They needed to move quickly.

Yure paused, then gestured at Birtua. "We'll hide them behind the barn, so they can't be seen from the balcony."

Holding her breath, Elitsa helped Yure and Birtua drag the guards around the side of the building. She used another essence to clear the air in front of them and then shot a nervous look towards the guildhall as Yure slid the left door open and slipped inside.

It was a large, high-roofed chamber, shelving looming in the darkness like waiting beasts. Birtua located a lantern — turning it to its lowest setting — and raised it overhead, casting dim illumination on a collection of trays and small crates, stacked and placed atop and alongside the shelves. It was evident they'd been moved recently by their messy organization. Yure grabbed an object from a tray wrapped in strips of cloth and quickly unwrapped it. It was a magesilver gauntlet, lustrous in the lantern light.

Putting the relic back into the tray, Yure grabbed several more cloth-wrapped items, then pointed to a stack of crates by the door. "Be quick. We don't have long before they notice the guards are missing or someone wanders back here for a chat. I'll extinguish the lights outside, then gag and tie up the guards."

"What are we going to do if the wagon doesn't show?" Elitsa asked, eyeing the large stash. Their entire plan hinged on an easy getaway, and for whatever reason, the wagon hadn't yet arrived.

"Hide in the woods," Birtua said, shrugging. She'd already started carelessly scooping trays off the shelves into a crate braced against her stomach. Pausing, she picked up a ring and stuffed it into her pocket. She gave Elitsa an arch look, catching her stare.

"They'll be here. Hurry up." Yure slipped out the doors.

Gritting her teeth, Elitsa moved to help. She didn't like how precarious this was. Their success hinged on the guildhall's staff being preoccupied with dinner. They should have staged a distraction, something that would ensure the guards' attention would be elsewhere, but Yure said they couldn't risk attracting notice. This night needed to feel normal, boring. The skin between Elitsa's shoulder blades itched as she turned her back on the door, the desire to run rising with every breath.

Dumping trays into a crate, Elitsa followed Birtua to the door. They peeked outside before hurrying across the grass to the edge of the trees where the overgrown road sloped down behind a split boulder, a spindly tree rising from the red-veined stone. The wagon wasn't there. Though they had no lanterns, the moon was bright overhead, making it easy to find their footing.

"Over here," Birtua called, setting her crate down several steps off the road. It wouldn't take long to locate the boxes if anyone came looking, but the slope and rocks made it invisible from the hall. "Hear that?" She straightened, looking down the grassy trail. "I think I hear a horse. Wagon must be coming."

Birtua started to head back, and Elitsa hastily set down her crate and jogged after her. As the barn and guildhall came back into view, Yure passed them, two crates stacked in his arms.

Elitsa wasn't certain how long the guards would be unconscious, and her anxiety continued to grow. *How do thieves deal with this wire-taut dread?* Inside the barn, she seized another crate, wishing they had a less conspicuous way to carry everything. She barely noticed what she grabbed, the relics passing quickly through her hands. She had to believe they could get away with this, that no one was going to get hurt. *That Mother and Pipene would understand.*

Finishing ahead of Birtua, Elitsa rushed back to the door,

stumbling over something on the floor. She was so focused on getting out that she didn't pause as she slipped outside.

There was a guard in the way.

Halting only a handful of steps from him, Elitsa stared at the uniformed man with wide eyes. She stopped breathing. His narrowed eyes — a dark blue that reminded her of Lake Odarka — shifted from Elitsa's masked face to the crate in her arms. Could she bluff her way past despite the mask and the missing guards? *No, it's over.* She tensed, preparing to act.

"You! Stay where you are!" The guard snapped, reaching for his cudgel. His eyes darted away from Elitsa to something behind her, and she heard Birtua's soft curse. "Put it down, and raise your hands!"

"Don't," Birtua growled softly.

Yure appeared in the trees, crossbow raised. He was going to kill the guard.

"No!" Elitsa yelled.

The guard started to turn towards Yure. Elitsa smelled the scent of balsam, pungent and overwhelming, and then she heard something heavy hit the ground behind her. Birtua lunged past, barreling towards the guard in a blur of motion. She slammed into his side, the force of her essence-powered blow sending the man sprawling, his weapon flying away from his hand. Birtua followed with a punch to the guard's jaw, his head snapping back, the sound like cracking wood. He crumpled instantly, eyes rolling back into his head.

Birtua reached for the knife at her belt, and Elitsa caught her arm. It felt like trying to grapple a bear.

"Don't kill him!" she said quickly, holding Birtua's furious glare. "We can put him with the others." She looked at Yure imploringly as he approached. He'd lowered his crossbow, still appearing calm and unflustered despite their near disaster.

"One less to track us," Birtua said, breathing hard. She yanked her arm from Elitsa's grip.

Yure looked down at the unconscious guard. The man's jaw was already starting to bruise, and there was blood on his lip, but he was still breathing. "Fine, but we leave; now. Grab what you can. Birtua?"

Growling, Birtua took her hand off the hilt of her knife and braced her hand on her knee, standing up. She yanked the crate Elitsa was still holding from her hands with enough force that Elitsa heard her elbow pop and then shoved past her to grab the box she'd dropped by the barn. Stacking them easily as if they were as light as two plates, she jogged past the guard — stepping on his ankle as she passed — and headed down the road.

"I'll move him; you take one more load," Yure said, nodding towards the barn. Shifting his crossbow on his back, he started to drag the guard towards where they'd hid the others.

Elitsa watched him indecisively for a moment, then hurried back into the barn. Taking a crate, she swept another shelf clear. She palmed a bracelet, checking it for essences. It was empty — not really a surprise, but she hoped she'd get lucky — and Elitsa shoved it distractedly into her pocket before rushing outside with what she'd grabbed. She wouldn't be able to fight for long if the mages came after them, not with what she had left in her magesilver.

When Elitsa reached the bend in the road where they'd left the relics, she found Birtua loading the crates in the back of a small wagon, then covering them with straw. The driver, an elderly man with a stooped back, battered gray hat, and a disinterested expression, kept his gaze on his shaggy black horse.

"Who is he?" Elitsa whispered to Birtua as she set her crate down into the wagon.

Birtua, rearranging the straw, glanced at her and shrugged. Her face looked haggard, as though the energy she'd had earlier had already drained out of her. "Don't know."

Yure jogged up and hid the bag in his hands beneath the straw, glancing back up the road towards the guildhall. "We have maybe forty minutes before they notice anything is wrong. Time to—"

A twig snapped, and everyone — minus the driver, who if he moved at all, Elitsa couldn't tell — looked towards the woods on the other side of the road.

Cas, dressed immaculately despite whatever he'd done to get here, stepped out from between the trees, grinning broadly. "There you are. Who are your friends?"

CHAPTER 19

Elitsa felt like she'd fallen through ice, her body frozen, her mind a panicked blank. How had he found her again? Motion to her right caught her eye — Birtua moving her hand towards the knife on her waist. "Just finishing a job," Elitsa blurted. She had to turn this around somehow.

"Mining survey," Yure said.

The wagon driver, undoubtedly picking up on the tension, tipped his hat to them and mumbled something in a quiet drawl before flicking the reins and setting off. As the wagon moved — Cas watching it leave — Elitsa took a step forward, worried what Birtua and Yure might do without the wagon between them. She resisted the urge to look in the direction of the barn. They needed to get going, but she couldn't risk making Cas suspicious. *What has he seen?*

"You wound me!" Cas said, feigning hurt with a hand over his heart as he walked forward. "You said you weren't working."

"I don't like partners."

"Mhm." Cas looked at Birtua then Yure, his eyes lingering on Yure's face. "So who are you two then? If not Elitsa's friends or partners." His cheek dimpled as he smiled.

"Nic," Yure said, face expressionless. If he was thinking about using his crossbow, there was no sign.

"None of your damned business," Birtua growled at the same time.

Cas grinned at her. "I like you." He tilted his head in the direction of the departing wagon. "Did I make you miss your ride?"

"We were going to walk," Elitsa said.

"Hmm, yes, this cold weather is quite pleasant." He was clearly probing for information.

Elitsa could practically feel the tension radiating off of Birtua, and she shifted a little to the right. Annoying as Cas could be, she couldn't let Birtua stab him. *I will not be responsible for innocent deaths, indirectly or otherwise.* "No need to follow us, Cas; we're just heading back to Rivna."

"Works for me." Another easy grin, then Cas looked back at Yure. "I feel like we've met before. At the Black Eyed Fish? I'm very good with faces."

One minute Yure was standing calmly beside her, and then the next, he was lunging towards Cas with a knife in his hand. He was fast, but Cas was like the wind. Elitsa smelled heated copper and spice-scented resin, and then the knife was stabbing into Cas's chest, only instead of a spray of blood, sparks showered the air as the steel scraped sideways.

All humor gone from his face, Cas twisted sideways, throwing Yure off-balance, except the Smoke Eye didn't fall. As he rolled back up to his feet, Birtua moved forward, the vanilla scent of white oak strong in the air.

"Don't hurt him!" Elitsa caught Birtua's arm, earning a curse, and then the woman shoved her. She was strengthened by her essence, and Elitsa flew back into the dirt, landing hard.

Hells below, he really is going to get me killed. Baring her teeth, Elitsa scrambled back onto her feet, ignoring the pain in her side from where she'd hit a rock.

Cas, moving sideways to keep both Birtua and Yure in view,

hadn't yet used his relics to attack. *What is he waiting for?* He recognized Yure, which probably meant he knew they were Smoke Eyes.

"He won't tell anyone!" Elitsa said, trying to move between them. She glared at Cas, annoyed when he arched his eyebrow at her. Even now, he couldn't take a damned thing seriously.

Birtua shook her head, drawing her knife. "We can't risk that. I see the look in his eyes. Your boyfriend is calculating what we're worth to him." Her mouth thinned, her eyes suspicious as she looked at Elitsa. "I'm starting to wonder if something drew him here."

"I didn't tell him!" Elitsa gave Cas a frustrated look, anger mounting at how relaxed he still seemed. He didn't care how complicated he'd made everything. How close she was to just letting Birtua do what she wanted. "He loves money. He can help us, help Verka."

Yure, who was stalking closer to Cas like a panther, gave her a sharp look.

She'd made a mistake, mentioning Verka's name, but Elitsa held his eyes with a glare. She couldn't afford to show even a trace of weakness or indecision.

Cas held up his hands non-threateningly, his damned grin returning to his face. "She's right. I do love money. If you want me to forget you were here ..." He trailed off suggestively.

"I say we gut him," Birtua said.

"Hey now. You're in a hurry, right?" Cas gestured over his shoulder towards the guildhall. "Can you afford to leave another body? I won't go easily." He wiggled his fingers, showing his magesilver rings. "Do you have time for a fight?"

Cas was right. Every minute they delayed made it more likely the guards would catch up with them before they could get far enough away. They needed to get back to the main road and disappear. "We need to go," Elitsa said.

Yure looked between Elitsa and Cas, eyes narrowed, then he

straightened. "He lives, but you pay him from your share."

Elitsa thought about her rapidly dwindling purse and felt another spike of irritation for Cas. *Why couldn't he have stayed in Pelisk and left me alone?* "Fine. Can we be on our way? If the guards—"

A fireball shot into the sky above Talsa, exploding in a distant burst of white light.

Cas whirled with a curse, hands raised.

"What was that?" Elitsa gasped as the light faded. She could hear distant shouts from the guildhall. She wasn't sure whether to run or fight. She looked back at Yure, heart pounding in her ears, and found him staring calmly towards the hall.

Birtua looked a little surprised but had recovered quickly and was resheathing her blade.

"That's our cue to leave," Yure said. "A distraction to keep the Guild from following us." He caught Elitsa's eye. "Pay him and catch up." Turning away, he started down the road, Birtua hurrying after him.

Elitsa thought about the busy market and the Mother's Masks. *Did Verka arrange for someone to attack the city? Is anyone hurt?* Questions flooded her mind, the desire to know tangling with fear. *I am responsible for what happens*, she thought, chest tightening. Who had she aligned herself with? Verka didn't seem the type of person who would kill innocent people. Had she misread her? *Can I risk sticking around to find out?*

Self-preservation winning, Elitsa locked her emotions away and dug into the inner pocket of her coat, removing a silver coin. "Here," she said, glaring at Cas as she pushed it into his hand. "Now go away." Shoving her hand through her hair with a frustrated sigh, she started after Yure and Birtua.

Cas fell into step beside her, and Elitsa stopped, whirling on him. "What are you doing?" she growled.

"We stay together. I have a job, remember? I have to keep an eye on you."

"I paid you to leave me alone!"

"You paid me so I wouldn't indulge my curiosity and see what you were up to at the guildhall." He tapped his pocket. "I won't tell the Guild you're working with rogues, but I'm still getting paid to follow you around, so …"

Clenching her fists, Elitsa aimed a silent scream at the sky and stormed down the road. *I'm being punished.* This was punishment for all the lives she'd harmed while thinking only of herself. It didn't matter she'd finally decided to change, that what she was trying to do was leave the Guild, start over. Lady Luck had favored her for too long, and now the wheel had turned.

"Did you hear about what happened in Kirtara?" Cas asked, easily catching up to her with his long stride. "Someone stole a bunch of relics." He glanced sideways at her. "Right after we were there, together. How about that."

"How about that," Elitsa said flatly. He was about as subtle as a bonfire. Why was he so interested in what she was up to? Cas was an opportunist, but was that all this was? And why would the Guild first try to kill her and then send Cas to shadow her? Was this unrelated somehow, something the Guild did for all agents at the end of their contract to ensure they didn't disappear with their relics? *Or did Vilis send the message?* It was possible he might be working independently; had a change of heart and now wanted to protect her. A part of her wanted to believe that. *Or did I see in him what I wanted to?*

"Guild thinks it was rogues," Cas said.

Elitsa made a noncommittal noise, increasing her pace. She adjusted her scarf. It was getting dark and cold as the night deepened, but that meant they'd be harder to find. They'd reached the main road but hadn't yet caught up with Yure and Birtua. It was probably for the best that they'd split up. *Now, if only I could walk faster than Cas.*

"Must have had inside help, no?" Cas continued, unconcerned by her lack of response.

He was trying to torment her, like a little boy tugging on a girl's braids. *Can I punch him hard enough to knock him out? Shove him into the ditch beside the road?* The thought was a satisfying curl of heat inside her stomach.

"You're in something, aren't you? You're working on your exit strategy." His teeth were white in the darkness. "I'm not judging you, Serlov. I'm impressed. We're more alike than I thought."

"We're not alike," Elitsa growled. "You only care about yourself."

"Someone has to." He fell silent for one blessed moment, the sound of his boots crunching on the gravel. "I want to meet the person paying you. Verka, is it?"

Elitsa looked at him, nearly tripping on the steep road. *Could I be wrong, and he knows why he's here to spy on me?* "Why?"

His clothing rustled as he shrugged. "Maybe I can help you."

"Or maybe you're going to tell the Guild and sell them out."

"Does it matter?" He glanced down at her, his hair falling across his eye, and Elitsa had the annoying desire to shove it back. "You don't really care about a bunch of rogues, do you?"

She didn't, but they weren't the ones trying to kill her. Verka had kept her promises so far, and that had to mean something.

"Take me to Verka, or I can take you to Vilis. I'm sure he'll be very interested in what you've been up to. I wonder what he'd pay to keep your secrets."

Elitsa stopped abruptly in front of him, the wind choosing that moment to blow her coat back in a dramatic snap of fabric. "I'd like to see you try," she snarled, a challenge in her eyes.

Cas grinned down at her, utterly relaxed despite her threat. "As fun as that would be, I'm guessing we shouldn't linger on the road. What was it you told your rogue friends that I love more than anything?"

"More than the sound of your own voice? Money."

"Exactly! Besides, if the Smoke Eyes or that Verka person don't want me to leave once we're in their secret lair, do you think I'll be able to just walk out of there? I mean, I *am* good, but I haven't taken on a whole room before. So, what's the harm with an introduction?"

"And if they kill you?"

"Worried about me, Eli?" He grinned at her glare. "They won't. I imagine two agents in their pocket is twice the fun as one."

"I'm not in their … Fine, but we're done talking." Turning away, Elitsa stalked off down the road. The sooner they reached Rivna, the better.

It was late by the time they got their first good view of Lake Odarka far below. Elitsa was exhausted, the urge to sleep strong, but she didn't want to risk being discovered near Talsa. So far, there was no sign of the guildhall's guards, so whatever Verka had arranged had either sent them in a different direction or kept them busy. She was grateful for the bite of the cold wind, as it was likely the only thing keeping her from falling asleep in the road.

Cas, somehow, seemed to be faring better, his stride never faltering. He glanced at her from time to time, and that was enough to make Elitsa set her jaw and keep their pace quick.

"Why don't we stop at that barn over there," he said, nodding to the side of the road, "get a few hours of sleep. If they were chasing you, they'd be here already on horses."

"We keep on," Elitsa said. Her tongue felt thick, her words slow. "We haven't seen Yu—" What name had Yure used? "Keep on." She concentrated on the crunch of dirt and gravel beneath her feet. One step after another. Elitsa was so focused on just keeping upright and moving that she almost didn't hear the sound of horses behind them until Cas grabbed her arm and pulled her off the road.

Alarm burned through Elitsa's body like a scalding shot of fresh-brewed cider. Was it the Guild catching up to them? Whether they had or not, it was too late to hide; she could already see the trotting horses and the sleek black carriage pulled behind.

Cas took a step forward and held up his arm.

"What are you doing?" Elitsa hissed.

"It's a private carriage. You want to get to Rivna quickly, don't you?"

"Cas!"

The horses drew even with them, the driver glancing at Cas as if he intended to go by, but then he looked back and pulled sharply on the reins. The carriage slowed. The window in the door was pushed open, and a woman's face appeared. She had on a tricorn hat, her dark hair pinned back except for two long curls framing her oval face. Red-painted lips parted in pleased surprise — the dark shade reminding Elitsa of Solveiga's favorite roses. Chandelier earrings hung from the woman's ears, the diamonds glittering in the light from the lantern affixed to the side of the carriage, and she was wearing a black dress, high-collared and embroidered with silver. Considering the woman's obvious wealth, Elitsa was surprised she wasn't traveling with guards.

"Hello travelers," the woman said, her voice a near intimate purr. "What brings you out on such a fine night?"

Cas smiled demurely, then, tucking his chin, laid a hand over his heart as he dipped forward into a bow. "Greetings, Lady. Alas, a family tragedy. Our great-aunt has died, and my sister and I are traveling at all haste to Rivna." He glanced back at Elitsa, false sorrow plastered on his face.

Caught off guard and annoyed by the twist of sympathy she felt inside her chest, Elitsa could only manage a slight nod. *What are you up to, Cas?*

"Utterly distraught, as you can see," Cas said smoothly,

looking back into the woman's eyes. "Normally, we wouldn't dare risk the roads at night, but our mother needs us."

"Oh, you poor dears," the woman said, staring only at Cas. Elitsa thought she might be a minute away from running her tongue over her lip. "I'm heading there now. You will come with me. I insist."

The driver cleared his throat without taking his gaze from the road ahead, but the woman ignored him.

"Come in!" the woman said again, unlatching the door and pushing it open. "Symon! Symon?" She narrowed her eyes at the driver, who didn't move. "Forgive him, just climb in."

"Cas," Elitsa hissed at his shoulder. "Are you sure this is a good idea?" Whatever the woman's motive for picking them up, Elitsa doubted it was sympathy.

Cas glanced back at her, lips curving in the dark. "Better come along to protect me, *sister*." Grinning, he grabbed the handle and climbed into the carriage, leaving Elitsa standing in the road.

Tension heightened, Elitsa gave the driver Symon a careful look then stepped into the carriage. Pulling the door shut with a loud click, she seated herself on the plush bench beside Cas.

The woman stopped ogling Cas long enough to thump her fist against the roof of the carriage. "Onward, Symon!"

The carriage lurched into motion, throwing Elitsa forward into Cas's arm, who caught her with a slight smirk. Biting her cheek to keep from flushing, Elitsa leaned back into the seat and turned her attention to the stranger across from them. Unlike the external lantern, the soft lights in the carriage were lightprisms, fixed to the paneled wood on either side like glowing diamonds. The woman was clearly wealthy; the broad collar of her black mourning gown covered with hundreds of tiny black pearls. Strands of onyx and emerald beads draped around her neck, and rings glittered on her fingers. When Elitsa glanced at Cas, she saw he'd removed his rings, the only visible indication he worked for the Tower. *Smart*, she thought grudgingly.

"May I ask the name of our rescuer?" Cas asked, all charm.

Elitsa glanced at him, annoyed by the careless way he lounged against the seat with his legs outstretched and crossed at the ankles, his boots brushing the woman's skirts. He seemed utterly at ease in the presence of someone Elitsa suspected either had ties to royalty or owned half of Rivna.

Why does he bother me so much? Elitsa returned her gaze to the woman, worrying she'd catch her scrutiny, but she was too busy undressing Cas with her eyes. Was that a *relic* hanging around her neck, in plain sight? Elitsa had missed it earlier, distracted by her other jewelry. It was exquisite, finer than most relics Elitsa had seen, shaped like a delicate dragonfly wing several fingers in length. *Damn you, Cas, you put us right in the hands of a Tower mage!*

"I am Lady Zorine Ourada."

"Oh, a lady of the court! We are indebted to you, Lady Zorine."

Lady Zorine beamed and raised a ringed hand to her cheek as if to cover an invisible blush. "Just a minor cousin of King Dmitrei. No one terribly important."

Right. Just someone who could purchase the entire Aerie out from under Solveiga's fingers. "You came from Talsa, Mistress?" Elitsa asked bluntly, ignoring the what-are-you-doing look from Cas. If Zorine was a noble, she probably wasn't a Guilded mage, but that didn't mean they could trust her.

Zorine raised an eyebrow, almost as though she'd forgotten Elitsa was there. "From Chertava. I imagine you're wondering why I'm traveling so late as well?" Her green eyes slid back to Cas. "I admit to a certain fondness for my own bed and would rather reach home than sleep in an inn." She glanced back at Elitsa, head tilting to the side. "You have different features. Separate fathers?"

"Half-siblings," Cas said smoothly. "I must say, I love your earrings. Is that one of Zora's designs?"

"They are, yes."

They started talking about the masterful work of some designer Elitsa had never heard of, and she felt herself begin to tune them out, her exhaustion rushing back to drag her under. Worry about the Guild, about Vilis and Pipene, about finding her mother's killer, swirled inside her head. Elitsa grabbed her wrist, idly twisting her mother's bracelet, her fingers brushing over the beads.

"That's a lovely bracelet. Where did you get it?"

Elitsa blinked, pulling her attention back to Lady Zorine and Cas. She hadn't realized they'd stopped talking. The woman was staring at her mother's bracelet.

Elitsa closed her fingers over the painted beads, baffled by the stranger's interest. It was hardly as fine as the jewelry Lady Zorine was wearing. "My mother."

"Hmm, well, it is a lovely antique. The painting on the beads is exquisite." Lady Zorine tilted her head, studying Elitsa with as much attention as she'd given Cas.

Cas stared at Elitsa's profile, brow furrowed, then leaned forward to catch Lady Zorine's eye. "Tell me, Lady Zorine," he said, smiling, "have you ever attended a winter fete at the House of Swans?" The conversation quickly shifted to favorite drinks and gossip about people Elitsa didn't know. Relieved to have lost Zorine's attention, she pulled down her sleeve and looked out the window, watching the darkened countryside move swiftly past.

They reached the city at dawn, Cas waking Elitsa with a jab from his elbow. Wiping her mouth, Elitsa sat up and blinked bleary eyes at Lady Zorine. She looked older in the brighter light, a sharpness to the woman's gaze that Elitsa hadn't noticed before, but she was too tired to be wary of her.

At Cas' apparent previous direction, Lady Zorine let them out at the southern edge of the River District just west of the Tower, slipping Cas a small card as he exited the carriage. Bowing with his hand over his heart, Cas slipped the card into a pocket with a bright grin, holding Zorine's gaze as Symon, without so much as a glance in their direction, snapped the reins, driving back over the bridge towards the Moon Court.

"Sure you don't want to follow her home?" Elitsa asked sarcastically as she stamped her feet to get the blood moving in her legs. She felt stiff and had to admit, the idea of her own bed sounded wonderful.

Cas grinned, flecks of gold glinting in his brown eyes. "Are you jealous of Lady Zorine?"

"Of her? No. I just feel like I need a shower after sitting in a carriage with the two of you."

Laughing, Cas interlaced his hands behind his back and stretched. "Just a little harmless flirting. I got us to Rivna quickly, didn't I? We probably beat those friends of yours." He looked around at the graying buildings. "I don't suppose I could convince you to go for breakfast first."

"No," Elitsa said, taking off down the street. She wanted to get this over with so she could check on Pipene and hopefully beg a bath.

Sighing, Cas strode after her. As they cut between two tall buildings in the direction of the Black Eyed Fish, he started to whistle.

"Could you not?" Elitsa glared at him. "It's best not to draw undue attention to ourselves here. I—"

A hooded figure stepped out from behind a stack of crates and punched Cas in the stomach, yanking a sack down over his head as he hunched forward. Before she had time to process what was happening, Elitsa felt something sharp press into her back. She froze, meeting the blue-eyed gaze of Cas's attacker, and then rough canvas dropped down over her face. Mindless of whatever weapon the person behind her held, she reached for her essences, panic clawing up her throat, then something hit the back of her head, and all went black.

CHAPTER 20

Elitsa woke in darkness, her head throbbing madly. She still had a sack over her head, but she could see faint light through the rough weave. Was she indoors? It smelled damp and musty. Her arms were tied behind her back, and she was on a chair. Pushing up with her toes, she was able to rock back a little, but she let the chair settle back down, not wanting to knock herself over. Cas ... was he still with her?

"Cas?"

"Elitsa?" Cas's voice drifted to her from the left, and she reflexively turned her head towards him, though she couldn't see through the hood. He sounded groggy and sober. Had they knocked him out too? He cleared his throat, and Elitsa heard the sound of something scrape against the floor. "Well, if you're here," Cas said, "we're probably not in Lady Zorine's boudoir."

Elitsa rolled her eyes, impressed he could still find humor in their situation but also annoyed. If he hadn't been distracting her, she might have realized they were being followed. She squashed a flutter of fear by forcing herself to think about the situation. It was possible the Guild had grabbed them, though it would have been easier to murder them in the alleyway instead of going through the effort of hauling them somewhere private. They would have had to drag her and Cas out of the River District, something she doubted would be easy with the Smoke Eyes patrolling the streets. And as far as she knew, the Tower didn't have a dungeon. It smelled like … it smelled like they were underground.

"Is this usual for you?" Cas asked. "I confess, this is my first abduction."

Elitsa didn't bother responding. If it wasn't the Guild, then were they Verka's? Why tie her up then? She was on their side. *This is Cas's fault*, she thought, anger bleeding into irritation.

Ahead of her came the echo of footsteps splashing through water — from a tunnel, perhaps? The light through her hood brightened. Someone was carrying a lantern. Elitsa could hear the rustle of clothing, and the murmur of a voice, followed by an answer.

The footfalls stopped, and the hood was ripped off her head. Blinking in the sudden light, Elitsa squinted up at the figure above her. It was Ivo, wearing all black, his long coat buttoned up to hide his tunic beneath. He took a step back and crossed his arms, revealing Verka behind him. She was dressed like a merchant from the Kurdaima with a gold scarf tied over her hair and an embroidered vest over her white blouse, the stiff fabric covered in stitched blue and black stars. Her blue skirt, the edge of her white tunic visible beneath, was covered by a linen over-skirt with a matching pattern in red and blue stripes across its base. She leaned over and set a lantern on the floor.

Looking to her left, Elitsa saw Cas. He was tied to a chair, like she was, a black hood still covering his head. They were in some storage chamber of grayish stone. On the other side of him, in the rough-hewn floor, was a channel of dark water that ran the length of the room. *Is that the water that feeds the fountains in the city?* To its right, more light glowed from inside the mouth of a passageway, presumably where Ivo and Verka had entered. Elitsa looked back at Verka with narrowed eyes. "Is this really necessary?"

Verka crossed her arms and gave her a considering look, as though she had cause to be suspicious. "Why did you bring an agent here?"

"Hello?" Cas said, turning his head towards their voices. "I'm Cas; who are you? Mind taking off this hood?"

Ivo glanced at him, then started to pick at his nails with a knife.

"I didn't have much of a choice," Elitsa said. "He found me in Talsa and wanted to speak with you. I thought you'd prefer meeting him before he returns to the Tower."

Verka held her gaze for several moments, then looked at Ivo and nodded.

Ivo didn't move — did he not like receiving instructions from Verka? — then reached forward and yanked the hood off Cas's head.

Cas blinked, squinting, then jerked his head to the side in an attempt to toss his hair out of his eyes. Taking in the room, he looked from Ivo's knife to Elitsa. He almost seemed concerned as he looked her over, but when he shifted his gaze to Verka, whatever sincerity was there disappeared into a bright, salacious smile. "So, you're the money. Whatever you're doing, I want in."

Verka walked up to him with a decidedly chilled expression, apparently unaffected by his friendly attitude. "Cas Rosya, reclamation agent, son of Borys Rosya. He was a cobbler, wasn't he? Disappeared some years ago." She pursed her lips, eyes moving over his clothing. "You live above The Stone and Song."

Elitsa stopped pushing against the ropes around her wrists to look at Cas. He lived in an inn in the Kurdaima? She thought he had a room in the Spears. If Cas was surprised by what Verka knew about him, he didn't let on.

"You've done your research on me," Cas said, "so you know I like to live well. Honestly, I'm not sure why you didn't approach me first. It's no secret I'm open to varied work." He glanced at Elitsa. "But Serlov here; she's always been rather tight-laced."

Elitsa glared at him and received an infuriating wink. He wasn't entirely wrong, but it galled her that he thought he had her figured out.

"Tell me, Agent Rosya," Verka said, "who do you think would be more useful to me. Someone above suspicion, or someone known to break the rules?"

"I get it, but considering your recent acquisition in Talsa and that lovely light show of yours, I think your plans are near their end. You need all the help you can get." Cas looked between Verka and Ivo.

"What do you think, Elitsa?" Verka asked. "Will he be useful?"

Elitsa considered, not missing the fact that Verka had dropped 'agent' from her name. If she vouched for Cas, and he double-crossed them, she was sure they'd take it out on her. Still, it was probably better to keep an eye on him than worry about what'd happen if he returned to the Guild. "He fights well."

Cas beamed and gave Elitsa a look that heated her belly. She glowered at him.

"All right, Agent Rosya," Verka said, drawing Cas's eyes. "I'll pay you ten silver per job, but if you breathe a word about our plans, about me, to anyone outside this room, Ivo here will carve up that pretty face of yours. Do we have a deal?"

"Consider me yours." Cas glanced at Ivo, who was still playing with his knife. "You can put that away, mate."

"Will you untie us now?" Elitsa wiggled her fingers. "My wrists are going numb."

Verka nodded at Ivo, and he cut the ropes around Elitsa's wrists and then for Cas. Flexing her hands, Elitsa stood up. Her shoulders felt stiff, and she dug her fingers into the muscles of her back, grimacing. "Have Yure and Birtua returned?"

"They made it back, as did our … donations." Verka's lips

curved into a tight smile. Reaching into a pouch at her waist, she handed Elitsa a small coin purse. Her payment.

Elitsa slipped it into her pocket, fingers brushing the bracelet she'd stolen from the guildhall's barn. Her skin prickled. Had Ivo searched her when she was unconscious? "The distraction," she said. "Did you—?"

"No one was hurt, Elitsa. I told you, unlike the Guild, I aim to save lives, not take them."

Elitsa felt a surge of relief. She glanced at Cas, who was scrutinizing Ivo. Now that the job was done, she felt restless. She needed to decide on her next steps. The money from Verka wasn't enough to disappear, and she still needed to confront Vilis. Could she convince Cas to go to the Tower and bring him to her? Cas hadn't been burned yet, but that wouldn't last long. Did he understand that working for Verka might destroy all future employment with the Guild? *Is Cas being impulsive, or does he know something I don't?*

"There's something you should know," Verka said. "There's a contract out on you. Dead or alive."

Elitsa's stomach dropped like a stone. It was official then. Her life in Rivna was over. "Did you know about this?" she demanded, turning to Cas. "About the assassin? Was your plan to get me back here so they could finish the job?"

Cas frowned, and damned if he didn't look concerned. "Assassin? Of course not. Why would they ..." He trailed off, maybe thinking about Kirtara.

Someone other than Vilis had to be feeding the Guild information on her. They'd need compelling proof for an official contract, and they couldn't know about all her interactions with Verka unless ... Unless Verka had let their association become known. *Why, though?* It seemed unlikely the procurer would burn a potential ally before getting more use out of her. Or had news of the assassin convinced Verka that working with Elitsa would draw too many eyes?

"I can see what you're thinking, Elitsa," Verka said, "but you're no use to me dead. Our time for secrecy and shadows is almost over, and even if the Guild is hunting you, I have need of your skills and expertise." She glanced at Cas. "Whatever your true reasons are for following Elitsa here, you should know that your employers will think you are helping her. Playing both sides won't work."

"I wouldn't worry about me, Verka," Cas said, smiling. "I always land on my feet."

Elitsa snorted and pressed her fingertips to her temples. How had she ended tangled up in this with Cas, of all people? *And now he can't even bring me Vilis.* Could Solveiga? She had connections inside the Tower. But if Elitsa returned to the House of Swans, she risked putting Pipene in danger. She couldn't risk that, no matter how badly she wanted answers.

After her mother's death, Elitsa had pushed everyone away to work for Vilis. She'd been distant and cruel, trying to separate herself from her old life, but Pipene had refused to hate her. She hadn't let go of their friendship, and when Elitsa had been unable to continue on her own, Pipene had welcomed her back as if nothing had happened. Elitsa would not let her be drawn any deeper into this.

I might not be able to say goodbye. Elitsa's stomach hollowed, the guilt a physical pain inside her chest that almost made her miss the preoccupied look on Verka's face as she murmured something to Ivo. "What is it?" she asked.

Verka pursed her lips and rested her hand on the woven belt around her waist. "I'm deciding how best to use you. I apologize for grabbing you off the street like we did, but I wanted to ascertain Agent Rosya's intentions. I'm actually surprised you made it inside the gates without notice."

"But you said the ... donations made it back."

"You can say relics, Eli," Cas said. He rested his forearm on her shoulder, but she shook him off.

Verka nodded. "Yes, but we didn't bring them inside the city."

Elitsa thought back to how quiet the streets were when Lady Zorine had dropped them off by the bridge. It'd been early, but there were usually always a few people heading to their jobs or returning from fishing on Lake Odarka. People could always sense when there was going to be trouble in the city. "The Tower already knows about Kirtara?"

"The messenger towers," Cas said. "They probably sent a message before we got back." He rubbed a hand over his chin, brown eyes keen. "You've hit more than Kirtara and Talsa, haven't you. The Guild might attribute a handful of missing relics here and there to the actions of unorganized rogues, but a brazen theft from a guildhall? You couldn't risk giving them time to improve their security, to prepare."

Ivo grinned, teeth sharp in his bearded face. "The ferret thinks he's got it all figured out."

"I thought you intended to hide until you were ready to challenge them," Elitsa said, frowning. "If the Guild suspects you, why aren't they storming in here?"

Verka walked over to the chair Elitsa had been tied to and sat down, crossing her legs. "Last night High Mage Kyrylo, chief advisor to the king, was found dead, an apparent victim of the Night Sickness. Within an hour of his passing, the Guild recalled every mage to the Tower, including their knights that have been part of the King's Guard for the last sixty years."

Elitsa didn't understand. If the Guild was behind the illness, why would they kill one of their own and then leave?

Cas barked a laugh. "You're telling me that a non-communicable illness has sent the mages running from the castle. Why would they abandon their position, unless ..." He broke off, then shook his head. He seemed impressed. "I didn't think he had it in him."

Who was Cas talking about? Elitsa hadn't told him she suspected the Guild was involved in the Night Sickness deaths.

"You think the king killed his advisor and passed it off as the Night Sickness." Elitsa looked at Verka. "You think he forced the mages out." Merely considering the idea felt ridiculous. The king was not subtle, nor had he ever expressed a shred of strategic thought. Someone else had to be involved. A noble? Someone clever behind the scenes?

"War is coming," Verka said, "and the Tower will respond, but we can have a hand in the outcome."

"But why leave at all?" Elitsa asked. "Surely, the mages in the castle were stronger than King Dmitrei's guards. Why step into a position where they'll have to force themselves back inside? Isn't that the opposite of what the Tower wants? To be seen challenging the king?"

"Whatever their reasons," Verka said, folding her fingers, "the Guild won't be distracted for long. They will gather and make their move either against us or the king. Rivna is a tinderbox, waiting to explode." There was a crack in Verka's impassive exterior, a look of genuine concern in her eyes. "You may have to fight alongside us, Elitsa, if the Tower marches on the city. People will get hurt, and I worry we don't yet have enough resources to prevent fighting."

Elitsa ran her hand through her hair, sharing a look with Cas, who, for once, seemed at a loss for words. Out of all the scenarios she imagined to find herself in, she'd never considered being caught in the middle of a brewing war. Would the Guild really move against the king? They'd watched him for years, ignoring his antics. Why abandon the charade? Had someone else seized control of the castle? *Could it be the queen?* She seemed clever enough.

What seemed more likely, was that the Guild would tear through the city looking for the Smoke Eyes. *And here I am in their company.* The only upside of the Tower's current preoccupation was that they might not bother sending another assassin after her. Elitsa could slip away, disappear. *But where would I go?*

And what about Vilis? She'd never know if he'd lied about her mother's killer. He might have the answers she'd been chasing this whole time. She couldn't walk away from that. *And Pipene?* Elitsa had to warn her of what was coming.

"I can tell you where a big stash of relics is," Elitsa said, "near the city."

Cas's head swung in her direction. "Elitsa," he said warningly, "Do you think that's wise …"

"It's largely unguarded." Elitsa turned to Verka. "I'll tell you where it is, but I want something first."

Ivo took a step forward, his knife flashing between his fingers. "Or you could tell us where it is now."

Cas tensed, eyes darkening dangerously, but Elitsa moved between them, seizing one of her essences and filling the air with the scent of fire.

"No need for that," Verka cut in smoothly. "What do you want, Elitsa?"

"I want you to bring me someone." If the Guild had recalled everyone, it was possible Vilis was inside the Tower and therefore untouchable, but there was a chance he'd still follow his usual routine.

Verka raised an eyebrow.

"His name is Vilis." Elitsa glanced at Ivo. "He's a high mage and will most likely be at Liudmyla's Athenaeum in the reading rooms." A sprawling building within the Kurdaima, the library could be accessed by everyone, though the reading rooms were more often than not reserved for Rivna's wealthier residents, including high mages like Vilis.

Ivo huffed a laugh. "You want us to bring you a mage, here. It'd be easier if we kill him."

"I don't want him dead," Elitsa said quickly, "but if you don't think you're up for the challenge …"

"That might work on someone younger, but my people are not so reckless." A woman walked out from the tunnel. She was around Cas's height with silver hair, tied back from a good-natured face. Dressed in a dark gray coat, trousers, and sturdy leather boots, she seemed oddly at home here beneath the city despite looking like someone's grandmother. Her clothing was fairly plain but well-made, with diamond-shaped stitching across the waist and chest. Hanging from her ears, in plain sight, was a pair of sword-shaped magesilver earrings.

Following her was a burly man with a broad, sun-tanned face and shoulder-length brown hair. He was dressed in a long-sleeved, milk-white tunic with a thick stripe of diamond-shaped embroidery down the front of his chest. Loose wine-red trousers draped over his leather boots, and a wide woven belt of blue and white wrapped his broad waist.

Verka, having turned her head at the sound of the woman's voice, seemed apprehensive about their interruption.

Why does she seem worried?

"It's more crowded than I'd expect down here," Cas murmured.

The woman stopped between Verka and Ivo, and though her smile seemed open and friendly, Elitsa felt a barely imperceptible tension with her arrival. "You must be the reclamation agent Verka's been working with. I'm Leida."

"Elitsa." She glanced at Ivo, drawn to a change in his posture. He'd lost his haughty attitude and was looking at Leida with near reverential deference. This was the person the Smoke Eyes obeyed, not Verka.

Leida tilted her head and gave Cas a cursory look. "And you ... You're also a Tower agent."

Cas smiled broadly and brushed at the collar of his coat. "Can you tell by my dashing clothes?"

Leida smiled indulgently. "You're a bit of an entertainer, aren't you." She circled him as if she were a grandmother judging her grandson's wardrobe, trailing the scent of rum and oranges. "I make it a priority of mine to know everyone with ties to the Tower. I bet you'd love The Stone and Song."

"They have the best piragi," Cas said, still smiling. "The cook's a wonder." Leida seemed to have the same information about Cas that Verka did.

"Mmm." Leida gave him an affectionate look. "Yes, and a wonderful place to catch a song. You look like someone who enjoys music. There's a man there with a beautiful voice, a true master."

Elitsa saw Cas's face drain of color, his eyes darkening with unmistakable wariness. His smile tightened.

"I love a good melody," Cas said.

"I thought so." Leida stopped in front of him, clasping her hands over her waist. "And your name, young man?"

"Casimir Rosya."

"Mmm. Do you have family in the city?"

"Not a one."

"It can be lonely on your own. Everyone should have someone." Leida sounded sympathetic, and Elitsa felt a shiver of wariness as she turned to her. "And you, such misfortune to lose your mother so young. It is good that Solveiga has kept an eye on you. Luckily you and young Cas, here, found the Tower, hmm? Though it seems loyalty is in short supply these days."

Elitsa narrowed her eyes, not bothering to hide her suspicion like Cas. She didn't like what Leida was implying. "Yes, well, hounds get hungry when they're not fed, and loyalty only extends so far when someone wants you dead." She didn't bother reminding Leida her contract had ended.

"It is a difficult place to be when you've been entrusted with your master's secrets but no longer required. Sometimes confidences must be buried, bridges burned, and old dogs put to ground."

That sounded suspiciously like Leida approved of Elitsa being hunted. "You think the Tower should kill off their agents?" Elitsa demanded angrily. She shot a look at Verka, who was simply listening.

Glancing at Elitsa, she cleared her throat. "I don't think that's what Leida is saying," Verka said smoothly. "I think—"

Leida turned, her blue eyes cooling. "I think, *Verka*, that you should not presume to explain my words. I see no problem with the Tower discarding their tools when they are no longer useful. All I care about is when they try to extend their hand over *my* people, *my* territory." She turned back to Cas and Elitsa, the softness gone from her face. "I don't see why we should trust you any more than your Guild does."

"I helped you in Talsa," Elitsa retorted. "I think I've shown I keep my word when you keep yours, and now I'm offering you something immensely valuable. You want to stand up to the Tower? This stash is more than whatever you've grabbed so far, I'm sure of it." It was a bold assurance, but if it kept Leida from dumping her and Cas's bodies in the river, it was worth the risk. Elitsa glanced at Leida's magesilver. Could she fight her way out of here with Cas? Would Verka help or just stand by?

"Perhaps." Leida rested a hand on Ivo's shoulder. "But as Ivo says, we don't necessarily need your willing participation."

"You'd waste two agents?" Cas asked, arching an eyebrow. "Two *skilled* mages?" He took a step forward, prompting the mountain-sized man behind Leida to take a mirroring step. "We may not wear the Guild's seal, but we're just as good, if not better, than those fools sitting in their posh tower. We can be useful."

Verka took a step closer to Leida. "We have a deal, Leida. We work *together,* and in return, you are generously paid. You agreed that I get to choose the people I work with."

"We do have an agreement," Leida said, "but sometimes terms change. There's a war coming, as you so aptly said, and I don't want to worry about the people inside my lines."

"You need relics, right?" Elitsa cut in, heart pounding at the glacial cast to Leida's eyes. "For the River District. You want to make money, to be able to use your relics openly, set your essence prices, but first, you need to survive whatever happens next. Who is the Guild more likely to move against first? You or the king?

"I don't owe the Tower anything. All I care about is earning enough money so I can leave, and I'm willing to help you to get it. And Cas, here? He'd sell his own grandmother if it meant a big payday."

"Well, I wouldn't go that far, but pay me well, and my loyalty is yours." Cas's eyes crinkled at the corners as he smiled. "You may think that is a weakness, but who else is willing to pay more than you, or rather Verka here, right? I recognize the winning horse, and I'm going to bet on you."

Elitsa winced. Did Cas just compare Leida to a horse?

Leida folded her hands and tilted her head to the side. If she was offended, Elitsa couldn't tell. "What are you proposing?"

Elitsa exchanged a look with Cas, lips twitching at the triumph in his eyes. "The Cartographers' Guild," she said. "There's an underground storeroom at their estate outside the West Gate. A group of agents, including Cas and me, helped move a cache of relics there over the summer that was discovered in the White Forest. I'm not sure why — maybe they didn't have room in the Tower? — but whatever their reason, most of it is still there."

Leida studied their faces, then looked at Ivo. "Have you heard about anything like this?"

"There were rumors of something big out in the White Forest," Ivo said, rubbing his jaw. "A logger was talking about it at The Smoke and Hammer, but he was quite drunk and known to tell tales, so many didn't believe him."

"You spoke with him?" Leida asked.

"No, he disappeared, as did the rest of his crew. Presumably on another job."

Elitsa felt a chill and looked at Cas, whose brow was furrowed. He ran a hand over his jaw. Several people had stumbled across the old ruins where the relics had been found before the Tower caught wind of it. She'd never stopped to consider what happened to them after they'd taken over.

"What about you, Verka?" Leida asked.

"We heard of it, as well," Verka said, "but thought it'd been taken into the Tower."

Leida crossed her arms with a thoughtful expression, tapping her fingers against her bicep.

"You'll need us." Cas leaned his arm on Elitsa's shoulder, gesturing at Ivo with his magesilver ringed fingers. "There's a trick to getting inside."

"I think we can manage a couple of dusty old cartographers," Ivo snorted. "I'm sure they'll be more than happy to open the door for us."

"They don't know about it," Elitsa said. Cas's arm was heavy, but she didn't shrug him off like before. As distasteful as it was to admit, even to herself, she found his presence comforting. She couldn't count on Verka to have her back if Leida decided to kill them, but she was certain Cas wanted to live as badly as she did.

"I'm sorry?" Leida narrowed her eyes.

"The building was gifted to them by the Tower. The cartographers don't know what's under their feet or how to access it."

"And the Guild would just leave this priceless stash unguarded," Leida said doubtfully.

Cas grinned. "No, there are guards, but they think they're there to protect the maps. Guild owns all the merchants, you know? And their trade routes?"

Leida pursed her lips. "And all you want in exchange is this mage of yours. Why?"

"Personal business," Elitsa said flatly.

"Should have asked for more, Eli," Cas murmured. He

straightened, removing his arm from her shoulder. "For my part, I want to keep one or two of the relics."

Leida chuckled and shook her head, rubbing one of her earrings between her fingers. "All right, here's what we'll do. Cas, here, will take me to the Cartographers' Guild so I can see this place for myself. Ivo will bring you this Vilis person, if he's not locked up in the Tower with the others. If you're lying to me about the cache, I will kill the pair of you and your mage friend."

Elitsa's pulse quickened as she stared into Leida's eyes. She believed her.

"You will wait here with Verka," Leida continued. "If you try to leave or if your conversation with your mage results in an escape attempt, I'll kill your partner."

"I understand," Elitsa said, glancing at Cas. *He won't try to run, will he?* Leida really only needed one of them to get into the storeroom — something neither Elitsa nor Cas had voiced — but Leida was likely to see it as some kind of betrayal if Cas disappeared.

Cas's lips curved as he stared down at her, his eyes heating. "Don't worry about me, Eli. I'll be back."

Elitsa frowned and slipped her hand into her pocket, palming the bracelet she'd taken in Talsa. As Cas turned to follow Leida, she caught his hand, stomach flipping at the surprised look that crossed his face. "Make sure you do," she said, transferring the bracelet to his palm. It didn't have any essences in it, but she felt a little better about his chances. He was the only ally she had right now, and she needed him to come back.

CHAPTER 21

"I don't trust her," Elitsa said flatly after Leida, Ivo, and her hulking bodyguard had left with Cas. "And I'm not convinced her goals for Rivna are the same as yours. Are we really better off if she takes the relics?" Elitsa had never met the Smoke Eyes's leader before today, but she'd heard stories. Leida was not someone you wanted to cross.

Verka blew a slow breath between her teeth and made a smoothing gesture over the fabric at her waist. "I apologize for Leida. She is concerned with the safety of her people and can be … blunt. Leida is the reason the Guild hasn't tried to raid this district. They are wary of her, which is what we need."

"You and whoever employs you." Elitsa rubbed a hand over her forehead. She could still smell Leida's perfume lingering in the cold air. "I thought you had more authority with the Smoke Eyes." Verka had been so confident when they'd first met, but it was clear her influence hung on Leida's goodwill.

"Our ties are much the same as yours and mine," Verka said. "An exchange of services, and, when this is all done, legitimacy."

Legitimacy … among Rivna's elite? "Leida wants the Smoke

Eyes to become some kind of guild? Your employer must be quite influential if you can make that happen."

Verka smiled, then gestured at the austere room. "Might as well get comfortable. It may be a while before they return. I have business to see to, but you'll be safe here while you wait." She turned in a slow circle, as if looking for something, then pointed out a crate by the wall. "There's some food there and water, if you're thirsty, though the channel is also drinkable."

Elitsa pulled her collar against her neck and stuck her hands in her pockets. "And what about heat?" Though decidedly warmer than the streets above, there was a chill to the stone beneath her feet.

"You have your essences, but we shouldn't need to keep you here long. After I return, we'll figure out more comfortable but safe lodgings. Do what Leida asks for now." Verka tucked a curl of hair behind her ear and raised her chin. "If the cache beneath the Cartographers' Guild is as big as you say and we're able to take it, I'll pay both you and Rosya twenty silver each. As I said before, you may have to fight alongside us, but I'll make sure you have the means to decide your future after this is all over."

Verka adjusted her cloak and started towards the passageway. As she reached its arch, two figures leaned out from the shadows on the other side. They looked her over and then glanced at Elitsa before moving out of sight. Verka looked back over her shoulder. "If you were thinking about exploring, I suggest waiting until I return."

Elitsa narrowed her eyes. "So I'm a prisoner now?"

"They're merely here to keep you safe. The Guild is searching for you, remember?" Her brows raised in warning, then she disappeared into the tunnel.

Sighing, Elitsa looked around her prison. Leida's involvement was a dangerous complication. She'd been wary of Verka, but the Smoke Eyes' leader gave her chills. *If Verka hadn't spoken up for us ...*

Elitsa shook her head, turning her mind back to the room. She hadn't missed anything in her initial sweep; the channel cut into the floor the only interesting feature. Wandering towards it, she bent down and stuck her fingertips in the dark water. It felt like freshly melted snow, and she yanked her hand back as a shiver rolled down her spine. Something was creating a gentle current that propelled the water towards a pipe in the opposite wall.

What time was it? It was impossible to tell underground. Pipene would undoubtedly be worrying about her if she wasn't still mad Elitsa had left again without saying goodbye. Was Verka right? Would there be actual fighting in the city? The Guild had always tried to keep the peace. Would they really turn their relics on Rivna's citizens? Against the king? *What was he thinking kicking them out of the castle?* She could understand not wanting to be a puppet anymore, a powerless figurehead, but what was King Dmitrei planning to do? Or the queen, for that matter?

I need to get Pipene out of the city. Could she persuade Solveiga to take all the Swans? They sometimes traveled during the summer, so Solveiga had to have someplace safer they could stay. But how could she convince Pipene to leave without her, and Solveiga — the only one who had the power to force her to leave — unless she told them what was going on?

Time crawled past, and Elitsa forced herself to sit in one of the chairs. Sinking into the high collar of her coat, she tucked her hands against her ribs, and she must have dozed off, for she suddenly heard motion in the tunnel. Had they managed to find Vilis? Apprehension settled between her shoulders, and she stood up, shaking out a cramp in her leg. *I should have thought this through.* What if he'd killed Ivo or another member of Leida's crew? Elitsa wanted to confront him, *needed* to, but Vilis was unlikely to be forthcoming after being kidnapped by the Smoke Eyes. She should have approached him on her own.

Ivo strode through the doorway. On his heels were two men

— including the mountain that'd been with Leida earlier — dragging the limp form of Vilis between them.

"I said I wanted him alive!" Elitsa rushed forward, examining Vilis' hanging head as they carried him into the room. There was a bruise on his forehead and blood on his cheek. Ivo's men also looked worse for wear, their clothes disheveled. The new one, lean with long brown hair, had a broken nose, already swelling, and the mountain had blood matting his hair by his left ear. Vilis had not come easily.

They dumped him into one of the chairs, shoving his head back to prevent him from falling forward, then the long-haired one roughly bound his hands behind him. It looked like one of Vilis' hands was broken. The magesilver buckles had been ripped off his coat.

Elitsa gave Ivo a sharp glare, noticing that he looked the same as when he'd left.

"It's not an easy thing grabbing a mage," Ivo said. He held up a hand, tossing a handful of magesilver rings into the air before catching them again. "We've taken his relics. Leida says you have one hour to talk to him; then it's time for you to go to work." He jerked his head at the two men, and they followed him out, stopping to talk to the guards outside.

Elitsa looked back at Vilis's unconscious form, dread, and anger like a band across her chest. This man had pretended to be her mentor for eight years. *Why? Why go through all that trouble?* His chest was rising and falling; his blue tunic ripped where they'd removed the buckles. His brown hair hung down over half his face, moving as he breathed. She felt a stab of guilt and worry that his injuries were her fault, but she shook it off. Vilis had to know why her mother died, maybe even knew her killer. He didn't deserve her pity. Elitsa gathered her hurt and anger around her like a cloak, then reached out and shook his shoulder.

"Vilis," she said, her voice flat and controlled. The scent of him, cedar and apricots, tangled with the metallic tang of blood. "Vilis, wake up. Vilis!"

He stirred, a bone-deep cough rattling from his chest, and Elitsa snatched her hand back, her heart thumping wildly. Blinking slowly, Vilis spat blood on the floor between Elitsa's feet. He tested his bonds, awareness returning quickly, then he lifted his head and glared venomously up at her.

The rage in Vilis's eyes nearly stopped her heart, and Elitsa wasn't sure how she didn't back up to get away from it. *Who is this man in front of me?* The hope that she'd been wrong, that she actually meant something to him withered and died.

Then his expression changed, and he seemed confused before his familiar calm control settled over his face like a mask, but Elitsa knew she'd never forget what she'd glimpsed beneath. "Elitsa, I did not expect to find you aligned with the Smoke Eyes." Despite his injuries and immobility, Vilis was projecting confidence as though he was the one in control.

"No?" Elitsa's anger roared back, brought to life by the judgemental arrogance in Vilis's eyes. "Where did you expect to find me after leaving an assassin in my home?"

His calm remained unbroken. "The contract on you was not my doing."

"And I suppose you didn't steal from me or hurt my friend?"

"Your *friend* was a rogue; were you aware of that?" He eyed their surroundings with distaste. "Of course, as I find you here with rogues, perhaps you did."

"It's not illegal to keep essences that I harvested and paid for."

"It is, if found in the possession of someone with an unregistered relic. And after discovering your *connections* with criminals, I had to assume you've been corrupted."

Elitsa shook her head, face flushing with anger. Vilis was lying. Pipene had caught him taking her essences before he saw her relic.

"You knew the Guild kills agents who decide to leave, and you didn't tell me. Were you hoping your assassin would kill me so you wouldn't have to yourself? I thought you cared about me; I thought ..." Elitsa's eyes started to burn with tears, but she blinked them away. She would *not* break in front of him. *I should have seen this*, she thought. His reserve, his harshness, she'd thought it was just who he was, but he'd been trying to keep her at arm's length. He'd never cared about her at all. "Did you kill my mother?" she asked, staring hard into his eyes, looking for any sign of guilt.

There was a tiny twitch in his left brow. "Branka died from the Night Sickness."

"Don't ..." Elitsa clenched her fist, an overwhelming urge to seize an essence flooding her senses. She wanted to hurt him. "Don't lie to me, *Vilis*. I know the Guild is involved; what I don't understand is *why*. Why kill my mother? Why kill any of them?"

"The Tower is not killing those who die from the Night Sickness."

"Stop *lying!*" Elitsa released an essence of air as she threw her hand towards the second chair beside him. Wood splintered as the wind flung it across the room into the wall.

Vilis didn't flinch. "Neither I nor the Guild killed your mother, Elitsa. She was a rogue."

Elitsa laughed and shook her head. "That's absurd. My mother didn't have any relics. She restored books."

"You were too young to pay much attention to the books she worked on, but the ones she'd buy were expensive, rare. Books from private collectors, including some that'd been stolen from the Tower when the dissidents caused the split. It took me a while to figure out where Branka was earning her money. For a time, I thought it was left from your father."

"No," Elitsa said, shaking her head. Vilis was lying again, but why? She thought about the books her mother would work on by candlelight, the broken bindings, timeworn leather covers, and the soft pages filled with symbols and elegant handwriting.

They'd looked valuable, sure, but she had never questioned their origin. Her mother had never taken her along to acquire books; she'd always left her behind with Orson and Sofija. Would Elitsa have known if her mother was performing magic? She'd never seen anything that looked like magesilver on her. Her only jewelry had been the bracelet Elitsa now wore.

Could she have hidden magic from me? But why? Was Vilis suggesting her mother had harvested and sold essences? "So what ..." Elitsa said, throwing up her hands. "You're telling me a rogue killed her? I don't believe that. The Guild wouldn't be covering it up, making it look like an illness, not to save a rogue."

Vilis' eyes were steady. "It is a sickness, Elitsa. A poison. Harvesting essences is what killed Branka. I took her relic when she died, and I spread the story that a rogue had killed her. You would have never been allowed into the Tower if they'd thought your mother was a rogue. I did what I could for you both."

Elitsa shook her head. All this time hunting for her mother's killer, a search that Vilis himself had set her on, and he was telling her it'd been random? "I don't understand; you're saying that harvesting essences is killing people? I harvest essences, as do hundreds of other people. I'm still here."

"There are always traces of pollution in the essences we harvest, elements that can cause illness if you absorb too much into your body, but in the past fifty years, we've seen an increase, an imbalance. Take food, for example; sometimes, it can become poisoned by its environment, absorbing minerals from the ground that can kill or make you sick. We're seeing the same thing happen with the essences we harvest. Occasionally, someone will collect the wrong thing, and it will be fatal."

Elitsa thought back to her conversation with Melnyk along the road. Could essences be weakening because of this pollution? *Is that what is causing the imbalance, the famine, the seedbeetles?* "If this is true, then why aren't there more dead?"

"The fatal doses are rare. Most people experience only minor fatigue."

Elitsa narrowed her eyes, studying Vilis's face closely. "Why is the Tower hiding this? If people knew that harvesting might kill them, then—"

"They'd panic. This is why we seek to acquire all essences that are farmed. The Tower has a purification process that not only refines the essences, strengthening them, but it cleanses the pollution. We believe that this mitigates the accumulation."

Elitsa shook her head. She'd never heard of a purification process before, not even from the essence market in the Kurdaima. Why would the Guild keep all of this secret? If people knew it was safer to bring them their essences, then maybe they wouldn't take them to the Smoke Eyes. "Your purification process isn't working. People are still dying, and you're doing nothing." She made a disgusted sound and crossed her arms. "This is about money. The Guild doesn't want harvesting to stop. They don't care how many of us die, as long as they don't have to do the work themselves. That's why so few mages die from the Night Sickness. Does the king know about this?"

"I can only speculate," Vilis said.

Anger flashed across Elitsa's skin. The Tower was truly rotten to its core. They didn't care about the people of Casekraia or their agents or if the world itself burned. She'd felt guilty for betraying her oaths to them, but what promises mattered to a guild with blood on their hands? They had killed her mother as surely as if they'd taken a knife to her throat. Elitsa wanted to destroy them, to watch the Tower fall, but what could she do? If she tried to tell anyone about the Sickness, about the pollution, the Guild would hunt her down and kill her. They'd already tried once, and the longer she stayed here in Rivna, the more likely it was they'd succeed. She was a loose thread.

And Vilis ... why was he telling her this? Did he think she wouldn't survive? Elitsa turned her glare back on him, rage flaring at the impassive way he watched her. He hadn't even demanded to be untied or ask what she planned to do with him. He wasn't worried. "Why tell me all this? About the pollution, about my mother?"

"You deserve to know. Whatever you think of me, know that I cared for her." Vilis glanced past Elitsa's shoulder towards where Ivo waited with the others. "Your time with the Tower is over, and if you still desire a chance at another life, I suggest you leave Rivna now."

The skin prickled on the back of Elitsa's neck, but she didn't follow his gaze. "You think I should run from your assassin."

"I did not order the contract on you, Elitsa, but I cannot rescind it either. You should reconsider your current allies."

Elitsa stared into his eyes, trying to read him. *Why is Vilis so unconcerned about being held here? In fact, how did Ivo manage to grab him at all? Is he expecting rescue?* Was the Guild going to make a move against the Smoke Eyes?

Spinning on her heel, Elitsa strode to the passageway, leaving Vilis alone with the lantern. Through the arch, on the other side, the men were sitting on overturned crates in a small alcove, playing cards.

Ivo peeled off the wall. "Done with your mage, are you?" he said, removing a toothpick from between his teeth.

"I want to talk to Verka."

Leaning into the hall, Ivo looked at Vilis, then tossed the toothpick onto the floor. "All right. You two, stay here with the mage."

Ivo headed away down the passageway, not bothering to grab one of the lanterns. The further they walked from the guards, the darker it got, but Elitsa kept close to Ivo's heels. It never grew pitch black, as there was some kind of hair-like fungus glowing along the top of the walls. They made several turns, moving through numerous narrow tunnels and larger rooms. Ivo didn't speak, so the only sound was their footsteps against stone and the drip of water.

Finally, when Elitsa was starting to wonder if Leida had decided to keep her down here forever, Ivo led her to a narrow set of stairs and up to a door, beneath which Elitsa could see the glow of light. Yanking it open, he preceded her into a small closet-like room. They squeezed between a shelf of bottles filled with what Elitsa thought were dyes and out through another door.

It was a textile storeroom, the shelves along the wall filled with bolts of brightly colored fabric. An older woman sat in a chair in one corner, embroidering a dark blue skirt draped over her lap. Standing by a table in the center of the room was Verka and an elegantly dressed man with shiny brown hair, pinned at the back of his neck with a jeweled pin. Leida and Cas weren't there.

Verka glanced up, looking at Ivo before her gaze settled on Elitsa. She murmured something to her companion, who nodded and then rolled up one of the documents on the table before carrying it out of the room. There was the muffled sound of voices as he opened the door, quickly cut off as he closed it again. "You're done with your conversation?"

"We should leave."

"Leave?"

"She didn't kill him," Ivo volunteered, leaning his hip against the table.

Elitsa scowled at him. "Of course not, but I think the Tower is coming."

"We weren't followed," Ivo said.

"I don't think they're necessarily coming here, wherever here is." Elitsa glanced around the windowless room. "But I think they're going to move against the Smoke Eyes." She glanced at Ivo then moved closer to Verka. "I know you have a deal with them, but Leida isn't going to stand against the Guild, is she? Not in a direct fight. The cache won't be much use to you if we're all dead."

Ivo chuckled dryly. "Smoke Eyes don't run from a fight, *Agent*, especially if we're being paid."

"I'm not an agent anymore," Elitsa said, feeling oddly relieved and pensive. It was just a title. Why did it bother her to let it go? The Tower had been her life, her focus, the path to finding her mother's killer. What was she without it?

Verka shook her head. "It doesn't matter. We need the relics."

Elitsa glanced at Ivo again. She couldn't understand Verka's trust. Why was she so confident the Smoke Eyes would fight? Why wasn't she worried? The gang had never moved against the mages directly before. And even if they were willing to protect their territory, what assurances did Verka have that they would win?

Ivo grinned. "You haven't figured it out yet? Verka works for the king. No one has deeper pockets than him."

"What?" Elitsa looked back at Verka. She'd thought that she must be working for a rich merchant or even a noble, but the king? "Do you mean the queen?"

Verka gave Ivo a displeased look and rapped her fingers against the table. "No, King Dmitrei is my employer."

"He's ... but why?" Conceivable or not, why would the king work with the Smoke Eyes?

"Come on, ferret, I thought you were smart." Ivo tapped his temple. "The king is stealing relics from the Guild."

Verka's mouth thinned. "King Dmitrei is redistributing the balance of power."

"The advisor," Elitsa said slowly. "He really did kill him." That was why Verka was pushing for more relics. The king wanted to stand against the Guild, to show they couldn't control him, but he'd forced their hand. Did he anticipate what would happen to Rivna if he failed? If the Tower chose to attack?

"Ivo will take you to Rosya," Verka said. "Leida has decided to take the cache, but the cartographers have a meeting this evening, so we'll move at first light."

"And the Guild?"

"Still locked in their tower, but we have eyes on them." Verka's gaze was steady. "I'd prefer your help, Elitsa, but we do have your companion, so it's up to you. Though I doubt Leida will release you until this is over."

Elitsa crossed her arms, resentment spreading heat across her chest. "Fight or be caged, is that it? You're not treating me any better than the Guild."

"The difference is you will have the goodwill of King Dmitrei. He will pay you well when this is done and is likely the only person who can remove the Guild's contract against you."

Verka was right. Vilis wouldn't help her now, and if the king lost … well, she doubted that would be good for anyone. The best she could hope for was Verka's plan to work and for the king to gain control of Rivna and the Guild. Besides, if things went sideways, Elitsa had a better chance at escaping in the street than from whatever dark hole Ivo decided to stash her in.

"I'll help, but I'll hold you to your promises."

CHAPTER 22

Elitsa was fairly certain she'd kill for a hot cup of tea. She was going on three days now with minimal sleep, and between the hard floor and Cas's long limbs jabbing into her spine, she'd spent the majority of the night thinking of ways to smother him. Better that than imagining the destruction a hundred mages could rain down on the city.

But an attack never came, the night passing quietly save the snores and restless movements of the seven Smoke Eyes sharing the cramped room. They were in a warehouse south of the docks, the smell of drying fish imbued in the walls. Elitsa guessed it was an hour or two before dawn. She heard the scrape of a door sliding open, so when Ivo stalked into the room and began to wake everyone, she was already up and folding her blanket.

Cas, awakened by Ivo's boot to his ribs, jerked upright with a grunt, a knife he'd procured from somewhere held in his hand. He shoved sleep-tousled hair from his eyes and blinked at the room.

"Morning, sunshine," Elitsa said. "Do you often stab people when you wake?" There wasn't much by way of water to refresh herself, so she roughly ran a hand through her hair and shook out her clothes. When her fingers brushed her Guild pin, she froze, then quickly removed it from her coat collar and shoved it into her pocket. *I don't need that anymore.*

Cas smiled at her, the drowsiness disappearing from his eyes as he lounged back onto his elbows. He looked her over — his slow scrutiny bringing a flutter inside her stomach — teeth catching on the edge of his lip as he slid the knife into his boot. "Only if they deserve it. You look tired. Did you get any sleep?"

The flutter died. "I might have," Elitsa said, narrowing her eyes, "if you hadn't kept jabbing your knee into my kidney. You're worse than Pipene."

"Pipene?" Cas's smile widened.

"Friend of mine." *Who is most definitely mad at me by now.* Elitsa glanced towards Ivo. She needed to get a message to Pipene, but the Smoke Eye was unlikely to let her speak to anyone until after the job.

One of Ivo's men — narrow-shouldered with a scar across his cheek — passed out bruised apples and day-old cornbread. As the man moved to the other side of the room where Ivo was, Elitsa crouched down beside Cas. "How did it look?" she asked quietly.

"The cartographers know how to party." Cas grinned, twisting off the stem from his apple. "No, it was quite boring, actually. I guess the king requested some new maps or something, which is why they were gathering last night, but I only heard a little of their discussion. Leida and I saw the guards — that woman is surprisingly sneaky, for her age — they were dressed like researchers. They seemed more alert than usual; maybe the Tower warned them about the relic thefts? But there were only a handful of them. I don't think they're expecting trouble."

"Do you think they moved the relics and are just making it appear like it's a worthwhile target?"

Cas glanced at her, the apple poised over his lips. "A trap? I do love how your mind works, Eli." His lips curved, the edge of his boot tapping hers. "Could explain why the night was so quiet, though as far as the Guild knows, the Smoke Eyes are unaware the stash is there, right? Seems like a risky waste of resources unless they know for sure what Verka is after."

He was right. Vilis knew Elitsa was helping Verka, but he was still being held underground. He'd only had suspicions before Kirtara, nothing concrete to tell the Tower like he did now. *Why did they try to kill me when I had two days left on my contract?* Was Vilis still lying?

"We'll let Ivo and his friends go first," Cas said. "They have to ensure we're still breathing to disable the door." He bit into the apple, wiping juice off his chin with his sleeve. "Did you get what you wanted from High Mage Vilis?"

What she wanted … funny Cas would phrase it that way. Elitsa took a bite of her cornbread to avoid answering. Vilis had told her more than she'd expected, but what should she do with what he'd told her about her mother? Had Elitsa wasted the past eight years? *Where would I be now if I hadn't become an agent?* She couldn't see herself working for Solveiga like Pipene nor finishing her apprenticeship with Master Davor. What if she'd never experienced magic? Elitsa's thoughts shifted to what Vilis had said about pollution. "Have you ever felt sick after harvesting?"

"Sick?" Cas frowned, tossing the apple core into a corner. "What do you mean?"

"Like—"

Ivo stopped in front of them, anticipation glinting in his gray eyes. "Time to go, ferrets."

"Just waiting on you," Elitsa quipped. Standing up, she shoved the remaining piece of cornbread into her mouth and brushed the crumbs off her hands. She saw Cas watching her, brow still furrowed in question, then he stood up and gave Ivo a jaunty salute.

"If you try to run—" Ivo began.

"We won't." Elitsa held his steely gaze. "We want to be paid just like you do."

Ivo watched her for a moment, then jerked his head at the others.

They left the warehouse through a side door that let out into a dingy alley filled with thick, gray fog. Only hints of the main street were visible, the lamp posts rising like thin trees from the enveloping haze. Elitsa couldn't even see the sky or the tops of the buildings above them. Something clanged in the distance — a hammer on metal? — but the fog quickly swallowed the sound. Per their discussion the night before, they would head for the West Gate then across the barley fields to the Cartographers' Guild.

A dark-haired woman named Fanya went first, slipping out from between the warehouse buildings with a quiet but confident stride. Three men, possibly brothers, followed her; Elitsa hadn't caught their names. Ivo sent Elitsa and Cas next, bringing up the rear with two others. Elitsa didn't like feeling boxed in, but with the bounty on her head, the Smoke Eyes' presence did offer a certain level of protection. *If I can trust them*, she thought, thinking about Ivo at her back.

How much money had the mage guild placed on her? Enough to entice one of the Smoke Eyes to turn her in? Considering the current tension in the city, she probably didn't have to worry about that. No one would risk getting close to the Tower today.

The streets were hushed. It felt like they were alone in the city. Cas, walking beside her, was watching the sides of the buildings. *Did he hear something?* He seemed uneasy, the muscles taut in his jaw. Elitsa's pulse quickened, dancing beneath her skin like a fox-hunted hare. Was that the flutter of fabric? Laundry caught in a breeze? The fog seemed to thicken, snaking between them like white smoke. She looked back at Ivo. The Smoke Eye was staring into the mist, body taut with tension. He reached for his belt.

There was a whistling sound, and something struck Ivo in the side of the head, sending him spinning. Whisper-soft whines filled the air from multiple directions, and then the thud of stone against flesh as the Smoke Eyes started dropping. Elitsa sank into a crouch, spinning around, hand out, not sure who or what to attack. The scent of the fog sharpened, bringing to mind the chilled winds that crossed the surface of the lake, of marsh grasses and melting snow. Someone was burning essence. She reached for her own, but the sound of a bird froze her hand. *Was that one of Solveiga's cygnets?*

Fanya sidestepped one of the projectiles, the stone cracking against the wall of a building with a loud thud. She flung out her hand, the scent of smoke and burning wood pungent in the air, as fire burned a path through the fog. Elitsa heard a sharp exhalation of breath, and the scuff of a boot against stone, the fog swirling as though someone was inside it.

Another whistle from the left and Fanya fell sideways. All the Smoke Eyes were down.

Elitsa felt Cas move, sprinting towards the buildings to their right. He only made it two steps before something struck him in the back. Flying forward, he tucked into a roll, coming up on his knee. He turned, determined eyes looking past her, hand rising, the scent of fire flooding the air, and then a figure rose from the mist at his back and struck him across the head. Cas crumpled onto the ground.

Elitsa winced and then glared at the back of his head. He'd been running away. Was he going to leave her here? The figure behind him moved forward, and Elitsa straightened, heart hammering as she held out her hands non-threateningly. More figures stepped free from the fog, several bending down to check the pulses of the Smoke Eyes on the ground. She could see ten of them, wearing hooded cloaks of black feathers over form-fitting tunics and dark gray trousers. The feathers reminded her of Pipene's cloak, though they were a different color and looked more durable. Why were they dressed like Solveiga's Swans?

"What do you want?" Elitsa demanded, trying to keep everyone in sight. Was this another gang she'd somehow never heard of? Or had the Guild taken to wearing feathered cloaks?

One of the figures tucked a slingshot into their belt as they glanced at the person on their left, then, raising gloved hands to their hood, pushed it back off their head, revealing blond hair tied back into a bun. Though a mask covered their eyes and nose, there was no mistaking Pipene's bruised jaw or her blue eyes. There was a splint on her right wrist and forearm.

"Pipene? What—" Elitsa dropped her hands in confusion.

Pipene's smile was anxious as she stepped forward. "I'll explain, but first we need to go."

Elitsa stared at the others, picking out men and women, some of whom she realized she recognized from the House of Swans. "What's going on, Pipene?" What were they doing here, and why had they attacked the Smoke Eyes?

"Later, I promise." Pipene glanced to the right.

Following her gaze, Elitsa saw black smoke rising into the sky. "What's happened?"

"We have to get off the street. Please come with us, Elitsa. You trust me, don't you?" Pipene grabbed her hand, squeezing her fingers. "Let me take you to Solveiga."

Solveiga … what had Pipene's boss gotten her into? And why had she kept this a secret? Feeling worried and hurt, Elitsa looked down at Cas, still motionless on the ground. She'd thought she might be able to rely on him, but when it came down to it, he was only interested in saving his skin. "All right, Pippe, but then you tell me everything."

CHAPTER 23

Elitsa stared at the pale walls of the king's castle north of them, frowning into the cold wind as her hair blew sideways across her face. The rising sun, breaking through the thick fog, lit the spires atop the slate gray roofs of the towers, making their moon-shaped finials glow gold. From here, at the top of the intake tower, she could see across the trees in the park between them and the castle. To the southwest, smoke still rose into the sky from the Black Eyed Fish that'd caught on fire early that morning. A fire that hadn't spread to the surrounding buildings as a Guild mage had just happened to be in the area. The Tower had struck against the Smoke Eyes, but only a questing blow. *What are they planning?*

Elitsa could feel Pipene staring at her, her friend's brow creased with worry, and she brought her mind back to what she'd told her. "When?" she asked after a moment. How long had Pipene had a secret life? The Pipene she knew abhorred violence, and yet Elitsa was supposed to believe she'd been running around challenging the Smoke Eyes?

"The year when you were apprenticing to that reclamation

agent. I'd been at Solvegia's for two years, and she ... asked me to join."

Elitsa gestured at Pipene's black cloak as the wind ruffled the numerous feathers. "What exactly are the Swans? Are you supposed to be Solveiga's enforcers?"

"We're not like the Smoke Eyes if that's what you're thinking. We're not thieves. We keep the neighborhoods safe, keep Leida and her crew out of the Aerie."

Pipene knows about Leida?

Elitsa frowned as Pipene braced her hands on the stone railing and stared in the direction of the mage guild. "You know the split in the Tower a hundred years ago when a faction of mages was forced out? The mages who left created the Swans. They wanted to share the relics and magic with everyone, not just keep it for themselves."

"You're saying the Swans are mages?"

"A few were." It was Solveiga who answered, stepping out onto the narrow walkway with Irusya. They were both dressed like Pipene, though they'd removed their masks as she had.

Elitsa moved back against the stones beneath the roof's shadow to make room. She'd guessed that some of Solveiga's people held relics — how else could she manage to maintain the Aerie's autonomy from Leida — but Elitsa had never considered they'd come from mages who'd left the Tower. *What else did they share with Solveiga?* "Does the Guild know?"

"No," Solveiga said. "They believed the dissidents, as they called them, had fled beyond their reach."

"Why risk staying here? In Rivna?" Elitsa asked.

"Their — our — mission is still the same. The preservation of life. The Guild is destroying Casekraia, and without our intervention, it is only going to get worse."

Irusya caught Elitsa's eyes, her dark hair — curls braided into a crown — shining as a ray of sunlight touched the tower. "I'm sure you've seen the imbalance in nature through your use of your Tower relics. The weakness in the wind and rain? The disappearing diversity in plant and animal life?"

Elitsa thought back to her conversations with Melnyk and Vilis. *Was everyone aware of it but me?*

"We've been using magic wrong," Irusya said.

"Wrong?" Elitsa frowned. Vilis hadn't said anything about that. "What do you mean?"

Irusya spread her hands, her eyes brightening with enthusiasm. "We didn't always take magic as we do now, harvesting it like grain to store and keep, to trade for money." She gestured at Elitsa's ears, her magesilver visible as the wind blew her hair back from her face. "Our use of magic should be a borrowing, a melding of our essence with that of another — a momentary transfer of energy. Then, when our intention is achieved, we release what we borrowed, allowing the energy to return to the collective. We should only ever take what we need, not stockpile essences like food for winter."

Elitsa touched her earrings, the rings and chains cold beneath her fingers. "Are you saying that mages in the past didn't store essences? What about the Winter War, when the Guild fought the frost wyrms? Without storing essences, they would have been forced to use whatever they had on hand." There would have been no fireballs, something Elitsa would expect was useful for fighting creatures of ice unless the mages had had a torch or fire burning nearby. What Irusya was saying had obvious complications for fighting and defending themselves.

"Harvesting," Solveiga cut in, "is not so much the problem as the storing of it. Do you know how much essence the Guild has locked away? They take more than they need, hoarding it like gems. They could use it to help the city, to keep the fountains running through the winter, but they don't."

Iruysa nodded. "The old war is what first led the Guild to store essence, but they were only kept for a limited time, not like today. We've had peace for hundreds of years. There's no need to harvest in this way. Their claims that they are standing ready in case the wyrms return? It's a lie."

A bird diving down into the surface of the lake caught Elitsa's attention. "The pollution …" she said, thoughtfully. "It's being caused by essence storage."

"Yes," Irusya said.

"You know about the pollution?" Solveiga asked, studying Elitsa closely. "He told you then."

"How …" Elitsa narrowed her eyes, an ache beginning in her chest. "You've been watching me?" How did Solveiga know what Vilis had told her? How did she know him at all?

Pipene nodded, tucking a strand of blonde hair behind her ear. "When you came back to Rivna, once we heard about the contract on you."

"We've been watching High Mage Vilis for longer than that," Solveiga said.

Elitsa frowned, trying to read the expression on Solveiga's face. "You knew my mother …" Realization pricked her skin like shards of ice. "You know how she died, the real reason."

"Yes." There was no guilt in Solveiga's voice, just calm acknowledgment.

Nausea twisted Elitsa's stomach, and she shook her head. *No.* No, if Solveiga knew, that meant that … Anger roared through her like a wildfire. They'd let her hollow herself out for the Guild. "You let me believe Vilis' lie; let me nearly kill myself to join the people responsible for my mother's death!" Her glare swept over Pipene, who shrank back against the railing, eyes brimming with mirrored tears.

"I didn't know, Eli. I swear."

"I couldn't stop you once you set your mind on it," Solveiga said. "Not without drawing Vilis' attention to us. He covered up Branka's death, and I wasn't sure why until I realized he'd stolen her research and had driven you towards the Tower."

"Her research … I never saw her with any relics," Elitsa said, pulling away from the wall to grip the railing. It took every shred of willpower she had to drag her thoughts away from the fury. She wanted to break something, to scream into the cold wind until her throat was raw. Elitsa swallowed, nails scratching at the stone beneath her hands. "What was she doing, then?"

"Branka was trying to figure out a way to cleanse the essence pollution. To make it safer to harvest."

"People will die until we can end the long-term storage of essence," Irusya said. "We can't predict who or where, and unless we can force change inside the Guild, the practice will continue. If we could stop using relics ..." She glanced at Solveiga as if wanting to say something else but instead closed her mouth.

"If you want to end essence harvesting, why not tell everyone about the Night Sickness? About its cause?" Elitsa demanded. Why couldn't her mother have shared this with her? She could have helped. *Why did she keep this secret?*

Solveiga's mouth thinned, and she looked out towards the city. "The Guild would silence us before we could convince anyone of what's happening. Despite the animosity many feel for the Tower, the majority of Rivna's citizens believe what they tell us about essences, about the dangers of uncontrolled magic, even the lands beyond our borders."

If they thought the Guild was too powerful to overcome, what were they even doing here? Why not leave? Solveiga certainly had the money. "So you do nothing?"

Solveiga's eyes chilled like the lake at winter, but it was Irusya who answered.

"We've been working quietly. It can take a long time to change people's minds when they cannot see another way of living. Another path." Irusya put her hand on Solveiga's arm. "To restore Casekraia, we must first erode trust in the Tower."

"This is our goal at the House," Pipene said, her voice soft. "Not all the nobles and merchants who visit us care about the people like we do, but they fear loss of power and money. We have been convincing them that the Guild's leadership will destroy us."

A knot formed in Elitsa's chest. They'd chosen not to tell her. She could forgive her mother, despite the sting, for that's what parents did, after all, try to protect their children. But Pipene? *Did she think I wouldn't care?* The knot tightened. The one person she trusted in the world had let her hunt, vainly, for her mother's killer, had left her wondering who and why, feeling more and more like a failure. Pipene had chosen to leave her in the dark. *She thinks I'm no better than the merchants.* And the worst thing? The worst thing was that maybe she was right.

It was too much. The secrets, the lies, the betrayal, the seemingly unsolvable problems threatening to destroy not just Rivna but all of Casekraia. What could she do? What could any of them do? Elitsa's chest tightened, the pressure expanding until she couldn't breathe.

Brushing past Pipene and Solveiga, she stalked away from them to the other side of the tower where she couldn't see the city, just the dark blue water of the lake and the mountains rising beyond it. She sucked in a breath of cold air, then another, focusing on the icy burn inside her lungs, on the chill against her cheeks. The pressure eased, her emotions slipping one by one into the nothingness.

Elitsa felt Pipene behind her, and looked back over her shoulder.

Pipene flinched, but still took a step forward to stand beside her. "I'm sorry, Eli. I should have told you."

The nothingness frayed, and Elitsa clawed at it, trying to pull the coldness back around her heart. "Why didn't you? How long have you known?"

"A year."

"A year?" Elitsa hissed out a breath and hunched forward, leaning her forearms against the thick railing. Her hurt and guilt welled back up, returning the ache inside her chest. Deserving or not, it still hurt to know what they thought of her, what Pipene thought.

"You were so angry after your mother died, but hunting for her killer gave you purpose, direction. And last year ... being an agent had become everything to you, and I thought ..." Pipene bit her lip and looked away. "I was worried what might happen if you thought the Guild was responsible."

She thought she was protecting me? "I deserved to know, Pipene. Were you planning to keep this from me forever?"

"No, of course not. I just ... You've been so unhappy. I could see the toll reclamations were taking on you and how you were trying to remake yourself into someone else, someone hard and ruthless. And when you started talking about leaving, I felt hope. Hope that you could get away from all of this. You were finally ready to move on, and if I'd told you then ... then you would have stayed."

Elitsa closed her eyes, relief easing her fear. Pipene hadn't given up on her. *But she thought this would break me.* Instead of asking Elitsa for help, including her in whatever plan Solveiga had to stop the Guild from harvesting, she'd left her on the outside. Pipene had left her on the *wrong* side. Elitsa could have died just like her mother had without even knowing why. What was she supposed to do with that?

She straightened, looking past Pipene's worried face to Solveiga and Irusya, who were talking quietly. Why had they brought her here? If Pipene had been trying to protect her, what had changed her mind? *Or had it been Solveiga's decision?* "Why did you bring me here?" Elitsa asked, striding towards them. Pipene's feelings aside, why would Solveiga risk tangling with the Smoke Eyes to rescue one person? And why now, when the Guild and king were on a collision course? "Why risk antagonizing Leida?"

"A child warned us you were there," Irusya said. "They thought you might need help."

"A child?"

"He said his name was Miros."

"Oh." With the unexpected events of the last few days, Elitsa had forgotten about the children she'd tasked to bring her information. "Did he say anything else?"

"No, just ate his weight in sticky buns."

No new Night Sickness deaths then. *Some good news,* Elitsa thought.

"You are one of us," Solveiga said. "You live in the Aerie. As far as why we are here ..." She nodded at the castle. "We've been tasked to help King Dmitrei."

Elitsa barked a laugh, and a look of vexation crossed Solveiga's face. "I'm sorry, you're *also* working for the king?"

"Also?" Pipene moved up beside her, the feathers from her cloak brushing Elitsa's arm. "What do you mean?"

Elitsa glanced at her, a complicated tangle of emotions rising to the surface. She knew she shouldn't be mad at Pipene, but it was there like a sliver in her palm. "Supposedly, I've been helping the king; indirectly anyway." Elitsa crossed her arms, tucking her curled fingers against her sides. "After you were attacked, I started working for a woman, Verka, who's using the Smoke Eyes to gather relics. She claims the king is her employer."

Pipene's brow furrowed.

"Yes," Solveiga said. "The king has several procurers like her throughout the kingdom."

"When I sent you after Orson—" Pipene said.

Elitsa cut her off, not wanting to get into that discussion now. They'd never talked about what happened at the Black Eyed Fish. "Verka claimed, when we first met, that they were trying to help the people by challenging the Tower's authority, but I find it hard to believe that the king is involved. He's hardly shown much concern for the plight of his people and has never fought back before. Is someone else behind this? The queen, or some noble who has King Dmitrei's ear?"

"It is the king's plan," Solveiga said. "He desires to lessen the

Guild's hold on the city, so magic can be shared and not controlled. There is more to him than most realize, but despite his compassion he is still a king, ultimately concerned with his own power and autonomy. The Tower has controlled him since his father died."

Compassion? Elitsa had certainly never thought the king to be cruel, but it was hard to believe he cared about more than having fun. Was this about the people at all or a dangerous scheme to break free of his confinement? *If a man who painted his horses blue can be called confined.* "So he's gathering relics to fight against the Guild."

Solveiga inclined her head. "I don't believe King Dmitrei wants war, but whatever the outcome, I doubt he'll back down. If he loses this battle, it is unlikely he'll have another opportunity. What happens now will define his reign."

And Rivna's future. "Where do you fit in? And the Smoke Eyes, why are they helping him?"

"The Smoke Eyes are in it for the relics and silver," Solveiga said, "and the king's promise that he will allow the legitimization of new guilds."

"Sanctioned relic use outside the Tower," Elitsa breathed. So Verka hadn't lied about that. But what about the Night Sickness? If more people began using relics, they needed to share the dangers.

Irusya nodded. "It would benefit everyone. If we can openly use relics and decide their use, we can move away from harvesting to healing and growing food. We can address the problem of pollution on a larger scale. The king could convince the Guild's scholars to share their research on purification."

The research her mother had been working on. What had Vilis done with it? Did it have something to do with what he was working on with Freythen? "Have you been procuring relics too? How did the king find out about you?"

"He didn't," Solveiga said. "Our history with the Tower has

been a closely kept secret, but when I became aware of what the king was after, I approached him and offered our assistance."

"What was he after?" Elitsa frowned.

"There's a stash in the castle," Pipene broke in, eyes shining with excitement, "and the king doesn't know where it is."

"In the castle?" Elitsa peered across the water at the sun-lit spires.

"A war stash of relics and essence," Solveiga said. "Hidden before the split in the Tower. The king was unaware of it until he came across its mention in his great-grandmother's journal. It's why he's kicked out the Guild mages. He's hoping to find it before they do."

"The Guild knew it was there?"

"Yes, but not where. And, as they didn't want King Dmitrei to know about it, they could do no more than cursory searches."

A hidden war stash? How did it compare to what they'd found in the White Forest? If the Guild wanted it, it had to be big. *Which means, they won't stay out of the castle for long.* "So you're going to help him find it before the Guild does?"

"We're going to find it before either of them do," Solveiga said. "We can't be certain what the king will do, so we need to locate the stash ourselves before this ends in war."

The Swans wanted to break into the castle? Elitsa eyed them each in turn but found no levity in their expressions. She pinched the bridge of her nose. This sounded like one of her and Pipene's games from when they were children. Taking relics from guild-halls was one thing, but getting past the king's guards? And what would they do with the cache if they found it? Sneak it out piece by piece? They wouldn't just have to worry about the king, but the Tower and Smoke Eyes as well. "There has to be more to this," Elitsa said, shaking her head. "You're gambling with treason."

Irusya put her hand on Solveiga's arm. "There is a powerful relic with the war stash that can open portals to other worlds. I know how that sounds, but it's true. We can't let the king or the

Guild find it. I ... we were tasked, by the mages who founded us, to keep it hidden."

"Portals." Elitsa looked at Pipene in disbelief.

"Isn't it exciting?" Pipene said.

"Or farfetched. Wouldn't we have heard about it before? Seen some kind of sign?" Elitsa gestured at the sky and the unseen stars above.

Pipene's smile broadened. "As inconceivable as the frost wyrms that crossed the Crystal Sea and attacked Casekraia? We believe that, even though the only traces are large bones in the forest."

"Yes, well, perhaps we shouldn't. We have proof that the Guild lies." Elitsa looked at Solveiga and Irusya. They didn't appear irritated by her reluctance, more judicious, as if they were waiting to see what she'd do.

This was all so ridiculous, fanciful, like the myth of King Crow, a bird with a wealth of relics who used magic. Pipene had always been the one who'd dreamed of grand adventures and mysterious plots. Those stories had been fun for a while, but life wasn't some grand adventure. It was cold and hard. It was about survival, and this ... this felt precarious and dangerous and every sensible thought in her head was telling her not to get involved. They couldn't take on the Guild and the king.

"What's wrong?" Pipene touched her shoulder, brow furrowed in concern.

"I ... I can't get involved in this." Elitsa took a step back. How funny it was that the hurt she'd felt at being excluded had been replaced with the need to get away. But they hadn't asked her to help, had they. They'd told her what was going on, their plan, but not once had anyone asked if she would help. *They thought they were rescuing me, for Pipene.* They didn't need her, not really, and with her career over and the mystery of her mother's death solved, what was left? She wouldn't be able to convince Pipene to leave with her. She had a place, a purpose, a family. All Elitsa could offer was more danger and attention from the Guild.

Brushing past Irusya, Elitsa wrenched open the tower door and started down the spiraling staircase. Several of the Swans who'd retrieved her were standing on the stairs, and she had to squeeze past them, avoiding their curious looks as she rushed to get outside.

"Elitsa! Wait!"

Elitsa halted on the landing, mere steps from the door that led outside, and looked back. Pipene was hurrying down after her, her feathered cloak fluttering behind her like a sail. "Pipene, I don't—"

"Here." Pipene pressed a pouch of coins into Elitsa's hand and curled her fingers around it. "I know how you feel about taking money, but I want you to have this. I've been saving." She smiled as Elitsa opened her mouth to protest. "Don't worry, it's not *all* I have, but this is enough to get you started somewhere. You'll need it. Please, Eli, let me help."

"You're not going to ask me to stay?" Elitsa nodded up the stairs. "To help the king?" A part of her wished she would.

"We both know no one can make you do what you don't want to." Pipene smiled, her eyes bright with unshed tears, but before Elitsa could say anything, she shook her head. "No, if you need to get away, I want to help you. You're smart and strong, and I know you haven't figured out what you want to do yet, but I'm certain you'll find the perfect place. Just send me a letter whenever you get settled, so I know you're alright."

The ache returned to her chest, and Elitsa tightened her fingers around the pouch. She needed to find a new path, and it was clear it wasn't here in Rivna. *If I stay, I'll endanger them all.* "What about you? Pipene, if the Guild and king go to war, you could be killed. And this plan to rob the castle? Have you thought this through?" *You could come with me.* But she didn't say the words aloud.

"I'm a Swan, Eli." Pipene's smile wavered. "I wish I could go see the world with you, have one of those adventures we've always talked about, but Solveiga needs me. If there's fighting, I can help protect those who don't have relics."

Elitsa searched her face. "Does Solveiga have something on you? Is she making you do this?"

"No, of course not. I chose to help. Solveiga has done a lot for me and Rivna." Pipene hugged her suddenly, arms tight across Elitsa's back.

How different our paths have been, Elitsa mused, heart aching. All this time, she'd thought she was the one setting her sights high, following a noble calling. *Pipene never lost herself, like I did.*

"Take care of yourself, Eli." When Pipene let go, there were tears on her cheeks, but she still smiled brightly. Sniffling, she squeezed Elitsa's arm then hurried back up the stairs.

The ache spread, knotting the muscles across her chest and shoulders. Elitsa shoved the money pouch into her coat and opened the door, stepping out onto the stone bridge that connected the intake tower to the shore. She began to walk briskly towards the park. She had to get outside the gate, head south maybe, towards Tristi, but the further she got from the intake tower behind her, the heavier her feet felt.

Elitsa slowed, eyes on the expanse of green lawn ahead of her. She looked to her right towards the castle. Pipene was going to go in there, with only a handful of Swans at her back. *I can't let her do this alone, whether she wants my help or not.* Pipene was her family. Whatever secrets she'd kept, and whoever she owed loyalty to now, Elitsa couldn't abandon her. For what, anyway? A life of running, taking whatever job she could find? Pipene was willing to risk her life for the people of Rivna, and though Elitsa couldn't say she felt the same, she would do anything to ensure Pipene's safety.

And what about Orson and Sofija? When the tower split a hundred years ago, there'd been fires in the city and essence-fueled fights that'd killed civilians. How much worse would it be if the Guild fought the Smoke Eyes?

Maybe they wouldn't succeed, and Verka and Solveiga's plans would fail, but if the king could regain control of Rivna and Casekraia, then this was likely the only way the Guild would be held accountable for her mother's death. *And the deaths of all the agents before me.* She still had no idea why they were being killed.

Setting her jaw, Elitsa spun around and marched back to the intake tower. Crossing the narrow bridge, she jerked open the door, startling one of the Swans who was crossing the landing. His alarm shifted to curiosity, and he gave her a small nod before continuing past to the stairs that headed down. More Swans followed on his heels, and Elitsa had to step sideways along the wall to enter the tower.

"Back again?" Solveiga appeared on the stairs, followed by Irusya.

The taller woman smiled, seemingly pleased she'd returned. "Elitsa, we are glad you are here," Irusya said warmly. Her words mattered more than they should.

"I've decided to help." Elitsa looked for Pipene but didn't see her. "Where are you going?"

Irusya nodded towards the descending stairs. "There's a tunnel at the base of the intake tower that carries water into the castle."

"You're planning on swimming?"

Solveiga's lips curved. "No need. A secret passageway was added during its construction as an escape route for the royal family. Surprisingly King Dmitrei is unaware of it. One more thing lost to time."

"Does the Guild know?"

"We don't believe so, but we'll guard our exit just in case."

"And if the king finds us?"

"He is expecting our help, but he won't be thrilled to discover us inside without permission, which is why we're aiming to avoid detection."

Elitsa's stomach twinged nervously. As little thought as she'd given the king all these years, the idea of sneaking into the royal castle filled her stomach with butterflies. "Do you know what we're looking for?"

"The castle is built atop a warren of tunnels," Solveiga said, starting down the stairs after Irusya, "some that extend out beneath the lake itself."

"Tunnels? Like crypts?"

"Some are probably used as vaults for the royal family. According to our records, there are natural caverns beneath the foundation, bisected by tunnels left behind by the ice wyrms, and someone — one of our kings or queens in the past — used them to create secret rooms."

"Wyrms ... aren't they depicted with wings?"

"They have different stages," Irusya called back, "like many insects; if the accounts are true, that is." She cleared her throat. "Some of the tunnels were likely used as storerooms, but I expect they'll be covered in dust and cobwebs now."

"The king is unaware of them too?"

"No, he knows about them," Solveiga said, "but they are numerous, and right now, his attention is on the upper floors of the castle."

Irusya, steadying herself with a hand on the wall, glanced back up at Elitsa. "The Queen Dowager referred to the war cache as being hidden by the King's Mirror. King Dmitrei thinks that means it's in the palace."

"But you don't," Elitsa said. They'd reached the bottom of the tower, where a complicated array of pipes and valves took up space in the center of the stone floor. Pipene leaned out from a slim doorway in the wall across from them, holding a lantern. Her blue eyes brightened as she caught sight of Elitsa, and Elitsa felt her heart warm. She was glad she'd come back.

"If it was in the castle," Solveiga said, nodding at Pipene, "he would have found it already, or the Guild would have. The only place it can be is somewhere below."

"And the King's Mirror? What do you think that means?"

"We don't know what it means," Solveiga admitted, brows pinching in irritation. "But we have a delving trick that locates essence. If something is down there, we'll find it."

"It's a bit like stitching wounds in the dark," Irusya said, "but we're out of time."

"And if the cache isn't here?" Elitsa asked.

Irusya shook her head. "It's here."

Pipene slipped out of the doorway to stand beside Elitsa, making room for Solveiga and Irusya to enter the dark passageway.

Looking past them, Elitsa saw several of the Swans ahead, carrying small lanterns that illuminated a slightly curved wall. It looked wet in places, as though water was seeping through the stone. A rusty metal grate had been laid down on the floor, providing a narrow but flat surface to walk on.

Elitsa looked back up towards the stairs, where it spiraled high overhead. It was like standing in the bottom of a deep pit. "Are we the last?"

"Solveiga left Taisa and Maks at the top of the tower to keep watch, but we're the last going into the castle." Pipene gestured for Elitsa to enter the tunnel, then ducked in after her, pulling shut the metal door.

The darkness deepened, Pipene's lantern casting shadows on the wall. Elitsa could hear the drip of water, and smelled the earthy scent of things left to rot and decay. The air smelled older than the tunnels beneath Rivna, as though it hadn't been used in quite a long time.

"It's kind of exciting, isn't it?" Pipene said, the glow from her lantern reflecting in her eyes. "Sneaking into the castle. I've always wondered what it looks like inside!"

"Yes," Elitsa said dryly, "I'm sure the secret underground tunnels are quite lovely."

Pipene laughed and reached for Elitsa's hand. "I'm glad you came back, Eli. I should have told you about your mother as soon as I found out. I am so sorry. I hated feeling like we were on opposite sides."

A rush of relief and affection softened the hollow inside her chest, and Elitsa squeezed Pipene's fingers. She was not alone. Not as long as she had Pipene. "Me too. I kept parts of my life from you too; it just … it never felt like a world I wanted to bring you into."

"I understand. No more trying to protect each other, all right? Unless it's from actual physical danger of course."

Elitsa smiled. "Deal."

CHAPTER 24

T he secret tunnel opened up into a room where fresh
water entered the castle, with a pump and thick pipes
running up into the rough stone ceiling overhead.
Closing the tunnel's hidden door — a heavy slab of stone that
blended seamlessly into the wall — they left the chamber, stepping through an open archway into a massive stone cavern with
curved sides. Smaller tunnels and corridors disappeared into
darkness in the rocky wall across from them.

As the Swans gathered around Solveiga and Irusya, Elitsa
paused by the wall, resting her palm against the rough stone.
Something had clearly tunneled through the earth here, leaving a
strange sideways diamond pattern, offset every few paces as if
whatever made the imprint had been slowly twisting. She shuddered, trying to imagine the frost wyrm as it moved through the
ground beneath the castle. *How had it not destroyed Rivna?*

"We'll leave where we entered," Solveiga said, raised voice
drawing Elitsa back to the others. "So make sure you can get back
here." She held up a piece of white chalk. "We'll search in
different directions in teams of two. As we have no map, mark
the ground at each fork with the number of paths back to

prevent getting lost. If you search a room, draw a line across the threshold to indicate it's been explored. We're looking for hidden doors or hollows in the rock, places where the cache could be located."

"Or a door that says 'secret stash here!'?" The woman who'd spoken had a round, pale face and a purple ribbon braided through her red hair. She grinned as laughter rippled through the chamber.

Irusya laughed, the lantern shaking in her hand.

Solveiga raised an eyebrow, but she seemed amused. "Keep to the west and north, areas that are below the castle. The lake is off that way …" She gestured down a branching of tunnels to Elitsa's right. "We can't be sure how safe the rooms are in that direction, and what we're looking for is more likely to be beneath the castle grounds than the lake."

The Swans nodded, a few exchanging whispered words with each other.

"And it goes without saying to be as quiet as possible," Solveiga continued. "I'd prefer not to leave any traces that we were here, but speed is the priority, so let's get to work."

"And if the kings' guards find us?" a tall woman asked with long black hair hanging in a braid down her back. Her feathered cloak looked dirty on one shoulder, perhaps from brushing against the tunnel's wall when she'd entered, and Elitsa resisted the urge to reach out and wipe it off.

"Hide, if you can, and if that's not possible, tell them you are here by order of the king." Solveiga's smile was self-assured. "King Dmitrei has already tasked us to find the cache, so our presence here is not entirely unsanctioned." She started passing out the chalk, giving one to Elitsa and Pipene.

"Want to team up?" Pipene grinned.

Elitsa nodded at a young man with brown hair streaked with blond. "I thought I'd ask him, actually."

Pipene rolled her eyes and shoved Elitsa's shoulder. "Yeah,

right. You don't even know his name! Come on. I don't want to pass up this opportunity to explore and find lost treasure."

"We're more likely to find old bones and water damage," Elitsa said, thinking of the deep lake somewhere above their heads.

"Maybe, but still more fun than stealing relics for the Smoke Eyes, no?"

Elitsa pursed her lips, allowing Pipene to pull her towards one of the dark tunnels ahead of them. As they entered the hall with their lantern, she thought about Cas, briefly wondering what Leida and Verka would do when they found Elitsa gone. Who would they think had taken her? Would they blame Cas for her escape? They could still carry out the job with his help. *He'll be fine*, she thought, annoyed that she was thinking about him at all.

They passed an opening to their left that seemed to be just a short connecting chamber to a pathway opposite, through which they glimpsed another team. "Not that way then," Pipene said, bending over to draw a chalk line across the entrance. Continuing on, the path curved towards the right, then split into two. Pipene chose the right-most hall to put some distance between them and the others and drew the number one on the floor.

It was hard to track the passage of time as they searched the warren of tunnels, the darkness absolute, broken only by their lantern. They found a room that seemed to have promise with a wall that looked just a little too clean for the grime in the rest of the room but delving revealed no strong essences on the other side. They found broken doors with rusted hinges and others sealed beyond repair, rooms with nothing but dust and tiny bones and one small but pretty crystal formation that shimmered with iridescence when their light reflected upon the ceiling above. One series of rooms felt warmer than the others, and Pipene shoved her cloak back behind her shoulder, complaining about the lack of a breeze.

Wiping sweat off her forehead with her sleeve, Elitsa picked a new direction for their search. It was impossible to tell where they were in relation to the castle above, but the corridors began to look more cared for, the walls smooth stone, bearing signs of the workers and mages who'd built the tower. "I think we've entered the castle's foundations," Elitsa said. Passing through a room with arching ceilings and heavy pillars, they heard Solveiga's voice in a room ahead of them.

"Oh good," Pipene said, "maybe they've found—"

Elitsa stopped dead in the doorway, alarm rising through her body as she caught Pipene's arm. Solveiga and Irusya weren't alone; they were facing two of the king's guards.

One of them — a bearded man in his fifties with hard brown eyes and a downturned mouth — snapped his head in their direction, his hand tightening on the hilt of the short sword at his waist. He was dressed like the city watch, though his overcoat was dark green instead of gray, with silver embroidery along the tops of his shoulders. Pinned above the king's sigil on his left breast was a large, magesilver medallion, the metal rods curving up over his shoulder like splayed rib bones.

"Everything all right?" Pipene asked cautiously.

"Stay where you are," the bearded guard barked.

"As I said, Captain," Solveiga said in a calm voice, "I have a team working with me."

Captain? Elitsa glanced at the scowling man's collar and saw a small silver sword pinned to the fabric.

"King Dmitrei did not advise me of your presence here, *Mistress* Solveiga."

"Our task is sensitive. Take me to Marshall Oles or King Dmitrei. They know me and will confirm what I've told you."

The captain exchanged a look with his companion, a woman with pale skin and short blonde hair.

"I believe Marshall Oles is a client of the House of Swans, sir," the second guard murmured. Her deep green eyes were decidedly more friendly than the captain's.

Irusya lifted her chin. "We haven't done anything threatening, have we? And we're certainly not carrying anything dangerous."

"You are trespassing," the captain said. "And I am concerned that you have entered without the guard knowing. We will speak with Marshall Oles. And you two." He glowered at Pipene and Elitsa. "You will come as well. Leave your lanterns."

"This way," the younger guard said.

The captain gestured Solveiga and Irusya forward, followed by Elitsa and Pipene, then took up the rear, his hand firmly on the hilt of his sword. "Run out of feathers for your cloak?" he asked.

Elitsa glanced back and saw the captain was watching her shrewdly, probably wondering why she was the only one not wearing black. "Never had one," she said.

The captain narrowed his eyes, and Elitsa looked away, her heart thumping. Did he recognize her somehow as a reclamation agent? She couldn't remember ever crossing his path before.

The guards led them into a dim hall and then up a flight of stairs through a heavy wooden door that'd been left open. Here lightprisms were attached to the walls, and they passed a guard sitting and reading. He jumped up off the wooden bench, his book hitting the floor as he snapped to attention.

Elitsa winced at the fallen book, a memory of her mother's horror when she'd once folded a novel's page to mark her place.

Leaving the blushing guard behind, they entered a room with several narrow cells, then passed through a hall of storerooms to another broader staircase that spiraled up to what Elitsa guessed was the castle's main floor. The pale gray stone was polished, the floor overlaid with wood tiles arranged in geometric patterns. There were more lightprisms here high on the walls, and lead glass windows let in a measure of light from the cloudy sky outside.

Taking the lead, the captain marched them past several attendants — wearing white tunics and gray skirts or trousers — to a wide hallway, carpeted in red. Huge framed paintings covered the wall, a mix of colorful landscapes and gilded portraits. Elitsa craned her head to look at them as they crossed to a closed set of doors. The captain rapped his knuckles on the wood, listened, then opened the door, striding in and leaving the second guard to ensure they followed.

The room was four or five times larger than Elitsa's apartment, with high ceilings and massive windows that opened onto a balcony. Through the glass of the gold-framed doors, carved with climbing roses, she could see the dark blue water of the lake and the snow-capped mountains beyond.

Tearing her eyes away from the incredible view, Elitsa took in what had to be an audience chamber. Surely this was too grand for the marshall's office. There was a deep blue rug covering much of the floor and elegant dark-wood furniture, the sides carved into an intricate design of blooming flowers and forest creatures. On a table, between the armchairs facing the window, was a stack of leather-bound books and a tray with the remains of a recent meal. Framed art and portraits hung on the wall and … and there was a lean figure standing beside a desk near the wall, staring at Elitsa and the others. Her stomach dropped.

"Your majesty," the captain said, surprise in his voice. "Forgive me, my king. I was seeking the marshall." Clasping his fist against his chest, he bowed his head, the other guard immediately following suit.

Lanky and narrow-shouldered, the king was even more colorful up close than the distant glimpses of him Elitsa had seen. His dark brown hair was tousled and flecked with what she assumed was blue paint — remnants of some art project? — and his smiling lips were painted a soft shimmering orange-pink, like the shade of a sunrise. He had a sharp chin and sharper cheekbones. She could see intelligence in his greenish-brown eyes and a feeling of welcome, almost as if he were glad of their interruption. His long, rich blue coat, embroidered with gold suns and silver moons, hung open over a slightly rumpled tunic and trousers. Blue paint, like what speckled his hair, smeared across the left toe of his shiny black boot.

King Dmitrei closed the book in his hands with a loud snap, then thumped it down on the table. He rushed forward, and for a brief, horrifying moment, Elitsa thought he meant to hug them, but he skidded to a stop an arm's length away, examining their faces with eager intensity.

Pipene made a soft exhalation and gripped Elitsa's hand, her fingernails pressing into her skin.

"Captain Nazar!" The king's voice was soft and playful, and though Elitsa had no trouble hearing him, she felt herself lean forward as though drawn by his cheerful tones. "Are these the rats that tripped our alarm?"

Alarm? Elitsa thought with a spike of curiosity. She'd seen no tripwires or alarm devices. Could he have used an essence somehow to alert the guard to movement below the castle?

"Yes, sire," the captain said, straightening. Surprisingly he seemed to treat the king with respect, not as though he were merely tolerating his presence. It was a different attitude than what she'd experienced in the Tower.

"Your Highness." Solveiga bowed, crossing her right leg over the other and laying a hand over her heart.

Irusya gave the king a warm smile and bowed deeply.

Elitsa and Pipene hastily copied their movements.

"Forgive the intrusion," Solveiga said. "I was eager to get to work, as you requested."

"Mistress Solveiga. And your lovely wife, Irusya! As effervescent as ever." The king beamed, smiling at Irusya, who actually seemed to blush, then reached for Solveiga's hands. Instead of the desirous look people often gave her, he seemed to be looking at her with genuine affection. Almost as if they were friends. "Have you charmed your way into obtaining the veiling powers of the mists? I expected you to come through the front gate, not appear beneath my foundation like a ghost. How did you get past my guard?"

Elitsa tensed, waiting for the stormcloud of displeasure, but the king seemed … amused, not angry. *Does he trust so easily?* If so, she could understand why the Guild had controlled him for so long. What had changed his mind?

Solveiga smiled, squeezing the king's long-fingered hands. "Through the intake tower, Your Highness. Our mission is of the utmost priority to me, as it is to all Casekraians, and I did not wish to burden you until I knew whether the passage was a true vulnerability."

The king pursed his lips and arched an eyebrow, eyes dancing. "A secret passage, and just beneath my nose this whole time. Captain Nazar, have the passage seen to immediately."

Nose and ears reddening, the captain turned to the younger guard and issued a quick series of commands.

The guard clasped her hand over her heart then bowed deeply to the king before quickly leaving the room.

"Are there more of you?" the king asked, eyes moving again over Elitsa and Pipene. He stared at Elitsa's face until she felt a blush begin in her cheeks. "I love your hair," he said, eyes sparkling. "It's fierce and daring."

He … what? Elitsa exchanged a confused look with Pipene. Her hair was short, but she'd always just thought it practical, nothing more. She stared into the king's friendly eyes, unable to look away, and saw the man behind the title. This was him, spirited and vibrant, but there was a cunning there too. *He's letting us underestimate him. See what we want.*

"Nine others, Your Highness," Solveiga said.

Releasing her hands, the king sat down in the chair behind him. He spread out, draping his arms along its winged sides, and tilted his head, giving Solveiga an appraising look. "You have always been a bit presumptuous, appearing without warning." His voice was dry with a dangerous edge. "I do admire your delicious abandon, Mistress Solveiga, but it would not do to presume *too* much."

Solveiga lowered her head in mock-chagrin, a smile playing at the corners of her mouth. "Forgive my impetuousness, sire." Her voice was soothing, lacking any tension or worry over the king's apparent censure. How many times had they had this conversation? "With the recent movements of the Guild, I worried we were running out of time."

Mention of the Tower seemed to steal some of the mischievous light from the king's face, and he looked toward the doors to the hall, brow furrowing thoughtfully. "So? Have you found it?"

Straightening, Solveiga glanced sideways at Irusya. "Not yet, Your Highness. But Irusya and I are confident it is here."

"Thanks to your mysterious source from the Guild," the king said. "I admit I am dying to know who this person is." He pursed his lips. "But I will allow you this secret." Turning his head to the right, he stared at a point high on the wall.

Elitsa followed his gaze and saw a large gold-framed portrait of a woman in her late years in a pale blue dress with a jeweled crown atop her head. Her face was in profile, her white hair braided into a coil at the base of her neck. Was this the Queen Dowager Irusya had mentioned? Why hadn't she given more useful clues in her journal, and why did no one seem to be aware of the cache's location? It seemed rather crucial to be able to locate the royal reserve. *Why didn't you explain what the King's Mirror was?* Elitsa thought.

The king stood up, face surprisingly somber as he looked back at Solveiga. "I have always admired you Solveiga, and I allowed you into my confidence not only because of Verka's assurance that your influence within the city is on par with that of the Smoke Eyes, unscrupulous though they may be, and I believe that your skills and, should we say, ingenuity will help me unlock the mystery of my missing cache. You know what is at stake ..."

Elitsa listened with half an ear as the king reminded Solveiga that without the cache, Casekraia would continue to deteriorate beneath the Guild's control. His tone reminded her of Master Davor's lectures, meant to stoke her guilt and commitment to her apprenticeship. Though she knew she should listen, she let her gaze drift towards the windows. What was the King's Mirror? If it was as simple as an actual mirror, the king would have likely found the cache by now. *Could it refer to something that looks like a mirror? A location?*

She took a step towards the balcony, staring at the surface of the lake, the blue darkened by the graying sky overhead. The wind had died down, the water rippling as the waves softened. Then, as if someone had run a hand over its surface, the lake smoothed, the mountains reflected in the dark glossy water. Elitsa stared, transfixed by the stillness, then the wind started back up again, disturbing the reflection. The windows rattled slightly as the air pushed against them, and she blinked. The lake had been so smooth, almost like glass, almost like ... *Almost like a mirror.*

Heart thumping, Elitsa took another step forward, tuning out the sound of the king's voice. She heard Pipene whisper something, but she was too focused to hear what she said. *Could the lake be the King's Mirror?* It could be seen from his office, and Solveiga had said the tunnels extended out beneath it. Perhaps the war cache was somewhere under it, which meant they'd been searching in the wrong direction.

Awareness raised the hair on the back of her neck, and Elitsa turned her head. The queen was standing beside her. Heart stopping, confusion, and embarrassment rushed heat into her cheeks. Where had the woman come from, and how had Elitsa not heard her arrival?

A woman of soft curves in contrast to the king's sharpness,

Queen Nefeli was the picture of composed elegance. There was no hint of gaiety in her square-shaped face. Dark brown eyes sat beneath slashing brows, and her wavy brown hair, half-pinned back from her face, was draped over one shoulder. Unlike her husband, she wore her crown atop her head — a silver circlet with turquoise gems from Kreanos. A daring amount of tawny beige skin was revealed by the deep cut of her neckline, a gauzy blue dress visible beneath a long-sleeved overcoat in dove gray. Embroidery that reminded Elitsa of waves ran from the end of her sleeve, up her shoulder to the rounded high-necked collar. A silver necklace gathered high in the hollow of her bared throat dangled several long chains of varying lengths upon which hung silver birds and black pearls.

"Queen Nefeli," Elitsa said stiffly, making a belated and embarrassingly awkward bow. She'd thought the queen avoided the king's company, at least that was the gossip on the street. What had brought her into the office?

As she rose, the king bounded up beside them, grinning out at the lake. "It is a beautiful view, isn't it! It often steals my breath." He laid a hand against his chest, cheeks flushed pink, and stared as though lost in his thoughts.

The queen, despite her stern expression, inclined her head. "It is striking, my king." Her voice was lower than King Dmitrei's, her words more pronounced and clear.

Elitsa took a careful step back, closer to Pipene and Irusya, trying to distance herself from the royal couple.

Irusya, catching her eyes, gave her a sympathetic smile.

Seemingly transfixed by the view, the king continued to stare out the window.

Solveiga softly cleared her throat. "Let us return to our task, Your Highness. I would like to check in with my people. Perhaps they've found something."

King Dmitrei spun, eyes shining with excitement. "Yes! Of

course. I will have Captain Nazar send an escort with you to assist in your search. The cache must be found tonight."

The queen clasped her hands in front of her, draping ringed fingers over faint scars on her left hand. "Perhaps, we may also provide them with food and water, my king?"

The king nodded, eyes softening as he looked at the queen. "An excellent idea. Captain, see to it that they have whatever they require."

"As this may be a long day," the queen said, "I will speak to Steward Belov to prepare spare rooms. There should be no need for our guests to retire elsewhere while the search is ongoing."

"Yes!" The king smiled at her with admiration, and Nefeli almost looked pleased. "An excellent idea, Nefeli! We certainly have the space."

They respect each other, Elitsa thought, surprised as she watched the royal couple closely. Rivna, it seemed, was so distracted by what they thought they knew about Dmitrei and Nefeli that no one bothered to look beneath the surface. *We've dismissed them, but they are more complex than we give them credit for.*

She narrowed her eyes at the queen. *Complex and clever.* Was Nefeli being helpful, or had she effectively made them all prisoners? *What will happen if we don't find the cache?*

"Thank you, Your Majesties," Solveiga said, bowing deeply. "You are too kind. We will not disappoint you."

The queen's hawk-eyed gaze suggested they better not. Turning her back on them in obvious dismissal, Queen Nefeli caught the king's attention with a light tap on his arm. "I would like to speak with you, my husband," she murmured.

King Dmitrei cocked his head, lips still caught in a smile. "Yes? Of course, Nefeli." Looking back at Solveiga and the others, his face brightened like the burst of sunlight after dawn. "Happy hunting, Mistress Solveiga!" he called, flapping his hand in the direction of the door. "I eagerly anticipate your success."

This mask of exaggerated merriment is all the Tower sees, Elitsa thought, bowing along with Solveiga and the others. It was a weapon, just as much as Elitsa's size was hers.

The captain, face pinched with barely concealed displeasure, gestured at the door, likely disappointed he wasn't taking them on a trip to a prison cell.

Elitsa glanced back at the king and queen, who had stepped out onto the balcony. They were speaking, their heads close together. *What are they up to?* Unable to overhear their words, she looked past them to the lake. The cache is what she needed to focus on. *Could I be right about the King's Mirror?* Tearing her eyes away from the lake, Elitsa followed the others into the hall and down underground.

They were a procession by the time they reached the bottom floor, their ranks swelled by the king's soldiers. One of the Swans — the woman with the purple ribbon in her hair — was waiting in the vaulted room with a guard, her tense expression softening at seeing Solveiga and the others. "Is everything all right, Solveiga?" the woman asked, eyes skipping from soldier to soldier as they filed into the room around them. The guard beside her, a gray-haired man with a vaguely badger-like look to him, nodded at one of the arrivals — a young woman who Elitsa guessed was a relation.

Solveiga let go of Irusya's hand, though her wife didn't seem to notice. Irusya was watching the guards with a tense expression. *She's probably worried about the relic she was looking for.*

"We are fine, Dita," Solveiga said. "Has anyone found anything?"

Dita shook her head, though Elitsa noticed her fingers twitch by her thigh. "Not yet." Was she communicating with Solveiga?

Eyes slanting down to Solviega's hand, Elitsa saw her make a similar gesture with her fingers. Whatever they were saying to each other, Dita seemed to gain confidence.

"Listen up!" Captain Nazar said, making eye contact with a handful of his guards. "Anyone in a feathered cloak is here at the king's behest, and I want at least one guard per team. We are searching for a reserve of relics, hidden somewhere in these tunnels, and they will be assisting us." He glanced at Solveiga and Irusya. "They will be using essences to delve for the cache but remain alert."

Elitsa glanced at the assembled guards. Did Captain Nazar think the Swans would try to attack them? She'd noticed iron torches on the walls, but the guards hadn't lit any of them. Instead they carried handheld lightprisms with metal rings and thick glass sides. *Better to be safe than sorry*, she thought, thinking of the Tower.

"Check in every two hours, and report to Lieutenant Inta here, if you discover anything." He nodded at a short figure beside him with braided blonde hair and tawny skin, holding a notebook. Beside them, someone had hung a lantern from a tall metal stand. "I will be conferring with Marshall Oles. Guardian Lapina, you are with Mistress Solveiga." He nodded at a dark-haired man in uniform. "And Guardian Priede, you're with these two here."

A woman with warm brown skin and black hair, braided and pinned at the back of her head, turned to look at Elitsa and Pipene, who'd slipped over to talk to Solveiga. As the captain and guards headed into the tunnels, Pipene slipped back to Elitsa's side.

"Aren't the Swans going to be alarmed if the guards find them?" Elitsa asked as Solveiga and Irusya left with Guardian Lapina.

Pipene gestured at Solveiga. "That's why Solveiga and Irusya are heading back to the intake tunnel. If anyone tries to slip away, that's where they'll go, and Solveiga can tell them what's going on." She glanced at Lieutenant Inta, who was talking to Guardian Priede and another guard with a thick scar running up the back of their neck into close-cropped hair.

"Should we pick a new direction?" Pipene asked, removing

her chalk from a dark gray belt wrapping her waist. She grimaced at the powder on her fingers.

"I think we should search in the direction of the lake," Elitsa said.

"You sure?"

"Yes, I think ..." Elitsa trailed off as Guardian Priede headed their way, holding a lantern. Priede had a short sword, like all of the guards, and was wearing a magesilver ring on her thumb.

"Greetings," Priede said, making eye contact with both of them. "I'm Priede, I've been assigned to help you."

Pipene smiled warmly. "I'm Pipene, and this is Elitsa."

Priede returned the smile, though a touch cautiously as if she wasn't quite certain what to make of them. "Should we begin?"

"Yes!" Pipene turned to Elitsa, eyeing the dark tunnels that branched off from the vaulted room. "So ... do you remember how we got here?"

CHAPTER 25

"O k," Pipene said, brandishing her chalk. "We think the lake is that way?" They'd returned to the immense cavern with the diamond pattern on the walls and followed the rounded tunnel in what they thought was northeast, away from the castle's foundation. After discovering an old cave-in of dark gray earth and shale, they backtracked to a branching set of smaller tunnels.

"Should we turn back?" Priede asked behind them, her voice uncertain. "The ceiling could collapse on us like the tunnel." Her nostrils flared, her brows knotting over her gold-brown eyes, as she held her lantern close to the wall. "Aren't we beneath the lake here?"

Elitsa glanced back, raising her lantern. "The tunnels are old, but the walls look solid. I think if it were going to collapse, it would have flooded a long time ago." She looked at Pipene, who was staring at the ceiling. "Here, I can check." Passing her the lantern, Elitsa pulled the essences of earth and yarrow — a grass-lands plant with a savory, herby scent — from earrings in her left ear and combined them to expand her awareness into the rough stone above their heads. She imagined that she could see through the expanse of earth and rock, relaxing her vision until she saw past what was in front of her. The colors were dark and deep, save several shapes of lighter gray — small stones or bones trapped in the earth, perhaps? — and Elitsa couldn't see their end. If the deep, dark waters of Lake Odarka were indeed above them, she didn't think it could easily leak through.

Releasing a slow breath, Elitsa let the essences she'd used for delving dissipate into the space around them. "We should be fine," she said. "And I can say with certainty that the cache is not above us."

Pipene laughed, and Priede actually cracked a smile. "Onward!" Pipene said, raising the lantern and chalk. "I want to be the first to find it."

"IT'S ANOTHER DEAD END," PIPENE SIGHED, BLOWING A LOCK OF hair out of her face. Groaning, she walked several steps back down the hall toward Priede, who'd lost her informal stiffness and was leaning against the wall drinking water. She'd even told them her first name — Jana.

Elitsa wearily rubbed a hand over her face and stretched her shoulders, then, setting her lantern down, stepped closer to the smooth stone wall. It had to be here somewhere. Solveiga and Irusya believed the cache existed, and why else would the Queen Dowager mention it in her journal? They'd been searching for over an hour, and like before, they'd found nothing but dirt and spiderwebs. Not expecting to find anything but unwilling to walk away without at least trying, Elitsa delved into the stone. She'd had to borrow essences from Pipene, having burned through her own meager supply.

Elitsa blinked. There was a hollow on the other side of the stone, her enhanced sight revealing box-like shapes as smudges of lighter color. Skin prickling in nervous anticipation, she put her hand against the wall. Was this a door, or was she seeing into the side of a room? Elitsa couldn't tell how large the chamber was. *But what else can this be, but the war cache?* If mages had been involved in hiding it, then maybe they'd used some kind of mechanism to lock it away, like the room beneath the Cartographers' Guild.

"There's something here," Elitsa said. Excitement chased away her exhaustion. She hadn't expected to find anything, not considering her luck the last few days.

"What'd you say?" Pipene called from behind her.

Elitsa sharpened her focus, feeling the delving spell start to slip, and found a narrow, tube-like channel connected to a blurred knot of gold and brown. *A channel through the stone ... can it be activated with air?* Brushing her fingertips over the nearly invisible opening, Elitsa seized an air essence and pushed it through into the mechanism inside the door. She felt it twist as a lock disengaged. Yanking her hands back, she watched wide-eyed as the sheet of rock slid sideways into the wall.

Heart pounding in her ears, Elitsa snatched her lantern off the floor and cautiously walked forward, holding it high to illuminate the way ahead. Excitement coiled inside her stomach, sending tingles down her covered arms. As she crossed the threshold — stepping over some kind of track cut into the floor — Elitsa turned back to see Pipene and Jana hurrying forward, excitement in their faces. She grinned, feeling giddy. "We found—"

The wall rushed back between them, the door slamming shut with an audible click.

"Elitsa? Elitsa!" Pipene's yells were muffled on the other side.

"I'm here!" Elitsa anxiously ran her fingers over the wall, trying to find a similar hole to the one on the other side, but the stone was intact, the mechanisms that opened and closed it hidden inside. *It doesn't matter anyway*, she thought. Even if there was a way to reopen the door, she'd used her last essence. All she had now was the ebonweaver, which was useless in the dark. *Why did the door close?* Elitsa took a step back, shifting her feet over the ground to see if she'd stepped on something like a lever or tripwire.

"Elitsa? How did you open the door?" There was a thump. "You better not have found something amazing without me!"

Releasing an incredulous laugh, Elitsa raised the lantern and examined the door again. There was no visible way that she could see to reopen it from this side. "I can't open it from here!" she yelled. "It's an air lock! Find the hole and blow some air into it!" She heard a curse and the sound of something banging against the door.

"I'm out!" There was a pause, and then, "Jana doesn't have any either!" Another muffled curse. "Jana's going to get some from her captain or another guard. You'll have to sit tight unless you find a way to open the door from there!"

"All right! I'm not going anywhere!" She couldn't, could she? The door had shut so quickly, Elitsa hadn't seen what was in the room. Maybe there was another exit. Turning around, she moved away from the door, holding her lantern high.

It was a long room, filled with numerous crates, baskets, and shelves, and objects she couldn't quite make out, stretching back into the darkness beyond the reach of her light. Unlike the passage that'd led them here, the walls were rough and uneven. *Like a natural cave.* In front of her — the indistinguishable shapes she'd seen in her delving — were wooden chests with iron bands, the lids closed and covered in a thick layer of dust.

As Elitsa moved deeper into the room, she found stands of magesilver armor. Unlike the individual pieces she'd seen the Tower's elite knights wear, these were entire suits, capable of holding enormous quantities of essence. This was it, the war cache everyone was looking for. And based on what she'd seen so far, this find was priceless. Reaching out, Elitsa brushed her fingers over the chestplate, her thrill quickly turning to shock.

There was an earth essence stored inside the armor, and it was strong. Why had they left it here to gather dust?

Curiosity getting the better of her, Elitsa crouched down in front of a chest and pried at the lock. The lid creaked as she raised it, soft light spilling out from numerous essence-filled bottles resting in fabric. Whirling, she pushed up another lid. It was filled like the first, the essences adding their light to her lantern. *This could fund a new life, take me beyond Casekraia.* She picked up one of the bottles, the vine-like essence inside slowly changing shape as though responding to the motion.

Hope and need shifted beneath her skin as Elitsa allowed herself to imagine a future free of the Guild, of Rivna. With this, she could afford to do anything she wanted. She could support Pipene and pay off Orson's contract. If Cas were here, he'd already be filling his pockets, and plotting his escape, sparing no thought for what would happen in his wake to the people of Rivna. *If the king falls, they won't be able to fight back.* The Tower would be swift to extinguish any hint of rebellion. This fight Elitsa had become entangled in would leave its mark on Casekraia forever.

Elitsa put the bottle back, feeling a rush of shame. If she were using Cas as a role model, then something was seriously wrong. Still, it was hard not to consider it, but it didn't matter anyway. She was trapped with no escape and knew she'd be unable to convince Pipene to grab what they could and run.

There was also the matter of Jana. She'd probably return with more guards, maybe even Captain Nazar. *I chose this,* Elitsa reminded herself. She would not endanger or disappoint Pipene. She would not run away.

Elitsa thought about the relic that Solveiga and Irusya had wanted to find. What did something that closed portals even look like? Looking for the relic felt easier to focus on than the tangle of emotions trying to flood her head, so Elitsa stood back up and surveyed the room. It was unlikely that she would find it, especially having no idea what she was looking for, but it'd pass the time while she waited.

Skirting a stack of crates, Elitsa stepped up to a set of wooden shelves built into the wall. She raised her lantern, casting light over a collection of small items — rings and bracelets and something that resembled a tinderbox. Her hand, sleeve pulling back from her mother's bracelet, passed over a shallow silver bowl holding a raven's beak. Her wrist warmed, the beads of her bracelet like soft sunlight against her skin.

Gasping, Elitsa yanked her hand back, the lantern swinging. The paint on the beads was disappearing, fading away in a wash of iridescent color before settling on pale white. How had the color vanished, and why did the bracelet still feel warm? She hesitated, then ran her fingers over the beads. She had the perception of something in the back of her mind, like a moth flitting just out of sight, but the awareness faded quickly. *Did I imagine it?*

She looked at the beak in the bowl. Had it transformed her mother's bracelet somehow, or was it the bowl beneath it? Setting the lantern on the shelf, she picked up the beak. As her fingers curled around the hard bone, Elitsa felt a jolt of energy pass through her fingers down into her wrist beneath her bracelet, her second sight expanding like when she'd delved the tunnel walls. There was something *alive* inside the beads around her wrist, like an essence before a harvest, and at the energy's touch, it became aware of her. The warmth pulsed, and she felt what she could only describe as a rush of fondness, of familiarity. Whatever was inside her mother's bracelet *recognized* her.

Goosebumps rushing up her arms, Elitsa transferred the beak to her other hand and turned her wrist over, examining the bracelet closely. Was it some kind of relic her grandmother had painted to disguise it? It wasn't magesilver. And whatever essence it held was nothing Elitsa had ever felt before.

There was a scrape behind her, the sound of the door sliding open, and Elitsa spun around, letting her sleeve fall back down over her bracelet. Light spilled across the floor from a dozen handheld lightprisms, and an unfamiliar guard wedged the door open with something to keep it from closing. She saw Pipene shoving her way forward and then her gaze snagged on the suit of armor she'd touched earlier. Elitsa's breath caught. She could *see* the essence, a shimmer of pale brown inside the overlapping magesilver plates across the chest.

CHAPTER 26

"You found it!" Pipene squealed.

Elitsa forced her gaze back to Pipene as her friend barreled towards her with wide, excited eyes. Behind her was Jana and five other guards, including Captain Nazar, then Solveiga and Irusya. The captain surveyed the room as though he found the whole thing suspicious, eyes narrowing as they landed on Elitsa's face. "Did you touch anything?"

"Of course not," Elitsa said as Pipene grabbed her arm. She tightened her hand on the beak, hiding it against her coat.

The guards fanned out, staring at the cache with a mixture of awe and disbelief.

Solveiga strode forward, lips thin with concern, but it was Irusya that Elitsa stared at. Walking at her wife's side, the center of Irusya's chest glowed with multicolored light, undimmed by the feathered cloak pinned beneath her throat. Whatever relic she was wearing beneath her clothes was filled with more essence than Elitsa had ever held at one time. Some she recognized by their color, but there were many she couldn't identify. Her stomach fluttered. *Why can I see them?*

"Grab as much as you can," Captain Nazar snapped at the

guards. "You, and you, get that armor on and take the rest to the marshall in the courtyard." He turned sharply and jabbed a finger at Solveiga and Irusya, and then Elitsa and Pipene. "And you lot! Take a crate and follow my guard. Quickly now!" He strode deeper into the room, snapping orders to the soldiers about what to take.

Elitsa looked at Pipene, confusion momentarily distracting her. There was an undercurrent and an urgency to the guards' movements she didn't understand. "What's going on?" She could see the glow of essence on Pipene's upper right arm. Her friend was likely wearing magesilver bands.

Pipene opened her mouth, but Solveiga answered first.

"The Guild's marching on the castle," she said, watching Jana hurry to a stack of crates.

The flutters in Elitsa's stomach erupted into a rush of wings, a chill dancing down her spine as she tightened her hand on the beak clutched inside her palm. "What happened?" What had pushed the Tower's decision? *Did they discover the king's dealings with the Smoke Eyes?* She thought about Cas and felt a rush of worry. Maybe they'd gone ahead with the heist and been captured.

"I don't know; perhaps they're worried we'd find the war cache if they waited any longer." Solveiga exchanged a look with Irusya, who, kissing her cheek, disappeared into the maze of objects. "They'll attempt to reclaim the castle, but King Dmitrei intends to prevent them from entering the gate."

It was happening too quickly. Were the guards prepared to fight against Tower-trained mages? They'd found the war cache, but they didn't know what was here. Was there even time to use what they'd found? This might end up being short and bloody, and they were on the losing side. Elitsa studied Solveiga's face, finding only resolve. The Swans' leader intended to stay. *Does she actually believe we can win?* "You're going to stand with the king."

"Yes. He'll need us." Solveiga lightly touched Elitsa's shoulder.

She wasn't sure if the gesture was meant to be comforting or if Solveiga could see the doubt in her eyes. "The decision to stand with us is your own, but whatever happens today will decide Casekraia's future."

"And if we lose?"

Solveiga smiled. "We continue." She nodded at Pipene, then waded into the sea of crates, balancing her lantern atop one before picking it up. It was strange watching her fall into step behind a guard to leave the room. Solveiga seemed just as at home here performing manual labor as she did gracefully sweeping down the staircase in the House of Swans.

"We knew this day would come," Pipene said, threading her arm through Elitsa's. "A fight against the Guild, but this time all of Rivna will be watching."

"Will they?" Only once had someone tried to intervene during her reclamations, and that person had been a family member, not a neighbor.

"The mages can hardly come in force without someone noticing."

Pipene was right, but that didn't mean that the people would do anything or affect the outcome. Would Verka be able to convince the Smoke Eyes to help? *We're going to die here*, Elitsa thought. The Guild might keep the king alive, but she doubted they'd care about the lives of anyone else in their way. She looked at Pipene, but if her friend had come to the same bleak conclusion, she'd hidden it deep.

"I was hoping we'd have time to examine all this." Pipene lowered her voice, grinning. "To take a souvenir at least." She let go of Elitsa's arm and reached for a wooden box. Opening the lid, she ran her fingers over a set of magesilver rings.

Elitsa flushed, thinking of her earlier thoughts of weakness, but Pipene was already picking up a basket and dumping the rings inside. *You're a better person than I am*, she thought, affection warming her heart. Looking away, she watched two guards pick up one of the large essence chests and carry it toward the open doorway. She could see the multi-colored light of the cargo inside despite the thick wood. Wonder and concern brought another rush of goosebumps to her skin, and she touched a hand to her throat.

It was then she saw Captain Nazar staring at her, his narrowed eyes lit by the lantern in the hands of a guard lingering at his elbow. She held his gaze defiantly. She hadn't freed herself from the Guild to live under another heavy hand. *No more masters*, she promised herself. She was here, but not for the king or Captain Nazar; she was here for Pipene and the memory of her mother.

More soldiers appeared, along with the rest of Solveiga's Swans, the room quickly filling up with bodies and light. Turning her back on Captain Nazar, Elitsa shoved the beak into her pocket and bent down to pick something up — a crate of mage-silver helmets that were empty of essence. As she lifted it into her arms, she paused. The room felt darker than before and more quiet, muted despite the additional people. Elitsa looked around the room, trying to pinpoint what was different until she realized that the colors of essences were gone. She couldn't see them anymore. *The beak*, she thought, feeling lightheaded. She was no longer holding it. What *was* it? A relic that allowed her to see magic?

"Eli, you coming?"

Elitsa turned her head at Pipene's voice. She was holding a basket, and had a thick magesilver belt of overlapping chains draped over one shoulder. "Yes." Elitsa cleared her throat, her voice sounding oddly breathy. *I can figure this out later.* After whatever happened next with the king and Guild, she'd find a moment to herself and examine the beak and her bracelet and figure out what was going on.

As she started to follow Pipene from the room, she saw Irusya swiftly tuck something into her pocket before hefting several pikes that were tipped in magesilver. Had she found the portal relic? If it was as important as Irusya and Solveiga claimed, Elitsa hoped so.

Caught in the stream of bodies, Elitsa and Pipene had no opportunity to slip away from the guards as they carried the relics up into the main castle. Everyone seemed focused on getting as much of the cache upstairs as possible, but Elitsa didn't miss that the captain had set guards where they'd come in. There would be no leaving that way, though that hopefully meant the Guild wouldn't be using it either.

They took a different way at the top of the spiral staircase, the guards ahead leading them towards the front of the castle where they'd set up a staging ground in the courtyard before the Peoples' Gate. Enclosed within a high stone wall, the courtyard was a large, open space, wide enough to accommodate multiple carriages and horses. The gate itself was closed, which was generally unheard of, though you could see through the stone archway and iron filigree to the bridge beyond. With the double doors sealed together, the large gold sun at its center sat inside the curve of a silver half-moon. It would not stop the Guild. The intricately woven metal had been crafted to be decorative, not defensive, and Elitsa guessed they would push it open as soon as the mages arrived.

The sun was setting, the sky overhead a weld of pink and blue. Lightprisms, arranged around the courtyard by the king's staff, would provide light once night fell. The air felt chilled, and Elitsa welcomed the coldness on her face and neck. Her coat had been a touch too warm while they'd wandered the tunnels, but she hadn't wanted to carry it.

The relics were being stashed beside the stables, overseen by two sharp-eyed women in officer livery, who, with the aid of several scribes, were making a list of everything brought to them, then assigning them according to some criteria Elitsa didn't understand. There were more guards here, multiple units, perhaps the king's entire force armored for battle. Instead of being sent back down to fetch more from the cache, Elitsa and Pipene were directed to one side with Solveiga and the rest of the Swans.

A flurry of activity drew Elitsa's eyes to the palace doors, and she saw King Dmitrei stride out with Queen Nefeli, followed by a squad of guards wearing the new magesilver armor. Her hand went to her pocket, the desire to see the essences again overtaking her worries. What would it look like, she wondered, with so many relics and essences all packed together? The king stopped next to a man in a dark green overcoat standing on the stairs overlooking the courtyard with Captain Nazar. The stranger had black hair, peppered with silver, and a thick mustache and Elitsa could see a gold sword pinned to his collar. *Is that Marshall Oles?*

Irusya appeared around a knot of soldiers and touched Solveiga's back, whispering something to her.

Solveiga nodded and touched Irusya's cheek, then turned, drawing the Swans' eyes to her. The Swans' leader looked solemn, her gaze unwavering, as she looked at each of them in turn, and Elitsa curled her fingers away from the beak in her pocket when their eyes met. "We know what has brought us to today. We are the Mother's guardians, protectors of this city and Her people. I see your hearts and your courage, but your lives are your own. Tonight, we stand against an army, so if your wings carry you away, know that you still walk in Mother's light."

Solveiga was giving them a choice. Elitsa looked at the Swans, and though she saw a few nervous faces, no one made a move to slip away. They believed in Solveiga and were willing to fight. *Maybe she should be king*, Elitsa thought. She could see the people of Rivna being roused to help her, but would they rise for the king?

Captain Nazar approached with Jana, the guard carrying a

box of bottled essence. "King Dmitrei has need of you and your people, Mistress Solveiga."

Solveiga raised her chin, her soft smile proud. "We are honored to serve the king, Captain Nazar."

"The marshall is dividing the guard into squads of four, with one primary relic user per group." He looked them over with sharp eyes, gaze lingering on Pipene and Elitsa. "Do any of you have combat experience?"

"We are prepared to fight."

The captain eyed them again, perhaps skeptical that they could survive what was coming. Were they ready? The Swans had surprised her in the street, but open battle was something else. Elitsa had fought, had even faced death several times, but nothing like this. She looked at Pipene, beautiful, kind, softhearted Pipene. Elitsa wanted to spirit her away from all of this, but she could see the stubborn tilt to her head. Pipene was nervous, they all were, but she was as committed as Solveiga.

"Very well," Captain Nazar said. "I will assign each of you."

Solveiga nodded. "What will be our placement?"

"We have set up blockades on the bridge. Heavy infantry will go first, followed by our squads. You have relics?"

"We do."

"Guardian Priede will give you essences. If you require an additional relic, see Lieutenant Berzins." Nazar pointed at the women overseeing the relics. "When you receive your squad assignment, join your team."

"And then?" Dita asked.

Captain Nazar glanced at her. "We move to the bridge and wait."

"Captain," Irusya said. "I am a healer. I would like to assist your medics, if I may?"

"Very well. They will hang back by the gate. Report to Doctor Soroka by the stable. They are tall like yourself; dark hair, blue coat."

"Thank you, Captain." Irusya caught Solveiga's face in her hands and kissed her, the women locking eyes for several breaths, before she headed off in the direction Nazar had indicated.

Solveiga watched her leave, the cords in her throat taut.

The captain turned to Jana and nodded. As she started handing out the essence bottles, Nazar moved off towards a group of guards drawing essence into their armor.

Elitsa and Pipene grabbed a bottle each from the box and shifted back to allow the others access. Elitsa pulled out the cork and drew the fire essence into one of her earrings, gasping a little as she felt the heat of its power. There were over twenty of varied strength, and for a moment, she thought she felt a pulse from the bracelet on her wrist.

The air filled with the scents of essence. Somewhere, above the sound of voices and preparations for battle, Elitsa heard the loud whinny of a horse. She could almost taste the tension on her tongue. Her focus contracted, and she pushed her fears to the back of her mind.

Pipene caught her arm. "Are you all right, Eli?" she asked softly.

"Yes, why?"

"You may be fighting friends today."

Elitsa shook her head, accepting another bottled essence of air from Jana. "I have no friends in the Guild."

"And your mentor?"

Elitsa froze and glanced sideways at her. She'd forgotten she hadn't told Pipene who had attacked her or that the Smoke Eyes were holding Vilis beneath the city. The secrets were piling up but now didn't seem like the time to get into it. Somehow, despite Elitsa's years of service with the Tower, Vilis and Pipene had never met. *Not until he tried to kill her.* Her anger returned, and Elitsa let it build inside her chest, chasing away the jitters in her hands. What mattered right now was surviving the battle.

"The Guild wants me dead, and I doubt they're coming here to talk. I have no problem defending myself." She glanced at the splint on Pipene's wrist. "Will you be all right?"

"Of course." Pipene's eyes sparkled. "You remember the summer I broke my arm and still picked more apples than you."

Elitsa's lips curved, and she nodded at the essence in Pipene's hands, setting her concern aside. Her friend knew her limits. "Store as much as you can. There will be a fight, I'm certain of it."

CHAPTER 27

E litsa was standing with her assigned squad when a young guard raced into the courtyard through the Peoples' Gate and signaled the marshall.

"Here we go," Nikandr said, his penetrating green eyes fixed on the king atop the stairs. The queen had disappeared inside the palace, perhaps to watch from one of the towers.

Nikandr was the leader of their squad, broad and bearded with a large shield, pike, and a short sword on his belt. Covering his thick brown hair was a magesilver helmet with a pointed tip that brought to mind an acorn cap. His green wool overcoat, split at the hips like Elitsa's, was covered by a chainmail vest that ended mid-thigh. The other two guards were Vasyl — a slim, gray-eyed man with a full-lipped mouth quick to smile — and Ganna, a black-haired woman with an athletic build and a half-moon scar over her lip. They were dressed like Nikandr in thick wool clothing, but their hats were polished steel.

Elitsa glanced past Vasyl to Pipene, where she waited with her squad. The Swans were spots of black among the greens and grays of the king's soldiers. Eyes briefly meeting, Pipene smiled nervously before adjusting her feathered cloak around her shoulders. She'd put her mask back on, reminding Elitsa of the eerie attack in the fog. Elitsa looked for Solveiga but didn't see her.

King Dmitrei said something to the marshall, who turned to Captain Nazar. Orders were shouted, and a line of ten soldiers in full armor headed towards the bridge. The squad ahead of them began to move, and then Elitsa was walking forward with her team, hand gripping the dagger at her waist. If everything went as planned, she should never have to use it.

The press of bodies around her tightened as more guards closed in behind, most wearing chainmail or metal plate over dark green tunics. As they passed beneath the large archway and gilded gates, Elitsa reached into her pocket and gripped the beak, the glow of essences appearing on the guards ahead of her. The bridge was wide enough for two wagons side by side, and the armored guards in the front spread out in a line, halting at the first barricade.

Elitsa's team stopped by the guard wall on the left side of the bridge. She cast a glance skyward, body tensing as the sound of stomping feet hushed into uneasy silence. The torches that usually blazed on the bridge had been doused, and Elitsa could see the stars. The evening was uncharacteristically clear, the wind crisp and biting, blowing her hair across her mouth. She could hear the snap of the king's flags, and the rustle of fabric; the breath of the people around her, and the clink of weapons and armor.

Craning her head to see around Nikandr's broad shoulders, Elitsa stared past the armored guards and barricades to the end of the bridge. The view of the park was framed in the old stone archway that mirrored the one behind them, the trees and grass indistinct in the darkness. She saw the Guild before she heard them, a starlike array of rainbow-colored light that grew to fill the width of the darkened portal. The carried essences were strong and numerous, and Elitsa's mouth went dry as eight heavily-armored knights, wearing the Guild's best magesilver, marched out onto the bridge. They were followed by figures in long coats, emblazoned with the Tower's seal. There were maybe fifty of them, but the strength of the shimmering light was staggering.

Elitsa's stomach flipped, and she let go of the beak, the glow of essence disappearing from her sight.

One of the mages lifted his hand, and small orbs of light shot up to fill the sky in the space between them. They looked like stars, as though he'd plucked them from the heavens above. There were gasps and murmurs of alarm from the king's guards, the sound of creaking armor and shifting feet, but everyone held their positions. Though accustomed to the Guild's casual use of magic, Elitsa's heart shot into her throat. Unease settled heavy on her shoulders, and she licked her lips.

"Not as many as I expected," Ganna said softly, "but I suppose they wouldn't want to leave their tower unguarded."

A mage stepped through the Tower knights in front, dressed in a high-collared, ice-blue coat that shimmered as though embroidered with starlight. The gold, tasseled sash around his waist fluttered as a gust of wind arched over the bridge. It was Arch-Mage Silina, one of the elder mages of the Vertex of Flame and Starlight, the council that ruled the Tower. "Let us pass!" His voice echoed loudly. "We have business with the king."

"Mother's Blessings, Arch-Mage Silina." The king's voice echoed behind her. It sounded louder than it should, amplified by device or magic. "I regret that the castle is closed this evening. An illness among my staff, you understand." Though his dulcet voice carried its usual playful tone, there was an undercurrent of iron inside it. He sounded confident, like a king.

Silina cocked his head, face folding like he'd tasted something sour. "The king's gates have always remained open. Is that not one of the tenets of our fine city? Of your rule?"

Elitsa's lips tightened. Why bother with this false display when they were clearly poised to attack?

"Yes, an edict I whole-heartedly support," King Dmitrei said. "You know how much I adore guests." He sounded almost fond. "Let us also speak of the Tower's oath to protect this kingdom and its people. Who is watching our skies and borders this beautiful evening?"

Skies? Was the king speaking about the frost wyrms?

Silina was silent for several breaths, conferring with another beside him. "Speaking of our oaths, we have learned you discovered a large cache of relics. We will take them to the tower for study, as agreed."

"Unfortunately, I cannot accommodate you in that regard, Arch-Mage Silina." The king sounded regretful, as though he truly wished he could. "Whatever relics we may or may not have discovered within the castle's grounds are part of the royal armory, and therefore must be kept here, for the safety of the realm."

"This is highly irregular." Silina's voice had lost its lazy arrogance, irritation and anger coloring his words and posture.

"I am king, am I not? All final judgments are mine. Or do you not recognize my rule?"

"Forgive me, King Dmitrei." Silina didn't sound at all apologetic. "But we cannot allow that. Order your guards to stand aside, or we will remove them."

"No." The king's voice was as soft, calm, and cold as the snow in winter. "If you advance, Arch-Mage Silina, I will be forced to defend my castle and the royal seat of Casekraia."

Elitsa looked back at King Dmitrei, feeling an odd mix of pride and fear. She would not have thought she could ever admire the seemingly frivolous king, and yet here he was, standing against the Guild, refusing to back down. It was clear from their interaction earlier and his poise here on the bridge that there was more to him than his extravagant behavior suggested. *I just hope he doesn't get us all killed.*

"So be it." Silina stepped back behind the armored soldiers.

This was it then; a face-to-face fight with the Guild. Sweat trickled down Elitsa's chest. She looked for Pipene, but couldn't see her. The kings' guards had relics, but she doubted they were as well trained as the Tower mages. *Hells, I might have more training than they do.* Could they hold against the Guild? Ganna was murmuring something under her breath. It sounded like a prayer to Mother Moon.

We'll survive this, Elitsa promised herself, unwilling to let the idea that they would fail take root inside her head. There was a future beyond the Guild; there had to be.

"Hold," Nikandr said, tightening his grip on his shield as he stared at the mages on the bridge. His other hand was on the hilt of his short sword, ready to draw.

Elitsa glanced at Vasyl. He held a shield like Nikandr, and his hand was on the axe at his belt; a magesilver medallion, the chain still around his neck, caught between his teeth. *That's one way to do it*, Elitsa thought distractedly. As long as he kept it in his mouth, he could use the essences inside and keep his hands free.

Ganna held a pike in both her hands, eyes fixed forward in fierce focus. If she wore any magesilver, Elitsa couldn't see it.

The sound of boots struck the bridge. Elitsa breathed in, ready to seize an essence. The Tower's knights were advancing.

A command was given behind her, and Elitsa heard the whistle of arrows as they passed overhead, striking the ground at the Guild's feet. A warning shot. Undeterred, the knights took another step, shields raised below their helmeted faces, ready to thrust overhead once they reached the range of the archers.

Suddenly a ball of fire shot from the Tower mages, flying over Elitsa's head with a crackling whine. She followed it back with her eyes as it shot towards the archers arranged several paces from the king and his heavily armored guards. One of them thrust forward their almond-shaped shield, a winged magesilver wolf fixed to its painted surface. The fireball — a metal sphere wrapped in flame — deflected up and sideways, flying down into the water to the right of the bridge.

"Defend the king!" someone bellowed from behind her — presumably one of the officers. From somewhere to Elitsa's right, a responding fireball was tossed over their front line towards the Guild. She heard a loud thunk as it struck someone's shield.

The bridge erupted into chaos.

Heat flashed back across Elitsa's face and legs, as the guard in front of her and Nikandr caught a burning ball of fire against their shield. She smelled earth as they moved to deflect it, forcing the fire into the stones at their feet. It'd come too quickly to do anything else.

She lost sight of their attackers, jostled into Nikandr's back by a squad behind them as the mages struck inside their ranks. Anticipation, fear, and sweat tangled with the scents of releasing essence. Ganna put her hand out, touching Vasyl's back, and through the space between them, Elitsa saw Pipene across the bridge. She was raising her hand, her blonde hair swirling around her face. Magesilver glinted on her fingers, and she threw a sheet of wind-shaped daggers with a sweep of her arm. The motion looked practiced, and Elitsa was caught off guard with the ease and familiarity with which Pipene used her essences.

"Serlov!"

Elitsa's eyes snapped to Ganna's face. The guard's brow arched in question, and she flushed. What was she doing, standing here motionless? Her mother's bracelet warmed on her wrist, pulsing like a faint heartbeat, and she looked forward, trying to see past Nikandr and the guards in front of them. She didn't know who to attack. She'd never stood like this, a soldier caught in a battleline, unable to run or take cover. It felt like she was balanced on a ledge, excitement and hesitation wrestling for control. When had she lost her edge?

Gritting her teeth, Elitsa drew on her essences. She smelled the acrid odor of a blacksmith's shop and soil after rain as she formed a hasty sphere of metal-studded earth. Wrapping it in fire, she propelled it over Nikandr's shoulder with a push of sea-scented air. The wind essence she'd gotten from Jana must have come from the sea.

Elitsa didn't see where her thrown fire hit. One of the guards in the front roared "Stand!" and the Tower's knights slammed into their line. Nikandr shifted back as swords struck shields, forcing Elitsa to step sideways, and for several seconds, she could see through the soldiers to the mages beyond.

A woman, staring at Nikandr, raised both hands, and Elitsa shoved her hand into her pocket, gripping the raven's beak. Red and orange shimmered into existence down her arms, unspooling like thread from a magesilver necklace tight against her throat. The mage was gathering fire.

Elitsa seized an air essence as magic coalesced between the woman's palms, the red-orange shimmer turning purple, becoming a tangle of heated lines, of purpose. She could *see* the spell's construction, the mage's intent. Magic became visible fire, and it lanced through the air towards Nikandr. He'd dipped his shield, thrusting with his sword past the falling guard ahead of him. Elitsa swept her arm up, blowing the stream of fire into the sky with a shield of air. She focused on holding it, jaw clenched as the mage's eyes flared then narrowed. If her essence weakened before the mage's fire, it would resume its path forward.

Nikandr swung his shield back around as Elitsa's essence dissipated. Unobstructed, the mage's fire splashed across Nikandr's shield then disappeared.

Elitsa dropped her hands, breathing hard.

The battle continued, fierce and fast, moments passing through Elitsa's awareness like scenes captured in lightning flashes. Nikandr, Ganna, and Vasyl fought around her as she attacked and shielded against magic. Wind and ice and lightning crackled to Elitsa's right and left, striking flesh and armor or shooting into the sky or off the sides of the bridge. Someone beyond Ganna fell, their helmet knocked free, their tunic burning.

Another guard fell in the front line, a sword wound, not magic. The king's guards shifted, closing the gap, Nikandr now one of them.

Blood slicked the stones by Vasyl's feet, flying motes of ruby red catching Elitsa's eye as his axe drew back.

Ganna, hand against the guard's shoulder in front of her, leaped up and stabbed down with her spear, trying to drive the knights back.

A Swan appeared in a blur of motion, his brown hair and feathered cloak streaked with ash. He raised a slingshot, sending a metal sphere over the front line, trailing green-tinged smoke. Elitsa blinked, and he was gone again. *Speed enhancement*, she thought — a trick she'd yet to master.

A flaming arrow hissed overhead, and one of the barricades exploded, throwing mages off the bridge with screams and fire.

Squads broke and reformed or rotated back, seeking more essence or healing.

Elitsa lost track of how many essences she used and released. She slipped the beak into her pocket, stretching her cramping fingers. With her magic sight gone, the world felt muted, but amidst the disconcerting loss, she could feel her mother's bracelet more strongly. Their connection had strengthened somehow as the fight wore on. A result of the beak's power?

Beyond its comforting warmth against her skin, Elitsa could see *into* it. The beads were not glass or stone but ossified eggs of a moth-like creature she could almost visualize inside her head. It was unlike anything she'd ever seen before, and though it felt alive, aware of her in some small way, it seemed more like an echo than an active consciousness. Whatever it had been before, the bracelet held magic, magic that felt like the essence of air.

Someone staggered into her, knocking Elitsa off-balance. She regained her footing and caught sight of Dita, her cape singed and a slingshot in her hand, and then a woman moved between them, tossing a spear up over the heads of the holding line of guards.

Stepping back behind Nikandr, Elitsa saw a mage creating a spear of ice. She grabbed the raven's beak, goosebumps rushing down her arms as her sight expanded. She could see the spell as it came together, the threads of essence solidifying in the air. The mage's eyes caught hers — narrowed in focus — and then they let the spear fly towards Vasyl. He was shoving someone back, his axe raised to strike, his chest exposed to the oncoming spear.

Elitsa reached for an air essence and came up empty; she'd used every one she had. Panic rushed through her. Her bracelet pulsed, a swirl of gold light appearing in her mind like an unfolding essence. She seized the magic, throwing out her hand in a broad sweep to break the spear of ice. The magic from her bracelet didn't manifest as a slice of air but tore through the spell itself, severing the mage's intention that bound the essence together. A cold spray of shattered ice struck Elitsa's face and scattered over Vasyl's head as he slammed his axe into the shoulder of the Tower knight.

Vasyl ducked, belatedly throwing up his shield as he looked back. He was breathing hard, sweat dampening his hair. Their eyes met, held, then he nodded and turned back.

Elitsa's pulse went wild, drowning out the sounds of the battle. What had she just done? She was still trying to wrap her mind around it when the air seemed to warp ahead of them, turning red. Without thinking, she threw her arms forward past Nikandr's shoulder, the beak still clenched in a death grip in her left hand, seizing the golden power once again. She broke the fireball inches from their faces, her hair blowing backward as scorching hot air blasted across her. Blocking her eyes with a bend of her arm, she felt tiny rock-hard fragments from the projectile scatter across them. Some struck her, burning and drawing blood.

Nikandr raised his shield, looking back at her. He had several bleeding cuts on his face, his cheeks and beard singed from the heat. "You're breaking the essence." There was a hint of wonder in his voice. His arm shook as someone shoved against his shield. "When you break it, direct the spell up with air. You'll avoid burning yourself."

Elitsa shook her head. "I'm out." She swayed, then steadied herself. She felt so tired. How long could they keep this up? How long *had* they? Elitsa probed her magesilver, finding only the ebonweaver and several essences of earth and fire. There were no shadows here, caught in the midst of a battle, and as exhausted as she felt, she would not try to sneak away or run. Not without Pipene. *Please be safe,* she thought.

She concentrated on the bracelet. The golden, air-like magic felt powerful, strong, but she doubted it could last forever. She certainly couldn't. Did her use of the bracelet require more of her energy than magesilver?

There was no time to think about it; another spear of ice came streaking down towards her, not Nikandr, on the heels of a span of wind daggers that he caught against his shield. Elitsa broke fireballs and bolts of lightning, blasts of air, and lashes of water. Frost and ice lay scattered around her; water drenched her clothes. For every strike she broke and redirected, another nearly made it through. Even with Nikandr, Vasyl, and Ganna around her, the attacks kept coming again and again. The mages were targeting *her*, Elitsa realized. They must think she had a relic from the king's war cache.

There was a cry, and then someone broke through the guard wall. Nikandr was struggling, Vasyl was simply gone, and Elitsa saw something barreling towards her from the corner of her eye. She started to turn, a wave of dizziness almost making her fall. *Ganna ... where is Ganna?* Elitsa's heartbeat stuttered as she waited for the strike of a blade or shield, but then the knight slipped on the ice, coating the ground around her feet, and someone grabbed her by the back of her coat, yanking her away.

Ganna appeared, driving her pike into the knight's back. The soldier rolled, but then Vasyl fell atop him, ripping free a mage-silver pauldron to slam his axe beneath the soldier's arm. The king's guards were fierce and efficient, stripping away the knight's magesilver and ensuring he would not rise again.

Whoever gripped Elitsa's clothes continued to pull her away from the chaotic front line of battle. The squads were breaking and reforming as the mages pushed forward, shouts and explosions filling the air. Head spinning, exhaustion pressing black at the corner of her eyes, it took Pipene repeating her name several times before Elitsa realized who had pulled her away.

"Eli. Eli! Are you all right?"

Relief at seeing Pipene dissolved the cloud of confusion wrapping her head, and Elitsa clasped her friend's arm. "Yes, tired." Impossibly, she hadn't dropped the beak, and Elitsa shoved it back into her pocket, fingers shaking. The magic in her bracelet felt dimmed, maybe enough for one or two spells more.

Pipene nodded, brushing her hair off her forehead as she scanned the crowded bridge. She'd lost her mask, and there was blood and water on her clothes.

Elitsa looked back at the gate. The king was still standing with the marshall and his guards, though there were fewer archers than she remembered. She caught a glimpse of Irusya to the side, kneeling over a guard on the ground. "Solveiga?" she asked, thinking of how it'd feel to lose someone in the battle. Unexpectedly, the scent of her mother — oakmoss and vanilla — flooded her senses, and Elitsa could see her face with crystal clarity.

"Still standing," Pipene said.

Elitsa nodded, breathing through the pang of loss as her memory faded, and looked up at the net of light in the sky, cast by the Guild mage at the start of the fight. The lights were fewer now, undoubtedly disrupted by the chaos of thrown magic. *Why did they put them there?*

A group of guards shoved past her and Pipene, jostling them towards the middle of the bridge. In the front, an armored soldier was blown backward, knocking another to the ground. The king's guards broke and bowed inward. The lights overhead exploded, sparks of blinding light searing Elitsa's eyes. When she could finally see again, the Guild was plowing through their ranks on a direct path to the king. It was like watching a fox tearing forward through a mass of birds. The attacks from guards and Swans were rebuffed, bodies thrown back as if they were no more than feathers.

"Protect the king!" someone bellowed above the noise of fighting.

Two of the king's armored guards rushed forward, swords drawn and shields raised, but before they could reach the mages, they were violently thrown sideways, knocking down multiple guards as they slammed into the sides of the bridge.

Three mages advanced unobstructed, their clothes showing no signs they'd been caught inside the battle, with Arch-Mage Silina in the lead. Ice lanced through Elitsa's stomach, and she grabbed the raven beak. As the bone touched her skin, lines of light appeared between the mages like shimmering strands of spider web. Elitsa's dread turned to horror. She could *see* what their spell would do, and the essence Silina held — the life force of a massive bear.

The guards realized too late what the mages intended, their faces registering alarm and disgust as an enormous glowing specter of a bear appeared in front of them. It roared and charged forward. Guards moved to intercept, including one of the Swans, and as the glowing lines touched them, they collapsed instantly, the mages' spell tearing away their souls as if they were no more than paper.

Pipene screamed and dashed forward, whether for the mages or bear, Elitsa wasn't sure.

Fear flashed through her chest, and the magic in her bracelet rose with it, burning away her exhaustion. She threw herself past Pipene into the bear's path, flinging up her arm in a wild slash as she flung the bracelet's golden magic into the death spell. She felt the specter's hot breath on her face, and then it broke with an audible snap that she felt inside her chest. The bear's shape came apart, washing over her in wisps of torn light. Elitsa heard a distant roar, the sound seeming to vibrate the bones of her skull, and then the animal's essence faded away into nothing.

There was silence on the bridge, every eye on Elitsa as she stood unsteadily, breathing hard. The mages had halted in their tracks, fifty paces from the king, with Elitsa in between. Pipene, no more than an arm's length from the mage on the left, was staring back at her with wide, disbelieving eyes. Elitsa's body hurt; she felt close to collapsing, the magic in her bracelet nearly expended as though it were low on energy like she was, but she straightened. The mages were shocked, off-balance, and she had to react before they did. *It's just like bluffing a contract-breaker, right?* She would be fierce, in control. "You will move no further!" Her voice was firm, strong. "We are not enemies. No more Rivnans will die today! You saw me break your spells. Stand down or you will see the full use of my power!"

Elitsa's heart pounded in her ears as sweat trickled down her spine. Surely they'd call her bluff, question her power, her age. She summoned all her anger and distaste for the Guild and what they'd done and used it to hold Silina's gaze, daring him to challenge her.

The mage on the left — gray hair braided into twin knots atop their head — urgently grabbed Silina's arm and said something Elitsa couldn't hear. Silina glanced at them disdainfully. He seemed to consider, and then Elitsa saw when his uncertainty changed. *Just one more time*, she thought, reaching for the bracelet's weakened magic. Silina thrust out his hand, and a spear of ice sped towards Elitsa's chest.

Seizing the golden magic, she broke the arch-mage's spell with a close of her fist, slivers of ice and water exploding harmlessly out to either side of her as Silina staggered. Elitsa's arm dropped numbly to her side, fatigue overwhelming her. All sensation in her bracelet vanished. *Are you dead?* she thought, though she didn't expect an answer. She'd used everything. If Silina attacked her again, she'd be powerless to stop him.

Shoving away his companions' efforts to help him, Silina straightened and stared at her with a look of consternation that made her want to laugh. Was she smiling? Elitsa was too tired to know for sure. *Does he remember me?* She'd bled for the Guild for years, and still, no one knew who in the hells she was. It was both a relief, and horribly depressing.

Elitsa heard the scrape of boots on stone, and then the king's guards were moving past, enfolding her. She smelled roses and golden pears, and then King Dmitrei stepped up beside her, a nimbus of essence-fueled light glowing around his head. He looked luminous and proud, his sharp cheeks flushed, his chin lifted. Draped around his neck and narrow shoulders was a magesilver capelet of draping chains — had it come from the war cache? And then there was something else, the sound of hundreds of footsteps, and then the light from lanterns and light-prisms as people appeared at the end of the bridge; Rivna's citizens. *Is that Verka and Leida in front with the city watch?*

Silina looked back, face tightening at the murmur of voices, of shock and outrage. The silence had broken.

"I have always seen the value in alliances, Arch-Mage Silina," King Dmitrei said, clasping his hands behind his back. "You have underestimated us." He laughed, a bright, joyous sound. "I believe that you have no idea what we are capable of, what the *people* are capable of."

The mages still standing shifted, heads turning nervously

towards the townspeople at their back. Though bloodied and bruised, the king's guards straightened proudly, and Elitsa saw Solveiga, holding up a Swan with burns on their face. *Irusya will be relieved,* she thought.

Pipene slipped through the king's guards to Elitsa's side and wrapped an arm around her waist. It was taking every stubborn ounce left in her body not to collapse onto the stone beneath her feet, but she let herself sag, just a little, leaning on Pipene for support. She could not afford to show weakness, not beside the king or beneath the mages' watchful eyes. *We won,* she thought, not quite believing it. Somehow they'd stood against the Guild and were still alive.

"That was incredible!" Pipene whispered against her cheek. "How did you do that?"'

Elitsa gave a helpless shrug, too tired to speak, and very aware of the king on her other side. She stared at Silina. He had to know he was beaten. The mages wouldn't turn against the people, would they? They'd already broken their own accords, unleashing a bear's essence in view of everyone. *How far are they willing to go?*

Silina faced the king. He looked confident and unafraid. "It is good we came when we did," he said loudly, amplifying his voice. "To help you turn away these rogues."

The gray-haired mage whispered to him.

Silina's face tightened. "We will ensure the removal of any additional agitators within the Tower, and acknowledge your aid in this joint endeavor." His lip curled. "The Tower, and Rivna, are stronger together."

"As mad as a spitting snake," the king murmured beneath his breath.

Surprised, Elitsa glanced at him, but there was no outward sign he'd spoken at all, his gaze on Silina.

"Indeed, Arch-Mage Silina," King Dmitrei said. "We cannot abide the use of blasphemous magic." He looked past the Guild to the townspeople beyond. "Despite this tragedy, today is a historic day, for today brings change! Magic should not be reserved for the elite few, for then it can turn people desperate, it can corrupt, as we've witnessed before the Peoples' Gate. I have seen your suffering, my beloved Rivna! It is time to bring back the old ways, to *share* magic, not just hide it away.

"When the new day dawns, my proclamation is as follows — new guilds may be legitimized, relics may be used to heal, for agriculture, for art, and for innovation!"

Art? Elitsa thought, trying to imagine what that might mean.

Murmurs rippled through the crowd, including a few raw cheers that Elitsa thought might have come from the Smoke Eyes.

The king raised a hand, his fingers reflecting the light behind his head, turning them gold. "In a fortnight, you may bring your petitions to register for a guild to the castle. We have had a busy night, as you can see, and must complete our preparations. Return to your homes, good people! Share this news with your neighbors. Our future will not be one of hunger and struggle. We will see beauty return to Casekraia!"

The crowd erupted once more into conversation, the city guards who'd accompanied them beginning to encourage the people back to their homes. The mages on the bridge drew together, exchanging whispers, their body language tense. Only two knights were still standing, their weapons lowered.

Arch-Mage Silina, nodding to a huddle of mages, glared at the king. "We will return to the Tower."

Return? Elitsa felt Pipene's fingers tighten on her waist.

"Nonsense!" The king bounded forward, the guards on either side moving to flank him.

Behind the mages, Elitsa could see several of the city guards turn back to block their escape, with a line of Smoke Eyes standing behind. Was that Ivo, with his arms crossed, and Cas?

Elitsa felt a flush of relief, which she didn't know what to do with. *So, Leida didn't kill him.*

"You will stay here tonight," King Dmitrei continued, voice warm as if he were smiling, "as my guests, for your service to the crown."

Silina stiffened, his displeasure clear on his face. His eyes, filled with ugly contempt, shifted to Elitsa. "Of course, King Dmitrei. If we may send a messenger? To alert the Tower of our delayed return."

"I will see to the message." The king nodded at the guards, who moved to encircle the mages, ushering them into the castle through the open gates. He turned back to Elitsa and Pipene, glancing at Solveiga, who had moved up beside them, before fixing his attention on Elitsa. Barely concealed excitement shone from his face, his eyes bright and wondering. "We must speak," he said, looking at her like someone who'd discovered a new exotic bird.

Elitsa just stared back, too tired to bow or worry.

"And you, my dear Solveiga!" The king spun, reaching for her hand, the spell-light around him fading as a guard appeared with a lantern. "There is much we need to discuss." He shook his head, lips pursed. "You continue to surprise me."

"Of course, Your Highness. I aim to satisfy." Despite the obvious signs of battle on her face and clothes, Solveiga looked as composed as ever. "Might we get some rest, sire? My people are tired."

"Yes." The king blinked, and he squeezed her hands. "Yes, of course. You have acted admirably today, which is not a surprise, of course." He grinned mischievously, and Solveiga's lips curved.

Just Solveiga? Elitsa thought. *Not all the Swans?*

Letting go, the king braced his hands on his hips. "You will remain here until we've had a chance to speak and celebrate! Nefeli will have already notified the staff." He nodded at Captain Nazar, who stepped up beside him. "Return whatever relics you were given to Captain Nazar. Procedure, you understand. And now, I'm going to plan a party!"

Captain Nazar cleared his throat. "I believe it is three in the morning, Your Highness. If you wish to retire—"

The king flapped his hand dismissively. "Nonsense, Captain! This is when I do my best thinking. Perhaps we should have dancing?" He took off in a fast walk across the courtyard, his guards rushing after him.

Pipene hid a giggle behind her hand.

Elitsa didn't know what to make of him either. She'd seen another side of him when they'd faced off against the Guild, but this was him, too, the man who loved midnight parties and moon moths.

Captain Nazar scowled, his knuckles whitening where he rested his hand on his sword. "If you would take your people to the castle, Mistress Solveiga?" he growled.

"Of course, Captain." Solveiga smiled and touched her fingers to Pipene's shoulder, starting forward.

"Thank the Mother," Elitsa murmured as Pipene pulled her along. "I'm about to fall asleep on my feet."

CHAPTER 28

An enthusiastic maid with a long braid and a thin, sharp-nosed face showed them to a room in the castle's guest quarters. It was a massive chamber that Elitsa and Pipene would share with Solveiga and Irusya. Pipene murmured something about how elegant it was, but all Elitsa noticed were the two large beds. As the maid excitedly chattered about the room and the battle — her tumbled words as fast as a galloping horse — Elitsa collapsed face-first onto the gold comforter. *What was the girl saying?* she thought blearily. Something about the steward being horrified that they were in one of the nicer rooms?

"… move to somewhere more appropriate," the girl said, "but for now you get to stay in the same room as Lady Zorine!"

Lady Zorine? Elitsa cracked open an eye.

"… and Sylvie says we're going to have a party. The king throws the *best* parties, he …"

Solveiga finally managed to chase the maid away, and as soon as Elitsa heard the heavy door click closed, she fell asleep. She had so many questions about her bracelet, about what she'd done, but her mind refused to cooperate.

She wasn't sure how long she slept, but she woke to the door softly opening. Bolting upright, Elitsa blinked to clear her eyes and saw Irusya, pressing the door shut with her hand.

Looking over her shoulder, Irusya winced. "I'm sorry," she mouthed. "I didn't mean to wake you."

Pipene sat up with a flail of limbs, her hair a messy blonde cloud. "What? Who?" She rubbed her eyes and wiped the corner of her mouth with the back of her hand. "Irusya?" Pipene looked at the second bed, the blankets rumpled. "Where's Solveiga?"

Fussing with the sash on her long green robe, Irusya walked over to the second bed and sat on its edge. There were robes for each of them in the room, the silken fabric embellished with blue flowers and silvery moons, though Elitsa doubted her skin would look as luminous against the emerald shade as Irusya's did.

Elitsa was still wearing her rumpled clothing, and she surreptitiously sniffed at her sleeve, wrinkling her nose.

"The king summoned her," Irusya said, "so I walked her over to his office. You can go back to sleep. It's dawn, but the castle staff is bustling around prepping for a party."

"A party?" Elitsa raised an eyebrow.

Irusya shrugged. "King Dmitrei wants to celebrate."

"Seems premature to declare what happened last night as a victory."

"It is," Pipene agreed, "but it'd probably be strange if the king *didn't* throw some kind of outlandish gala. He likes to live boldly." She touched Elitsa's arm. "He said he was going to plan one last night, remember?"

"Did he?" It seemed vaguely familiar, but her memories of before she'd fallen asleep felt hazy. Crossing her ankles, Elitsa leaned against the tufted headboard. She'd never had a headboard before, but she understood the appeal. It was certainly more comfortable than the wall. Running her hand through her hair, she looked down at her bracelet. Was it still drained? Elitsa was worried that she'd damaged it irreparably, but as she focused on the ring of beads, tuning out Pipene and Irusya, she felt a faint pulse of energy.

Pipene nudged her, and Elitsa looked up with a start. "What happened to your bracelet?" she asked, leaning forward. "Weren't the beads painted?"

"They were. They turned white after I found the war cache." Elitsa glanced towards her coat, draped over the back of a chair by a glossy wood table. She didn't remember removing it. *Should I tell them about the beak?* she thought, anxiously hoping it was still inside her coat pocket.

"Your bracelet is a natural relic," Irusya said.

Elitsa looked at her with a frown. "A what?" The origin of magesilver — which her bracelet clearly was not — was unknown, though she'd never heard anyone call it unnatural before.

Irusya gestured towards her hand. "May I?"

Nodding, Elitsa scooted towards the edge of the bed — Pipene shifting to the side — as Irusya moved to join them. She perched beside Elitsa and held out her hand. After Elitsa rested her fingers in the older woman's palm, Irusya turned her wrist gently from side to side as she examined the bracelet.

"I don't think these are beads but fossilized eggs."

Elitsa's pulse quickened, thinking about the moth-like creature she'd seen.

"Eggs?" Pipene leaned across Elitsa's knee, her hair brushing her arm. "From what? A small bird? They're so tiny."

"A moth," Elitsa said.

Pipene looked up at her, nose wrinkling. "A moth? Do they lay eggs?"

"Yes, though they don't usually look like this."

Irusya nodded. "Could be. Before the Tower, it was common for mages to form bonds with intelligent creatures to perform stronger magic. They were called the Bonded. When the creature passed from injury or age, it would often leave behind a piece of itself — a natural relic, for lack of a better word — that was an accumulation of the energy they worked together, like a renewable well of magic."

"It predates magesilver?" Pipene asked.

Irusya let go of Elitsa's hand and tucked a dark curl of hair behind her ear. "Yes."

Elitsa rubbed her finger over one of the beads and felt a heavy flutter of wings at the back of her mind. "So it's not alive then?"

"No, it's more like a memory of the creature."

Living or not, it responded to her. *Do you have a name?* Elitsa thought. Her connection to the bracelet, a faint gold thread inside her mind, seemed to pulse, but there was no real answer. Was it a response, or was she reading too deeply?

Pipene straightened, her shoulder pressing into Elitsa's back. "Is it more powerful than magesilver then? What Eli did to that death spell …"

Irusya folded her hands in her lap. "It can be. It depends on the wielder's knowledge and ability. Natural relics aren't empty containers like magesilver; they hold their own renewable power, and what it is and how it manifests varies. It depends on the creature and the magic they performed with their mage." She nodded at Elitsa's hand. "You can draw essences through the relic, like magesilver, but you can't store it."

"Well," Pipene said, grinning, "I, for one, am glad you had the relic last night. The bracelet's power is like wind essence, right?"

"That's what it feels like," Elitsa said, thinking back to how the golden magic had cut through the charging bear. "Wind or air." She remembered the avaricious gleam in the king's eyes after the battle and looked at Irusya. "Will the king try to take it from me?"

"He can't," Irusya said. "Or at least, he won't be able to use it. Only descendants of a Bonded mage can use their relic."

Elitsa nodded, the tightness in her chest easing. She had no intention of letting anyone, king or not, take her mother's bracelet.

"The bracelet was your grandmother's, wasn't it?" Pipene asked. "Do you think she was Bonded?"

"I don't know. I never met her." Elitsa glanced at Irusya. "Are there still living Bonded?"

Irusya seemed to hesitate, her lips parting as she twisted the gold wedding band on her right hand. The metal was engraved with orange blossoms and twining vines. "I don't know. I believe the knowledge of how to create that kind of relationship has been lost."

That could be problematic, Elitsa thought. If what she carried was rare, then she had to assume she had not only the king's attention but the Guild's as well. *They'll want to know how I stopped them.* That was probably why the king had summoned Solveiga. He thought Elitsa was a Swan and that she would do whatever Solveiga told her.

"I'm going to the privy," Elitsa announced, standing up. She'd worry about the king's intentions later. Retucking her blouse into her split skirt and trousers, she crossed to the chair and grabbed her coat, shrugging it on. There was a slight chill in the room, despite the lit fireplace, and she assumed it'd be colder out in the hall. She also wanted to have the beak back in her possession. "Will you be here?" Elitsa asked, looking back at Pipene and Irusya.

"I thought I might go in search of breakfast," Pipene said. "Meet you near the kitchens? They're one floor down, left of the stairs. The maid said they'd have food for us."

"I'm going to wait for Solveiga," Irusya said.

Elitsa nodded and opened the door, eyes catching on a fine ceramic vase delicately painted with golden bees and twining flowers. Selling something like that would probably pay her rent for half a year. It was a good reminder of the disparity between them and the king. *The sooner we get out of here, the better*, Elitsa thought, stepping into the hall.

Locating the privy at the end of the long corridor, she used the facilities and washed her face and hands in a basin of cold water. There was a mirror on the wall, and Elitsa scrutinized her face. She looked grim, her blue eyes suspicious, a permanent line between her dark brows. She did not look very approachable, which probably explained why her marks had always run. Pipene would have had an easier time with her warm smiles and pleasant expressions. Still, would the Guild have backed down if Pipene had yelled at them? Looking grouchy had its uses.

Elitsa thought about the bridge, a shiver running down her arms as she gripped the counter. What happened didn't feel real. She'd reacted without knowing if the golden light could stop the spell.

Her stomach growled, and Elitsa pushed away from the table. *Reliving it doesn't change the outcome.* She'd made a choice and came out the other side. All that mattered now was under-standing what she carried and where to go next.

Leaving the washroom, Elitsa headed down the staircase to the first floor. She started to turn left towards the kitchens, then paused, staring at a wooden panel on the opposite wall. It was a depiction of Mother Moon and Father Sun reaching down to Casekraia. Standing on the peak of a snowy mountain, a woman with long, braided hair was accepting a gold and silver crown from the gods in the sky. It was an old story of their world's creation, clearly adapted to refer to the royal family, but it reminded her of a book her mother had repaired for someone in the Moon Court.

Elitsa turned to the right, the awareness of where she was like a draught of spiced tea. *I'm inside the royal castle.* An opportunity that would likely never occur again. Curiosity swallowing her unease, she tucked her lip between her teeth. She'd heard the castle had several libraries. What rare volumes might they have? This might be her best chance at learning something about the Bonded or the beak in her pocket. Anticipation whispering through her body, Elitsa quickly followed the rightmost corridor, opening several doors to various salons and sitting rooms until she found a room filled with books. Slipping inside, she quietly shut the door.

Lightprisms, shaped like blooming glass flowers, trailed across the upper walls on metal branches. There were no windows, and bookcases lined the perimeter of the room, unbroken save a gap across from her where long curtains half-covered a collection of gilded portraits. Comfortable-looking chairs and couches, upholstered in rich green fabric, were arranged in the center of the room.

Impressed, Elitsa started examining the books to her right. The first few shelves were of various histories, the red and green leather spines marked with years in gold foil. She found a section of accounts from explorers and thinking of her father, started to pull one free — it was about the Frostlands — when she heard footsteps and voices in the hall. They were coming closer.

Pushing the book back into place, Elitsa looked around for somewhere to hide, deciding the best place was behind a green-upholstered settee, but before she could take a step forward, the door swung open. She immediately stepped back into the shadowy space where the curtains hung, her shoulder brushing one of the portraits. Heart thumping wildly, she mentally reached for her magesilver as two figures stepped inside. The ebonweaver essence unfolded, the scent of spice and darkness filling her nose, and then she wrapped herself in the shadows around her.

The door clicked shut, and Elitsa's eyes widened as she saw who had entered the library. *What are they doing together?*

"Tell me where the gateway is," Cas said, holding the door shut with the flat of his hand. He was without his coat; his white, long-sleeved tunic belted at the waist over loose black trousers and worn leather boots. A thick stripe of vibrant embroidery ran down the front of his chest, a pattern of blue and green trees and diamonds.

Taller than he was, Irusya fixed him with an unimpressed stare and crossed her arms. "I know who you are and what you want. I'm not going to help you."

Who Cas was? What did she mean by that?

Cas let go of the door and ran a hand through his hair. "I don't work for the Augor Council. I'm on my own. I just want to return home."

Return home? Didn't Cas grow up here in Rivna? Elitsa frowned, careful not to move. If they heard the curtain rustle and came over to investigate …

Irusya didn't look like she believed him. "As I said, I won't help you. I don't trust you, and I'm not sure why you're spending so much time around Elitsa either."

Cas sighed with what sounded like frustration. "There's nothing suspicious about that. We're in the same line of work."

That was true, but Cas did seem to cross her path more than most. A small part of her — a tiny part — had always wondered if he liked spending time with her, but she'd never let her suspicions go about his motives. Was he after money? He'd never tried to interfere or steal a job from her, and successful as she'd been, she wasn't the highest-earning reclamation agent. If Cas had hoped Elitsa would give him access to Irusya, he would have had more success gaining Pipene's favor.

"Don't try to corner me again," Irusya said coolly. "I'm not sure how you ended up here, in the castle, but I suspect your welcome is more tenuous than mine." Wrenching the door open, she slipped back into the hall.

Cas remained in front of the door, staring at the empty space in front of him. He braced his hands on his hips, a muscle flexing in his jaw. Then, running a hand over his face, he left the room and closed the door behind him.

Elitsa released her breath in a rush, losing her grip on the ebonweaver's lingering magic as her belly relaxed and her hands flexed at her sides. What *was* Cas up to? Whatever this gateway was, it seemed to be important to him. Why did he know to approach Irusya, and how did she know where it was?

I should follow him for a change, Elitsa thought, though she dismissed the idea quickly. As much as she wanted to demand answers, she didn't have the time to become involved in another complicated scheme. Cas wasn't dangerous, and she expected Irusya could handle him. Besides, Solviega was probably done talking with the king. Whatever his plans for her, she needed to be ready to disappear.

Putting her hand in her pocket, Elitsa curled her fingers around the raven's beak. She raised her other wrist and examined her bracelet. She could see faint wisps of multi-colored light swirling around it, drawing essence from somewhere. Her stomach flipped. It was restoring itself, just like Irusya said. *If Pipene could see this ...*

Pipene. She was probably wondering where Elitsa was. Her stomach growled then, loudly enough that she gave the room a furtive look. Using the ebonweaver essence had brought on a sharp hunger. Skirting the furniture at the room's center, Elitsa put her ear to the door. She didn't want Cas to see her leaving the room, but she heard no one in the hall. Was the castle usually this deserted in the hallways? Maybe all the staff were either cleaning up the signs of battle on the bridge or preparing for the king's party.

Retracing her steps to the staircase, Elitsa headed towards the kitchens. She had just reached what she thought was the correct wing when a young woman in a long-sleeved tunic with the king's symbol on it hurried up to her, cheeks flushed and breathing hard. "Agent Serlov!"

Elitsa stiffened, automatically looking for members of the Guild nearby who might have overheard. It was ridiculous — they were still under guard, as far as she knew — but every muscle in her body had tensed. "Not an agent anymore."

The woman's brow furrowed. "Apologies, Mistress. The king requires your presence."

Elitsa's pulse quickened. She'd expected this was coming, but she thought she'd get the chance to speak to Solveiga first. "Right now? I was going to get breakfast."

The woman cocked her head as if confused by Elitsa's question. "Immediately, Mistress Serlov."

"All right. Where—?"

"I will take you to him. This way, please." The woman spun on her heel and set off at a quick pace, back the way Elitsa had come. As they neared the hall with the library, they veered off to the right into the wider corridor with the red carpet and art-covered walls. Instead of going to the king's office, as Elitsa expected, the secretary led her out into a small open courtyard and towards a glass conservatory with a peaked roof, the front doors guarded by two of the king's guards. The structure was still within the castle walls but elevated so that you could see the lake and mountains from inside.

A gust of wind followed them as they entered, and silver bells dangling from the wooden eaves overhead chimed softly. Along the glass walls, ceramic pots held small fruit trees, sculpted bushes shaped into foxes and swooping birds, and blooming camellia shrubs with soft pink flowers. A large eagle owl — with milky gray feathers and a disapproving expression — stared Elitsa down from a stand by the far wall, decorative troughs to either side planted with hellebores and bell-shaped snowdrops. In the room's center, large cushions in creamy whites and soft grays lay scattered across the floor, overlapping each other, and it was there the king of Casekraia lay on his side, head propped up on one arm, and a goblet of wine in the other. He was laughing at something Verka said, who was stiffly kneeling on the corner of a pillow opposite him.

Between them was the queen, with her back to the owl and Lake Odarka. She was sitting on the only chair and appeared to be making rope, having secured the pale fibers to a rod tucked beneath her shoe. It was an incredibly odd thing for a queen to be doing, and Elitsa stared at her for several moments before she noticed Solveiga.

She looked as relaxed as the king, looking back over her shoulder at Elitsa and the woman who'd brought her here. When their eyes met, she gave a slight nod.

"Mistress Serlov, Your Highness," the secretary announced loudly. Bowing deeply, she quickly exited, letting in another gust of air as she pulled the doors shut.

The king, eyes sparkling, looked in Elitsa's direction. "Ah! Yes!" He gestured with his goblet, spilling wine on his coat, but he didn't seem to notice. "Our unexpected guardian. May Mother Moon shower you with blessings!"

Off-balance, Elitsa bowed. He didn't seem drunk but genuinely delighted by her arrival. "Just doing my part, Your Highness." She had no idea how to speak to the king properly. This gathering felt informal and relaxed, as though she'd inter-rupted an intimate meeting of friends.

"Verka tells me you are a Tower reclamation agent. Is that where your bracelet came into your possession?"

Elitsa straightened, cheeks flushing cold. Was he implying she had stolen it? "No, Your Highness. It was my mother's. And I'm a former agent, Your Highness."

He tilted his head to the side, smiling, brown hair curling around his ears. Light blue powder sparkled across his eyelids and beneath the arch of his brows. "Yes, Verka tells me you've decided not to seek another contract."

Elitsa shot a look in Verka's direction. She didn't remember ever voicing that aloud, but it was a fairly obvious assumption based on their interaction. "Yes, Your Highness."

"Should I assume you make a habit of these sorts of daring rescues? Jumping to my defense on the bridge."

A habit? "No, Your Highness. This was my first large battle."

He smiled. "No, I suppose not. We would have heard of you before today then, I imagine." He glanced at Verka and Solveiga. "I do wish we had begun to work together sooner, Mistress Solveiga, had I known you could reach inside the Tower itself."

Elitsa kept her face carefully blank. So he did believe she was a Swan.

"What is it that you want, Mistress Serlov?" King Dmitrei asked. His gaze was clear and reassuring. He reminded her a little of Pipene.

"Want?" Elitsa glanced at Solveiga.

"Out of life, career." He grinned devilishly. "Do you enjoy hunting people, like you did for the Tower? Or perhaps you're a secret painter? Maybe you aspire to be king?"

"Aspire—? No, of course not, Your Highness." Elitsa's eyes darted to the queen, who had glanced at her husband with a veiled look of disapproval. "I'm ... not certain. I've only been out of the Tower's service for three days." *Am I really having the same conversation I had with Pipene with the king of Casekraia?*

"Mmm." King Dmitrei nodded as though she'd said something utterly agreeable. "It can be hard to make decisions when the opportunities seem endless. Opportunities we should protect, no?"

What opportunities? What is he talking about?

"I find myself intrigued by you, Mistress Serlov. I'd thought the Bonded were nothing more than myth. I'm still not certain what to do with you."

"The contract, Your Highness?" Solveiga murmured.

"Oh, yes! Thank you, Mistress Solveiga." He laughed and shook his head, touching the lip of his wineglass to his forehead. "I've been informed that the Tower is trying to kill you, which seems an odd choice for someone with an exemplary record in their service. But! In gratitude for what you did for all of us, I will ensure your safety. We cannot afford to lose our nation's only Bonded."

Elitsa blinked, still unsure how to react. She hadn't spared much thought recently about the death sentence hanging over her head, but once she left the castle, she had to assume the Guild would try again. What did the king want for helping her? *And will the Tower even listen?* "Thank you, Your Highness. Are you ... are you intending to involve yourself in the running of the Guild, then?"

"Don't forget, Serlov, who you are addressing," Verka said coolly.

King Dmitrei grinned. "I don't mind, Verka. It's a good question. Why do you ask that?"

The queen looked up, watching Elitsa as though she also wanted to know her answer.

Elitsa shifted her weight to the side. She'd never, in her wildest dreams, expected to be having an open conversation with the king. What should she say? "The people deserve to know about the Night Sickness, Your Highness, about the pollution in essence harvesting. About the Tower killing retired agents. They've hidden so much, and their secrets must be brought to light. They should be held accountable." She waited, heart thudding. Was it her imagination, or did Nefeli seem pleased by her response?

The king nodded thoughtfully. He didn't look surprised by anything she'd said. "I intend to make changes, Mistress Serlov. We have discussed the Night Sickness at length and how to approach this problem. I have no intention of carrying on like the Tower. I am glad you brought this up. As I promised on the bridge, I intend to restore Casekraia. To brighten our future. I see that this is your dream as well." He set down the cup. "Thank you, Mistress Serlov. I have more to discuss with Solveiga and Verka."

Elitsa bowed, recognizing the dismissal. "Thank you, Your Highness." She bowed to Nefeli, who had resumed her weaving. "Thank you." Giving Solveiga a quick look, she backed towards the doors, then quickly slipped outside. Ignoring the guards, she shoved her hands into her pockets and headed back into the castle in search of Pipene.

CHAPTER 29

"T his is not how I expected the day to go," Elitsa said, plucking at the sleeve of her dress. It was fine fabric, but the abundant layers of silk and velvet would be a horror to run in. The only practical use she could see for the ridiculous dress was that the thickness of the fabric might very well stop a blade. "I want my trousers."

"But it's fun to dress up every once in a while, isn't it?" Pipene beamed. She swayed, her skirts bumping against Elitsa as she smoothed her hands over the beaded embroidery across her waist. "Especially for a celebration."

"You're just saying that because the maids didn't have to use a hundred pins to get your dress to fit."

Pipene laughed. "That green looks gorgeous on you, though, you have to admit."

Elitsa wrinkled her nose, turning her head to eye the room. "I still think this party is a bad idea. Who's to say the Tower will actually accept what's happened?" Or if they'd listen to the king when he interceded on her behalf. How long was he going to hold Arch-Mage Silina and the others?

They were in a grand banquet hall with floor-to-ceiling

windows that looked out at the lake. The walls gleamed with gold and polished wood, and overhead, the vaulted ceiling bloomed with painted flowers. A banquet of food, mounded on silver dishes, was laid out on long tables covered in moon-white cloth. Gilded chairs and couches, upholstered with plush red fabric, were scattered about the room offering places to sit. In the back corner, a trio of musicians played stringed instruments.

People milled across the tiled floor, a mix of nobles, wealthy merchants, some of the king's officers, surprisingly Leida and Ivo from the Smoke Eyes, Verka, and the Swans who had fought to hold the bridge the day before. As uncomfortable as it made her being in this room, rubbing elbows with the 'elite,' Elitsa was impressed that the staff had somehow managed not only to clean all traces of battle from the bridge — save some broken stone and scorch marks — but they'd prepared a feast in the span of ten hours. Where had they gotten all this? It was a reminder that despite the king's talk of change, he'd been dining on cooked goose and cloudberries while the people outside his walls starved. As powerless as he might have been under the Guild's hand, there was more King Dmitrei could have done.

Elitsa turned, tracking Ivo, and saw Cas by the doors. *What is he still doing here?*

"Yes, there is still much that has to be done," Pipene said, "but we can finally use our relics openly. Irusya can heal without reprisal. I'd count that as a good day. And you! Who knew your mother was holding such a powerful relic all these years?"

Elitsa lowered her arm, her lace-edged sleeve slipping down to cover her mother's bracelet. It had regained more of its power. It wasn't back to full strength, like when it'd awakened beneath the castle, but maybe by the end of the day? She wasn't sure how long it'd take. Elitsa knew if she were to hold the raven beak right now — which she'd tucked into the sash around her waist — she'd see wisps of multi-colored light swirling around it like she had in the library.

"It's also brought me more attention than I like," Elitsa said. She'd noticed the way the king's guards, spaced around the room, would casually look her way. King Dmitrei hadn't tried to take her relic, but she couldn't see him just letting her disappear either. He had all but taken credit for her on the bridge, setting her apart in the eyes of the Guild, and though he'd promised her safety, she wasn't yet convinced he could influence the Tower as swiftly as he claimed. He hadn't before today, and not every Guild mage had been on the bridge. Would the others, whether or not they'd openly moved against him, be willing to let King Dmitrei have his say?

Their perception, Elitsa guessed, was that he was young and impulsive, easily distracted by beautiful things. She couldn't see them taking him seriously without strong proof that he could be a capable king. *Maybe it will just take time*, she thought. Time without the Guild's control. Maybe he'd fail, but at least they'd see him try.

"If you two aren't the picture of Lady Luck herself," Cas said, appearing from behind two women in expensive dresses.

Elitsa arched an eyebrow, searching his face for the frustration she'd seen in the library, but he looked relaxed. "Pipene, maybe."

Pipene gasped and smacked her shoulder, smiling. "Oh, stop it, Eli."

Cas's smile widened as he looked between them, giving Pipene an appraising look before turning back to Elitsa. "Yes, she is indeed golden and elegant, but you! You're the favored one."

"If that were true," Elitsa muttered, "you wouldn't be here."

Cas laughed, the sound so bright and joyous that he drew more than a few eyes. Though Elitsa was loath to admit it, he did deserve the admiration. He'd cleaned up too. The fine jacket was a bit short on him, the skin of his wrists visible, and his trousers were tighter than the other men in the room, but somehow he still managed to look dashing. Watching her scrutinize him, he ran a hand through his hair, letting it fall in a swoop over his left cheek.

Elitsa hadn't bothered to style her hair, despite Pipene offering to help, and had left it down over her ears. She was still wearing her magesilver earrings though they were empty. The lack of essence to draw on made her uneasy, but there hadn't been an opportunity to obtain more. *It's a royal party*, she reminded herself. How dangerous could it be?

"How'd you get in here?" Elitsa asked, grabbing a drink from a server passing with a tray. She looked for Irusya but didn't see her.

"I was worried about you."

"Worried about me?" Elitsa raised an eyebrow, trying to ignore Pipene's knowing smile.

"Last I saw you, we were being attacked by rogues in feathered cloaks." He cocked his head as he looked at Pipene. "It was quite the surprise to see them again on the bridge, standing among the king's guard. You were there, weren't you? One of Solveiga's swans? I have so many questions about that, by the way."

Pipene's smile sharpened. "If you run with jays, you're going to find yourself snared."

"Ah yes," Elitsa said, archly, swirling her drink. "The River District, where you tried to run."

Cas crossed his arms, lightly resting a hand against his throat as he looked between Pipene and Elitsa. "I can see how it would have appeared, so I hope you know I wouldn't have left you. I was trying to get out of the open."

"Mhm. Leida make you finish the job?"

"Job?" Pipene asked.

"You interrupted a heist with your apparent rescue of Eli." Cas grinned. "I could have carried on without you, but we didn't do it. After we came to — regretfully, Ivo woke before I did — Leida called it off. Not sure why; maybe related to what happened here."

"So for not performing the job she threatened our lives over, Leida decided to bring you here?" Elitsa said. "From the Smoke Eyes, she only brought Ivo, and I doubt you've had enough time to worm your way into her inner circle." Considering the king's comments about the gang, Elitsa was surprised he'd allowed any inside.

"Charm my way, you mean. I made a deal."

"A deal?" Pipene pursed her lips.

"With Leida." Cas nodded at the leader of the Smoke Eyes, who was in conversation with Ivo and, oddly, Captain Nazar. "I decided to give up my Tower contract and work with her."

Elitsa barked a laugh. "That was stupid."

"I second that," Pipene said.

"Is it? The Smoke Eyes have legitimacy now. I can't imagine another time when they've been invited to the castle to dine with the king."

"It's always about money and power with you, isn't it?" Elitsa shook her head. Maybe the gateway he was after had something to do with relics.

"They're still thieves," Pipene said.

Cas raised an eyebrow. "And the Swans are …?"

"Protectors."

There was a loud popping sound and gasps of surprise and awe, and Elitsa, Pipene, and Cas turned to see what was going on. The king, wearing a long jacket covered in purple roses over a white tunic and trousers, was standing on a low stage near the windows with his hands raised. Several large butterflies were gently floating down in the air above him. Elitsa guessed they were made from paper, their wings glittering like the gold on the king's tunic in a rare moment of sunlight before the sun moved back behind the clouds.

Queen Nefeli stood to the king's right with her hands clasped at her waist, her posture nearly as straight as the marshall's. Her purple dress, a close match in color to the roses on the king's coat, exposed her shoulders, and long bell-like sleeves hung from her braceleted forearms. It was in a Kreanosian style, suited for a warmer climate than Casekraia. Her hair was braided into two thick plaits, decorative gold wires — strung with pearls — woven through the brown strands, and she was wearing her crown. The queen's eyes were keen and watchful, and though she didn't look displeased, Elitsa saw more than a few people straighten when her unsmiling gaze passed over them.

It was the third time Elitsa had seen them together. Something had definitely changed between the royal couple. She no longer believed the queen was secretly controlling the king's actions, but they did seem to be working together.

The musicians stopped playing, leaning their instruments against their knees.

"Now that I have your attention," King Dmitrei grinned, reaching for a glass from a table nearby. "Thank you, honored guests, for joining me today in celebration of Casekraia's future!"

There was a scattering of polite applause from the nobles, though Elitsa noticed that Leida and Ivo just stared. They were both dressed in black, their clothing well-made but unembellished, and they stood out amidst the profusion of colors worn by the other guests. *Have they released Vilis yet?* Elitsa wondered. She looked at Pipene. She'd covered the bruises on her face with cosmetic powder, the broken blood vessels in her left eye beginning to fade to yellow. Whatever concern Elitsa felt for Vilis evaporated.

"It has been a difficult year, but the light is finally shining on us again." King Dmitrei's lips quirked, a nod to the moment of sunlight earlier, and the nobles laughed. "In large part to the return of the Bonded." He threw out his arm in Elitsa's direction.

Her stomach dropped into her feet, her fingers tightening on her glass as all eyes shifted to her. Cas beamed as if the attention was on him.

"Thank you, Mistress Serlov, for your service. You are a true asset within my court." King Dmitrei raised his glass again, and there was another light scattering of applause. "To Casekraia! To the kingdom, and Her people." He took a drink, prompting everyone to raise their glasses to their lips.

Elitsa just stared, mind spinning. He'd all but said she worked for him. This was how he would protect her from the Guild by shoving her up on a pedestal? What he'd done is make her more of a target. She'd accepted no offer from him, and yet he'd planted the seed that she'd acted by his command. The Tower would think she'd betrayed them long ago. *He's backed me into a corner,* she thought angrily. The Guild wouldn't just try to kill her anymore. They'd want to capture and interrogate her.

Unaffected by her frozen stare, the king grinned up at the paper moths as they floated out towards the crowd. They hadn't fallen yet, likely held aloft by someone using essence. King Dmitrei kissed the queen's cheek and then jumped off the dais to mingle with his guests, the noise of conversation rising again to fill the room.

Elitsa breathed in through her nose, her body tense. She could feel people watching her. The sharp, star-like cuts of the wine-glass in her hand pressed painfully into her skin, and she eased her grip on the crystal before it shattered. She looked longingly at the exit. She wanted to run and get away from the attention. *Maybe I can convince Pipene that we should slip out into the gardens.*

Turning to Pipene, she saw Cas was staring at her, eyes bright with fascination. "I never thought to see you in service to the king. How did you accomplish that?"

Elitsa frowned at him in exasperation. *He thinks I maneuvered myself into this position?*

"He must have plans for you," Pipene murmured. "Perhaps it'll be something you'll enjoy."

As friendly as King Dmitrei seemed, Elitsa doubted her happiness was a point of consideration in his plans. He'd expect her to do what he wanted because he was the king. "I doubt the Guild will be too pleased once they realize I'm an agent."

"*Retired* agent," Pipene said. "They can hardly be mad after trying to kill you. Technically, you're a free woman now. You can do whatever you want!"

Elitsa watched the king move around the room, the guests' attention moving with him as though they were all flowers following the sun. It couldn't be that simple. The Guild had tried to kill her because they thought she was no longer valuable to them. What would they do now if they saw her protecting the man they'd been trying to control? And King Dmitrei, he would want to keep her close, wouldn't he? She was not free, maybe even less than before.

Solveiga joined them with Irusya on her arm. They seemed comfortable in their stunning garments, and though neither wore expensive jewelry like the wealthier guests, Elitsa thought they outshone them all. Admiring Irusya's braided hair, she didn't miss the way her lips pressed thin when she looked at Cas.

"You might consider smiling once in a while, Elitsa," Solveiga said, lips curving. "I'm all for scowling when you feel like it, but I think you're making some of the more *sensitive* guests nervous."

"What?" Elitsa frowned out at the room, meeting the eyes of a woman with white feathers woven into her braided blonde hair. The stranger's eyes widened, and she quickly looked away. *I don't look that scary, do I?* Remarkably, the thought that she was scaring the guests eased some of the tension coiling inside her stomach. "What are we doing here, Solveiga? This is all so ..."

"Fake?" Solveiga scanned the surrounding crowd, her face somehow both friendly and stately. "Yes, King Dmitrei does enjoy putting on a show. He has limited time, you see, to convince the public that things have changed, that he's in power now. The nobles are fickle and cautious. They've always shown respect for the crown, but they will back whoever appears the strongest."

"Will he legitimize other guilds as promised?" Pipene asked.

"I don't think he has much of a choice," Irusya murmured, linking her hands over Solviega's arm. "He needs us. Needs the threat of the 'rogues' to stop the Tower from attempting to reassert their authority."

"They might not have backed down if the Smoke Eyes and townspeople hadn't arrived to witness," Cas said, ignoring the sharp look Irusya gave him. He grinned at Elitsa. "That and whatever it is you did to break the arch-mage's magic. Could have used that in Kirtara. More secrets, aye Serlov?"

Outside of this circle, excusing Cas, only the king, queen, and Verka knew that the bracelet was the source of her magic. "What is the king planning to do with me?" Elitsa asked, eyes drifting again to the guards at the edges of the room.

"Well, as I'm sure you gathered from our meeting with him, he believes you belong to the Swans," Solveiga said. "A double agent of sorts."

"That is what I surmised," Elitsa said.

Solveiga inclined her head. "I decided not to disabuse him of that notion for your sake and mine. I have a certain … history with his majesty, so I thought he would see our connection as stabilizing." Solveiga studied her. "I won't tell you what you have to do, but consider that this provides an opportunity for you. One which may offer a path for your future and will not be without its rewards."

Cas seemed interested by this, and Elitsa sent a pointed look his way. *Want to take my place, pretty boy?* she thought. He didn't see the chains associated with this, the responsibilities. "What does he want me to do, join his personal guard?" Elitsa quipped. She doubted Captain Nazar would enjoy that very much, based on the looks he kept giving the Swans and Smoke Eyes.

Solveiga smiled. "Yes, after he suggested you pose for a rather large statue, but I persuaded him to give you a merchant commission instead."

Elitsa frowned, not understanding. The king didn't want to keep her here? *Wait ... a statue?*

Pipene gasped, eyes shining. "He wants to give her a *ship?*"

Elitsa shook her head. "I don't understand. Why would he go for that?"

They all fell silent for a moment as a pink-cheeked man with a thick beard and tall brown hair slowly strolled past them as though trying to listen to their conversation. After hovering for several minutes beneath their quiet stares, he finally moved off with a disdainful sniff.

"What do you think it tells the Guild," Irusya said after the man left, "if he sends away what they believe to be his greatest weapon?"

Elitsa was hardly his greatest weapon. At least she hoped not. Surely once King Dmitrei finished going through the war cache, he'd find something that'd take his attention away from her. She reached for her bracelet, feeling the shape of the beads beneath her sleeve. So, the king wanted the Guild to think he didn't need her?

"Clever," Cas said with a knowing grin, likely coming to the same conclusion Elitsa had.

It was utter madness, that's what it was, but it did present an opportunity. Elitsa couldn't see herself as a merchant, though. *What do I know about making trade deals?* Also, as far as she knew, most of the existing merchants seemed to work for the Tower. Was the king hoping she'd be some kind of spy?

Irusya tightened her hand on Solveiga's arm, and the women shared a private look.

"If you're not considering the offer," Solveiga said, "I'd advise you to disappear soon, leave the continent. The king, for all his youth and sweet cheer, is a clever man, and will make whatever decision he sees fit, whether or not you desire it."

"I'd be wary of the mages," Cas said. "They'll want to study whatever relic you have."

Elitsa thought again of Vilis. He'd claimed to have taken a relic from her mother when she died. Had he suspected Branka held a Bonded relic? Is that why he'd kept an eye on Elitsa? Not because of affection for her mother, but because he wanted to know if she ever found it. *Maybe Mother didn't know what the bracelet really was.* Or maybe she had known but had been unable to figure out how to activate it.

The music suddenly surged, a wild cacophony of sonorous strings, and the crowd began to shift, compress, opening up a space in the center of the room. Three figures were crouched on the floor, draped in different colored cloaks — one blue, one green, and one yellow. The blue figure stood, extending their arms and revealing a rainbow of color on the inside of the cloak. They were wearing a pale blue bodysuit that hugged their curves like a second skin.

Elitsa's cheeks warmed as the green-cloaked figure rose — a man with clearly defined muscles and a square, rugged face. As the last figure joined them, the trio began to dance with the music, their bodies weaving around each other in a flurry of loose-limbed shapes as if they were butterflies caught in a strong, churning wind. It was quite different from the traditional Casekraian partner dances with sweeping movements, spins, and hops. There seemed to be more freedom to it, as though the dancing was meant to mimic natural movement.

Then the king, surprising no one, flung himself into their midst and began to spin, arms reaching out and up, his long-fingered hands graceful. He'd discarded his coat somewhere, and the loose sleeves of his tunic fluttered as he moved. He looked utterly happy, and Elitsa had to admit it stirred something inside her watching him dance with such abandon.

Curious what the queen thought about her husband's perfor-mance, Elitsa found her near the wall with Marshall Oles. Nefeli seemed to be admiring his dance, one hand pressed over her heart as she watched. *Is she actually smiling?*

"He moves well," Cas said, breath stirring the hair at her ear.

Elitsa's skin prickled, a rush of heat down her spine. She hadn't been aware he'd moved so close, but now the scent of him filled her nose, firewood and pine, and blackberry chocolate. He was looking down at her, the gold flecks in his smiling eyes like stars. Mind going blank, the sounds around her turned into an indistinguishable buzzing; then, Cas turned his head away with a grin. Still staring at him, Elitsa could see where he'd nicked his jaw shaving.

"Want to dance, Serlov?" Cas looked down at Elitsa again, eyes dropping for an instant to her mouth.

Elitsa swallowed. "No." She needed to be wary of him, especially after what she'd overheard, but he always acted with such ease around her. If Cas had bad intentions, wouldn't Elitsa be able to see at least a shred of guilt or hesitation? *Why do I even care?*

"Too bad." He raised his glass and then moved off through the crowd, head turned to watch the dancing.

A hand clenched around her elbow, and Elitsa jumped.

"Eli!" Pipene hissed, her smile wide and bright. "Were you *flirting?*"

"What? No!"

"I think he likes you."

"Cas?" Elitsa flushed, much to her annoyance, and she drained the sparkling pear wine from her glass. "No, he flirts with everyone."

Pipene smiled. "He doesn't flirt with me."

Elitsa looked back at Cas, finding him beside one of the nobles — a full-figured man with a pleasant face and shoulder-length blond hair combed back from his broad brow. They were laughing. Leaning in, Cas curled his fingers around the other man's hand and took a sip from his glass. Her chest tightened, and she cast about for a server, leaving her empty glass on their tray.

"Well," Pipene said, "he is flirting with that man, but that doesn't mean he's not into you. He treats you differently, have you noticed?"

"Maybe he wants something from me," Elitsa said, thinking about the library.

Pipene laughed. "Yes, I think he does, but not what you're implying with that suspicious tone. It's hard to hide attraction!"

Yes, but attraction to what?

The music quieted, and Elitsa glanced back towards the dancers as they slowly folded themselves back into their starting poses. The king, flush-cheeked and laughing, sprang back onto the dais by the window and started clapping. The guests took up the applause, Pipene and Elitsa joining in, and then the dancers left, and the crowd slowly reclaimed the floor.

Elitsa felt a headache begin behind her eyebrows. She didn't belong here in this dress, with this crowd. She couldn't pretend this felt normal, like Irusya and Solveiga, who stood nearby, arms around each other, heads pressed close as they whispered and smiled.

The merchant commission was starting to sound more appealing. It was better than staying here, watched by everyone. *I've done enough for Rivna, haven't I?* All she could do now was hope the king kept his promises.

Leida walked up to them, and Solveiga's smile tightened, the two women eyeing each other like rival wolves.

"You look well, Leida," Solveiga said, her voice lined with frost.

"As do you, Solveiga." Leida turned her grandmotherly smile onto Irusya, who gave her a cool look. "We will see much change, I think, in the days ahead."

Elitsa's skin prickled. There was an ominous undercurrent to Leida's words, despite her mild tone.

"What do you want, Leida?"

"It has been long since we have sat down together. I believe it's time we met again, as you seem to have forgotten our peace, Solveiga." Leida's eyes slid to Elitsa.

"Yes," Solveiga said coldly. "We will talk about finding one of your shadows inside my House."

Leida's eyes crinkled as she smiled. "A meeting, then, after the Night of Souls. Enjoy the party, Solveiga." Raising her glass, she moved off, Solveiga and Irusya watching her until she'd disappeared into the crowd.

"Was that about me?" Elitsa asked, alarmed. She hadn't thought about the fallout of the Swans intercepting her in the Smoke Eyes' territory. *I should have warned Pipene what I was doing.*

"In part." Solveiga returned her arm to Irusya's waist. "Leida is unhappy we bested her in her territory."

"She sent someone into the Aerie first," Pipene said, "so she can't exactly point fingers."

"Yes. We're just due for another chat." Solveiga nodded towards the food. "Should we get something to eat?"

Wonderful, Elitsa thought, rubbing her temples. There was something else to worry about. Trailing Pipene and the others to the banquet tables by the dais, she cast a despairing glance towards the windows. If she could pry open the glass, she could escape over the balcony. It couldn't be that far of a drop to the lake below. She was debating the likelihood of injury when the ballroom's grand double doors slammed open with a thunderous bang.

CHAPTER 30

A gale-scented wind rushed inside, the guards by the door flying outward. Startled screams filled the air as guests were knocked down or pushed back. The music cut off with a discordant wail, plates and glasses shattering as they were dropped or blown onto the floor.

Elitsa jumped back to avoid a tray of honeyed pears as it slid off the banquet table in front of her, the magic-charged scent of the fading wind essence ruffling her hair. She reached for Pipene's arm as three mages strode through the open doors in Tower garments. Before she registered who they were, she was already pulling Pipene down behind the table. Solveiga and Irusya had done the same to their left, but the king was still staring towards the doors with a shocked expression, the marshall and Captain Nazar scrambling to stand in front of him.

Cursing her heavy skirt as she crawled to the table's edge, Elitsa craned her head around it. The intruders had arranged themselves in front of the doors. She caught her breath. They were the remaining members of the Vertex of Flame and Starlight, the Tower's ruling council, each one a powerful arch-mage. Verka had been wrong. The Guild was not going to stand by as the king threatened them. This was a coup, the puppeteers publicly taking control.

Arch-Mage Zaets — a deceptively pleasant-looking man with white hair and owl-like eyes — waved his hand, and Elitsa smelled the brine-filled scent of wind again as the doors slammed shut.

The mage to his right, Arch-Mage Caune, turned and ran her hand in an upward motion, sealing the doors with something that looked like viscid spiderwebs, while Arch-Mage Belous — who Elitsa had always thought looked rather goose-like with their thin neck and beaked nose — stared at the crowd.

"What is the meaning of this, Zaets?" the king demanded, his voice echoing in the stunned silence. He had lost his gleeful smile, his face as close to anger as Elitsa had ever seen. "You dare use your relics here, endangering my guests?"

Queen Nefeli was standing a step behind him, her hand on the king's back. She looked off-balance, disbelief, and anger showing through her cracked composure.

The guards who'd been knocked over scrambled to their feet. They drew their weapons, eyeing the mages uncertainly, some looking to the king and marshall.

The king straightened. He hadn't put his coat back on, but despite his underdress, he was still projecting proud confidence. "I am willing to overlook this breach of protocol and decency if you leave now." His tone was assured, the initial anger smoothed. "As I told Arch-Mage Silina, who is still my *guest* at present, the cache will stay—"

"We are not here for Silina," Zaets interrupted. "You are a puppet, King Dmitrei, a paperman *we* allowed to remain on the throne. We've let you play at ruling, and it has suited us thus far that the people believe you have some measure of control. But that time is over. The pup that bites the master's hand—" Zaets' eyes cut sideways.

The guards rushed the mages from either side, perhaps

signaled by Captain Nazar or Marshall Oles. They swung their swords, and Elitsa held her breath, expecting blade to cut through flesh and bone. Instead, she smelled the acrid scent of something *wrong*, and dazzling blue light, so bright it left traces across her vision, crackled through the air like a fast-expanding lattice between the guards and the mages. They were moving too fast to evade it, and as the first guard fell against the web, he screamed, body convulsing, eyes glowing blue as the light forked through his body. The guards toppled one by one, smoking on the floor.

Bile surged in Elitsa's throat. That was no essence. Whatever unnatural force the mages were channeling did not belong.

"What in the Mother's name was *that!*" Pipene gasped in Elitsa's ear, her fingers digging into her arm.

The guests screamed, erupting into motion though they had nowhere to go. In the confusion, Captain Nazar and Marshall Oles pulled the king and queen down beside Solveiga and Irusya.

"Silence!" Arch-Mage Caune thundered, her voice loud enough to rattle the chandeliers overhead. "Don't move, don't scream if you wish to leave this room alive! Rivna belongs to the Tower!"

Elitsa's heart pounded in her ears as she shot a look towards the windows. The sky had darkened outside, and as she stared at the amassing storm clouds, she heard the angry rumble of thunder. It was as if the weather was responding to the mages' strange magic. *We need to get out*, she thought desperately.

She glanced towards Solveiga and Irusya to see if they had a plan. Irusya looked stricken and was whispering something fast and intently to Solveiga.

"We are your rulers." Caune's smile stretched thin and horrible as she looked over the crowd. "Do you see how your king hides? Says nothing as his guards die?"

The king tried to stand and was pulled back down by the

marshall. Giving his commander a frustrated look, King Dmitrei yelled over the makeshift barrier. "You attacked us! *You* moved against the castle. I did not start this!"

Solveiga caught Elitsa's eye and gestured sharply, indicating she wanted them to join her.

Exchanging a look with Pipene, Elitsa glanced up over the table. The horrified guests between them and the mages provided some cover. Grabbing Pipene's hand, Elitsa scrambled sideways. She waited for Caune to shout or attack, but they reached Solveiga and Irusya's table without incident.

"No?" Arch-Mage Zaets called. "You thought we wouldn't notice your childish grab for power? Your *alliances?*"

The king shoved the marshall's heavy hand off his shoulder and peeked over the table. "What magic are they using?" he whispered, half to himself. "I've never seen it before."

"Whatever it is, it displeases Father Sun," Marshall Oles said as lightning struck the surface of the lake, followed by another loud retort of thunder.

He follows the old ways, Elitsa thought, studying the marshall's serious face.

The queen's brown eyes were round, but if she were on the edge of panic, she had not yet given in to it. The knuckles of her hand were pale where she gripped the king's sleeve. She looked at Elitsa, and then her eyes narrowed in recognition. "You! Your relic. Can you stop this?"

Me? Elitsa swallowed, her chest tightening painfully. What could she do against their frightening magic? She didn't even understand what they were using. "I'm not a mage."

"We can't fight their magic, Your Highness," Solveiga said. "They are not using essence."

"It is pointless to hide, King Dmitrei!" Arch-Mage Zaets called, his tone sounding like a teacher scolding a troublesome student.

Marshall Oles looked at Elitsa expectantly, and then when she said nothing, he turned to Captain Nazar. "We must get the king and queen out of here." Leaning sideways, he looked out over the crowd. There were still several guards, but they were watching the mages, unsure or unwilling to approach.

Irusya shook her head. "We need to stop them! They're drawing magic from another world."

"Don't be ridiculous," Captain Nazar spat.

Solveiga gave him a murderous look, and for a second, Elitsa thought she meant to stab him.

"Are you going to cower behind your subjects, King Dmitrei?" Caune demanded. "Maybe he doesn't think we're serious."

There was a scream, but Elitsa couldn't see what'd happened.

A flicker of anguish crossed King Dmitrei's face, and he moved as if to rise, but the queen tightened her grip.

"No!" she said. "They will kill you!"

The king shook his head, his eyes determined. "It will be easier for them if they don't." Prying her fingers from his arm, he sprang to his feet.

Cursing, the marshall stood too, half-blocking the king with his body and drawing his sword.

"What is your plan, Zaets?" King Dmitrei demanded loudly. "Do you believe the other nations of Cerana will support you? You think I am ridiculous, naive, but I am still a king, and you are not."

"We can't let them leave the castle," Irusya hissed as the king talked. Her face was as serious as Elitsa had ever seen it, her eyes filled with distress.

"Leave?" the queen said, frowning fiercely. "That is exactly what we want!"

"No!" Irusya leaned forward, looking up at Dmitrei, who covertly glanced down at her. "They are not what you think! The essences they store, they're selling them off-world. If you want Casekraia to survive, we must close their open portal!"

The portal, Elitsa thought. She'd forgotten about Irusya's relic. *Did she know this would happen?*

Zaets laughed, unaware of their conversation behind the table. "You have no true allies beyond this city, young king. You think Kreanos will move against us? Who gave us their third daughter? They may send their regrets when they learn King Dmitrei has succumbed to the Night Sickness, but that is all."

"You're mad," Nazar hissed at Irusya. He seemed uncertain if he should stand up with the king and marshall or remain where he was with the queen.

"Listen to her!" Solveiga growled, catching the queen's gaze. "If you want to survive, you must listen."

"Stop stalling, King Dmitrei," Zaets said. "I am growing impatient."

Elitsa stared at Irusya, mind spinning. How had the Guild even opened a portal in the first place? And who were they selling to? What happened to the essences that left Cerana? She pressed her fingers to the sash at her waist and felt the raven beak. Maybe if she could see their power, she could understand it and break it like the spell on the bridge.

Slipping it free, she curled her fingers around the beak and peered around the table. She couldn't see the mages through the guests, but above their heads, channels of shimmering blue light rose up and through the ceiling. Elitsa gasped, drawing back against Pipene.

"What is it?" Pipene asked, steadying her.

"I see it." Elitsa's skin felt cold as everyone looked at her. "Their magic ... it's coming from somewhere else." *Is something in the sky above us?*

King Dmitrei glanced down at her, then back at Zaets. "What guarantee do I have that you will let my guests go unharmed? What are your plans for Queen Nefeli?"

"You can see the magic?" Solveiga asked intently.

Elitsa nodded. "I can see essences." She did not explain how.

She didn't want to talk about the beak, not with the queen and Nazar staring at her.

"Come to me now," Zaets commanded, his voice sharpening.

"What is she talking about?" Nazar's gaze shifted to Solveiga and Irusya. "What is this?"

"I am not going to submit myself into your hands without assurances," the king said.

Marshall Oles bent his head. "Wait, sire," he urged quietly. "More guards will be coming."

"You saw it yourself, Captain," Solveiga said, tone controlled despite the flash of irritation in her eyes. "On the bridge."

"I have to close the portal now!" Irusya pulled what looked like a palm-sized mirror from inside the neckline of her gown, the space where the mirrored surface should be, glinting a strange, opaque purple.

Queen Nefeli's eyes widened. "What is *that*?"

"Sire," Marshall Oles said, "I urge you to—"

The table exploded.

Elitsa was thrown backward, the air driven from her lungs as she slammed painfully into the stairs of the dais. Food and pieces of wood and glass rained around her. People lay bleeding on the ground, others rushing to the sides of the ballroom. Pipene had been blown to Elitsa's right and was lying on her side, half-covered by a section of broken table.

Captain Nazar, bleeding from the side of his face with a mangled leg, crawled towards the king. Dmitrei had also hit the dais, and he struggled beneath the marshall's limp body. Oles was dead, impaled by a candelabra through his back. He must have tried to shield the king. Elitsa couldn't see the queen.

Irusya was on the ground with Solveiga covering her. The back of Solveiga's dress was shredded, and it was difficult to tell what was blood or wine.

Ears ringing, Elitsa reached for her ribs as she watched Solveiga force herself up on one elbow. The woman's eyes swept

Irusya's face, then she rolled onto her side and raised her arm, her magesilver bracelet glinting as she released a blast of wind-shaped daggers at the approaching mages. One took a noble woman in the arm as she tried to scramble out of the way, another cutting Caune's cheek. A step behind Caune, Belous threw his arm out in an arc, breaking the shimmering daggers against a shield of purple energy.

Sound rushed back, and Elitsa could hear screams and cries of pain. There was shouting on the other side of the main doors, and they shuddered as something thumped against them. *The other guards*, Elitsa thought.

As she struggled upright, she saw Cas by the back wall. He was slowly inching behind the mages. *What are you doing?* she thought, skin prickling with alarm. Was he trying to open the doors? Where was Leida and Ivo?

Irusya, looking dazed, raised a hand to her head, then her eyes flared wide. Turning her back on Caune and Zaets, she started searching the ground, hands shifting frantically through the debris.

"There's no point fighting," Caune sneered. She didn't bother wiping the blood off her face, as though unaware she'd been cut by Solveiga. "You can't counter our power." She glanced towards the nobles, trying to force their way out through a hidden door at the side of the room, but made no move to stop them.

Irusya grabbed something — the relic? — and ducked behind a long red couch, the fabric torn and spilling feathers. She cradled it in her hands, and it looked like she was talking to it.

King Dmitrei stood up, swaying as he gripped his side. His tunic was turning red beneath his fingers.

The captain, struggling up despite his injured leg, took a stance half in front of him and drew his sword.

"You won't get away with this!" the king said, his voice tight with pain and anger. "The people will not stand for it!" He looked in Elitsa's direction, and her throat went dry.

He wants me to do something, she thought, her heartbeat racing.

"Oh, I think the people will follow along with whoever is in charge," Zaets said mildly. "Look how they run, no one trying to help you except for these … rogues." He narrowed his eyes at Elitsa. Was that a spark of recognition in the arch-mage's eyes?

Pipene started coughing and dragged herself out from beneath the broken table.

Relieved, Elitsa looked back at Zaets and saw that Cas had reached the doors. He met her eyes over Belous' shoulder with a half-smile, then, turning back to the doors, raised his hand to the carved wood.

Elitsa stood up. She had no idea what she was going to do without a single essence, but she had to give Cas a chance. She had to hold the mages' attention. "Unlike you, we care about our city," she said, adjusting her grip on the raven beak in her fist. It was hard not to show how unnerved she was by the lines of blue light connecting Zaets, Caune, and Belous to the ceiling. They looked like puppets on glowing strings.

Zaets tilted his head to one side. "I recognize you. You're a reclamation agent."

"Was," Elitsa said.

Cas splayed his hands over the sealed doors, his shoulders rising as he took a deep breath. There was a flash of light, and then flame dashed hungrily across the seam in both directions. He grabbed a handle and pulled. The door didn't open.

The mages turned, Arch-Mage Belous flicking their hand towards Cas's back.

"Cas!" Elitsa shouted.

Unexpectedly Leida rose from behind an overturned couch, knocking the mage's spell away with a discharge of meadow-scented air. Despite Leida's strong push, Elitsa saw Belous' conjured blade deflect mere inches from Cas's right shoulder, punching a hole in the dark wood door in a spray of splinters.

Cas staggered back, arm raised, then Leida grabbed his arm and hauled him away.

King Dmitrei released a peal of laughter, drawing the mages' attention. His eyes looked wild, his lips drawn back from his teeth. "Not expecting resistance, Zaets? Casekraia is *mine*." He leaped over a fallen table and raised his arm, a stream of fire shooting away from his ringed hand towards Zaets and Caune.

Caune raised her hand, deflecting the fire up with a snarl.

The king continued to pour energy into it, forcing her to block him. "Nefeli!" Dmitrei yelled, holding the fire. "Nefeli, where are you?"

Belous stepped forward, and Elitsa saw blue energy pouring down their arms. With the beak in her hand, she could see what Belous intended, their spell's construction as clear to her as it'd been on the bridge — it was a severing spell.

Solveiga was getting back up, eyes darting sideways to where Irusya still whispered at the relic.

Caune paused, chin raising as though she were scenting the air like a dog. The blue lines of light connecting them shivered. "Zaets! The portal!"

King Dmitrei staggered, the flames cutting off as his essence ran out. He fell, tripping over something on the ground.

Lunging after him, Captain Nazar caught him, both men hitting the ground together.

Zaets, face alarmed, turned towards the couch where Irusya hid.

"No!" Solveiga yelled, battering the mages with a blast of air. She lunged forward at the same time, enhancing her speed, knife in her hand.

Elitsa tensed, grabbing her skirt so she was ready to run. *Where did Solveiga hide her dagger?* she thought, regretting her lack of a weapon.

Belous moved, body shimmering blue as they drew more power through the channel with a wave of their arm. Solveiga flew sideways, her body slamming into the wall, knocking down a gold-framed portrait.

"Dmi! I am here!" The queen had appeared from somewhere, the side of her face red with blood. She had picked up the captain's sword and was standing over them, hands shaking.

Pipene seized a silver pitcher from the floor and threw it as hard as she could at Caune. The mage cursed, ducking sideways, eyes hateful as they snapped to Pipene. Blue energy crackled down into her hand as Pipene leaped forward.

Panic clenching like a vise around her chest, Elitsa felt the magic of her bracelet surge in response. She seized it instantly and broke Caune's spell, staggering as she felt a responding drain on her energy. There was a pulse from the bracelet, the rush of exhaustion tapering off, then its power went dormant.

Caune's eyes flared in alarm, flailing backward as Pipene slammed into her, her knife stabbing into the arch-mage's side with stunning speed. Even before Caune fell onto one knee, Belous turning in alarm, Pipene was falling and rolling away, scrambling behind an overturned table.

Elitsa felt a pressure in her chest, like the vibrations of a faraway explosion, and then the blue cords of light disappeared, the mages staggering as though they'd felt the cut strings. Caune, half-rising, gave a startled cry, Belous pulling her upright.

"It's closed!" Irusya yelled.

The main doors splintered inward with a loud crack, guards pouring into the room in defensive positions.

To the left of the room, where guests were still attempting to flee through a side door, several more guards forced their way inside.

Elitsa breathed a sigh of relief. They had reinforcements now, the mages' otherworldly magic cut off. With the beak's sight, she could see that they still held essence, but the arriving guards were prepared too, decked out in magesilver armor.

But before Elitsa could move to Pipene's side, Caune, Zaets, and Belous took a collective breath, and the orange-red hue of fire flared between them then exploded outward. Several of the guards screamed as fire washed over them, the others forced back, diverting the flames with their magesilver shields.

Heat licking her face, Elitsa dove for cover.

CHAPTER 31

From behind an overturned couch that was starting to smell more than a little charred, Elitsa looked for the others. Captain Nazar and the king and queen had taken cover along the side of the wall behind a large cabinet. Irusya was scrambling towards Solveiga, still lying on the floor by the wall. Glancing the other way, Elitsa could see Cas, Leida, and Ivo bunched together by one of the broken tables, the glow of an earth essence fading as they struggled to shield themselves against another barrage of fire.

Elitsa saw a flash of blonde hair. Pipene was peeking out from behind another of the tables. She gestured at someone, then ducked back down.

Elemental spells flew between the mages and the guards trying to push through the doors. Caune grabbed Zaets' arm and hissed something.

The owlish arch-mage nodded, then met Belous's eyes.

Foreboding iced Elitsa's spine and she gripped the beak in her hand so tightly it felt like she'd cut her skin. Bands of gold light appeared from the mages' chests and wove around each other, connecting them. It thickened in front of Zaets, the light coalescing, the web of the destructive spell clear to Elitsa's eyes, almost as if she was watching it drawn line by line. She could see its purpose. *They're going to bring down the castle!* Her bracelet was drained, slumbering, its presence faint. She had no essences, no weapons; how could she stop them?

Her emotions surged — frustration at being powerless, anger at the Guild, and fear that this was the end. *I'm not ready to die.* For the first time, Elitsa's future felt open, and she would not let them take it from her. She moved into a crouch. She started to put the beak back into the sash at her waist when it warmed inside Elitsa's palm, startling her as a wave of awareness spiraled up her wrist. It felt like it was coming alive, awakening as the bracelet had beneath the castle. It wanted to help her. Understanding unfurled in Elitsa's mind as clear as if someone had whispered into her ear. Her heartbeat thundered. She could break the mages' spell, but not just that. She knew how to capture their essences.

The mages' power surged, the destructive spell started to expand, release. Elitsa reacted; she dashed forward, saw Caune's amused, disdainful face, then reached out with her hands and grabbed the essences out of the air before they could discharge. Energy rushed into her body as though she were nothing but the wind. The scents of everything overwhelmed her, colors and sensations exploding in her mind. She could see millions of stars overhead, glimmering faintly in velvety blackness like tiny fireflies. She was coming apart.

Then connection to Elitsa's own body rushed back, and she felt the power move through her bracelet, recharging it, filling it. She felt it race through her hand into the beak, felt her mind expand, felt its awareness press against her, saw the shape of a raven as clear as could be in front of her eyes, wings unfurling, encasing her. She had to let it go; she couldn't hold this much power.

Staggering, Elitsa let the energy go, pushing it back towards the stunned faces of the mages. White-hot power, a tangle of essences more powerful than she'd ever held before, flashed away from her like a wave. The beak cracked inside her clenched fist. The mages threw up their hands as if to shield or block their eyes, but the power roared over them, burning through flesh as though Elitsa had unleashed the sun.

Blackness rushed in at the corners of Elitsa's vision, and she felt herself falling, her body unresponsive. The side of her face pressed against the floor, and she heard Pipene distantly call her name. *Why does she sound so far away?*

Someone rolled her onto her back, and Elitsa glimpsed the bodies of the mages, the blackened fingers of a hand, a soldier standing over them with pike lowered, the elaborately painted ceiling — a profusion of flowers in gold and red — and then Pipene's worried face looming over her. "Elitsa! Can you hear me? Are you all right? Irusya!"

Elitsa closed her eyes, the motion feeling abnormally slow, snippets of conversation drifting past her as the ringing in her ears rose and fell like the sea's tide.

"I want the tower surrounded!" King Dmitrei's voice? "Gather all the—"

"… she *burned* them like lightning was—"

"Sire! They're not human! Look at the—"

"I got you, Elitsa." Pipene's hand on her cheek. "You're going to be fine. Just hold—"

"Let me see her! I need—" *Was that Cas?*

Elitsa felt herself being lifted, start to sink into blackness, then her eyelids fluttered open, and she was in another room. Irusya and Solveiga were there, a warm hand pressed against her head, and she felt a rush of coolness like a soothing breeze moving softly beneath her skin.

Elitsa's eyes cracked open again, and the room was dark, the faint glow of candlelight at the edge of her vision. Her bracelet felt warm, pulsing with energy, recharging. Had it saved her?

Someone was talking in the corner of the room. She wanted to turn her head, but her body felt leaden ... like a tree grown down into the earth. *Is that Irusya's voice?*

"They know about us now. It's only a matter of time before—"

"Not about you." Solveiga's voice, soft, insistent. "He won't find out."

"He's going to ask how I knew about the portal, about ..."

Elitsa drifted, missing Irusya's words.

"Promise me you won't do anything." Solveiga. "Not yet. With our legitimization, we can bring back the old ways, but it will take time. For now, we have to ... he's more likely to hoard essences now. He's afraid of ..."

"... no longer shipped off-world." Irusya. "I must ..."

CHAPTER 32

E litsa woke to warmth and light, a glaze of sunlight washing out the blankets' colors on the bed. She lifted her arm and groaned, muscles protesting at the movement. Everything ached, pinpricks of overwhelming sensation starting at her feet and calves.

"You're awake!" Pipene's voice. "Careful, don't move too quickly."

Elitsa sat up, receiving a resigned look from Pipene, who had been reaching out to help her.

Lips pursing, Pipene climbed onto the end of the bed and leaned against the carved wooden side as Elitsa looked out at the unfamiliar room. It was a little bigger than her apartment with a second alcove bed in the opposite corner, the painted cabinet between holding a pewter hand mirror and a pair of candlesticks.

"Where are we?" Elitsa asked. Her mind felt a little foggy, but she remembered the battle in the banquet hall and the burned bodies. *I stopped them*, she thought. She'd danced with death again, and was still breathing.

"The castle, in the staff quarters. Irusya didn't want to move you far." Pipene scratched at the painted wood where someone had carved their name. "I think the king should have put you up in one of his fancy guest rooms again. Seems only fair for someone who just saved him *and* his castle."

Elitsa cracked a smile and rested her head against the wall. She felt relaxed, her brain not offering its usual quick critique of what had happened. *I'm probably in shock*, she thought, looking down at her chest. Someone had changed her out of the dress from the party into a linen nightshift. She put her hand over the bracelet on her wrist, rubbing the warm beads.

The wings fluttered in her mind, and for a second, she could smell the mist-touched grass of a field at night.

Pipene pulled her knees up, wrapping her arms around her embroidered skirt. "How did you do it? How did you make a spell like that?"

"It wasn't a spell." Elitsa's stomach fluttered as she remembered the horror in Zaets' eyes right before he started to burn. "I broke theirs and then …" She gestured. "Sent back the essence." The raven beak. She straightened, eyes darting around the room, searching for her dress. "The beak I was holding; where is it?"

"Oh." Pipene slid out of the bed and walked to a chair where Elitsa's coat and trousers sat folded. "It was in your hand. I had to pry your fingers open." She turned, holding up the beak. "I didn't know what it was, but I thought you might not want anyone to know about it." She carried it back to the bed, handing it to Elitsa before returning to where she'd been sitting at her feet. "Did you get that from the war cache?"

Elitsa turned it over, rubbing her fingers over a deep crack through the blue-black bone. She could feel it now, a presence at the back of her mind, but it was weak. Looking up at Pipene, she didn't see any essence glow around her friend. "Yes. I picked it up after … when it changed my bracelet. I don't know why they responded to each other."

"Do you think the beak is a bonded relic too?" Pipene asked as if reading her thoughts. "I don't feel anything when I touch it."

Her eyes widened. "So that's how you did it. It let you harvest the essence from another person! That's incredible, Eli! I've never even heard of such a thing. Could it be from your family too? But why was it here then? In the castle?"

Why had the beak bonded with her? Based on what Irusya had said, it didn't seem possible. And if it had been connected to her family like the bracelet, why had it taken so long to wake up?

Pipene scrunched up her face, thinking. "Well, if you're the only one it works for, then the king can't take it away from you."

Elitsa studied Pipene's bright grin. There was no jealousy in her friend's face, just genuine excitement. Elitsa's chest tightened, tears pricking the back of her eyes. She didn't deserve her. No one did. "I think they're similar, but I'm not sure why it bonded with me. It feels different … but it's connected somehow to my bracelet, so maybe that's why?" She turned the beak over again. "I think I broke it when I held the arch-mages' power. I wish I knew more about what it is so I can fix it."

"The Tower might know something, though I'm not sure they'll be easy to talk to right now. King Dmitrei is not very happy with them at the moment. They're claiming not to know about the … the creatures."

"The creatures?"

"Oh!" Pipene straightened, eyes wide. "You didn't see? The mages, there was something wrong with their bones. You ah … well, the power kind of ripped away their skin, quite nasty, but they had these crystalline growths on the bone like they were *made* from crystal. Solveiga thought maybe they'd been warped by the power they were channeling from … wherever? But I don't believe it. They weren't human."

Elitsa felt a chill, recalling the snippets of conversation she'd overheard between Solveiga and Irusya. Irusya had said 'us,' 'they know about *us.*' *What had she meant?* What was their connection to strange beings and portals to other worlds? She thought about the frost wyrm's tunnel beneath them, the creatures who had supposedly come from the Frostlands and then disappeared at the end of the war. *Why have we never seen another wyrm?* Could they have come from somewhere else? How long had that portal been open?

What *was* Irusya's connection? As suspicious a person as Elitsa was, she couldn't imagine Solvegia's wife having some dark purpose. Irusya was always helping people. *I was wrong about Vilis.*

"Makes you wonder how many in the Tower knew about them," Pipene said. "Though I suppose it'd be easy to keep secret, right? If the only way you can tell they're not human is beneath their skin. Do you think there are more of them? Elitsa?"

Elitsa blinked, pulling her thoughts away from Irusya. "I suppose." How else would they have taken over the council? Could Vilis be one of them? She didn't think so, but then, she'd never suspected the council to be hiding such an astonishing secret. Even if the truth had gotten out, Elitsa doubted anyone would have believed it prior to the arch-mages' assault on the castle. "Did you know they were selling essences off-world?"

Pipene, twisting her hair around her fingers, shook her head. "No, Irusya didn't tell me. I was curious, when they told me about the portal relic, what it had to do with everything, but I'm used to Solveiga holding information back sometimes." She shrugged. "Annoying as it is."

Elitsa tugged on her earrings, thinking. What would the invaders — whatever they were — even do with the essences? Could they even use magic from Cerana off-world? *They'd need relics, wouldn't they?*

"The portal must be why things have gotten so bad here," Pipene said. "Stored essence disappearing out there some-where." She gestured at the ceiling and presumably the sky beyond. "Now that we've stopped them, and the king is taking control of the Guild, maybe it will get better. There's a lot to be done, but I finally feel hope, you know?" She grinned suddenly, lacing her hands over the tops of her knees. "So, are you going to accept his offer? The king and guilds can sort out whatever comes next, which I suppose includes me." Pipene shook her head, laughing. "But you, you can get away. Sail away, to be precise."

Elitsa smiled; it was hard not to around Pipene. "I haven't had much time to think about it with the party crashers and everything." She looked down at the beak. "I've been thinking about my father. My mother said his ship disappeared in the Crystal Sea. She said he was a map maker, an explorer, but you know what I think he really was? A relic hunter. I think he was headed to the Frostlands. We don't know what's there, you know? We've just heard stories about the wyrms the Tower fought to protect Casekraia."

Pipene's eyes brightened. "You think something is there."

"Maybe, we don't know, do we? None of the ships we've sent have ever returned. And these ... invaders, for lack of a better word, where did they come from? The portal Irusya closed, I don't think it was here, or at least it wasn't in the castle where we could see it. I couldn't see it." It had to be covered in magic, didn't it? Holding the beak, she would have seen if it was nearby.

"You think there are more there? Doing what?"

"I don't know. I'm not convinced they are in the Frostlands — what would be the need if they can hide among us so easily — but something's there. I want to find out what it is." As soon as she said the words, Elitsa knew what she wanted to do. She'd been so uncertain before, unable to choose a direction, but the thought of following in her father's footsteps? That felt good and certainly more honorable than working for the Tower. "If the king is as nervous about the strangers and their magic as I think he must be, I don't think he'll refuse me."

And, considering that she might be unable to repeat what she'd done in the ballroom, it'd be better if she could disappear for a while. She needed time to figure out more about these bonded relics and find a way to repair the beak. Elitsa looked at Pipene. "You should come with me."

"To the Frostlands?" Pipene tucked her lip beneath her teeth. She was clearly intrigued by the idea.

"This is what you've been talking about since we were girls," Elitsa said, leaning forward. "Exploring. What's more adventurous than this? Leaving for lands unknown?"

Pipene's smile widened, and she released a breathless giggle. Elitsa could see the mirrored excitement in her eyes, the consideration. "We could go to Agathenis. See Lightwall. Can you imagine what that city must look like?" She laughed again, then her brow furrowed, and she seemed to deflate. "I can't," she said regretfully, twisting her hair around her fingers again. "It would be amazing, and I would love nothing more than to join you but … Solveiga might need me."

"For what? I don't …" Elitsa frowned. "Actually, I have no idea what you do for Solveiga besides your work in the House of Swans."

"I'm not her right hand or anything like that, but I believe in what she's trying to do here in Rivna. We're making a difference, and now … if we can truly use our relics openly, if Irusya can heal, we can make life better. I would love to go with you, you know I would, but I made Solveiga promises."

Elitsa felt a pang of disappointment. She did understand, but a part of her had been certain Pipene would agree. This is what they'd wanted, after all. Her disappointment didn't totally dampen her excitement, though, and Elitsa leaned back thoughtfully. This was something she needed to do, wanted to do, for herself, and just because they had to say goodbye now didn't mean it was forever.

Someone knocked loudly on the door, making Pipene jump. Looking at each other, they burst out laughing, and then Pipene called out permission to enter.

Dita stuck her head in. She wasn't wearing her feathered

cloak. "Solveiga wants to see you both, in the red room. Do you know where that is?"

"I do," Pipene said. She looked at Elitsa questioningly. "Feel well enough to get up?"

"Good enough." Elitsa flexed her feet. She still felt too relaxed, like she'd spent too many hours in a steambath, but she didn't want to stay in the king's castle any longer than she had to. What he'd offered her before might have changed.

Dita nodded. "I'd hurry. That woman is there ... the king's advisor or something? The one who's been living with the Smoke Eyes." From the expression on her face, she didn't much care for someone who'd willingly stay with the gang. Pulling her head back into the hall, Dita shut the door.

Verka? What does Verka want?

Pipene hopped off the bed and grabbed Elitsa's clothes, tossing them to her playfully.

Getting out of the boxed bed, with minimal grunting — Pipene teasing that she sounded like an old lady — Elitsa dressed as quickly as she could. When she'd finished, she checked her reflection in the window, fluffing her bangs over her forehead, then ran her fingers over her magesilver earrings. *Do I even need to use them anymore?* Confirming the beak was in her pocket, Elitsa spun the bracelet around her wrist, and then nodded. "Ready."

Pipene grinned and flung open the door, leading Elitsa through the corridor and down a narrow flight of stairs to a wider hallway. They followed a slim blue and silver carpet beneath an exquisitely carved wood archway, almost bumping into an attendant carrying a basket stuffed with maps. Exchanging smiles and hasty apologies, they continued past a painting of an unfamiliar coastline then stopped at a dark-paneled door. They seemed to be in a different wing than where the king kept his office. Elitsa glanced down the hall as Pipene opened the door, catching sight of several guards before following her inside.

They were in a sitting room with tall ceilings and a window that looked out onto the park east of the castle. Elitsa could see the peaked roof of the intake tower in the distance. The halls had been cold, but here the chill was kept at bay by a large fireplace with a thick wooden mantle. Red-upholstered couches, currently occupied by Solveiga and Verka, were arranged around a low table holding a tray with a teapot and a rolled scroll tied with a gold tassel. Where was Irusya?

"Thank you for coming," Verka said, smiling pleasantly, setting down her cup on the table. "Please sit." She seemed happy and relaxed as if she'd shed her sharp edges, and Elitsa immediately felt suspicious. She did not recognize this version of her.

Solveiga, with her usual elegant poise, inclined her head.

Elitsa exchanged a look with Pipene before taking a seat on one of the couches. Pipene plopped down beside her and crossed her legs, putting an arm along the back of the couch.

"Tea?" Verka asked, gesturing at the pot.

"No, thank you," Elitsa said. She crossed her arms, trying to gauge the expression on Verka's face. Why was she here and not with the Smoke Eyes? *Does she have another job proposition?* She was dressed in finer clothing, with gold stitching on the throat and sleeves of her long blue coat, and she had silver combs in her braided hair.

Narrowing her eyes, Elitsa glanced at the scroll on the table. It was sealed with dark blue wax, but she couldn't make out the stamped design.

"I'll have some." Pipene reached forward and grabbed a porcelain cup from the tray, pouring herself some tea.

Verka smiled, folding her hands in her lap. "King Dmitrei expresses his appreciation and recognizes your service to the crown."

"I should hope so," Pipene said after sipping from her cup. "Elitsa saved his life *twice!*"

Annoyingly, Elitsa flushed. "Not alone."

"His majesty would like to know if you accept the offered commission." Verka gestured at the scroll on the table.

"To be a merchant?" Elitsa asked. She was relieved the king hadn't summoned her himself, but he was probably overwhelmed with dealing with the Tower.

Verka inclined her head.

"And if I don't?"

"Then the king will request your presence here, in the castle, as a member of his guard."

"What Verka is saying," Solveiga cut in, "is that one way or another, you will be in service to the king. The Tower has expressed interest in you and your relics, and he does not want them to interfere or for you to return to their service." She glanced at Verka, who had leaned back into her chair. "Verka is the only reason you're being offered any freedom at all and why you are still in possession of your bracelet."

Elitsa frowned. "You told him about the Bonded?" She'd assumed it'd been Irusya or Solveiga.

"Yes, some records survived the Tower's split and were brought here, but they weren't very detailed. In truth, we don't know who the Bonded were or much about how their bonds work. More relics than yours must have survived, but we don't know where they are."

"Maybe their descendants have them," Elitsa said. "They might not know what they have." Would they need to be awakened as hers had?

Verka nodded. "It is certainly possible. The king knows he can't simply hand your relic to someone else, but considering how powerful yours seems to be ..."

"He wants your loyalty," Solveiga said. She glanced at Verka.

"And as a Swan, he knows you are loyal to the people, to Casekraia."

Elitsa bit the inside of her cheek. *Should I tell them about my limitations?* Her perceived strength was all she had to bargain with, but if they thought she was a weapon, they might try to use her in ways she was incapable. "I'm not certain I can do it again," she said, watching Verka closely. "I broke the relic somehow. Weakened it." Better they thought the bracelet was damaged than admitting she had two.

"We know," Solveiga said. "Irusya told us." Something flickered in her eyes. "Forgive her for betraying your confidence, but she was worried about you. She wanted to make sure you were protected."

Irusya? Elitsa hadn't told her about the beak. She glanced at Pipene, who gave a slight shake of her head. If she'd hidden it, then when had Irusya examined it?

"It's good she told me," Verka said, "especially if you don't want to stay here in Rivna. This is why the king agreed to let you leave. After what you did in the banquet hall, he wanted you beside him, as a reminder of his strength, but if your power is broken, it's better if you're not around for anyone to find out."

It made sense, but how had Verka convinced him? From what she'd seen of the king, he didn't seem easily swayed once he'd made up his mind. *It doesn't matter*, she thought. Whatever King Dmitrei's reasons, Elitsa was grateful. She would hardly enjoy being his personal bodyguard or paraded around like a prized bird. There were too many memories here, and if she wanted to be someone her mother could be proud of, she needed to leave and start over.

"I'll take the commission," Elitsa said, "but I don't want to be a merchant. I want to go north, to the Frostlands."

Solveiga straightened, her eyes sharpening.

Verka raised an eyebrow. "You want to go where no one has returned from for over a hundred years."

"Yes, I do. I think we must. We don't know anything about the people who attacked us or the source of their magic. For all we know, they could be tied to the frost wyrms, to the Winter War. What if the Tower mages didn't kill them all as they said?"

Verka picked up her cup, looking thoughtful. "It will be dangerous. You might not come back."

"Maybe," Elitsa said. "But it's probably no less dangerous than if I stay here. If the king wants me out of the way, then this is what I desire." Her heartbeat quickened as Verka studied her with pursed lips. She was going to say no. *They're not really going to let me run off with an entire ship.*

"There is more to you than I first thought," Verka said. I will present your proposal. I cannot promise King Dmitrei will agree, but your argument is persuasive. Enjoy the tea." Rising, she set her cup on the table and left the room, closing the door behind her and leaving Solveiga, Pipene, and Elitsa alone.

Solveiga uncrossed her ankles and leaned forward. "Your idea is excellent, Elitsa. We need to know what is north of us. Pipene, I want you to go with her."

Pipene blinked, her cup clattering against the table. "Really? You'd let me go?" A smile spread across her face, lighting her eyes. "You don't need me here?"

"Irusya is gone, and she may need your help."

"Irusya …" Pipene looked at Elitsa, eyes wide.

Irusya was missing? *Please don't let this have something to do with Cas,* Elitsa thought. He was capable of a lot, but kidnapping? *But a gateway could be a portal, and if that's what he was after …*

Solveiga leaned back against the couch cushions, running a hand through her hair. "She believes there are more portals, and she wants to close them." She sighed. "She didn't want me to go, said I needed to be here."

Elitsa tilted her head to the side. "She left on her own?"

"Yes."

Then I won't have to hunt Cas down. Elitsa settled back, relieved.

He was probably still here somewhere, skulking around the castle.

"Why do they want our essence?" Pipene asked. "The crystal people clearly have magic of their own."

"Crystal people?" Elitsa grinned.

"We have to call them something!"

Solveiga's lips twitched, but she didn't smile. "I don't know, but the Guild has been selling to them for centuries. Without the portal, anyone left will be stuck here, but if there are portals elsewhere, then it will take longer to restore balance to Cerana."

Elitsa studied Solveiga's face. How did Irusya know about the intruders in the first place? "How did Irusya find out about them?" she asked aloud. She couldn't be one of them, could she? A crystal person? But then, did that mean Cas was too? *No, no, that's ridiculous.*

Solveiga shook her head. "That is something you must ask her yourself." She smoothed her skirt over her knees, then laced her fingers. "Not only must we change how we use magic, but we must ensure the return of the essence that's been taken. If the off-worlders use the energy, it will find its way back, but if they store it like the Guild ... Well, one problem at a time." She leaned forward, reaching for Pipene's hand across the table. "I won't force you to go, Pipene, but I am asking. I can't let Irusya do this alone."

"I'll go," Pipene said, squeezing Solveiga's hand. "Of course I will. I didn't like the idea of Elitsa going off on her own anyway." She smiled, catching Elitsa's eye.

"And you're certain she went there?" Elitsa asked. "To the Frostlands."

Solveiga nodded. "She'd been planning this for a while, before the attack."

"Solveiga ... How long have you known Cas?"

"Casimir?" Solveiga raised an eyebrow. "He's visited the House off and on. Why do you ask?"

"I … Irusya doesn't seem to like him."

"Oh." Solveiga laughed. "She thinks he's ridiculous, that's all."

Elitsa forced a smile, nodding. *Maybe Irusya never told her about their conversation.* Were there other secrets she'd kept from her? Reaching for the teapot, she poured herself a cup and brought the golden tea up to her lips. She was surprised to find it smelled like peaches.

"Don't worry, Solveiga," Pipene said. "We'll find Irusya and bring her home."

Elitsa nodded. "We just have to hope the king gives us a ship."

CHAPTER 33

Five Days Later

Sailing Southwest from
Casekraia's Grand Harbor in Velasa

Elitsa leaned over the railing, watching Velasa's harbor become a distant blur as they sailed south. To the west were the islands known as Father's Crown. Covered in towering trees, they protected the bay, and according to the sailors, they'd have to travel past the islands to reach the strait that led to open water. There the ship would turn north, and they'd follow Casekraia's rugged coastline to the Crystal Sea.

The wind smelled fresh and salty, and as Elitsa reached out with her senses, she could feel that its essence was stronger than the winds and breezes she'd felt upon the mainland. She smiled. She was sad they'd miss the Night of Souls, but she felt lighter than she had in years.

In Velasa, Elitsa had found a shrine to Sister Luck by the docks and could still smell cinnamon smoke on her clothes. She'd thanked the goddess for Her favor and asked for good fortune for

341

the trip ahead, leaving gifts of coin and dried oranges. The hand-maid of the shrine, a blind woman around her age, with copper, braided hair, and a crooked smile, had given Elitsa a token to carry — a brass coin with the Sister's face in profile on either side. She had never seen the gods, wasn't sure what was myth or history, but Elitsa had witnessed her fair share of luck and figured it was better to be on the Sister's good side than not.

They'd be traveling outside the trade routes, but if they sailed west across the Gold Sea instead of north, they'd reach the other continent. *The queen came from there,* Elitsa thought, looking past the dark green trees to the endless stretch of blue beyond. What must it have been like to leave her family and everything familiar behind? Thrilling and terrifying? Elitsa tried to imagine how different it must be, how a lizard could be large enough to ride, or what an ocean of sand must look like, *feel* like. They were lands her father had visited, and someday she wanted to see them for herself. *After the Frostlands*, Elitsa promised herself. *I will cross the Gold Sea.*

Pipene rushed up to her, leaning so far over the railing that Elitsa almost grabbed the back of her white cloak, afraid she'd tip over into the frothy water. The sailors were unfurling the sails and doing whatever it was sailors did, and Elitsa was just keeping out of their way. She'd never been on anything larger than a small lake boat before.

"Isn't this wonderful? I had no idea the sea was so big! You can't even see land that way." Laughing, Pipene closed her eyes and shook her head, letting the wind blow back her hair and cloak. "We're adventurers now, Elitsa! Just like we dreamed."

Elitsa grinned. "I know." In truth, even as children, she hadn't thought it was possible to leave Casekraia, not really, and yet here they were, rewriting their futures.

She glanced back at the sailors as they moved around the deck. They were all dressed in dark blue, their high-necked jackets cut short at the hips over fitted trousers, and everyone had a knife strapped to their lower back. According to Solveiga, they were soldiers; King Dmitrei had put Elitsa and Pipene on some kind of spy ship. But that wasn't the strangest thing; he'd sent the queen. According to the scroll, waterproofed and secured in the locked box in Elitsa and Pipene's cabin, if anything happened to Queen Nefeli, Elitsa would take command. Captain Novikova had ultimate authority over how the ship was run, of course, but the queen would pick their direction.

Currently, Nefeli was up in the crow's nest, hands braced on the railing and face to the wind. "She looks happy," Elitsa said, staring up at her.

Pipene twisted, following her gaze. "She does. It's curious that the king let her leave with us. Who turns a queen into an expedition leader? Is he trying to get rid of her, do you think? The Tower *did* arrange their marriage."

"I don't think so. I got the impression they've been working together." King Dmitrei had sounded concerned when he'd called the queen's name during the fight in the ballroom. Perhaps they'd become friends, if not lovers.

"Well, it is very odd, but maybe it's a kindness. If Queen Nefeli had hoped to actually rule, she didn't find any power in Casekraia. However, that is likely to change now that the king is censuring the Guild." Pipene shaded her eyes with her hand. "Kreanos is known for their sailing. Maybe she'll be useful."

"I suppose we'll find out," Elitsa said. It was still hard to believe that the king had given them a ship. True, she didn't have total authority, but the thought of being in command of Novikova and her crew was admittedly frightening. *I've never been in charge of anyone but myself*, Elitsa thought. The queen's presence was unexpected, but Elitsa could understand King Dmitrei wanting to keep an eye on her. Still, it was strange to send his wife. Was Nefeli really the only person he could trust? Why not send Verka? Or Captain Nazar?

Looking away from the mast, Elitsa saw a sailor raise a glass bottle into the breeze. A swirl of blue appeared inside the glass as he captured some of the wind inside it. As he sealed the bottle, Elitsa put her hand into her pocket and curled her fingers around the raven beak. She felt a faint pulse — the beak still hadn't recovered — and then a tenuous connection to the trapped essence in the sailor's hands. Her heartbeat quickened. Something had changed. Elitsa could feel the strength of the harvested essence, now dimmed by its confinement, but it felt like ... *Like it knows it's trapped.*

Elitsa let go of the beak with a jerk. She hadn't realized she'd taken a step back until Pipene put a hand on her arm. Her heart continued to pound. She could still feel the essence as the sailor walked away, even without touching the beak. *This shouldn't be possible.* The wind brushed her cheek, and she shivered.

"It's going to take time," Pipene said, leaning against the railing. "Harvesting is all we know. Everyone with a relic will have to relearn how to use essence."

"It's alive," Elitsa said, touching her fingers to her cheek. The essence was living energy. It needed to flow, to move, but inside the bottle, it couldn't. It would weaken, become stagnant.

"What do you mean?" Pipene looked at her, brows furrowed.

"Irusya said natural relics predate magesilver. So what did mages use before then? Not everyone was bonded, were they?"

"I don't know."

Irusya had also said that magic should be a borrowing, a momentary transfer of energy. "Maybe they used their own bodies."

"That would be incredibly dangerous."

"Yes." Like when she'd collapsed in the ballroom. "That's how the Guild convinced everyone to use magesilver." Elitsa tugged on one of her earrings. She had not refilled them. "They've always told us that the other nations use magic foolishly. What if they're doing what we should be?"

"We can find out," Pipene said, looking back up at the queen.

"Maybe we can convince Queen Nefeli to visit Kreanos when we're done."

Captain Novikova appeared from the upper deck, striding towards them. She was a sharp-faced woman with russet-brown skin and black hair, pulled tightly back into a single braid. A scar ran through her lips from her right nostril to her chin. "Bonded Serlov, Mistress Skliar—"

"Please, Captain, call me Elitsa."

"And Pipene is fine!"

The captain's expression didn't change; doubtless, she'd continue calling them by their last names. "We have a stowaway."

"A what?" Elitsa blinked.

Novikova clasped her hands behind her back and stepped to the side as one of the sailors approached, pushing Cas ahead of him. "I would bring him to the queen, but she is otherwise engaged."

"Cas!" Elitsa gasped. "What are *you* doing here?" *He should be back in Rivna.*

"See?" Cas grinned at Novikova, running a hand through his hair before the wind blew it back into his eyes. "I told you I knew her!"

Novikova eyed him in much the way a cat observes a lizard, then looked back at Elitsa. "Did you invite this man, Bonded Serlov?"

"Did you?" Pipene asked, grinning, as she looked Cas over.

"No!" How had he made it on the damned spy ship without anyone noticing? "I thought you were working for Leida now." Had the Smoke Eye leader put him up to this? The ship's departure was supposed to be secret, though perhaps that was hard to ensure when the queen was on board. Or, more likely, this had something to do with what he wanted from Irusya. *He's here for her,* Elitsa thought, stomach sinking.

"I was," Cas said. "But then I heard you got yourself a ship, and I thought, adventure? Exploration? Money? I'm here to help."

He was lying; she was sure of it. "I don't want your help." Elitsa gestured at Pipene, who was grinning, her hands braced on her hips. "*We* don't need your help. Go home, Cas."

"Well, I'd say that's a little tricky now, considering we're no longer at the dock." He grinned confidently.

"Throw him overboard."

"Hey now!" Cas said, laughing.

Novikova seemed to consider, then she nodded at the sailor. "Lower the sails. We'll send him ashore. I will notify Queen Nefeli."

Cas's smile faded. "But I can be useful! Tell them, Elitsa. You can't deny we work well together. What about Vilis? Do you want to know where he is?"

Vilis … for all she cared, he could still be rotting beneath the city forgotten by Leida, but knowing him, he was probably worming his way higher inside the Tower. "You're a distraction."

Cas's face brightened, eyebrow arching. "Oh?"

"No, that's not …" Elitsa scowled at him, clenching her teeth as heat spread across her cheeks. "This isn't one of your larks." She looked at Novikova. "Captain, I—"

"I can help you find Irusya."

Elitsa's eyes snapped back to Cas, her body tensing.

"What do you mean?" Pipene demanded. "What do you know about Irusya?"

Cas glanced at Novikova then held Elitsa's eyes with a serious look. "Can we talk privately?"

"If we are sending him to shore," the captain said, "I would like to do so before we hit the Indyllnan current. We'll be fighting against it to head north."

Cas took a step forward, raising his hands as the sailor grabbed his shoulder. "Just for a few minutes."

"Fine." Elitsa sighed. She did have questions for him that she wanted answered. "Five minutes. You can leave him with us, Captain."

Novikova looked Cas over and then inclined her head. "Five minutes. I will notify the queen of our situation." She gave Cas a stern look, her lips thinning. "Be on your best behavior, sir. I do not tolerate violence aboard my ship, and I will not hesitate to put you in your place." Novikova walked away, followed by the sailor.

"Who are you, really?" Elitsa demanded before Cas could speak. There were too many questions swirling around in her head, and though she'd normally give him time to talk, to sweat, Novikova was already sending another sailor up the rigging on the mast to get the queen. "I overheard you talking to Irusya in the library. Is the gateway a portal? You wanted her to help you find it. Why? Where is your home? Who or what is the Augor Council?"

Pipene gave Elitsa a confused, speechless look as a mixture of emotions crossed Cas's face. Elitsa had caught him off balance. Cas didn't look worried exactly, but he didn't seem particularly happy about what she knew. His brows dipped, his mouth tightening before he released a heavy sigh and shoved a hand through his hair.

"We're from the same place, Irusya and I," Cas said as the wind blew his hair back into his face. "And no, I won't tell you where — the name won't mean anything to you anyway — but we were ... on different sides."

Elitsa stared at him. Was he saying they were from another world?

"Different sides." Pipene captured her hair as the wind turned. "Like enemies?"

"No, more like the organizations that we worked for had opposing goals. Different plans, which were sometimes at odds. But that was in the past before I came to Rivna."

Before. Had Cas worked for some mysterious organization as a child? It didn't make sense, not unless ... not unless he wasn't human. Could there be another explanation? But that would also

347

mean that Irusya was one of them too. *Does Solveiga know?* "How will the portal help you get home?" Elitsa demanded.

Cas smiled and glanced towards the mast where the queen was descending the rigging. "We're almost out of time. What's important is that I can help you. To put it simply, I can feel the energy the gateways release. I should be able to help pinpoint Irusya's direction. If she is where you're headed, I'm your best chance of finding her."

The queen landed on the deck with a thump, releasing the ropes as she turned to Novikova, who gestured at Cas with Elitsa and Pipene. She'd traded her lavish dress for a light blue, long-sleeve tunic secured diagonally at the waist with a long silver sash. It was split up the sides, like Elitsa's coat, showing dark blue trousers beneath. Across the front of the buttonless tunic, wave-like swirls were stitched across the fine fabric. Elitsa thought her clothes looked lighter and thinner than what most Casekraians wore in the fall, and she briefly wondered if Nefeli would be warm enough as they approached the Frostlands.

The smile Elitsa and Pipene had glimpsed was gone, and Queen Nefeli approached them with her usual sharp-eyed reserve. "Captain Novikova tells me we have an unexpected visitor." She looked Cas up and down. "We have met before, yes?"

Cas bowed deeply. "Very briefly, Your Highness. I am Casimir Rosya."

"You are a mage."

Cas's lips quirked. "Not exactly. I am or was — like Serlov here — a Tower reclamation agent, which is why I carry magesilver, but I have begun searching for new employment."

"And what is the difference between you and a mage? You cast magic."

Cas inclined his head. "I suppose you're right, Your Highness."

"We should put him ashore, My Queen," Novikova said, hands clasped behind her back. "We are approaching the strait."

The queen glanced at Elitsa appraisingly.

Does she think I hid him on the ship? "I was unaware he was on board, Your Highness," Elitsa said quickly. "But …" She knew she was going to regret this, but she had a feeling he'd show up again if they tried to leave him behind. She did not want him to find Irusya before they did. "He may be useful." Elitsa didn't know if the king suspected there were more portals or what the queen truly expected to find in the Frostlands. "We don't know what we will discover once we cross the Crystal Sea," she said carefully. "There's a chance we'll encounter more …"

"Crystal people," Pipene cut in.

"… like Arch-Mage Zaets," Elitsa said. "We may need his magesilver."

"You vouch for him?" the queen asked.

Elitsa gave Cas a flat look. Did she have another choice? She didn't know what he was up to or what he'd do if they discovered another portal, but if he was after Irusya, they needed to keep an eye on him. "He is a competent tracker, Your Highness."

"A bit light on the praise there, Serlov," Cas said, the dimple appearing in his cheek.

The queen looked up at the sky, and Elitsa and Pipene exchanged a confused look as a full minute passed. Then Nefeli nodded. "You will accompany us, Mr. Rosya. In Kreanos, it is bad luck to turn back once a journey's begun. It seems you are meant to be here, but you will follow my orders, as well as Captain Novikova and Bonded Serlov."

"Mine too?" Pipene piped up, raising her hand.

Nefeli glanced at her, but Elitsa was certain she saw a tiny upward twitch at the corner of her mouth. "Captain? If you will see to finding a place for Mr. Rosya?"

If Novikova was displeased that Cas would be allowed to remain, she hid it well. "Of course, My Queen. This way, Mr Rosya."

"Until later," Cas said, clasping a hand over his heart as he looked at Elitsa and Pipene. Bowing deeply to the queen, he strode confidently after the captain.

Queen Nefeli looked towards the front of the ship, the breeze catching her hair. "I will be at the helm," she announced, then abruptly turned and strode away.

Elitsa sighed and braced her hands on the railing.

"I can't believe he showed up here," Pipene laughed, joining her. "Why didn't I know Cas knew Irusya from before?"

"I overheard them talking in the castle before the party. He wanted Irusya to show him where the gateway was, which I assume now was the portal. Cas claimed he was trying to get home."

"Cas knew about the portals before we did?" Pipene whispered, though no one was close enough to hear, especially with the wind muffling their words. "You don't think ... You don't think Irusya is one of the crystal people, do you? I'd always thought she'd moved from Xiltarma."

"If she is, it's clear she disagreed with Zaets and the others. Maybe they're not all bad." Cas had said they were on opposite sides, but he'd also fought against the arch-mages. Could there be multiple factions? *Why come here in the first place? Why buy our magic?*

"I suppose that means Cas is one too." Pipene tucked her hair behind her ear. "Do you think he's dangerous?"

"I don't know. He's selfish and clever, but I've never found him particularly untrustworthy." Of course, just because he wasn't callous didn't mean he wouldn't betray them in some way to further his own agenda.

Pipene nodded. "I've never heard a single bad word about him at the House. He always brings the cygnets candies, did you know that?"

Elitsa shook her head.

"I don't know ... how he looked at you at the party, and how he looked at you now ... I'm not convinced he's here just to chase after Irusya." Pipene smiled. "I think Cas sees that you're bound for great things. It's hard to resist the call of adventure." She winked. "This trip is the start of something magical; I can feel it."

Elitsa smiled, unable to resist Pipene's enthusiasm. "Untold dangers and certain death does get the blood flowing."

Pipene laughed and threw her arm around Elitsa's shoulders. "I think we've earned a little reckless fun, don't you? How much trouble can one man be?"

Elitsa chuckled. It seemed only yesterday that she'd been talking with Pipene about taking a vacation. She'd thought she'd have to set off on her own, but here they were together, already farther than either of them had been before.

Out here on the water, Elitsa felt free and hopeful, feelings she hadn't experienced in a really long time. For once, she could believe her mother would approve. Her future was still uncertain, her path likely to hold unknown dangers, but she was with Pipene, and Elitsa couldn't think of anywhere else she'd rather be. "Here's to reckless fun."

SELECTIVE INDEX

The Aerie. A section of the Peoples' Suburb by the western wall within the capital city of Rivna, the Aerie is protected by Solveiga, the well-respected proprietress of The House of Swans.

Athara. A coastal city on the island nation of Kreanos, where the sea snails are found that create the purple dye (known as Atharan purple), favored by the wealthier merchants and nobles in Rivna.

Domra. A long-necked folk instrument with a round body, made from wood, and three or four metal strings.

Dmitrei Volkov. The current king of Casekraia and the youngest to take the throne in the last two hundred years. Dmitrei has no siblings and lost both parents in his teenage years in a boating accident on Lake Odarka. His wife, *Queen Nefeli*, is from the island nation of Kreanos, a marriage arranged one year ago by his Guild advisors from *the Tower*.

Father Sun. According to Casekraian mythology, Father Sun and *Mother Moon* created life on Cerana. The ability to thrive and grow is attributed to Father Sun, as his warmth and sunlight ensure all living creatures' survival. Father Sun's symbols are the sun, fire, roses, oak trees, and white horses.

Gadra root. A plant whose essence is valued by the Guild as it boosts cognition.

The Gold Sea. The sea west of Casekraia.

The Hearth. A neighborhood in Rivna east of the Moon Court and near the king's castle. It is where the wealthy residents of the capital live.

The Kalien. A river that runs from Lake Odarka through Rivna and south past Kirtara. East of Tristi, it becomes a delta and lets out into the Moon Sea.

Kreanos. An island country west of Casekraia across the Gold Sea, and Queen Nefeli's homeland.

The Kurdaima. The merchant district in Rivna.

Liudmyla's Athenaeum. A public library in Rivna.

Lightprisms. Mage-crafted lamps that hold a fire essence inside, providing constant light. They are an alternative to candles or oil lanterns and are frequently used by the Guild and royal castle, as they are more difficult to weaponize.

Messenger towers. A series of communication towers spaced to allow for quick conversations between the major towns of Casekraia and Rivna, the capital city. Using magesilver lantern relics and short and long flashes of light — created by a combination of fire, wind, and the essence of a firebeetle — the towers provide the quickest way to send messages, but it is also the most expensive.

The Moon Court. A neighborhood in Rivna between the Tower and the king's castle where the royal families of Casekraia live.

The Moon Sea. The sea south of Casekraia.

Mother Moon. According to Casekraian mythology, Mother Moon with *Father Sun* created life on Cerana. Mother Moon is attributed with giving all living things souls or essences, and is honored during the *Night of Souls* in autumn. Some Casekraians believe that using magesilver relics is immoral as all living things that possess an essence, including plants, animals, and humans, have souls and are therefore sacred. Mother Moon's symbols are the moon, owls, swans, and soul bells — small red flowers that bloom in fall.

Nefeli Lykaios. Queen of Rivna and wife to King Dmitrei. She is the third daughter of the royal family of Kreanos, an island nation west of Casekraia.

The Night of Souls. Also known as Mother's Night. A day and evening celebration at the beginning of fall to remember the dead and the spirits/essences that inhabit all living things. In the weeks leading up to the Night of Souls, Casekraians decorate with carved wooden masks, harvest wreaths, painted pumpkins, and *spirit houses.*

Night Sickness. A mysterious illness where a person collapses and dies very quickly, 'as though their spirit was stolen from their body.' There is no apparent cause or obvious transmission, and it can happen without warning.

Reclamation agents. Hired by the Guild, these contracted individuals hunt down contract-breakers, people who have borrowed relics from the Tower for harvesting essences and either failed to return their relics or pay their monthly fees. Agents have their own contracts, usually for four-year terms, which allows them to use relics to perform their job. It can be a dangerous profession, as agents are often targeted by rogues who want to steal their relics.

Rivna. The capital city of Casekraia where the king resides.

Rogues. Any mage with an unlicensed relic, either found while exploring the forest or old ruins or obtained through criminal means by stealing from a contract holder, reclamation agent, or other licensed individuals. Though it was not traditionally illegal to own a relic, pressure from the Guild, coupled with the current economy, has left the majority of relic ownership in the hands of the Guild, king, nobles, and wealthy families (including select merchants). Anyone outside these groups found to hold an unlicensed relic is assumed to have obtained it illegally and is forced to give it to the Guild. Despite no actual law controlling this, the king does not interfere.

Sister Luck. A goddess of chance, believed to be the daughter of *Mother Moon* and *Father Sun*. A wheel is one of her symbols to indicate the cyclical nature of good and ill fortune.

The Stone and Song. An inn in the Kurdaima where Cas has a room.

Sparkwyrm. A worm found in seaside caves near Sidek, on the southwestern coast of Casekraia. Their essence can create an electric shock when combined with water.

Spirit Houses. Small, peak-roofed houses, about the size of a birdhouse, that are hung over the doors or placed in the windows in the weeks leading up to *the Night of Souls.* Candles are placed inside to honor the spirits and guide the souls of the deceased home.

The Tower. The guild of mages who control all magical relics within Casekraia. Established after the Winter War, where they fought the frost wyrms that invaded from the Frostlands north of the continent, they have since evolved into the true power in the land, controlling even the king. The Tower is also the physical home and seat of power for the mages within the capital city of Rivna. The various branches of the Tower include:

- *The Vertex of Flame and Starlight* (the council of mages that oversee all operations of the Guild)
- *The Flame* (guards and battle mages)
- *The Hunters* (relic hunters and explorers)
- *The Scholars* (scientists and researchers)
- *The Hands* (the administrators)

The White Forest. A remote and wild timberland in the mountains northwest of Rivna. It is a popular, but difficult place, to explore looking for lost relics.

Xiltarma. A desert country west of Casekraia across the Gold Sea, that borders Agathenis and Hibera.

A larger map of Casekraia is visible on my website at www. byhollykarlsson.com/maps-of-cerana

357

AUTHOR'S NOTE

Thank you for reading *Kingdom of Essence*. If you'd like to find out about new stories (we will be returning to Elitsa and Pipene in the future!), you can join my mailing list or visit my website byhollykarlsson.com.

If you enjoyed the book, I'd love it if you left a review. Reviews help me craft better stories and help other readers find this book. Thank you for your support!

This book would not have been possible without the endless encouragement, support, and story planning sessions with my husband, Kent. Thank you for inspiring and challenging me.

A big thank you to my editor, Maria Fowler, and my friends and beta readers: Allison Carr Waechter, Beth Okamoto, Jim, and Verle-Ranae Fourcroy. Your critique and enthusiasm have been invaluable.

And thank you, my readers, for taking a walk in Elitsa's world. I'd love to hear from you, so please feel free to send me a message on www.byhollykarlsson.com or Facebook.

ALSO BY HOLLY KARLSSON

Daughters of Fire & Sea Trilogy

Daughters of Fire & Sea (Book 1)

The Dragon Flute (Daughters of Fire & Sea Book 2)

The Demon Queen (Daughters of Fire & Sea Book 3) *Forthcoming*

Blood of Erith

Dark of Night - A Novelette

Prequel from the world of Daughters of Fire & Sea

The Way of Thorn & Key

With co-author Allison Carr Waechter

Short Stories

A Wish in the Dark & Lawbringer (available on www. byhollykarlsson.com)

Unusual Diction: Volume One

Unusual Diction: Volume Two

Unusual Diction: Volume Three

ABOUT THE AUTHOR

Holly Karlsson writes epic & adventure fantasy. She weaves worlds filled with magic, dangerous quests, mythical creatures, and compelling characters. Holly is the author of the *Daughters of Fire & Sea* trilogy and *Unusual Diction*.

Made in United States
North Haven, CT
16 September 2022

24185945R00221